While I'm Falling

WHILE I'M FALLING

LAURA MORIARTY

HYPERION
• • • • •
NEW YORK

Library of Congress Cataloging-in-Publication Data is available upon request.

ISBN: 978-1-4013-0272-6

Hyperion books are available for special promotions and premiums. For details contact the HarperCollins Special Markets Department in the New York office at 212-207-7528, fax 212-207-7222, or e-mail spsales@harpercollins.com.

Design by Jessica Shatan Heslin / Studio Shatan, Inc.

FIRST EDITION

10 9 8 7 6 5 4 3 2 1

THIS LABEL APPLIES TO TEXT STOCK

We try to produce the most beautiful books possible, and we are also extremely concerned about the impact of our manufacturing process on the forests of the world and the environment as a whole. Accordingly, we've made sure that all of the paper we use has been certified as coming from forests that are managed to ensure the protection of the people and wildlife dependent upon them.

While I'm Falling

There is an expiry date on blaming your parents for steering
you in the wrong direction; the moment you are old enough
to take the wheel, responsibility lies with you.

—J. K. Rowling, Harvard Commencement, 2008

1

ON A VERY COLD DAY during my sophomore year of college, when I was living just an hour away from home in a dorm, my father returned from a two-day seminar on financial planning to find what he initially thought was a stranger asleep in his bed. Even after he turned on the overhead light, he didn't recognize the bearded face of the man sleeping openmouthed on one of the firm, supportive pillows he always missed so much while away. In those first confusing moments, my father later told me, he simply didn't comprehend the situation. He would soon forgive himself this slowness—his experience as a trial lawyer had taught him that people often cannot comprehend the unexpected; the human brain can fail to register what seems impossible. "Blinded by naiveté" was how he explained it to me, in one of his more vulnerable—or perhaps more calculating—moments. Even after he turned on the light, he said, it took him several seconds to recognize the blond hair and pleasant face of one of the men who had worked on our roof the previous summer. Naiveté aside, I'm surprised he recognized the man at all. My father worked long hours, and so the repair

f, like everything that had to do with the house, had fallen
ther's domain.

ne roofer's tanned shoulders were visible over the top of the duvet. He did not wake when my father turned on the overhead light. Bowzer, our dog, was curled up at the foot of the bed, his silver chin resting on a lump that appeared to be the man's right foot. When my father kicked the bed, the roofer turned and sighed, resting one pale arm over his eyes. He seemed to be groping for something— or someone—with his other hand, but still my father allegedly remained clueless. Our house was on a cul-de-sac in a suburb of Kansas City that is known for its safety, excellent public schools, and complete lack of public transportation; still, my father said that for far too long, he truly perceived the man as some kind of confused, unshaven transient who had broken in to take a mid-morning nap.

"I was exhausted," he explained to me later. "Okay? Veronica? You understand? I'd been on a plane all day. All I wanted was to come home, change clothes—maybe even, God forbid, have someone make dinner for me—and I walk into *that*."

He said the situation only started to make sense after he spotted the note. It was creased in half so it sat like a little tent on top of the roofer's work boots, which were on the floor next to the bed, wool socks still nestled inside. Before my father even picked up the note, he recognized the lined yellow paper, a pad of which my mother kept in the drawer of her bedside table for copying down interesting passages in books, and gift ideas from the catalogues that she also read while in bed.

"O CLOUD-PALE eyelids, dream-dimmed eyes . . ." *You look so beautiful asleep I can't bring my self to wake you. But make sure you are gone by three. (And take this note with you!) I will call you. And I promise you, all day long, I will think about being brave.*

The note was not signed, but my father of course recognized my mother's handwriting, the careful cursive, the neat and even loops.

He looked at her bedside table. There was the Philip Roth book she'd been reading before he left. StriVectin hand cream. A tube of the raspberry lip balm she had, for years—and in his opinion, very irritatingly—woken to put on in the middle of the night. His brain was able to register what was clear, but he was so surprised, he said, that his legs literally gave way, and he had to sit on the edge of the bed. Because of my father's occasional back problems, my parents slept on an expensive mattress, the kind made out of the material that has something to do with astronauts—and apparently, it really could withstand the weight of a grown man sitting on the edge of it without disturbing a sleeping man, or even an elderly dog, lying in the middle. So my father had several seconds to look at the roofer's slackened face, and to notice—to his even further surprise—just how young the interloper was. When I first heard the story from my bewildered and disgusted older sister, the roofer was reported to be about thirty years old. That may have been an exaggeration—to this day, my mother maintains he was closer to forty.

But we can all agree that my father—once he collected his wits—responded to the crisis with characteristic forethought and logic. I wouldn't put all of this on his training as a lawyer. He is a huge fan of true crime—in his spare time, what little there is of it, he watches cop and private detective shows, *Unsolved Mysteries,* etc. He dropped the note where he'd found it, stood up, and took a large step away from the bed. His phone had a camera on it. He took it out of his pocket and took a picture of the sleeping man. He found the man's flannel shirt lying on the floor, and he used it—as he had seen so many television detectives use latex gloves—to pick up my mother's note. He slipped both articles behind her big oak dresser for safekeeping, and then crept over to his dresser, where he kept the small handgun he had purchased three years earlier after a house several streets away was burglarized—though it was a much nicer house, and the owners had been away at the time, skiing in Aspen.

"He bought that gun so he could tell everyone he bought it," my mother had said. "He bought it to make me insane."

And truly, on the snowy afternoon that the discovery of the sleeping roofer gave my father some reason to finally load the gun, he didn't load it. He wasn't looking for vengeance, he told me, just the upper hand.

"He could have just asked him to leave," my mother pointed out later. "Mr. Drama. You know what? He probably could have just cleared his throat."

But my father did use the gun, the tip of the barrel, to nudge the roofer awake. "Get the hell out of my house," he said, very calmly, or at least that's how he told us he said it, with all the quiet bravado of someone who has watched several Clint Eastwood movies in the course of his life. My father does have a trial lawyer's flair for drama—he tells stories well, and he has a good memory for dialogue. But neither my sister nor I was ever completely convinced that his actual delivery was so tranquil—our father is a very excitable person. He screams when he loses his car keys. He wails when he stubs his toe. In any case, the roofer woke up quickly and found whatever my father said, however he said it, sufficiently clear, and the gun sufficiently motivating. He raised his palms in surrender. He asked permission to stand. To my father's surprise, the roofer was wearing jeans, his leather belt still buckled. And he wasn't that physically impressive, now that he was standing up. He was several inches shorter than my father, and though his arms were broad and muscular, he was a little soft in the middle. "Cloud-pale eyelids?" my father asked me later. "*Cloud-pale eyelids?*"

The roofer, his eyelids now invisible above his wide-awake eyes, asked permission to put on his boots, almost every word, according to my father, followed by an "uhhh" or a "duhhhh" that strongly hinted he was not just temporarily terrified, but also permanently stupid. Of course, my father's impersonation may not have been accurate or fair. Long after the roofer—his name, I later learned, was

Greg Liddiard—returned to Alaska to marry his pregnant girlfriend, and my mother had little reason to defend him, she told my older sister and me that there were many different kinds of intelligence and stupidity, and that Greg Liddiard—her former boyfriend, poetry pal, whatever he was—hardly had the market cornered on any of them.

My father, by his own admission, felt pretty stupid himself. He wanted both me and Elise to understand he'd been blindsided. You think you know a person, he said. You think you have a good idea of what's going on in your own home. Once he understood the real story, he said, he was all done playing the dupe. Less than two minutes after Greg Liddiard ran shirtless out the door and down our long, icy driveway to his van, which was still parked in the curb of the cul-de-sac, my father used his cell phone to call my mother on hers.

"She must have seen the number," he told me, still incredulous. "Okay? Veronica? She must have known it was me." He clearly remembered that my mother's hello did not sound particularly guarded, not particularly friendly or unfriendly. She did not sound like a liar, a betrayer, a thief of his life energy, of his very life. She sounded, he said, matter-of-fact.

"Oh," she said. "You're home?" There was activity in the background, people shouting. At first, he pictured her subbing at the elementary school or the junior high, answering her cell phone in front of a room of bored or hostile young suburbanites as they misbehaved and switched identities and asked when their real teacher would come back. But it was Saturday. My mother was working her volunteer shift at the food pantry for the homeless shelter. How altruistic! He imagined her stacking cans of soup, wearing an apron, a self-righteous expression, and also her wedding ring.

"Yes," he said. "I am home, Natalie. And I think you better come home, too. In fact, you better come home right away."

She must have picked up on his tone. He said she was silent for a long stretch. Even with the background noise, he could hear her breathing on the other end.

"Yes," she said finally. "We need to talk."

He laughed. He actually laughed. He was nervous, he said, freaked out, standing in their bedroom, looking in the mirror at his own middle-aged face and realizing just how much was about to change. My parents had been married for twenty-six years. My mother was a junior in college when they met, my father in his second year of law school. Their union had survived early parenthood, a flooded basement, and the deaths of both of their parents. They had been allies against my sister's first boyfriend, Kyle, who had been nice enough at first, but who threatened to set himself on fire in our driveway after my sister broke up with him. My parents were married when Reagan was president, when the first Bush was president, when Clinton was president, and then the second Bush as well. They had planned vacations, funerals, and my sister's wedding, together.

"Oh my dear," he said, almost tenderly, his voice wistful, or at least it was each of the several times he told this story to me. "Oh Natalie," he said to my wayward mother. "I'm afraid you have no idea."

From this point on, the story gets even more slippery. Though unsolicited, my mother and father have each given me a different account of the Day of the Sleeping Roofer, and what happened after she came home. My father said he confronted her with the note, the shirt. My mother said he didn't need to. He said she sat down at the dining room table, still wearing her long wool coat. She did not appear exactly devastated. If anything, he said, she seemed disoriented, her big eyes staring at the striped wallpaper and crown molding that she herself had picked out and nailed on, as if she'd never seen them before. My father repeatedly emphasized that she looked a little demented—her hat crooked over her curly hair, her cheeks bright red from the cold. He said she didn't have anything to say for herself. He said he watched her stare at the wallpaper for a while, her runny nose unwiped, and then he went upstairs to get his travel bag, which was, conveniently, still packed, ready to go. He carried it back downstairs, past my catatonic mother, and out the side door to the garage, his heart, he said, a brick in his chest.

He'd only driven to the end of the block when it occurred to him that he had not done anything wrong. He still wanted to take a shower, and he didn't want to take it in a hotel. He wanted to take a shower in the house that he had worked over sixty hours a week for over twenty years to pay for. So he drove back to the house and yelled this at my mother, his breath turned to vapor in the open doorway to the garage.

My mother agreed, according to my father. Or at least she understood he was right. She left for a hotel. She took only a suitcase the first time she left. Five minutes later, she came back for Bowzer, and all of Bowzer's medicine, worried, she said, because my father was unfamiliar with the dog's complicated care routine. My father admits she was contrite and dignified in both of her exits. Of course, he added, with no real malice, she could afford to be contrite at that point. She still had her credit cards.

The next afternoon, forty-two miles away, I went on my second date with Tim Culpepper. We went sledding on dinner trays I stole from the dining hall, and then spent an hour making out in his car, the heaters on high, Nick Drake on the little stereo. After he dropped me off, I was still so happy, and smiling so much, that people next to me on the elevator looked uncomfortable. When I got to my room, my phone rang. I had to tuck the cold dinner trays under one arm to get my phone out of my coat pocket. It was my sister calling from San Diego to tell me about the Sleeping Roofer. I stood still in my doorway, the light of the hallway bright, my room still dark, the phone pressed against my ear. My mittens were wet from the snow.

"Are you still there?" she asked. "Veronica? Did you hear me? Mom and Dad are getting divorced."

The dinner trays fell on the toe of my boot, and then clattered on the linoleum floor. I said, "What? No they aren't." I had just talked to my mother the week before. She'd been worried about my scratchy throat, my sniffy nose. It was just a cold, but she'd wanted me to go to the doctor. She didn't think I was getting enough sleep.

"I just got off the phone with Dad," Elise said. "He's already talked to his lawyer."

It was a typical Elise response: irrefutable, no way out. I did not argue again. But when she told me about the Sleeping Roofer, I silently shook my head, not believing her at all. I could not reconcile the idea of it with all I knew of my mother. She was not a careless person. She smiled a lot, but not just at men. She smiled at old ladies. She smiled at squirrels. She was not a seductive flirt. Our neighbor, Mr. Shunke, would whistle at her when she was out gardening, but she would only roll her eyes. She wore comfortable shoes. She read magazines that had mostly recipes. And more importantly, she had been my mother. I had grown up with her kindness, taking it for granted, using it up.

"I have to go," Elise said. She wasn't crying, but her voice was quiet. "Charlie's home, and we have dinner plans with someone at my firm. I'll call you later."

I was still holding the phone, staring at it, when Tim Culpepper knocked on my door. I'd left my hat in his car. He held it out to me, looking uncertain and very tall. I said, "My parents are getting a divorce."

He came in and sat next to me on my bed, and spent much of the rest of the evening listening to me say, in so many different ways, that I was just really, really surprised, that I had not seen this coming at all. He said, "I don't know what to say." But he kept sitting there. I told him I was sorry for crying in front of him when he hardly even knew me. He said, "Oh come on, if I had a dollar for every girl who pulled this . . ." But he looked at my eyes and didn't make any more jokes.

I didn't want to call either my mother or my father. I didn't want to hear them say it, and I didn't know what I would say. Tim nodded. He didn't say he had to go. I told him, again, how surprised I was. My family had just spent Christmas together. Elise and Charlie had come in from California. They stayed in her old room, and I stayed in mine, and on the afternoon of Christmas Day, we'd walked over to old Mr. Wansing's for the neighborhood pie party just like we had on every Christmas Day of my life. Everything seemed normal. My mother got my father a recording device that looked like a pen, something he could use at work. My father got her a juice machine. They'd sat next to each other on the couch in bathrobes and watched as we opened our presents from them. In my memory, they both looked happy.

After a while, Tim started to look tired, his green eyes squinty, his long arms going wide when he stretched and yawned. I told him he could go if he wanted. I would be fine, I said. But I knew I wouldn't be. I didn't know what I would do with myself the rest of the night. I wouldn't be able to sleep. I wouldn't be able to study.

He raked his hands through his brown hair and said, "This may sound stupid, but when you're this upset, sometimes TV is good."

I didn't have a television, so he took me to his apartment, where I watched infomercials and a documentary on coral reefs until I fell asleep on his couch. He slept in the chair beside me, his legs dangling over the armrest, one of his hands in my hair.

I never liked living in the dorm. Even as a freshman, I disliked the noise, the ugly, orange-cushioned furniture, the communal bathrooms halfway down the hall. During my first visit home, I worked out a careful budget to show my parents that their costs would actually go down for my sophomore year, even when taking utilities and food into account, if they let me move into an apartment with two other girls on my floor. My mother seemed persuaded, but my father would have none of it. He seemed preoccupied by the idea that I would somehow be killed as soon as I had to buy my own groceries. He didn't feel comfortable with the idea of me walking or biking to the store. He didn't care that one of my roommates would have a car. He worried my roommates would not be careful about locking doors and windows. He worried that they would skip out on their share of the rent, or suddenly start smoking, or have weird boyfriends. And then, he wanted to know, what would I do?

There was no arguing with him when he got like that, impervious to logic, talking too quickly to hear anything I said. Elise might have known what to say, or yell, back at him; but all I could think was that I had nothing to negotiate with, nothing to threaten, nothing to withhold.

Later that night, my mother tried to plead my case. She didn't know I was listening. She thought I'd gone out to walk Bowzer, but I was just standing in the mudroom, scratching Bowzer under his collar so he would stay quiet, my ear pressed against the door.

"You read way too many of those crime books." She sounded angrier than I was. "They are making you completely paranoid. And no, do *not* talk to me about everything you've seen in court. You have to quit talking to Veronica like that. I don't want to teach her to be afraid of everything." Here, to my surprise, her voice broke.

He started in with a "You don't kno—" but she made a yelping sound so loud and sudden that I pulled away from the door, and my father actually stopped talking.

"She is making a perfectly reasonable request," my mother said, her voice quiet now, her breathing even. "I think we could at least consider it."

A long silence followed. I leaned close to the door again, waiting. I smelled cookies baking, chocolate chip. She would send me back to the dorm with several bags, enough to give out to my friends.

"Okay," he said. "I considered it. And the answer is no. She's safer in the dorm. I'm paying for the dorm. I'm not paying for an apartment yet. Period."

He was calmer the next time we talked, though he didn't change his mind. He said I would have to stay in the dorm until he could get my mother a new car, so I could have her minivan, which was old, but big and safe and reliable.

I didn't press him after that. My parents didn't discuss finances with me, but I had a good idea of why my mother was still driving the same minivan that she had been driving since I was in grade school, and why we had canceled our membership to the country club, and why I was only encouraged to apply for a college where I could get in-state tuition. My father was still making a good income, but there had been some bad investments, and then the nursing homes for both grandmothers, and then the funerals, and then the problems with the house.

My mother had been the first to notice the dark patches on the ceiling in the upstairs hallway. The night they got the estimate for a new roof, they stayed up late and argued, their words rising up from the heating vent in my room. My father said they would have to go into the retirement money, but my mother didn't want to. He held firm. She was being ridiculous, he said. They had to pay off credit cards, and the home equity loan. The interest rates were killing them. She needed to do the math. They had plenty of time before he retired, and in just a few years, there would be no more nursing home bills, and no more funerals, no more poorly chosen stocks, and I would be the only one in school. He would reinvest in their retirement then. Smooth sailing, my father told her. For now, they just needed to get out of debt.

Of course, the roof repair ended up costing more than either of them could have known. After my father came home to find the Sleeping

Roofer in his bed, it was pretty clear to all of us he would not be buying my mother a new car after all.

"Divorce is expensive," he told me, not long after he'd moved out. "Damn lawyers." He tried to laugh, but he looked a little dazed, and still as shocked as I was by what my mother had done. He was just getting over the flu, he said. His courtroom baritone was croaky. He'd aready gained some weight in his belly—my mother had been the one to monitor how much butter and salt he used.

"I can keep up with your tuition, no problem," he said, his gaze avoiding my face. "I don't want you to worry about that. But money's a little tight. In fact, if you could think of any way to offset some expenses, I would very much appreciate that."

So I returned to the dorm my junior year, this time as a resident assistant. I got three meals a day and a single room. In exchange, I had to attend a two-week summer training rife with workshops on things like fire safety, eating disorders, and CPR; during the year, I had to be in the dorm from six P.M. on for seven or eight nights a month in case there happened to be a fire, an eating disorder, or a youthful heart attack. The only other thing I was supposed to do was come up with a variety of event programming to make the dorm feel smaller and less institutional, at least for the freshman girls on my floor.

"*I'm sorry,*" my mother wrote in an e-mail. "*I know you were excited about an apartment.*" I could not tell if she meant "sorry" in the universal sense, just extending sympathy, or if she were specifically sorry for her actions, namely, having a slumber party with the Roofer. It was hard to know if she felt sorry about that at all. In those first few months after my father moved into a condo by the Plaza, my mother actually seemed happy, though the Roofer had long disappeared; she presented herself as pleasantly uncertain about what her future held—she didn't know whether she would stay in the house or move to another part of town, or even to another city. She didn't know if she wanted to go back to school. "I'm catching my breath," she told both me and Elise. "I'm just going to wait a bit before I make any decisions."

But by the time I moved home for summer break, there was a Realtor's sign in the front yard, though she did not appear ready for any kind of open house. Elise's room, my father's study, and one of the bathrooms had been sealed off with some kind of plastic sheeting—my mother said she was trying to cut back on air-conditioning. She'd realized how bad it was for the environment, she said. It was the same reason she'd let the lawn go, she said—all that wasted water and energy and gasoline for the mower. I asked her, half-joking, if that was also why she had stopped using the vacuum cleaner, and the mop. And the dishwasher. Throughout my childhood, my mother had been an energetic housekeeper. She'd baked bread. She'd kept a little flagpole by the front door, with a different colorful flag for every holiday and season. But when I first came home that May, the Christmas flag, with its faded smiling snowman, was still flying over the doorway. Inside, small tumbleweeds of dog hair drifted under the ceiling fan of the living room.

She'd gotten a job selling accessories at DeBeck's; it was just for the summer, she said. In the fall she would start subbing again, and figure out what she really wanted to do. She brought home fast food for dinner—mostly turkey sandwiches from a sub shop in the mall, and she ate hers right off the foil wrapper they came in, sliding mine to me across the table. She insisted we eat dinner together whenever possible, but she was difficult to talk to. She jumped around a lot in conversation. She asked me the same questions twice.

I, on the other hand, did my best to ask her no questions at all. I did wonder if she had been in love with the Roofer, and if she was heartbroken for him, and not my father. But I could not bring myself to ask her this. She was different now, too open, more than ready to tell me too much. She seemed desperate in a way that my father did not. I was anxious to get back to school, to Tim, to my friends, to all my plans, and to my own unruined life. My mother and I looked alike. We had the same dark, curly hair, the same brown eyes and long noses. But we were not the same person. That whole summer, I could feel myself pushing away from her, like a swimmer trying to escape someone reaching out, about to drown.

A week after I moved back into the dorm to begin my junior year, she sold the house. The buyer, who apparently had the rare ability to look past an overgrown lawn and plastic-wrapped rooms, wanted to close in thirty days. My mother acted as if she'd won the lottery. She was *excited* about moving into a new apartment, she said. It would be *so nice* to have all the maintenance taken care of, and *so much* less space to clean.

I understand now that I was refusing to see what I didn't want to. I could have asked her more questions. I could have asked her how she really was doing. In my defense, I will submit that I was young. And she said, repeatedly, that she was fine, absolutely fine.

Just a few months later, winter descending again, she started to seem askew. I came to stay with her over Thanksgiving, and most of her things were still in boxes at her new apartment—she said she didn't have time to unpack. She kept newspapers spread out over much of the carpet in case Bowzer had an accident while she was at work. And then one night, she drove to Lawrence to take me out to dinner, and on the way back from the restaurant, we almost ran out of gas—by the time she realized it, the needle was on empty, and we'd coasted into a station on fumes. These were little things, but together, they were worrisome. They seemed part of a larger unraveling, her good judgment falling away.

Finally, against the probable advice of anyone she might have asked, she started to complain to me about my father. Almost a year had passed since the day of the Sleeping Roofer. But the divorce—or more precisely, the settlement—was far from over. She believed he was hiding money from her. Their lawyers were still battling it out.

"Elise didn't have to work when she was in school. And she went out of state. It's ridiculous. He could afford to help you more if he—"

"Mom." I turned to her quickly. "Stop. Don't bring me into it."

She leaned against her window, her fingers pressed over her mouth. We were in her minivan, parked in the circular drive outside my dorm. The floodlights by the main entrance had just flickered on automatically, tuned in to the dusk that now settled just after six o'clock. The day had been bright and cloudless, and warm for early December. Gold leaves lay dried and broken under the windshield wipers. She had driven to Lawrence to take me out for Thai food; I had a box of leftover Chicken Satay on the floor mat between my feet.

"It's not that big a deal," I said. "A lot of students work. Most, probably."

She leaned forward and rested her chin on the steering wheel, gazing out through the partially fogged windshield. Her black knit hat was a little too big; the edge of it fell just above her eyes. She looked befuddled, cute, a child dressed up for a greeting card.

"Sorry," she said finally. "I shouldn't bring you into it. You're right."

A truck with a camper shell parked in front of us. A stout woman wearing a Kansas City Chiefs jacket got out of the driver's side and walked around to the back, meeting a girl who had gotten out the other side wearing sweats and a T-shirt. The woman opened the shell and helped the girl take out a basket of folded laundry. They fussed with the basket for a moment, pulling something else out of the truck to cover the clothes. The girl gave the woman a quick kiss and carried the basket up the sidewalk to the front doors.

The truck pulled away, but my mother continued to stare straight ahead.

"Where do you do your laundry?"

I looked at her. She sounded strange, as if she were asking a question with an answer she could not bear.

"Here," I said. "They have machines in the basement." I watched the girl with the basket walk up the steps to the front doors. "Some people just do it at home because . . . I don't know . . . they go home."

"Home," she repeated.

I rested my head against the cold glass of the passenger door and gazed almost longingly seven floors up to the dark window of my room. I did feel bad for her. I knew her sadness was real. But I was tired, tired in general, and specifically tired of hearing how much she didn't like all the changes she had brought on herself. Her problems were not my problems. At that particular moment, my problem was this: I had an organic chemistry test in five days, and even if I spent every spare moment until then studying, I was still probably going to fail it.

"I'd better get going," I said.

"Just stay a little longer, honey. Okay? I hardly ever get to see you."

"I have to study."

She patted my knee. "Just a few more minutes. To talk to your mom who just drove an hour to see you."

"I have to be in the building by six. I'm on duty tonight."

Her mouth tightened. "It seems like a lot," she said. "This job seems to take up a lot of time."

Actually, it didn't. It should have, maybe; but I wasn't really doing the job. At the start of the year, I had every intention of being an excellent RA. I hung a sign that said "RA" by my door, and also a message board with a dry erase marker. But now the first semester was nearly over, and I didn't know the names of most of the girls on my floor. I was too busy. In addition to a lit class and Spanish, I was taking five credit hours of organic chemistry and five more of physiology. I woke every morning with a deep sense of impending doom, a never-ending worry that I should be studying more.

"I don't mind it," I said, lying. This year, especially, I hated the dorm. I felt ten years older than everyone else. "And this kind of job looks good on med school applications. Seriously. They tell you to do stuff like this."

"I just hope you're spending time on your schoolwork."

I registered the words, felt my body react: my teeth clenched, my breathing quickened. "Mom. I study. You have no idea how much I study."

"I'm sure I do have an idea, Veronica. I went to college."

I ran my tongue along my teeth, looking away. The comparison was too ridiculous to respond to. She had majored in education.

"I just . . ." She turned to me and sighed. "I imagine you spend a lot of time with Tom."

"Tim."

"Right. Sorry."

"For your information," I said to her now, "I do not spend all my time with Tim. I hardly spend any time with Tim. I work and I study. All the time."

"He's a lot older than you, isn't he? He's out of school already?"

"He's in graduate school. He's twenty-four."

"You're only twenty," she said, as if I didn't know. "You should be focusing on yourself right now, on your schoolwork." She looked away and clicked her tongue. "And twenty-four is significantly older."

He's the best part of my life, I thought. I slid my eyes toward her. "You're suggesting I go younger?"

She closed her eyes. She looked so unhappy that I felt bad.

"I have to tell you something."

I looked at her.

"You seem hostile, honey. Are you angry with me?"

"No," I said, because saying yes would take up too much time.

She straightened her shoulders. "I know this might make you uncomfortable, but it's important for me that you understand.

Whatever your father has told you, I was never . . . technically, unfaithful in my marriage."

I winced. There were things I did not want to know about her, images I did not want in my head.

"Veronica. Would you look at me, please?"

I raised both eyebrows. She had spoken with all the authority she'd really had over me several years ago, as if I were fourteen again and she wanted me to unload the dishwasher.

"Please look at me, Veronica. You're still not allowed to be rude."

I looked at her. My mother has pretty eyes. They are large and dark, and they make her look friendly and a little concerned, even when she's mad. I pursed my lips and waited.

"I know your father and his lawyer will make what they want of that note." She swallowed. "But I at least want you to know that Greg and I never . . . made love."

I clapped my hands over my ears.

"Fine." She fiddled with the knob for the heater. "I just wanted you to know. It was a friendship. It might have turned . . . later . . . There were feelings there. There were for me. But we had only talked. We talked a lot. That day he fell asleep—we'd just been talking."

"In bed?" I shook my head, annoyed with myself. I had just asked her to spare me the details.

"I was unhappy. I was unhappy with the marriage, unhappy in general. It was nice to talk with someone."

"Then why didn't you get a divorce then?" *Before you had a sleepover,* I meant. I didn't need to say it. My tone was condescending, an adult speaking to a child. It felt good, gratifying, and then it didn't.

She shook her head. That was all. Maybe she had no good answer. That was a difference between my parents. My father spelled everything out, making a clear argument for his indignation; but with my mother, I was left to guess, to piece together clues from my memories. I had had no idea she'd been unhappy. Or rather, I had not really thought of her as happy or unhappy. The last year I lived at home, my mother spent her days driving my grandmother Von Holten to doctor appointments and even to a butcher on the other side of the city that sold pickled pig's feet, a delicacy that made my mother nauseous but brought her mother-in-law back to her happy girlhood in Queens. My mother learned to read a glucose meter. She became an expert at folding up my grandmother's wheelchair, putting it in her trunk, getting it out again. Three times a week, they went to an indoor pool, and my mother walked with her through the water.

My father had been appreciative. I remembered him saying so, all the time. He wished he could do more himself, he said, but financially speaking, this wasn't the year for him to take any time off. Expenses were adding up: Elise was in law school. I would go to college soon. My grandmother's money had run out, and yet she continued to live. So every day, both my father and my mother were up early, and gone in their respective cars before I caught the bus for school; but at the end of the day, my mother seemed the more tired of the two. After dinner, she would go up to her room, saying she wanted to read; but if I walked by their room after eight, her eyes were usually closed. By the time I went to bed, my father would still be downstairs in his chair, watching the news with Bowzer's head in his lap.

"My goodness, that's a big building you live in." She leaned over the steering wheel to look up at the dorm. Her voice had taken on that chirpy, resolute quality I recognized from a few months back.

"Yeah." I turned and looked up as well. From this angle, my dorm was a big plain rectangle of brown brick. The inside looked pretty much the same. "They've got a thousand of us in there."

"That's too many." She clicked her tongue. "It wouldn't feel homey at all. You know, I don't know why you didn't rush, Veronica. I loved my sorority house. There were about thirty of us, living in. We were like a big family. We all took turns making dinner, setting the table. It was so much fun."

I said nothing. It was not a surprise to hear that my mother had loved this.

She looked down at my boots. "Oh good! You're wearing them. How are they?"

"They're great," I said. "Thank you." She had given me the boots for my birthday. They were nice, stylish, maybe expensive. She got a good discount at DeBeck's, though she only worked full-time during school vacations. When school was in session, she took substitute teaching jobs during the day, and worked at DeBeck's on evenings and weekends.

"I like your hair like that." She lifted a long strand from my shoulder. "It's very grown-up looking. You're straightening it?" Her hand moved over her own curls.

I shifted in my seat. I needed to go. I wanted to go. But I could tell that there was something else she wanted to say. She looked coiled up, ready to spring, her fingers tapping the steering wheel.

She turned to me. "Christmas is coming up."

I nodded. I wished it weren't true, but it was.

"Elise doesn't know if she's coming home," she said. "Or here, I mean. Her home is there now, I suppose." She laughed a little, and then stopped. "Anyway, it might be just the two of us, if you come to my apartment. We could go out for dinner. Or a movie. That might be fun." Her eyes moved over mine. "But if you already have plans . . . with your father, that's fine, too. You could stay with me, but eat with him. Or you could stay with him, and eat with me. That would be fine, too."

I looked back up at the dorm. In two weeks, it would close for winter break, and it would stay closed for a month. The year before, I'd loved going home for break. I'd gone back to the house on the cul-de-sac, and slept in my old room, my old bed. This year, no matter where I stayed, would be different. My father's new condo had a guest room with a fold-out couch. At my mother's little apartment, I slept in a sleeping bag.

"Can I get back to you on that?" I asked. I didn't want to promise anything. I'd stayed with my mother for Thanksgiving, so it seemed I should stay with my father over Christmas.

I straightened up. "How's Bowzer?" I asked. "How come you didn't bring him?"

She shook her head. "He doesn't like to be in the car now that it's getting colder, I think." She leaned forward and fiddled with the heater again. "I've got to get him in to the vet. He's stiff. He sleeps all the time. And he's so cranky."

"He's old."

"No. It's more than that. I've got to take him in." She nodded as if making a decision. "But don't worry about that." She looked out into the night sky. "So what are you going to do tonight?"

I rolled my lips together. There was no point in talking. She did not hear me. "I'm going to study," I said slowly. "I'm going to study like I do every night."

"Oh. What are you going to study?"

"Chemistry. I have a test on Tuesday."

"Honey. It's only Wednesday."

I looked at her. *Make up your mind,* I wanted to say. *Make up your mind about how I should be.*

She patted my leg. "I'm sure you'll do fine." She held her hand up to the heating vent. "Your sister is always busy. Always worried about the next big case, the next big meeting, can't talk on the phone, she's got to work. But you both always do fine." She sounded sad, her voice wrong for the words. "You both always do so well."

"Not anymore."

"What?" She leaned forward to look at me.

"Nothing."

"Honey. Tell me what you just said." She reached over and pulled her old move, tickling beneath my chin until I raised it.

I held up both hands to the dash. "I just . . . You don't understand the way that it's hard. The test."

She leaned back. "Oh."

We sat without talking for maybe a minute, listening to the idling engine. Three girls walked arm-in-arm across the lawn. They were coming from the direction of the dining hall, their faces bowed against the wind. I thought I recognized one of them from my floor. I couldn't be sure.

"I'd better go in," I said.

"Right," she said. "On duty."

I opened the door, but her hand fell on the sleeve of my coat. She held tight until I turned back.

"Don't forget your leftovers." She nodded at the paper box of Chicken Satay. "But, honey, if you don't have a refrigerator you can put that in, you should probably just throw it away. You don't want to mess with food poisoning."

"Gotcha." I stepped out of the van with the box.

She reached for my sleeve. I turned back.

"Honey." Her face was pale in the interior light. "I just want you to know that . . ." She kept her hand on the sleeve, holding me there. "I know I'm a little bit . . . maybe kind of a mess right now. But I still love you so much. I'm still here for you."

For just a moment, it felt like before, when she was just my mother, her gaze so focused and full of love and worry for me. But even now that she was smiling at me and saying these nice words, I could see something wasn't right, or at least not the same. My eyes moved over her face in a slow spiral. She'd stopped getting her hair done, getting it highlighted, whatever she used to do to it. I could see strands of gray even in the semidarkness of her car. I said nothing. I didn't want to interrupt her. I wanted to believe what she was saying was true.

"And maybe I don't understand the way that test will be hard, but

I'm still rooting for you. I want you to do great." She squeezed my arm and smiled. "You've got your whole life in front of you. I just want you to make good decisions. It's so important for you to make good decisions right now."

I nodded, my eyes on hers. Her eyes, at least, had not changed, and so I made certain they were the last thing I noticed before I shut the door. When I got to the dorm's front entrance, I could still hear the idling engine of her van. Whenever she dropped me off after dark, she always waited, headlights shining, until I was safely inside.

2

I DID NOT ALWAYS want to be a doctor. I had only known, for a very long time, that I did not want to be a lawyer. Elise is six years older than I am, and so growing up, I didn't feel competitive with her, exactly; it would be more accurate to say she overwhelmed me from the start. She overwhelmed a lot of people. When she was in high school, she won the state championship for speech and debate two years in a row. She was class president. She was valedictorian. The summer before she left for college, she went to a town hall meeting and argued with the mayor about curbside recycling, and ended up giving such a passionate speech that it made the local television news.

She didn't overwhelm my father. But she could more than hold her own with him, which was enough to impress me. If he got loud, she didn't care. Sometimes she got loud, too. They argued about everything—her boyfriends, Tibet, the wisdom of a property tax hike, and whether my father should keep using so much butter. They were both fast thinkers—neither required much time between hearing a point and refuting it. At the dinner table, my mother and father sat at opposite ends, with a daughter between them on either side. If we had ever changed it, and let Elise sit across from my father, my mother and I would have been like spectators at a tennis match, silently watching the volleys go back and forth.

He sometimes seemed unnerved by his inability to intimidate Elise in any way; but for the most part, he seemed very happy to have a sparring partner, and also to have helped create a younger, prettier version of himself. When Elise got into law school, he walked around the house whistling "Yes Sir, That's My Baby" for days.

So of course I wanted to try for something equally impressive. I didn't want to do what she was doing, or even anything like it. I wanted to try for something different, something I could be better at—my own thing.

The trouble was, I didn't know what that thing was. I had good grades. I liked to read. I could do a backbend. As a girl, I had entertained the usual career fantasies: marine biologist, horse trainer, dolphin specialist. But my parents had each, in their own way, discouraged me from a career involving animals. My father's concerns were pragmatic: "Goofball," he said. "Honey. A vet is one of the worst jobs you can pick. You've got to have all the school that a doctor has, and you make about a fifth of the money. Sweetie. Why do that to yourself?"

My mother agreed that I should consider a different path, but for a very different reason. She pointed out, repeatedly, that I didn't take care of my own dog. "You *promised* that if we got you a puppy, you would take care of it," she reminded me. "You whined. You begged. You said you would walk it, you would feed it. And now who takes care of Bowzer? Who walks him when it's five degrees outside? Who feeds him? Who makes sure he has clean water? Who cleans up after him?"

The answer, of course, was my mother. Bowzer was a cute dog, a bouncy little schnauzer mix, and in his youth, my sister and I had been happy to play with him in the yard on sunny days and to snuggle with him at night. My father used to watch the news with Bowzer on his lap, holding him like a baby and rubbing his belly. But it was my mother who truly took care of Bowzer, even before he got old and stinky. By the time I left for college, he was deaf, and somewhat blind, with a fat pocket sticking out of his back like a handle. When my parents separated, my mother got full custody of Bowzer, pretty much by default.

It wasn't until my sophomore year, not long after my parents' separation, that I started thinking about going into medicine. I had aced my freshman biology class. I liked the idea of helping people. I had always admired our family physician, a quiet, thoughtful woman who took an annual break from her middle-class clientele to vaccinate refugee children in Kenya. She rarely erred with her hunches and prescriptions, and even my father spoke to her with deference. I thought I might be good at medical research. I saw myself in a quiet room, doing something important with test tubes that would help save, or at least improve, many lives. I didn't care about money so much, at least not the way my father did. ("You will," he told me gravely.) But I cared very much about how excited he got when I told him I was pre-med.

"You're being very smart," he said, pointing at me, though we were alone in his car, on our way to pick up two of his suits at the dry cleaner. Apparently, he told me, it was a two-person job, because why in the hell would you expect a dry cleaner to provide adequate parking for customers? Why not just assume a paying customer could bring along his daughter during the only time he got to see her in over a month so he could wait in the car while she ran up to the store to get his suits back? He went on like this for a good three minutes, and I didn't say anything. Until very recently, my mother had picked up his dry cleaning. I didn't know where or how she parked.

"Medical school. Good." He opened the ashtray on his dash and fished out the ticket stubs for the cleaner. "I worry sometimes, having daughters. I read an article just the other day. You know what college majors have the highest percentage of female students?"

I shook my head. He handed me the stubs and held up bent fingers to count.

"Education. Social work. English. And the one about taking care of children, I forget what it's called. Guess what they all have in common?"

I winced as we came within a foot of a cyclist. "They won't make money?"

"Bingo." He nodded at the glove compartment. "There's a twenty in there. You can pay from that. Make sure you get a receipt." He turned suddenly, sliding in alongside a fire hydrant. "Guess what major has the lowest percentage of female students?"

I didn't answer right away. He snapped his fingers.

"Pre-med?"

"Engineering. But you get the drift. And then they wonder why women don't make as much money as men. Well there you go. These girls do it to themselves. Why? Why choose to be poor? You and Elise are being smart. You're looking out for yourselves."

He put the car in park and smiled, his eyes full of affection and pride. I smiled back. It took me a moment to realize he was waiting.

"Honey," he said gently. "The suits."

I went to my first pre-med advisory session the fall semester of my sophomore year. It was held in an auditorium—they must have known about two thousand of us would show up. Gretchen and I got there ten minutes early, but the only seats left were in the far balcony. I worried we wouldn't be able to hear, but when the advisor came onto the stage, his face also appeared, like the Wizard of Oz, on a giant screen that hung from the ceiling. Another screen listed the course requirements and the kinds of grades and MCAT scores medical schools would expect. "Look to your left," the advisor told us, and two thousand or so of us looked to our lefts. "Look to your right," he said, and so, good pre-med students that we were, we followed that direction as well. "Don't get too friendly with either one of your neighbors," he said. "Because only one of you is going to make it."

Even at the time, when I was still innocent of organic chemistry and just how miserable it would soon make me, it seemed a very bad omen that at that first pre-med meeting, my friend Gretchen had been sitting on my right.

"It doesn't really matter who you were sitting by," she assured me. "He just meant it as a statistic."

Gretchen sometimes didn't understand when I was joking. But on the whole, she was freakishly smart. If life were fair, if hard work and discipline really could trump pure aptitude, I would have easily been the one to succeed out of almost any group of three in that auditorium. Gretchen, on the other hand, went out a lot. She had three different fake IDs. Sophomore year, we had inorganic lab together at seven in the morning, and Gretchen would show up with mascara tracks down her cheeks, her blond hair tangled and reeking of smoke. But she never seemed particularly pained after she put on her lab coat and goggles. She worked through the most complicated titrations and equations as if she were just stumbling around the dining hall, getting herself coffee and cereal—nothing a girl with a little hangover couldn't manage. She usually finished early.

I did okay that year. I put in the time. I memorized the formulas, the periodic table, the thermodynamic laws. I stayed in and studied when Gretchen went out. And though it seemed a little unfair that I should have to work so much harder than she did, I was happy I could at least keep up. The future seemed bright and certain. My father started saying, "What's up, Doc?" when he left messages on my phone.

This year, however, was different. First semester was almost over, and I was already sinking. Organic chemistry was everything I had struggled with and barely understood in inorganic the year before—only now all the diagrams had gone 3-D. For the first time, it didn't matter how much I studied. As early as September, I went into my TA's office hours for extra help. But when I tried to explain what I didn't understand, he used the word "obviously" a lot, squinting at me as if I were playing some joke on him, as if I were a small child pretending to be a chemistry student—no actual twenty-year-old could possibly be so dense.

"You just have to get past organic," Gretchen said. "It's a hurdle, that's all. Don't let it psych you out."

I slid my box of Chicken Satay across the table, offering her a piece. We were studying in the ninth-floor lobby, the door to the women's wing propped open so Gretchen could see the door to her room. She was the ninth-floor RA, and she had told a freshman from Malaysia that she would be available until ten o'clock that night to help her study for her first driving exam. Gretchen was nice like that. She wasn't even on duty tonight; I was the one saddled with the walkie-talkie. It lay on the table beside me, and every time it made a clicking sound, I closed my eyes and wished it back to silence. So far, this tactic seemed to be working.

"Seriously," Gretchen said. "None of this crap we're studying now has anything to do with being a doctor." She waved off the chicken and took another gulp of coffee. It was nine o'clock on a Wednesday night, but she was on her second cup from the vending machine downstairs. Her favorite bar had Ladies' Night on Wednesdays—after we finished, she would go out. "You can forget all of this after the MCAT," she said. "Just go bulimic, you know? Stuff your brain. Take the test. Purge. Repeat."

I tried to look reassured so she would quit talking. I appreciated her studying with me, since it was charity, really; she was already a chapter ahead of me in the book. But I couldn't read and listen to her at the same time. *The R/S system also has no fixed relation to the D/L system. For example, the side-chain one of serine contains a hydroxy group,* −*OH.* I turned to the glossary in the back of the book. This was English. This was my native language. There was no reason I couldn't understand. I was a little warm. I took off my sweater. I looked back at the book. Gretchen wrote something in her notebook. She turned another page.

"Can we go over this again?" I leaned toward her. "I don't even really understand what chiral molecules are."

She nodded and drank more coffee. "Chirals aren't a big deal," she said. "The book makes it confusing. They're just, like, mirror opposites." She put her coffee down and pressed her hands against each other, extending both pinkies. "You just have to be able to, you know, picture what the molecule looks like and flip it around. Like imagine what it would look like in a mirror." She smiled and wiggled her fingers. Her fingernails were painted a pale and sparkly pink.

That was it, I thought. That was what I couldn't do. I couldn't flip molecules around in my head. The atoms drifted apart on the first rotation, and I lost track of what and where they were. I looked back at my book so she wouldn't see my face. I didn't want her to feel sorry for me.

"So what are you doing this weekend?"

"This," I said. I didn't look up.

"Oh. Well." She made an attempt to sound pleasantly surprised. "Since you'll be in anyway . . . cover for me Saturday? I'll trade you any weekday you have."

"I can't," I said.

I could feel her looking at me, waiting. I always covered for her when she asked.

"I'm house-sitting."

"Oh. Cool. For a professor or something?"

I shook my head. She waited again.

"For Jimmy Liff," I said.

Gretchen's surprised expression contained so many circles, her round blue eyes, her O-shaped mouth, the doll-like splotches of pink on her cheeks.

"How do you even know him?"

"He works here. He's a security monitor."

"I know that." She raised her eyebrows. "You two just don't seem like you would be friends."

I played dumb, but I knew what she meant. Jimmy Liff was a sixth-year sociology student who took his position in dorm security a little too seriously. His dedication to enforcing rules was a little surprising because of the way he looked: His head was shaved. He wore tight white T-shirts, even in the winter. Both his well-muscled arms were tattooed—a snapping crocodile on the left, a series of Chinese characters on the right. His nose was pierced with a silver, bolt-shaped object that looked both heavy and painful. But Jimmy Liff was no anarchist, no rebel. He wrote people up for music turned ever so slightly too loud. He was ruthless with early morning runners who forgot to bring along their IDs. And around Halloween, during a fire drill, he'd keyed open a room and found a small marijuana plant on someone's windowsill. As soon as the alarms stopped blaring, he'd called the police. There was some rebellion. Someone fearless had painted "FASCIST PRICK" on the door of Jimmy's orange MINI Cooper as it sat in the employee section of the dorm parking lot.

"He creeps me out." Gretchen wrinkled her nose. "Why are you doing it? Why does he need a house-sitter?"

"He's leaving town for the weekend. I guess he has high-maintenance plants."

Gretchen lowered her chin, suspicious.

"Orchids," I said. "He said orchids and ferns."

"Jimmy Liff raises orchids?"

"That's what he said." I looked back down at the book. "I just have to mist them every day and check the humidity. He also needs a ride to the airport." I lifted my head and smiled. "I'm going to drive him in, and then I get the car for the weekend." I leaned back in my chair and waved my hands above my head. I was that excited.

"Wow. The one that says 'FASCIST PRICK'?"

I frowned. I wasn't going to let her bring me down. She had a car. She didn't understand. "He got most of that off," I said. "You can barely see it now. He's giving me fifty dollars. And I heard his place is really nice. I think he has a Jacuzzi."

"Yeah, I heard that, too." She looked over my shoulder to check the door to her room. She looked over her own shoulder, too. "You know why it's nice, in my opinion?"

I shook my head.

"*Drogas,*" she whispered. Gretchen was taking Spanish, too. "He's selling *drogas.*"

I frowned again. This was information I did not want.

"You actually know this?"

She looked at me as if I were stupid, not just about chiral molecules, but about the world in general. "How many college students do you know who live in a luxury town house by the country club? And that car?"

"Circumstantial evidence," I said. It was what my father would have said, what Elise would have said. I could think like them sometimes. I just couldn't mimic the intimidating way they said things, sounding bored and ready to fight at the same time. I just sounded anxious. "Maybe he has rich parents."

"Then why does he have a job that pays minimum wage?" She fastened the lid on the chicken. "Please. It's for contacts. He's supplying the dorm, I bet. Maybe all of them."

I paused to consider what she was saying. It was a weakness of mine, this need to slow down and take information in, to always wonder if I was, in fact, in the wrong. Neither Elise nor my father ever seemed to do this. When I got quiet with either of them, they considered me stumped and, if we were arguing, conquered. But Gretchen was waiting patiently, her chin resting in her hand.

"It doesn't make sense," I said. "If it's true, then why did he call the police on the marijuana?"

"Because he's mean." She shrugged. "I heard he mostly sells pills."

I drummed my fingernails on the table. My fingernails were not painted sparkly pink. They were chewed to the quick, awful-looking. "You heard this from a lot of people? People who would know?"

She shook her head. "Just a couple of people."

"So basically you're telling me a rumor?"

She put her palms up and nodded.

I nodded, too. Fine then. So it probably wasn't true. And even if it was, really it didn't matter. I wasn't going to be Jimmy Liff's friend. I was just going to stay at his nice house, and drive his nice car. Also, I had already told him I would do it. He was counting on me.

Gretchen squinted. "No offense, but I wonder why he asked you. You in particular, I mean."

I shrugged as if I didn't know. In truth, the answer to this question was embarrassing. Jimmy Liff had actually looked me in the eye and explained that I was simply the most boring person he knew. "I don't mean that as a bad thing," he'd added quickly. "I don't mean you're like, boring to talk to. I mean you seem boring in a good way. In a way that would be good for my plants and my car. You don't even smoke, do you?"

It didn't hurt my feelings. I understood what he meant. Jimmy and I had landed in the same Shakespeare class the previous spring, and though I had been a little afraid of him at the beginning, we had been paired by the teacher to work on a presentation for *Measure for Measure* together. I went to work right away. I made handouts; I memorized one of Isabella's soliloquies; I found video recordings of several different productions. Perhaps I went a little overboard, but it was a good thing I did, as all Jimmy did was show up the day of the presentation. But group work was group work, and we'd both gotten A's. He'd acted chummy with me ever since.

"I don't care why he asked me." I reopened the Chicken Satay. A drop of sauce fell on a diagram of a benzene molecule in my book. "I just care that I'm going to get out of here for a weekend. It's like a prison furlough."

Gretchen laughed, and then stopped. "You hate it here that much?"

"Yes." I took a bite of chicken. "I hate it that much." I couldn't believe she didn't hate it. She was an upperclassman, too. In the last week, we'd had three fire drills, all of them pranks, the alarms going off between four and six in the morning. And on just my floor, two weekends in a row, someone had thrown up in the lobby.

"Is Tim going to stay with you?"

I shook my head. This weekend was his grandparents' fiftieth wedding anniversary. He was driving up to Chicago on Friday, and he wouldn't get home until Sunday night. I was actually relieved about this. I would need to study all weekend, nonstop, no breaks. The test on Tuesday would be weighed heavily for our semester grade: If I did well on it, I could still do okay in the class, and be on track for medical school. If I didn't do well on it . . . there would be no point in even taking the final.

"What a waste," Gretchen said. "You know. The Jacuzzi." She leaned back and smiled. "I like Tim. He's nice."

"Thank you," I said. "I think so, too."

"He graduates next year, right? A master's? Engineering?"

I nodded.

She bobbed her eyebrows and whistled low. "He's going to make a lot of money."

"What does that have to do with anything?"

"I'm just saying . . . Why is that a bad thing? Why are you getting mad?"

I looked down at my book and shook my head. I didn't know why I was mad. I only knew I wasn't ready for the test.

"Well," Gretchen said, "since the boyfriend who may or may not be rich someday won't be around, it might be fun to have a few people over . . . not a party, just, you know . . ."

I shook my head. "I have to study. That's all I'm doing."

"Okay." She sighed and turned a page. "I admire your dedication."

I barely smiled. My dedication, if that was even what it was, didn't seem like anything she should admire. I was just scared all the time. I had already told everyone—my parents, Elise, Tim—that I was trying for medical school. They would be understanding if I quit, of course; but they would be understanding that I was weak, or not as smart as they were, or that I just couldn't do it. I didn't want their understanding. I was the one I couldn't let down. I didn't want to have to go through life knowing that I didn't do something I wanted to do, just because it was difficult. Even relentlessly difficult.

I'd felt this way for a while. My sophomore year, when I was having a hard time in calculus, I found a talking Barbie at Goodwill, and I instantly recognized her as the Barbie who said "Math is hard! Let's go shopping!" She had come out when I was young, and she had been in the news—people were angry about the implied message, and the toy company finally changed her computer chip to make her say something else. But the Barbie from Goodwill was the original version. I propped her up on my desk. Whenever I was sick of calculus, struggling with derivatives or integrals, I would press the Barbie's button, and stare into her stupid eyes until I was motivated to get back to work.

Tim said he wanted to help Barbie—he made her wire-rimmed glasses from a paperclip; he drew a pocket protector directly onto one of her big Barbie breasts. Gretchen thought it was funny, too. Elise wanted one for herself. Only my mother, when she saw my Barbie, didn't laugh at all.

"Honey. Why are you doing this?" She held the mangled Barbie up, and then turned her worried gaze to me. It was always strange when she was in my dorm room. Even if she just stopped in for a few minutes, I felt invaded, taken over. The room was just too small.

"It's a joke," I said. "It's just a joke."

She frowned. "I didn't even let you play with these when you were little." She set the Barbie back on my desk. The doll tipped over, and my mother bent her at the waist so she could properly sit up. She looked back at me. "Veronica. You're a kind and thoughtful young woman. If calculus is hard, then calculus is hard. It doesn't mean you're a doll."

"It's a joke," I said again.

She did not appear convinced. "This doll has nothing to do with you." She stared down at Barbie with wary eyes. "Honey. She doesn't even look like us."

At ten o'clock exactly, Gretchen closed her chemistry book. "That's it for me tonight," she said. "You want to take a break? Help me figure out what to wear?"

I shook my head, my finger marking my place in the chapter. *The D/L labeling is unrelated to (+)/(−). It does not indicate which enantiomer is dextrorotatory and which is levorotatory.* "No, thanks," I said. "Have fun."

She was just standing up when the elevator doors opened, and Third Floor Clyde emerged. She smiled and sat back down.

I didn't know Third Floor Clyde. I only knew his name because everyone did. He was a dorm celebrity, famous for being attractive in a shaggy-haired, dark-eyed way that made him seem like he should be out starring in pirate movies, not living among us in a dorm in Kansas. Back in August, on move-in day, the lobby was so hot and crowded that a lot of guys, and even one of the dads, took their shirts off as they carried rolled carpets and gaming chairs in from cars and trucks; but when Third Floor Clyde, waiting for an elevator with a large potted fig tree at his feet, took his shirt off, some smirking mother had elbowed her daughter and whispered, "Check out Adonis over there." Only a week later, his real name was common knowledge, along with his floor number. Two weeks later, when I was brushing my teeth, I overheard one showerer tell another that Third Floor Clyde was not only beautiful, but an art major, and also a brave environmental activist. "He chained himself to a tree," she shouted over the curtain, her voice full of reverence. "So he's, like, beautiful, and he's also, like, deep."

His voice was certainly deep. "Hi," he said now, the elevator doors closing behind him. His T-shirt read "5K Run Against Cancer," and it fit snugly over his lean, lithe frame. He glanced at Gretchen, but he smiled at me. Sometime in September, much to my confusion, Third Floor Clyde had started looking at me with a friendly familiarity, his eyes lingering on mine for so long that I started to worry we did know each other, maybe from back home. But I surely would have remembered a face like his, even if he'd been two years younger.

"Hi," I said, my voice as dazed and pleasant as I felt. I was just saying hello. Tim said hello to other girls, certainly. And some people just happened to be very attractive. That didn't mean you couldn't say hello to them. He continued to smile, so I did, too. Nothing wrong with that. Here was a person trying to be friendly. I should be friendly back. His forearms, somehow still tan, were flecked with white paint, as were his jeans and T-shirt. Both Gretchen and I watched him walk to the door of the men's wing. When the door closed behind him, she turned to me.

"What was that?"

I was still smiling. "What was what?"

She didn't say anything. She was annoyed.

"I don't know." I shook my head. "I don't even know that guy."

"Everyone knows who that guy is." She looked back at the door to the men's wing. "And he was giving you *a look*."

"I don't think so." I laughed and shook my head. But it was flattering to think so, especially because I'd been sitting next to Gretchen, who was blond and, at the moment, wearing a scooped-neck shirt with a pair of smiling lips on the front. But he had looked at me. Not that it mattered. I had a boyfriend. I was in love with my boyfriend.

I looked back down at my book. *A molecule is achiral if, and only if, it has an axis of improper rotation; that is, an n-fold rotation followed by a reflection in the plane perpendicular to this axis that maps the molecule onto itself.* Whatever jolt I'd gotten from Clyde's smile was already draining away.

Gretchen poked my arm. "So what are you going to do? Are you going to try to talk to him?"

I was confused for only a second. "Clyde?" I looked back at the door to the men's wing. "No," I said. "I have a boyfriend."

She gave me a pitying glance. "You're not married. Yet."

"But I'm happy." I smiled and poked her back. It was the truth and, for me, an adequate response. But I imagined she wouldn't see it that way. When I was in high school, I only had a steady boyfriend for a total of two months. I always felt a little sorry for, and even a little superior to, the girls who started holding some guy's hand in eighth grade, and were still holding the same one when we graduated. It all seemed a little claustrophobic, meeting the love of your life at fourteen. And maybe this wasn't fair, but I sort of assumed that these girls who ate lunch with their boyfriends every day, who huddled against a boyfriend's arm in the courtyard while everyone else milled about, were the girls who probably weren't going to college. Their horizons already seemed limited. If that was what they wanted, fine. But I was a different kind of girl.

I even thought that way my freshman year of college, when I was just dating around. But then I met Tim, and all of a sudden I understood why some of those girls in high school had not been able to just let go of their boyfriends' hands. Tim was simply my favorite person to talk to, my favorite person to be around, my favorite person to look at. If I had known Tim in high school, I would have been a girlfriend myself. It was my first inkling of how foolish it was to judge harshly and to discount fate, and to truly believe I was one kind of girl, and not another, just because of some decision I thought I'd made.

It was almost midnight when I got back to my room. The hall was empty, all of my freshman charges ostensibly in bed. Someone had written "YOU ARE NEVER HERE. YOU SHOULD NOT HAVE THIS JOB" on my message board. I wiped it off with the sleeve of my sweater and, holding the walkie-talkie between my knees, pushed my key into the lock.

My room that year was a little sad-looking. When I'd moved into the dorm as a freshman, my mother bought me a new white bedspread and a little white lamp to put on my desk. White, she told me, would be a safe bet to match whatever my roommate brought with her. And that had turned out to be true, to an extent. My freshman year roommate, a theater major from St. Louis, had proudly brought an entire bedroom set printed with the markings of a cow. Everything— bedspread, pillows, curtains, even a throw rug—was white with Holstein splashes of black.

The first time my mother came to visit, she was amused. "Does it make you want to mooooooove out?" she asked. She stood on my side of the room, her hands buried deep in the pockets of her raincoat, as if afraid to touch anything cow. My roommate had left for a rehearsal.

"Just try to get along," my mother counseled. "Sometimes you just have to try to get along with someone." She looked around the room and smiled. "Think of it as a learning experience. You know? Milk it for all it's worth."

This year, I had my own room, and there was no cow print to contend with. But I hadn't really had the time or energy to decorate. I had a laminated poster of the periodic table of elements taped on my wall, so I could stare at it while I blew my hair dry. I'd pinned a calendar to the bulletin board, next to a picture of Tim standing on his head in front of his apartment. But that was pretty much it for wall art. I still had the white bedspread, and I put a white sheet over the other mattress. This looked okay in the early fall, when I still kept my windows open, the sun shining bright on the linoleum floor. But on gray days, and always at night, my room looked bare and stark.

As soon as I put my books down, I checked my phone, pleased to see Tim had called twice.

He answered yawning. "Good evening," he said. "Or good morning. What time is it?"

"It's late. Sorry. I forgot my phone. Did I wake you up?"

"No." He was eating something crunchy. "We're watching *El Corazón Verdad*. You're missing out. Lorenzo is about to find out who his real father is."

I sighed, envious. The graduate engineering program was famously difficult, but you wouldn't know that from all the free time Tim seemed to have. He lived in an apartment off campus, and he regularly got himself to the grocery store and the Laundromat. He went running every morning. When the weather was good, he played kickball with his friends. He and his roommate watched documentaries on the Civil War and bad reality shows. They watched the Spanish soap operas so often that they were actually picking up Spanish. And yet Tim had recently been invited to a dinner at the Alumni Center for maintaining a 4.0. He never would have told me this, but they mentioned it at the dinner, and he'd brought me as a guest.

"They're doing a marathon tonight," he said. I could hear dramatic Latin music in the background. "You should come over."

"*No puedo*," I said.

"Whoa. Whoa." I clearly had his attention. "Seriously. No television. I'll turn it off. But will you come over? I'll come pick you up right now. Just get your toothbrush. I'll be there in ten minutes."

"I'm on duty." The regret in my voice was sincere. I liked watching the Spanish soap operas, sitting with him on his big couch, my head on his shoulder. In the morning, his roommate sometimes went out and got doughnuts.

"This job," he said. "This babysitting job of yours."

I fell on my bed, the phone pinched by my shoulder. "You could come over here."

I knew he wouldn't. He didn't like staying at the dorm. There was the security check-in to deal with, and the real possibility of a late-night fire drill. And if he had to pee in the middle of the night, he had a long walk to the nearest men's bathroom, complete with a flight of stairs.

"Tomorrow night?"

I checked the calendar pinned to the bulletin board next to his picture. Thursday, like Wednesday, was blocked out with an unhappy face.

"On duty again."

"You know I leave on Friday?"

"I'm sorry," I said. "I can't leave."

"But you could still come to Chicago with me." His voice was quieter. He'd turned the television off, or maybe just moved away from it. "You wouldn't have to come to the dinner. You could just drive up there with me. I'd show you around. When I'm at the dinner, you could go see a movie or something. Or study. I mean, you're invited to the dinner, but if you don't want to—"

"I didn't say I didn't want to go. I said I would feel strange." I sat up and pushed my hair behind my shoulders. "I mean, it's a big deal. They probably just want it to be family."

"It's not that big a deal."

"Being married for fifty years?"

"Lots of people do it. My grandparents are just out to get presents. And attention. They always want attention, those two."

"Mmm-hmm." I smiled. Tim had a picture of his grandparents in his room. They were both in wheelchairs, holding hands. "So what are you getting them?"

"I was going to pick something up on the way. What do you get for a fiftieth anniversary? I mean, it's gold, right? But what do you get if you're young and poor? I don't know. Matching sweatshirts? I have no idea."

I reached up to the top shelf of my closet and took out the plastic bucket that held my toothbrush, toothpaste, and soap. "That's why you want me to go. You want me to pick out a present."

"I want you to go because I want everyone to meet you."

I was silent, looking out my dark window. I was so high up. If there really ever were a fire, I might not be able to get out.

"So . . . ? How about it?"

I had never been to Chicago. And he would probably let me drive, at least some of the way. But I couldn't go. I had to study. And this weekend, I would have Jimmy Liff's car. I could drive as much as I wanted, anywhere I wanted to go.

Tim took my refusal with little grace.

"You're house-sitting for that security guy? The one who used to wear those stupid contacts that made his eyes look like a cat's?"

I frowned. I'd forgotten about the contacts. "Yeah. But that's not the point. He's not going to be there."

"Huh. You know that Chinese tattoo on his arm? You know what it says?"

"I didn't know you read Chinese, Tim."

"I looked it up. It says, 'I don't know Chinese, either.'"

I stood up, sat back down. "You'll come over tomorrow night? You're my only hope. I'll be trapped in the tower here. Come save me."

He laughed a little. "Good night, lovely Veronica. I'll see you to-morrow night."

I sat there for almost a minute, holding the silent phone against my ear. I could have fallen asleep just sitting there, without even taking off my shoes. I would have to get up early in the morning. Jimmy Liff was picking me up at eight. He'd said it was the only free time he had before he left, and he wanted to show me how to get to the town house, and how to water the more delicate plants.

I changed into my pajamas and slippers, got my little basket of toiletries, and shuffled to the bathroom at the end of the hall. But even when I returned to my room, my face scrubbed, my teeth clean, I didn't get into bed right away. I dragged the heavy wooden chair by my desk over to the closet, climbing up to reach the top shelf. I had everything up there—yearbooks, photo albums, ice skates, a book report I'd gotten to read over the radio in junior high—all the things that a college student with still-married parents would probably leave in a bedroom back home.

I found the cardboard box I was looking for and lowered myself into the chair.

My mother made amazing photo albums. My sister and I each had our own, our names cross-stitched on the front. Inside, she'd labeled each picture with the date, the event, and the names of everyone pictured. In the early years, before digital cameras, she used scissors to crop distracting backgrounds. She colored in our flash-startled eyes with brown marker. Once she got a digital camera, she could put all her energy into the layouts. She used wallpaper scraps for colorful borders. She included party invitations and notes from teachers, and a pressed flower from my prom corsage.

I moved the albums out of the box, one at a time, until I came to my parents' wedding album. The last time I was at my mother's apartment, she'd asked me if I wanted to keep it. She said she didn't want it around.

I flipped through the pages slowly. The corners were yellowed, and some of the pictures were stuck to their shiny vinyl pockets. As a child, I had looked through this album so often, and so slowly, that every image was already burned in my mind: the little campus chapel where the ceremony took place, the priest standing in front of a magnolia in bloom; my father, young and skinny in his tuxedo, barely recognizable, his hair long enough to cover his ears. And my mother, her dark hair falling to her waist, in a white dress with a Cinderella hoop, a too-big bow on the chest. She was twenty-two. She looked happy in the picture, her smile wide, her eyes bright, the breeze lifting her hair and veil. There is a picture of her with my now-dead grandmother, and in it, they both look so vibrant, my grandmother wearing a bright blue hat, my mother's head resting on her shoulder. There is a picture of my mother and father cutting the cake together. He is looking at her and saying something, and she is looking at the camera, clearly trying not to laugh.

It was hard to look at that picture, especially, and not feel bad for both of them, considering how it all turned out. I didn't understand why my mother had done whatever she'd done with the Sleeping Roofer, why she'd let our whole world fall into this strange and unorganized landscape. She'd been unhappy, she said. I squinted down at her youthful face in the camera's flash, searching for some clue, some way she could have known from the very start, even a hint at the world of difference between what she expected on that happy day, and all she had not foreseen.

3

HAYLIE BUTTERFIELD WAS THE only person in the dorm I knew from home. Her family lived just a few blocks away from our cul-de-sac, in a palatial house with a circular drive and small fountain in front, their mailbox hidden inside a statue of a lion. When Haylie and I were very young, we had almost been friends. She had a castle-shaped playhouse in her backyard that was three stories high, made with real wood, with glass windows and a spiral stairway down the middle. Also, incidentally, Haylie was nice. So whenever her mother called my mother and asked if I wanted to come keep her daughter company, I was always ready to go.

Haylie's mother, Pamela Butterfield, was a runner. Even in cold weather, we would see her pushing Haylie's bundled-up little brother in a jogging stroller with quick, even strides up the hill past our house, her ponytail bobbing over a wool headband. "The kid has little pedals in there," my father said once, smiling at his own joke. "Lazy woman, making the boy do all the work."

Pamela Butterfield and my mother were friends, or at least they had been, when Haylie and I were little. According to my mother, they spent long days at the country club's kiddie pool, comparing pediatricians and sleep deprivation while they held us under our armpits and bobbed us gently in the water. Haylie and I went to the same toddler tumbling class, the same ballet class, the same Spanish sing-alongs at the library. We were in the same Girl Scout troop, and my mother was our troop's leader until my grandmother's failing health took up too much of her time. When Haylie's little brother was born, Haylie's mother resumed the daily routine of a stay-at-home mom with a small child; but my mother was just beginning her long journey into the world of elder care. And after my parents canceled their membership to the country club, we couldn't go to the same pool. But my mother and Pamela stayed friendly. If Pamela was running by when my mom was backing out of the driveway, they would stop to talk, both of them saying they would get together soon, to have coffee maybe, when they weren't so busy.

By the time I was in junior high, Haylie's little brother and his friends were playing in the castle, and Haylie and I had drifted apart. I wasn't exactly a pariah in high school, but by seventh grade, Haylie had risen to the top tier of the social order. She'd always been cute, with the kind of face that looked feminine even with her auburn hair cut short all around. But in ninth grade, she made three major changes: she went out for track and made the varsity team; she let her hair grow past her shoulders; and she started wearing lip gloss. All of a sudden, she was legendary. She dated seniors. There was a rumor that a scout for a modeling agency had spotted her at the mall and given her his card, saying to call if she grew even a few inches taller.

My first and only boyfriend in high school had been in love with Haylie Butterfield. He told me this several months after he'd broken up with me; to be fair, when he was breaking up with me, I had agreed to "just be friends," and I suppose friends can tell each other whom they are in love with. But I remember that the moment he whispered "Haylie Butterfield" with so much reverence and ridiculous hope, I instantly lost all respect for him. Having a crush on Haylie seemed so unimaginative.

"Jealous much?" he'd asked.

Maybe. At the time, it was hard not to to be. Not only was she a beautiful track star, her grades were as good as mine. Her father was an executive at a utility company, and her future seemed to hold every potential: I'd heard her talking to a guidance counselor about applying to UCLA and Yale. Still, she hadn't done anything to deserve my resentment. She was pleasant enough when I saw her in the hallways. Almost everyone liked her. She made the Homecoming Court sophomore and junior year. And senior year, several months after her father was arrested for embezzlement and tax evasion, Haylie was elected Homecoming Queen. Maybe people felt sorry for her—her father's name had been in the paper every day for months, and everyone knew her parents were getting divorced and the house was being seized and her little brother was in the hospital with a stomach ulcer. But it may have just been Haylie's beauty and charm, undefeated, trumping everything.

Shortly after that, she disappeared, and so did her mother and brother. Their house was on the market before the end of spring. My mother tried to call, but by then, the number was disconnected. My mother left a note in the mailbox inside the stone lion. She never heard back. Someone bought the house who didn't have any kids, and they tore down the play castle to make room for a fire pit and patio. I didn't actually see the castle go down, but the next time we drove past their house, my mother and I saw jagged pieces of it sticking out of one of those big portable Dumpsters parked on the street. "It's sad," I said, and my mother nodded, saying nothing. She was quiet the rest of the day.

Much to my surprise, two years later, after the implosion of my own family and home, Haylie Butterfield resurfaced, as a resident of my dorm. I didn't recognize her at first. In high school, she'd worn pastel cashmere sweaters and sometimes matching accessories for her hair. She wore small pearl earrings that she said had belonged to her grandmother, and the only time I saw her wearing makeup was at prom. The first time I saw her in Tweete Hall's elevator, she was wearing black leggings, a black skirt, and a black cardigan with a tightly cinched belt, and also spike-heeled boots, even though it was still early fall and maybe eighty degrees outside. She'd cut her hair chin-length and dyed it black.

I had to squint at her a good five seconds before I could be sure it was her. She wore red lipstick that made her skin look very pale. She was still beautiful, maybe more so, just in a different way.

"Haylie?"

She turned. She did not look happy to see me. It was as if I'd popped a balloon by her head.

"I go by Simone now," she said.

"What?" I asked. I wasn't trying to be a jerk. I really just didn't understand.

"Simone. It's my middle name. It's what I go by now." There was no hint of friendliness in her voice, though I was certain that she recognized me. "That's what you should call me, too." She spoke quietly, and with a tight, fixed smile, though the other two girls in the elevator were speaking to each other in what sounded like Korean, and they did not appear either concerned with or aware of what we were saying.

"I'll try," I said. I didn't know what else to say. "I . . . I might mess up a few times . . ." I laughed, stupidly. ". . . since I've known you almost my whole life."

She didn't laugh. Her red-lipped smile was still. "Try hard," she said. When the doors opened, she stepped out and glanced back over her shoulder. "If you don't think you can manage it, that's okay. You don't need to call me anything at all."

The next time I had a desk shift, I looked her up on the roster. She was listed as a freshman, with a hometown that I had never heard of. That was all I could find out: for the last two years since her father's arrest, while I'd been in college, she had been doing something else.

The next time I saw my mother, I told her about Haylie's dyed black hair, the dark clothes, and, of course, the new name. I didn't believe Simone was really her middle name. It seemed to me I would have heard her middle name at some point, and if it were really Simone, I would have remembered.

"I don't know if I can do it," I said, pulling wads of newspaper out of our old drinking glasses. We were in my mother's new kitchen; I was helping her unpack. "It would be like you all of a sudden telling me I should call you . . . Suzie, or something, instead of Mom."

My mother, lifting her big Crock-Pot out of the bottom of the box, listened with a somber expression. "I wonder what happened to her mother," she said, and she looked over my shoulder and out the window, as if she hoped to see Mrs. Butterfield running up the street in front of our house, though we were in my mother's new apartment, three flights up, nothing to see outside but the side wall of another building. She turned around slowly, looking back at the empty boxes scattered around the floor. "Give her a break, honey," she added. "Think of what she's been through. Her father is in jail. Everything changed for her. If the poor girl wants to be someone else, let her be someone else."

I actually agreed with the advice. I had no desire to torment Haylie, or to make whatever new life she was creating for herself more difficult in any way. The next time I saw her in the dining hall, I said, "Hi, Simone," without so much as a smile. But she looked uncomfortable, even annoyed, her black-rimmed eyes downcast as I passed. She clearly preferred that I would choose the second option she had given me and not call her anything at all.

So that's what I started doing. For the next three months, whenever I saw her, I pretended I didn't know her, and she pretended she didn't know me. It felt strange at first, but then, as with most everything that feels strange at first, it felt normal after a while. Or maybe I just didn't notice her as much.

We might have finished out the year like that, ignoring each other in the main lobby, riding the elevator side by side without so much as looking at each other. But the Thursday morning that Jimmy Liff picked me up so he could show me how to get to his town house, Haylie Butterfield—Simone—was sitting in the MINI Cooper's front seat.

"You two know each other?" Jimmy asked. He was still in the driver's seat, ducking to see me through Haylie's window. Haylie and I looked at each other and, in silent agreement, shook our heads. She opened the door and leaned forward so I could climb into the backseat. Jimmy introduced us.

"Valerie, Simone. Simone, Valerie."

"It's Veronica," I said.

He glanced up at me in the rearview mirror. "That's right," he said, as if I needed confirmation. "I knew that. Sorry. Is it okay if I keep my window down? It's so nice out. But just tell me if it's too much air."

By the time we pulled away from the curb, he had his hand on Haylie's leg. She was wearing ribbed tights, not black, but gray, and he moved his fingers up and down the textured lines as he drove. I tried not to appear startled, in case he looked in the rearview mirror again. But, apparently, Haylie was not just trying to look different and have a different name, she really was different than she'd been before. In high school, she had exclusively dated the clean-cut and obviously-destined-for-success—a quarterback, a student body president, and even—famously—a sophomore at MIT. "That *sounds* impressive," my mother had pointed out. "But why can't he date a girl his own age? And why not a girl in the same state?"

Jimmy turned on the radio at the same moment he started talking. "Before we go out to the town house, I want to stop somewhere and see you drive." He glanced at me over his shoulder. "No offense," he added.

The backseat was very small. My knees were not far from my chin. "Oh, I'm a good driver," I said. "No tickets, even." This was probably because I'd never had my own car, but I didn't mention that.

"Just the same. We'll make sure." He was difficult to hear over the music blaring on the radio, someone shouting in German over loud guitars. Sitting this close, I could see the skin around the bolt in his nose looked a little puffy and red.

Haylie turned around. "This car is his baby," she said, her voice friendly, but not familiar. I could have been meeting her for the first time. She had her hair pulled up under some kind of turban that would have looked really stupid on anyone else. "I drive it, too, but usually no one else. We're sure you'll do just fine. We're so grateful you could do this for us." She flashed a smile.

I nodded. So she was going on the trip as well. And apparently, before they left, she was going to be condescending. Maybe it was the only way she could think to be. But I didn't smile back.

Jimmy drove to the parking lot of the football stadium. He gave me the keys, and though I got out of the car on his side, he gestured for Haylie to move from the passenger seat to the back. In the back, Haylie sat with her feet on the seat. In the rearview mirror, she looked like she had no torso, her heart-shaped face resting on the knees of her gray tights. I put the car in gear and told myself not to be nervous. I was a good driver. I tried to remember this as we rolled around the parking lot, me braking, accelerating, and turning at Jimmy's command. I did all this with the stereo on, the German guy still shouting.

"Okay. Yeah. I feel okay," Jimmy said, using one hand to signal for me to stop. He got out of the car and walked around the front to the driver's side. By the time I had gotten out and walked around to the passenger door, Haylie had moved to the front seat. She leaned forward to let me in.

"But try not to drive too much." Jimmy readjusted the mirror and ran his hand along his shaved head. "The weather is supposed to get shitty tomorrow. Maybe ice. But not until the afternoon. Our flight leaves in the early morning. You'll be fine if you come straight home."

I frowned, looking out the backseat window, at the bright blue sky, the maple trees still dappled with a few gold leaves. I hadn't heard about any ice.

But I said nothing. The idea of the weekend, the cuteness of the car, the luxury of the town house, was already locked into my mind. And later, when Jimmy showed me the security code that opened the door, and I saw the floor-to-ceiling windows in the kitchen and the enormous bathtub that looked like it had just been scrubbed (it had—Jimmy informed me that a maid came once a week), I forgot all about the potentially icy roads. I was friendly and compliant. I nodded appreciatively at the rather disturbing paintings on the wall, all painted by Jimmy. ("They're all from the point of view of a serial killer," Haylie explained. "They might be a little edgy for you.") And I paid close attention when Jimmy opened the door to a glassed-in sunroom as warm and muggy as an August night, and full of exotic-looking plants. He showed me which ones needed to be misted daily and how to check the humidistat.

"Obviously I keep the sunroom warmer than the others," he said, shutting the door behind him. "The rest of the house is set at sixty-five. So if it gets really cold tomorrow night, just let all the sinks drip a little, and open the cabinets underneath."

I wasn't sure what to say. Jimmy, I knew, was from some city in California that started with "San," not San Diego or San Franciso, but some other place that sounded like the weather was usually lovely and mild. He'd apparently heard a little about Kansas winters and freezing pipes, and he was ready to take unnecessary precautions.

"That's ridiculous!" Haylie appeared in the living room and gave one of his big arms a playful poke. "It's not an old farmhouse. And she's going to be here, running water. The pipes won't freeze overnight." She looked back at me, smiled, and rolled her lovely eyes.

I had slowly begun to understand that Haylie lived at the town house, too. Now that I thought about it, I rarely saw her around the dorm anymore. Her coat was hanging in the front closet, and Jimmy had pointed out her desk in the downstairs study. But I also understood that really, the house, the car—everything—belonged to him. So even though I knew, regarding the possibility of frozen pipes, that she was right and he was wrong, I looked to him for the final word.

He seemed to appreciate my good sense. "Turn the water on if it gets cold," he said, looking at me, not at Haylie. His cell phone rang in his pocket. "I'll take this outside," he said. He kissed the back of her neck as he walked past her out of the room.

Haylie and I were silent, listening to his heavy boots move across the kitchen and out the front door. It was the first time we'd been alone together since high school, and I wondered if, with no audience, she might momentarily drop the act. She did not. When she noticed me watching her, she fished a tube of lipstick out of her skirt pocket, turned around, and looked at her reflection in the flat-screen television.

"He's really particular about his things," she said. "He'll notice right away if anything is different." She sounded angry, maybe at me. I could see her face in the gray screen, but I couldn't read her expression.

Still, all around me was quiet. I could hear a dishwasher, gently humming, but that was all. Sunlight streamed in through the enormous windows, settling on the overstuffed couch, the hardwood floors, the lush and leafy plants perched on pedestals. I leaned forward and looked through the bathroom doorway, catching sight of the edge of the Jacuzzi—"a garden tub," my mother would have called it. I hadn't taken a long, hot bath in over a year. And so even though I was unsure if Haylie had just made a threat or a complaint, I continued to be friendly and compliant.

I would think about it later, how I dove headfirst into that weekend. I only took in the information that I wanted, and I ignored everything else. My mother would later tell me, in her nice way, not to be so hard on myself; I wasn't the first person to ignore a risk. This is how we welcome both adventure and grief, as anyone who has done so will tell you.

That evening, Marley Gould, wearing piglet slippers and a long, ruffled nightgown, was camped out on the big orange couch that faced the elevators in the seventh-floor lobby. I was on a quick study break, headed downstairs to get a soda; but when I saw the back of Marley's long braid, I slowed. I felt bad for Marley. She was from a town in western Kansas that had a slightly smaller population than our dorm. She seemed much younger than the other freshmen on my floor. Her roommate was in a sorority and never around. I knew she read out in the lobby because she was lonely.

"Hi, Marley. How's it going?"

She looked up with such a happy, hopeful expression that when the elevator doors opened behind me, I didn't move.

"Okay! Just doing some reading!" She showed me the cover of her book: a princess, in full princess garb, was holding a sword to a dragon's throat. She glanced at my walkie-talkie. "You're on duty?"

I nodded. Two black girls—I didn't know their names—emerged from the women's wing, laughing hard into their hands. One of them smiled at me and then at Marley, but they kept moving, running into the waiting elevator just before the doors closed.

"It's finally getting colder out, huh?" Marley pulled her braid in front of her shoulder, and then just under her nose, as if she were sniffing the tip. "And the buses were running late all day. Did you notice? I have to get better shoes. I have these great boots back home, but I didn't bring them up yet, because it was so warm at

Thanksgiving, and now it's cold. So my dad said he would send them, but . . ."

Trying to smile, I watched her lips move. I fought the urge to look at my watch. I had physiology lab the next morning, and before I went to it, I had to be able to diagram the central nervous system and digestive tract of a dog shark. And Tim was coming over at eleven. *You can be kind,* my mother had often said to both me and Elise. *Nothing else you girls accomplish really matters if you don't know how to look out for other people.* When I was in grade school, she had methods of tracking my social ethics. She was always the room mother, coming to school with cupcakes or inviting herself along on field trips on which she would *strongly encourage* me on the bus to sit next to the kid no one else wanted to sit with. *Just say hello and be friendly,* she would say. *It only takes a minute.*

Marley was looking at me now, waiting. She had asked me a question.

"What?" I shook my head. "Sorry."

"I said, 'Do you want to come to the spring band concert this year?' I know it's a little early, but I can give you the date if you want to mark your calendar."

"Yes!" I said. "Yes! I would like to go!" I had to go. There was no way out. Marley played the French horn, and at the beginning of the year, she'd told me she would be playing with the marching band before the first football game, and it was clear from the way she'd looked at me that she wanted me—or someone, anyone—to come see her. I'd said I would. But then I slept late at Tim's, and I had a test the following Monday, and it was raining, and I didn't want to go—so I did a terrible thing: I stayed in, studied all day, and then told Marley that I'd spent the day shivering in the stands, clapping and cheering her on. "You were great!" I told her, maybe too enthusiastic. She'd known I was lying. I was sure of it.

"I wish I were doing the holiday concert." Marley pulled her blanket up around her shoulders. "You have to be selected for that, and most freshmen don't get it. But Christmas music is my favorite. My mom played the piano for every music group in our town, so we always went to a bunch of holiday concerts. I always liked them, even when the music was bad." She sighed. "And then we'd all come home and drink hot chocolate."

I pressed the elevator button. Marley would be fine. She had her happy, intact, childhood home complete with Christmas carols and hot chocolate. I didn't want to talk to her anymore.

"Well, it's almost time for finals," I said. I checked the lights above the elevator doors. "And then the big winter break, not long after that. You'll get to be home for a while."

"Right." She pulled a large bag of Cheetos out from under the blanket. "Hey, do you want to watch *Friends* with me? It's on in ten minutes. I'll make popcorn."

"I've got to study," I said. "Sorry."

This was the way it went with Marley. We ended each conversation with her asking for time I didn't have. She was never the one who was busy, never the one who had too much to do. I knew from experience that if I looked at her now, she would be staring at the floor, her brow furrowed, as if I'd just said something mean. So until the elevator came, I stared at the beige brick wall by the doors, where someone had written "I WAS HERE" in black Magic Marker.

My mother was wrong: It did not take just a minute to be kind. It usually took much longer, and I had things I needed to do. My mother would no doubt have sat down with Marley all evening, trying to cheer her up. But she had never passed organic chemistry. Her whole life, at least up until she met the Roofer, had pretty much been spent looking out for others, and not getting much else done.

"I'm getting you a space heater for Christmas." Tim inched back toward the center of my bed. He was almost a foot taller than I was. My top sheet and comforter didn't quite cover both of us, and his knees were cold against my toes. I moved my fingertips over the soft hair of his chest, his heartbeat still strong beneath it.

"I should probably leave by midnight." He picked up a strand of my hair and wound it around two of his fingers.

I hadn't expected he would stay over. He had to be up and on the road early—he had to be in Chicago by late afternoon to pick up other relatives who were flying in. Plus, of course, he hated the dorm. I glanced at the ceiling. My upstairs neighbor had been playing the same reggae song for the last hour, the steady drumbeat vibrating the exposed water pipes over my bed.

"I can stay for a while," he said, turning toward me. "I'll stay until you fall asleep." He followed my eyes to the leaning pyramid of books and notebooks on my desk. "But you're not going to sleep, are you?"

I shook my head. I would start working again as soon as he left, and maybe finish up with the dog sharks by two. That would give me almost four hours to sleep. Jimmy and Haylie's flight left at eight; they were picking me up in front of the dorm at six.

"My lab prep is taking me longer than I thought." I sighed, rubbing my eyes. "Because I'm stupid." I looked away, embarrassed. I hadn't meant to say that last part out loud.

He poked my shoulder. "Don't say that."

I yawned and waved my hands at him. I didn't want to talk about it.

"Veronica, you're smart. You're completely smart."

"No, I'm not." I pulled the sheet up, tucking it around me. I could feel him watching me, studying my face. I shrugged. "Not the way Gretchen is. I study twice as hard as she does, and she gets better grades."

He looked away, apparently considering the matter. I held my breath. Tim was usually both nice and honest. But in situations when he had to choose, he tended to go with honest.

"I wouldn't say you weren't quick," he said.

"Okay. Great. Thanks." I wanted to change the subject. I didn't want to be so pathetic, the pathetic girlfriend, whining about being dumb. I smiled. "You're right. I just got started late. There was a noise complaint on the fourth floor, and I had to go deal with that." I looked back down. In truth, the noise complaint had taken about two minutes to deal with. Even my conversation with Marley hadn't taken too much time. What had taken so much time was the fact that every time I tried to read a paragraph in my physiology book, I ended up thinking about something else—usually about how bad my grades were going to be that semester.

"Yeah." He sat up straight, scratching his neck. "This job does take up a lot of your time, doesn't it?" He suddenly looked very serious, and though my room was cold, the tips of his ears were pink. "I've actually been thinking about that." He cleared his throat. "I was thinking how nice it would be, for you and for me, if you didn't have to do this job next year."

I waited, my eyes moving over his shoulders, his hand resting on the sheet.

"You know Rudy graduates this year. He's going to move out."

Before he could finish, I was shaking my head. "I can't move in with you," I said. "I can't pay that kind of rent." It was true. I would have to apply to be an RA my senior year as well. The last time I saw my father, he'd asked me twice if I was on schedule to graduate, and what kind of financial aid I thought I might get for medical school.

"Right." Tim sat up so the sheet fell over him. He looked a little Roman, wearing a toga. "The thing is, you wouldn't have to. You know I got that scholarship. And I'm working at my dad's office this summer, and he . . . Let's just say he's happy about the scholarship, and he's making things easy on me. I'll have enough to pay for that apartment myself. Or we could move into a different one. I could pay for the bills, everything."

I didn't know what to say. I didn't want to mislead him. But I was so flattered that he'd asked. I wanted to just stay in this moment, his invitation, the romance of it, hanging in the air.

"Okay," he said. "It would be nice if you said something now."

My eyes moved around my dorm room, at the bare linoleum, the blank walls, the vibrating pipes overhead.

"I mean, otherwise, you're going to have to keep this job until you graduate, right?" He looked a little pained. "You're going to be living in the dorm your senior year."

I nodded, picturing his apartment, with its pretty wood floors and the balcony off each bedroom. One of the balconies was big. I could make a terrace garden. The kitchen was small, but it would be wonderful to get to cook for myself, to cook nice meals with Tim, and to not have to walk across a parking lot every time I wanted to eat. I would never have to see the dining hall again. I would never have to eat off another orange tray.

Someone knocked at my door.

"Hello?" I turned back to the door, checking to make sure it was chained.

"It's me. Marley."

"Do you . . . do you need something?"

"I just wanted to get your opinion on something. I wasn't sure about this shirt."

Tim's eyes moved from the door back to me. He looked as if he were about to say something that might make me laugh. I leaned forward, away from him. "Uh, can I tell you tomorrow? I'm sort of . . . I'm in bed."

"Oh. Sure. Sorry. I didn't think that . . ." Her voice was already growing fainter. "Sorry."

Tim smiled. I smiled back.

"What?" he asked. "Is it the living together thing?"

"No. No, I just . . . you know." I knew what I had to say, and how to say it. I just didn't want to. He looked so happy. "I have to think about, what if . . . something happens?"

His eyebrows lowered. He moved his hand through my hair. He really had no idea what I meant.

"What if we break up?" I whispered, as if a lower volume might soften the words. "And then what do I do? I wouldn't have this job anymore. Where would I live?"

His hand moved away from my hair. "I don't think we're going to break up. Do you?"

"I don't know."

We stared at each other. I had just blurted it out. It seemed such an obvious answer. Of course I didn't know. He didn't know. Neither of us could possibly know. But he looked hurt.

"I don't mean that I think we're going to. Or that I want to," I added quickly. "I just mean that, if I give up this job, that's kind of . . . it for me."

He appeared to be taking in this information. He rubbed his chin and squinted at the cinder-block wall. "It's ridiculous," he said slowly, his eyes moving over the water pipes. "It's ridiculous that they don't let you control the heat in each room. I wonder if there's a way to sort of . . . rig up a separate thermostat."

His brain really did work like this. There had been many times when, in the middle of a conversation about, say, our relationship or my feelings, he would be suddenly distracted by some question about a building's circuitry or heating and cooling system. It was like a tic he couldn't help. Still, in this instance, I was pretty sure he was acting. He was changing the subject to give me some time, to remove any immediate pressure.

And then, because it seemed so simple, so logical, and, more than anything, so true, I said, "I'd like to live with you."

My cell phone beeped on my desk. We both looked at it.

"You going to get that?"

I shook my head. "But I don't know. Not about the phone, I mean. I mean about moving in. I need to think. I just need time to think."

"Sure. Yeah. Of course." He leaned over and kissed my forehead. "When do you have to reapply for this for next year?"

"January." My cell phone had stopped beeping. Above us, the reggae song ended, then started again.

I woke in darkness, my comforter pulled over my head. I turned on the lamp beside my bed and saw it was quarter past two. I had a Post-it note stuck to my cheek.

Sleep well. Enjoy the Jacuzzi. Drive carefully. Love you.

Beside the word "you," he'd drawn a cartoon rabbit who looked just a little bit like me, in a neurotic, stressed out kind of way. I stood up and set it carefully on my desk, propped up against my calculator so I would be able to see it. My physiology book was open to the same page I had been looking at before Tim came over, but the dog shark diagram seemed completely unfamiliar, the words swimming together before my eyes. I had to sleep. I would learn about dog sharks in the morning, either before or after the drive to the airport. There would be time. There would have to be time.

I had started back to bed when I remembered that someone had called earlier. I sat on my bed and thumbed in my security code.

"Hey, it's your big sister. I know it's late there. Sorry. Are you in bed?" There was a pause. *"Forget it. I don't need to know. Listen, I want to know if you've talked to Mom lately. I just called her, and she sounded weird. Even for her. She was talking about changing her name to Natalie Wood. Maybe she was kidding. But she didn't sound like she was kidding. Veronica, she sounded kind of . . . crazy. I'm worried she's having some kind of breakdown."*

I yawned and moved the phone to my other ear. My sister was a little behind the times. My mother had been having some kind of breakdown for the last year. It was nice that Elise had finally realized this all the way out in San Diego.

"I don't know any of her new neighbors. So. I'm hoping you can at least

call her. But I wish you could go see her. I know you don't have a car. But . . . I don't know. Something is going on, Veronica. I've never heard her like this. Okay. Call me. Call me back tonight. I'll be up."

I set my phone down and crossed the room to my bed, turning off the lamp. It was too late to call California, or too early, whatever. And I was tired. I had enough in my life to worry about without having to wake my mother up only to affirm that she was still unhappy, still full of regret, still unsure of what to do with herself. The truth was, she was all of these things because of very bad decisions she'd made. As my father said, she was lying down in the bed she'd made. And so, steeled against her and very sleepy, I lay down in my own.

4

HER DAUGHTER HAD CALLED her crazy. Or told her she was acting crazy. (*I did not call you crazy,* Elise-the-lawyer would say. *I said you were acting crazy.*) True. And, Natalie admitted, thinking back, maybe she had sounded a little unhinged just now on the phone. She had been talking to Elise about her last name, about how she was considering a change. "Just something I've been thinking about," she'd said, bending down to pet the dog, trying to sound cheerful. Just before the phone rang, Natalie had actually been thinking of something far more pressing and worrisome than her last name. But she didn't want to burden either of her daughters—and with Elise, especially, she didn't want to sound pathetic. So she'd come up with something else to talk about, a distraction, the first thing to pop into her head. She may have rambled a little, perhaps. But she didn't think anything she'd said had sounded *crazy.*

It certainly wasn't that crazy for her to say she might want to change her name. Most of the women she worked with had gone back to their maiden names, and really, as she'd told Elise, she was starting to see how that made sense. The faxes from Dan's lawyer to her lawyer were all titled "Von Holten vs. Von Holten," which seemed an apt, but sad, commentary, an allusion to civil war, something whole torn in two.

Then again, Von Holten was the last name of her daughters, her life's work, and it seemed so unreasonable that at the end of it all, Veronica and Elise would have the same last name as their father, and she would be the one on the outside, as far as nomenclenture went. Also, she had to admit she was attached to the name. Natalie Von Holten had been her name for longer than it hadn't been. Until the day the Realtor advised her to paint over the mailbox, the side of it had read "The Von Holtens," even during those last few months, when she was the only one still living in the house. She was the one who had hand-painted the letters just a few years earlier, using custom-made calligraphy stencils she'd bought at a hobby shop.

"Mom?" Elise had asked. "Are you okay?"

Elise was always driving when she called, stalled in traffic on some California freeway, and so Natalie had just chalked up the uncharacteristic softness in her older daughter's voice to a dropped headset, a bad connection. She didn't know she was being *evaluated.* So she'd kept going, explaining herself, holding the phone with her shoulder while she lowered herself to the floor, using her hand to gently guide Bowzer beside her. Yes, she told Elise, she was fine. She was a little tired. Things were getting crazy at the mall, everyone revving up for the holiday seasons, marking down the old merchandise. Here, she worried she was complaining again, being negative about the job she hated, pulling her successful daughter down. She smiled, thinking it would show in her voice. She went back to talking about her name. The normal thing, she told Elise, would be for her to go back to her maiden name. But she'd never liked being Natalie Otter. *Like the animal,* she used to say, instead of spelling it. In grade school, she had hated it; the name had been the butt of many jokes. *Are your parents Otters? Is your mother an Otter?* There was also the slightly more subtle pun, each tormenter truly believing he or she had come up with something new: *Natalie Otter do this. Natalie Otter do that.* Teachers were the main offenders. They did it to lots of kids. *Hi ho!* to Gwendolyn Silver. *Mary, Mary, quite contrary. Do you have a question . . . Mark?* Even in her annoyance, Natalie had felt bad for these teachers: the profession itself seemed to force regular people to attempt comedy for a captive audience. But she had longed for a name immune to their desperation, a name with weight and dignity, one that didn't make people think of an animal that belonged to the same biological family as the polecat, the badger, and the weasel. She'd found all that, and so much more, at the age of twenty-one, when she'd fallen in love with Dan Von Holten.

"So why not just come up with a new name?" she'd asked Elise, though she was really asking herself. That's what Maxine had suggested. Maxine worked in cosmetics. She was almost seventy, and she spoke to all the younger workers with the same friendly authority she used when telling customers they shouldn't use so much blush. "Come up with something you like," Maxine had said, hands raised, fingers extended so her long, acrylic nails looked like talons. "It's your name, honey. It's your life. You know what I'm saying? At some point, you've got to stop and ask yourself: why should everything be decided for me?"

It was a good question, Natalie decided, and she started to give her ideal last name some thought. It energized her, this idea of getting to start anew, to choose something just because she liked it, or even just to make a name up. And then Elise had called. Foolishly, naively, just trying to distract herself, Natalie had run some of these names by her ever-so-rational and steady older daughter, all in a misguided attempt to sound upbeat. "Natalie Nevermore?" she'd asked Elise, with a little laugh, though she wasn't really joking. "Natalie Northrup?" She'd always loved alliteration. "Natalie Nouvelle? Natalie Valentino. Natalie Wood!" Irreverent, perhaps, but a conversation starter!

Elise got very quiet. And then told her she was acting crazy. And then told her there was an accident up ahead, snarled traffic, and that she had to go.

Now Natalie sat on the floor of her apartment and watched the news with the sound turned down, free to wallow in private, to think how unfair it was that she could have spent her most vital years pouring all of her wisdom and understanding of the world into her daughters, guiding and nurturing them to the best of her ability, only to have one of those daughters grow up and decide, in the middle of a very bad day, that she was nuts. Or acting nuts, whatever. Natalie looked at the phone with narrowed eyes. Elise was probably already calling Veronica, spreading the news of their mother's demise. Everything would be taken out of context.

The problem with the phone, she considered, was that you couldn't see the other person's face or surroundings. You couldn't know what kind of situation you might be interrupting with your friendly call from California just to say hello. Elise, for example, had no way of knowing that her mother had, only moments before the phone rang, come home from work to find this note taped to her door:

NO DOGS MEANS NO DOGS. IT'S GONE TOMORROW OR YOU ARE.

Lou

Furthermore, Elise, who only called when she was driving, her headset in place, her young, newly married body cradled in one of her lime green Volkswagen's custom-ordered leather seats, couldn't have known that during the entire conversation, her mother had been lying on the floor of her apartment, pretty much where a couch should be.

It wasn't as if she didn't have any furniture. On the other side of her living room sat the leather armchair she had purchased from Pottery Barn, 15 percent off, just three years ago. She'd convinced Dan they needed a new chair for the living room—they had to get rid of the stuffed armchair they'd had for over a decade, which still had large red marks across the cushion—Veronica, when she was three, had gotten to it with one of Elise's Magic Markers. Dan agreed, so Natalie had gone out and bought a new chair. They needed a chair, and so they'd gotten one. As simple as that. And she still had the chair. But right now, coming home from the mall to her own apartment, she hadn't wanted to sit in a chair. She wanted to lie down in the living room, and to do that, she needed a couch. But she didn't have one. She was forty-nine years old, and after the divorce, she'd been saddled with almost three decades' worth of family furniture and mementos and a Ping-Pong table and a bunch of other junk that was a chore to get rid of; and yet somehow, she didn't have a couch.

Dan, she imagined, had a couch. He'd moved into a furnished condo, leaving everything from their old life behind, like a crab scooting out of a shell. She had been left with the mess, the garage sales, the sorting, the throwing away. And in the middle of all this, the dog, moments after a seizure, had peed on one of the emerald green cushions of the living room sofa. Natalie had actually been a little pleased, the dog's infirmity providing her with an excuse to get rid of the sofa, which was symbolic, she'd decided, of her old life with Dan, which also seemed a little peed-upon, ready to be thrown away. It would be fun, she thought, and equally symbolic, to replace it with something new, something striped, maybe, something contemporary, with a hide-a-bed for when one of the girls came to visit.

She'd tried. Sometimes, after work, instead of leaving the mall, she headed straight to the furniture sections of the big department stores, just to see what was out there. She'd sat on striped cushions and pressed her fingertips against cotton twill. She'd quickly gotten overwhelmed by the selection, and also the massiveness of the decision. In those first few months, she was still so raw, and so unsure of herself. After the divorce, such a big failure, she just didn't want to make a bad choice.

So she'd waited too long on the couch. Now, even if she found one she liked, she wouldn't be able buy it.

She'd started to make new friends, other substitute teachers and sales associates at DeBeck's. When they stopped by, they teased her about not having a couch. "You're waiting for Prince Charming to bring his own sectional?" Maxine had asked. "I don't know. As cute as you are, it's a tough market, honey. You may want to break down and get your own." Natalie laughed, politely, and blamed Bowzer, though it wasn't as if he peed in the house all the time. He was still a proud dog, full of dignity, waiting by the door when he needed a walk. But still, with a couch, once would be enough.

Bowzer was beside her now, lying on his side, one ear flat against the beige carpet. She scratched the back of his head and looked up at the television. A man pointed at map of Kansas City, the word "ICE" spelled out in all caps, the letters themselves appearing frozen, hovering in the foreground. A crawler at the bottom of the screen warned of freezing rain coming earlier than expected, just before early morning rush hour. ". . . *treacherous sidewalks, downed power lines, a good day to stay home if at all possible . . .*" Natalie frowned, looking out the dark windows. Tomorrow was Friday, a big day for teachers calling in sick. She would probably get a call for a job in the morning. Beside her, Bowzer started to tremble so violently that the tags of his collar jingled. Chasing rabbits, Dan had called it. Maybe mild strokes, said the vet.

She waited until he calmed, and then moved her hand over his head, her fingernails gently working through his soft fur. She'd known, when she signed the lease, that the complex did not allow pets. She had not thought Bowzer would still be with her. She had planned to take him to the vet as soon as the house sold. They would give him the shot. It would be a clean end, Maxine had advised, humane. Dogs were physical creatures; they didn't live in their minds, but in their bodies; and we weren't doing them any favors when we kept them around long after the fun was gone. "Kind of like husbands," she'd added, laughing, but then grew serious again. She said Natalie needed to start thinking about herself. She knew what she was talking about. She had been through a divorce herself. And Natalie was still young. She still had so much potential.

Natalie said she didn't feel young. Maxine had waved her off.

"Trust me," she'd said. "You'll be surprised how young forty-nine seems once you're sixty-seven."

It was a nice thing to say, but something about this had gotten to her. Maybe it was that forty-nine did not seem so far away from sixty-seven, especially when she considered that she and Dan had raided his retirement account during those last, expensive years. She looked away from Maxine, at her own short nails, and tried to think of something else. But she could feel the tears welling. She bit her lip. She hated that she was a crier. They were on break, sitting on a table in the windowless back room of DeBeck's, their mocha smoothies already finished. Natalie had to be back on the floor in five minutes. She would refold scarves. She would verify credit cards. She would smile and say, "Can I help you find anything?" to teenage girls in designer jeans who would look through her as if she weren't there.

"Okay, then." With that, Maxine scooted herself off the break room's table and back into her high heels. "Be smart. Look out for you. You wanted an apartment with good security and a month-to-month lease? And miracles of miracles, you found one? You need to take it. Honey. Listen to me. You're hanging onto the dog because you're hanging onto the past. This is a big time for you, a crucial time. The dog, Methuselah, he has to go."

She knew Maxine was right. Yes. That was what had to be done. And really, how had she ended up with the dog anyway? Veronica was the one who had wanted the dog. Dan had told Veronica she could have a dog. Why, Natalie wondered, should she be the one left with him after everyone else had moved on?

And yet, when the time came, she hadn't been able to do it. Days after the house sold, when she was starting to pack in earnest, Bowzer rallied. He jumped up beside her in bed one night, just as he'd done as a puppy, nestling against her chest. During the day, he lay on the floor next to whatever box she was packing, chewing his rawhide, his very presence so reassuring, concrete proof that she was not as completely alone as she felt. During that month of packing, she'd tried hard to be ruthless. She had a garage sale and sold everything of Dan's. He had left only what he had not cared about, and there was little satisfaction in selling, for two dollars, the leather briefcase she had bought him upon his graduation from law school. Or in throwing away the poem she had written for him on their fifteenth anniversary. As for the photo albums, she couldn't throw them away—most of the pictures of Dan had Elise and Veronica in them. So she packed them all in a box and drove them to Veronica's dorm. She did not ask. She just handed them over, repeating in her head the mantra Maxine had taught her. *Be smart. Start looking out for you.*

The day before she moved to the apartment, she'd actually taken Bowzer to the vet. Maxine had offered, several times, to come along; but Natalie had wanted to go alone. That was her first mistake. And then, instead of giving the vet instructions, she'd asked for his opinion. The vet had sighed, bent over, and looked deeply into the dog's cataracted eyes. "He's still eating. And getting around okay. I'd say the old boy has some good times left." He'd scratched the dog's ears and looked down at him fondly. It was the same vet they'd gone to when Bowzer was a puppy, when the girls were young. Veronica, still in grade school, had cried when he got his distemper shot.

Veronica. Natalie looked out the window again, worried about the coming storm. She reached for the phone, but stopped herself. Veronica would be fine. She took the bus from her dorm to her classes. If she went to her classes. Natalie frowned. Veronica had warned that her grades would be low this semester, and Natalie wondered if she was spending all her time with the boyfriend. She herself had moved in with Dan when she was in school. She'd lied to her parents, her sorority sisters covering for her. They got married a year after she graduated. She'd been in such a hurry.

Someone knocked at the door. Bowzer raised his head and barked, looking in the wrong direction. She put the phone down and stood, peering through the peephole. She recognized the apartment manager's puffy face and jerked her head away.

"I know yous in there, lady." He sounded both bored and annoyed. "You want to talk with me through the door so everybody hears, that's fine. But in the end it's the same."

"Uh, just a moment. I'll be right there." She picked up Bowzer, one hand supporting his bad hip, and ran back to the bedroom. She'd already put a pillow for him in the closet. "Stay," she whispered, though she shut the door. Even before his senility, the dog had never been particularly obedient. She ran back to the front room. The hallway in front of her apartment was unheated, and when she opened the door, she felt a wave of cold roll over and through her. Oddly, and unhelpfully, she thought of Twain: *Shut the door! Not that it lets in the cold but that it lets out the cozyness.*

"Yes?" she asked brightly. She knew she had a friendly face, a bright-eyed suburban-mom-liness about her that many people liked and trusted. Her whole life, she had been asked to watch strangers' bags, bikes, and children. "What is it, dear?" she asked, maybe, in her desperation, piling it on a little hard.

"You know what it is." He didn't smile. The apartment manager was in his twenties, maybe, unappealing in every way she could think of, a red ski hat pulled down almost over his eyes. He stood with his legs spread wide, his arms crossed, his chin jutted out so his head tilted back just enough to gaze at her from underneath the hat. "I just talked with the owner. No dogs means no dogs."

"Oh." She didn't say anything else. She was thinking they could come up with some reasonable plan together. She smelled curry cooking, maybe coming from the apartment across the hall. When he said nothing, she started again. "Yes. I'm sorry I lied." She smiled. "I don't usually lie. I didn't know what else to do. You see, he's old. I thought . . . I just need to . . ."

"You just need to move out," he said.

She shook her head. She continued to smile. This was a misunderstanding. "No no," she said, as if he'd asked her a question. "I'll take care of this soon, maybe, um, within the week . . ."

"The owner doesn't care what you do now. He doesn't care if you ice the dog or not. You lied on your application, lady. For months I been telling you to get rid of the dog. Now we're done talking. You got twenty-four hours. The dog goes and so do you."

She stopped smiling. She stared at him, angry, and then, when she realized her anger would not affect him, afraid. It was true—she'd heard correctly. He'd actually used these words, "iced," "you got twenty-four hours." And something about this, his low language, punctured her where she was still soft, making her realize all at once that she had truly slipped down into a different world where kindness held no currency and age earned no respect. She would have to stop expecting mercy. She would have to adjust the way she talked, and the way she thought, about everything and everyone.

Be smart. Start looking out for you.

5

ON THE WAY TO THE AIRPORT, Jimmy blasted electronica from the car's stereo. I rode behind Haylie. The sky was still dark, the controls of the car a green glow, and only Haylie's swinging, glinting earrings were visible between the seat and the headrest. I couldn't see her face; there was no way of knowing what she thought of the music or the volume. But when we were on the final curve of highway, the lights of the economy parking lots for KCI already in sight, she made a sudden whimpering sound.

"Can we turn it down at least?" She made a quick swipe at the volume knob with a fingerless glove.

Jimmy turned off the music, saying nothing. We rode the rest of the way in absolute silence.

At the airport, he handed me the keys without a word.

"Bye!" I waved, the keys jingling in my hand. "Have a good trip! Call my cell if you want to check on things!"

But he was already walking up to the doors, the metal chain attached to his wallet swinging behind him. If he heard me, he did not turn around. Haylie was still getting her bag out of the trunk. When the automatic doors slid open for Jimmy, she looked up, and almost lost her balance. She was wearing jeans tucked into velvety black boots with spike heels that looked hard to walk in.

"He's not really a morning person," she said. She lifted her bag and glanced at me.

Apparently, despite all the pretense, some part of Haylie Butterfield remembered enough of her old life for her to worry what I thought of her new one. I walked around the front bumper to the driver's seat. Haylie was still looking at me. I shrugged, and lowered myself into the car. I didn't know what it was she wanted me to understand. She didn't need to apologize for him, or make excuses, if that's what she was doing. I didn't care if Jimmy was a morning person or not. She was the one spending the weekend with him. I just had the keys to his house and car.

When I was ten years old, I left my bike unlocked outside the library, and someone stole it. My parents refused to buy me another. "How many times did I tell you to keep it locked?" my father asked. My mother seemed distressed by my sadness, but she held firm as well: "I know you loved that bike," she said. "But if you have to earn a new one, you'll be more careful with it. You'll appreciate it more."

When I bought a new bike the following spring, I did appreciate it more, and I never once left it unlocked. And though my parents believed I was more careful because of what the new bike had cost me in hours spent raking, vacuuming, and picking up Bowzer's poop in the backyard, that wasn't really it. It was the year I spent without a bike, having to run fast alongside my friends when they all biked somewhere, or get on the back of someone else's, which was easier, but humiliating. The day I got my new bike, I rode until dark, energized on pure happiness, my legs coiling and uncoiling like springs.

I felt that same pure happiness when I was finally alone in Jimmy's car, slipping my own CD into the stereo. I know some people hate driving. But I would guess most of them have cars. When they want to go somewhere, they do not have to sweetly ask for a ride, or figure out a bus schedule, or just stay home. They get in their cars and go. And maybe they don't appreciate it, even if they paid for their cars with hard work. After a while, they don't think about the ease. But I did. By the time I rolled out of the airport's exit, I might as well have been flying, loving every second of all that freedom and speed.

I was just coming down the entrance ramp of the turnpike when a raindrop froze on the windshield. I saw another, and then another. And then there were so many that the glaze caught the windshield wipers, stalling their rhythm. An SUV in the eastbound lane fishtailed for several seconds before the driver regained control. I glanced in the rearview mirror, at the stretch of interstate behind me. There was just farmland on either side, barren fields, a silo. I wasn't even sure if there was a decision to make. It wasn't as if I could turn around.

I turned off the CD player. I sat up straight. I could do this. My mother had driven Elise and me home from school in an ice storm once. She'd held the steering wheel with tight hands and told us not to make a sound as we slowly passed cars in ditches and cars that had spun into each other. She talked as she drove, her voice calm, her eyes never leaving the road. If you started to slide on ice, she said, you couldn't just hit the brakes. Braking was the first instinct, but sometimes you had to override it. You had to just keep going, she said, and make yourself steer your way through.

The MINI Cooper, cute as it was, was hardly made for icy roads. But moving very slowly and going easy on the brake, I steered it through several miles of slick bridges and slippery turns. I passed a semitrailer jackknifed on the median, a van on its side in a ditch. I didn't stop at either of them: from a very young age, Elise and I had both been captive audience to our father's frightening stories about what could happen to a girl on the highway once she left the safety of her car. Don't stop for anyone, he'd told us. He knew it sounded harsh, but there were people out there who would fake a wreck, fake an injury, just to get you to pull over, and once you so much as rolled down your window, they had you if they had a gun. *I don't care if it's a man or a woman,* he said. And anyone could dress like a nun, or look elderly. Ted Bundy had worn a cast. It was nice to help people, my father allowed. But on the road, you had to look out for yourself.

So I kept going. But after I passed the wrecks, I reached into my book bag to grope for my cell phone, thinking I would call the police. It wasn't there. But I kept feeling for it, hoping, for at least another two miles. That's what I was doing when I wrecked. It happened, as car accidents do, very quickly, and I doubt it would have mattered if I'd been driving with both hands. I pumped the brake, trying to steer, even as the car spun closer to the ditch and then slammed into it, front first. I went forward as glass shattered. My seat belt held. I fell back.

For several seconds, I didn't move. I just sat there gripping the steering wheel, my foot pressed hard against the brake. The impact had dislodged the rearview mirror; it rested on the dashboard, tilted up at an angle where I could see my reflection, my wide eyes, my bared teeth. I took several deep breaths. I lifted my hands from the steering wheel, moved my fingers. I eased my foot off the brake and wiggled my toes. My neck and shoulder ached where the seat belt had yanked me back, but I wasn't hurt in any serious way. I touched my head, smoothed back my hair.

I was okay. My hands were trembling. I was okay. It was not that serious. The air bags had not gone off. But I'd heard glass breaking. Something was broken. I tried not to think about Jimmy.

What to do. What to do. The engine was still running. I stepped carefully on the gas and heard a wild spitting sound, but there was no movement. I put the car in reverse, tried again. Going nowhere.

"It's okay," I said out loud. My teeth chattered. "It's okay. It's fine."

I turned off the engine, put on my hat, and opened the door. The weeds beneath me crunched under my boot; each stalk and leaf was completely encased in a perfectly smooth sheath of ice. I pressed one hand on the hood, steadying myself as I worked my way around to the front of the car. The light from the clouded sunrise was faint, but I could see that the bumper was caved in over the right front tire. The glass I'd heard breaking was the right headlight.

I leaned against the car and rubbed my shoulder. It hurt where the seat belt had held. The wind blew hard, and tiny drops of cold rain hit my nose and cheeks. I rubbed my shoulder and looked around. There was just the gray ice, the low, silvery sky, and the empty interstate. A station wagon glided by in the eastbound lane. I watched it disappear over a hill in the distance. It was only fair. Nobody should stop for anyone. I could be a murderer, for all they knew.

I got back in the car and rummaged through my backpack for my phone, hoping I'd just overlooked it. But I hadn't. I'd brought along my physiology book, my magnetic-stripped meal card, my driver's license, a pack of Life Savers, and several pistachio shells. And that was it.

My father had, of course, given me plenty of advice on what to do if I ever wrecked a car. I was to stay inside with the doors locked and wait for the police or the highway patrol. When they arrived, I was to make them show me their badges before I rolled down the window. Before I did any of this, I was supposed to call my father with the phone that I was to always have with me, the phone that my father had purchased for me, not because he wanted me to better be able to, as he put it, "blah blah blah" with my friends all day, but because he wanted me to have one in case of an emergency.

I looked at myself in the rearview mirror. My nose was running. My face was pale. If he found out about this, he would yell. Later he would say he was sorry for yelling, and that he only yelled because he loved me and because he didn't want anything bad to happen to me. But before he did that, he would yell.

I'm not sure how long I sat there. I'd forgotten my watch as well. It felt like an hour, but it might have been less. The freezing rain turned into regular rain, and then stopped. I got cold. Hungry. I wanted caffeine. The rising sun was a pale dot in the sky, and I looked at it without squinting, trying to guess the time. My physiology lab started at ten. My lab instructor, a PhD candidate from Ethiopia who appeared to be maybe two years older than I was, had informed us that she was aware that people really did get the flu and grandmothers really did die and that there were all kinds of legitimate tragedies that could keep us away; but she also believed that these tragedies were not her problem. In the end, work was work, and it had to be done at a certain time.

And yet there was nothing I could do. In either direction, there was just cold highway and ice, no sign of Highway Patrol. I turned on the radio, moving the dial past country music and scratchy commercials until I heard a DJ's low voice warning of hazardous driving conditions. Bridges were especially dangerous. The storm was already in the KC metro area, moving north. People who had been in accidents were advised to wait in their cars, not to call 911 unless there was a true emergency, and to know they were probably in for a long wait.

"Really," the DJ said, the opening notes to "Hotel California" steadily increasing in volume, "you're probably better off to just get out and punch the other driver, you know, work it out yourselves. You're both idiots for driving when it's like this. Admit it, cut your losses, and go home."

When the light from the sun was a little stronger, I rubbed mist off the windshield and noticed what looked like a sign for a gas station rising up from the horizon. It didn't look that far away, a couple of miles at the most. I heard my father's voice in my head and stayed where I was a little longer. But the colder I got, the less sense his advice seemed to make. I put my hat back on and got out of the car.

I found I had better traction walking on the strip of icy weeds between the shoulder of the road and the ditch. I carried my back-pack in front of me for better balance. I had walked for five minutes, maybe ten, when it started raining again, fat cold drops that fell on the ice and made it more slick. I pulled my hood up over my hat and pulled the string so only my eyes peeked out. Things could be worse, I told myself. I had remembered gloves. I had on the good boots my mother had given me.

I heard the semi coming up behind me long before I saw it. The sky had settled low and foggy over a hill, and when I turned, I saw headlights, two yellow eyes shining through the early gray morning. I don't remember the color of the cab. I did not expect it to stop.

But it did stop, its big engine still rumbling, the cab almost right in front of me. I waited, unsure of what to do. As far as hitchhiking went, according to my father, a girl would have to be out of her mind. "Once you get in somebody's car," he told both me and Elise, "you've got no control. You're in their world, okay? They're calling the shots."

My father hitchhiked when he was young, of course. The summer before he started law school, my father, a guitar strapped across his back, had thumbed rides all over the country. But times had changed, he said. You just couldn't do that kind of thing anymore, especially if you were female. He was sorry if that sounded unfair—here, he'd held up his palm when Elise opened her mouth. Life was unfair, he said. Get used to it. He had an arsenal of examples to prove the world was predatory, and young girls often the prey. If we didn't believe him, we could read the paper.

I looked up at the truck, my eyes squinting, the rest of my face still covered by my cinched hood. My friend Becky Shoemaker from high school had hitchhiked all the way to California and back after graduation, and nothing bad had happened to her. On the contrary, she'd been invited to tour a cave with a church group traveling through Arizona, and a truck driver who had a family in Chula Vista gave her his wife's phone number in case, when she got to California, she needed a place to stay. When Becky Shoemaker got to California, she'd called the trucker's wife, and ended up staying with her for almost a week. When I asked Becky if she had ever been scared, getting in strangers' cars, staying in strangers' houses, she'd looked at me like I was crazy. "The only way you make something bad happen to you is if you think about it all the time and, like, attract it," she'd said, with the earned authority of someone who had managed to spend two weeks in California for less than fifty dollars.

The truck driver rolled down the closer window and peered down over the edge. He was wearing a John Deere cap.

"What are you doing?" His voice was reassuringly friendly.

I tugged the hood beneath my chin. "I wrecked my car." *My car,* I thought. I had just wrecked my car. I would not think about Jimmy.

"What?" He cupped his hand over his ear.

I cupped my hands around my mouth. "I WRECKED MY CAR!"

"Oh," he said. "You and everybody. Need a lift?"

I shook my head casually, as if refusing a cup of hot chocolate. My teeth were still chattering, and it was hard to speak. "Could you just call Highway Patrol for me?"

"Sure." He rested a hand on the rolled-down window. "But it's going to be a while." He nodded vaguely behind him. "They got their work cut out for them today."

I looked back and nodded, too, but said nothing. We were like farmers agreeing on the weather. Rain hit hard against my chin. I pulled my hood tight again. The truck's motor sighed and growled. When I breathed in, I tasted oil.

"You're going to get pretty cold out here. Where you headed?"

"Just to that gas station." I raised my arm, pointing, as if there were any other direction to go.

"Come on. Let me give you a lift. I'll have you there in a couple of minutes."

I looked up at him. He was clean-shaven, smiling, and not much older than I was. He did not look like a killer. It would be frustrating to be a nice man, I considered, to go through life trying to be helpful, only to have women wonder if you were out to kill them.

"You're going to freeze," he said. "And it's not safe, walking by the highway." He laughed in a way that showed he was, in fact, frustrated. He agreed with me. I was being dumb. I took a few careful steps toward the cab, and the door popped open. I had some trouble hoisting myself up—the step seemed to be made for someone with a much longer stride. But when I finally got up, there was a passenger seat with a seat belt. I felt the blast of a good heater, closed my door, and slid back into the seat with a sigh.

"Better?" He put the truck in gear and smiled, laugh lines branching out from the corner of the one eye that I could see. The cab smelled like onion rings, and a pair of black socks had been left to dry on the dash, but the heat felt good. A plastic sack stuffed with fast-food wrappers and empty paper cups swung from a hook just over my knees.

"Much better." I was embarrassed by my earlier hesitation. I hoped to make up for it with gratitude. "Thank you," I said. "Really. I appreciate it." The cab was warm enough that I was already uncomfortable. I pulled my hood back and took off my hat.

He glanced at me, then back at the road. I could hear ice hitting the windshield, but he appeared unfazed, even as the truck picked up speed. He wore just jeans and a flannel shirt, as if the weather outside had nothing to do with him.

He nodded at my book bag. "You go to school?"

"I do." I marveled at how high up we were. I had never been in a semi before. "KU."

"Right on." He snapped his fingers and made a gun with his finger and thumb. "Rock Chalk Jayhawk."

"Rah rah," I said, barely raising my arm.

"That's in Lawrence?"

I nodded.

He gave me the look of thinking I was being dumb again. "That's right up the road. Is that where you live? I'll just take you there."

I opened my mouth, but again, I could think of nothing. If he took me all the way into Lawrence, I could catch a bus to campus and probably still make it to lab. I could even go back to the dorm first. I could get some coffee and brush my teeth. We approached the sign for the gas station. He glanced at me and started to slow.

"Yes. Thank you. If you could take me to Lawrence, that would be great," I said. "Thanks." I put my balled-up hat to my mouth to stop myself from thanking him again. The cab was almost hot, but my teeth were still chattering. I felt strange, weirdly energized. I'd gotten hypothermia, maybe. Or I'd hit my head when the car wrecked, and I didn't remember. Or I was just worried about Jimmy.

I looked at the driver. His face was blank, his blue eyes focused on the road.

"I just wrecked someone else's car," I said.

He gave me a quick, curious glance, and that was all I needed. I told him the whole story, speaking too quickly, breathing in the dry heat. I simply needed to tell someone what had happened. He was an objective stranger, and I wanted his opinion.

He shrugged. "It was the ice. Not your fault."

"But you don't *know* these people." And then I was telling him about Jimmy and Haylie. I did my best impression of Jimmy, about Haylie's warnings against making him mad. The driver smiled, and I felt a little better. I could lighten it all up, turn the whole thing into a funny story, something I could control.

"Ha," he said. "Tell me more. I've been driving for six days straight. It's nice to hear another voice."

I kept going. I told him how I'd forgotten my cell phone, and how my dad was going to kill me. I told him about how I was probably going to be late for physiology lab, and how much I did not want to dissect a dog shark on this particular morning anyway. He remembered dissecting a frog in junior high, he said. He felt a little bad for the frog, but he'd loved it, seeing how everything worked inside.

We were getting close to Lawrence. I could see the campus rising up on a hill in the distance, the twin flags of Fraser Hall faintly visible in the gray air. I might just make it to lab after all. We were making good time, going fast. I squinted out into the fields surrounding the highway, dead wheat stalks flattened by wind and ice.

"I can get off at the next exit," I said.

"Tell me something else," he said. "You're better than the radio."

But I couldn't think of anything else to tell him. My fatigue was catching up with me again. My shoulder still hurt, and I was certain the seat belt had left a bruise.

"I'm sorry. I'm tired." I rubbed my shoulder.

He glanced at me. "Did you get hurt or something?"

"Oh. I think the seat belt just bruised my shoulder." I pulled my scarf and coat and sweater away, glancing down. When I looked back up, he was looking at me.

"Here's my exit." I pointed at the sign.

He didn't slow down. I looked at him to see if he'd heard me. His blue eyes were dulled, his jaw slack.

"Here's my exit," I said again. The sign for the exit seemed to be approaching very quickly. I was still pointing, my arm straight out in front of me. We passed the sign. We passed the exit. I pulled my arm back to my side. Pinpricks of sweat formed under my arms. My mouth felt dry and hot.

"That was my exit," I said.

"Oh," he said. "*That* was your exit. I'm sorry. I was thinking it was later."

I felt movement under my skin, blood warming in my hands, in my throat. "That's fine," I said carefully. I was looking out at the road, not at him. "There's another Lawrence exit up ahead. You can let me off there."

"Sure," he said. "No problem."

I stared out the window, listening to the growling engine, the scrape of the wipers. There was nothing wrong. Everything would be okay. He just hadn't heard me.

He leaned forward, catching my eye. He had a deep scratch on his left cheek. "You're not mad, are you?"

"No," I said. I caught sight of myself in the side mirror. Something in my expression made me think of my mother's face. "There's one more exit for Lawrence. I'll just get off there."

A car passed us, the tires spitting back slush. It looked small and low to the ground.

"You're not going to talk anymore?"

I shook my head, still looking away. Tiny snowflakes were falling now. They hit the side mirror and melted, trickling down. I watched for the next exit.

He waited ten windshield beats before he spoke again.

"You probably got a boyfriend."

This was the first time his voice sounded anything but friendly. The word "boyfriend," especially, was not said kindly. There was a hint of accusation in it, a wary annoyance. Everything inside me, my breath, my heart, felt still.

"Oh. So now you won't even tell me that?"

I could not have answered him if I'd wanted to. My jaw was clenched, my tongue tense against the roof of my mouth. And I didn't want to answer. It was hard to know which answer, a yes or a no, would be unwise. I thought of Tim. He was well on his way to Chicago by now, north of the storm and unaware. I pictured his face and felt tears.

"I'm sure you do," he said. He puffed his cheeks, breathing out a long, sad-sounding sigh. "Bet you talk to him, he asks you to." There was a pause, the windshield wipers thumping. "Bet you do about anything."

"There's an exit," I said, and again my arm and finger extended in front of me. I looked at him as blankly as I could. "This is the last exit for Lawrence. I need to get out here."

He didn't look at me. I turned back to my window and watched as we passed the exit sign. My eyes drifted down, to the faraway ground speeding by below. I looked at myself in the side-view mirror again. So this was how it happened. And this was how it felt. I was a fly in a web, a bear in a trap. I'd made bad decisions, or maybe just one, and it was too late to go back.

He was quiet for so long that I turned to look at him. His hands were clenched on the steering wheel, his posture straight. His breathing was long and deep, purposeful, his nostrils flaring as he inhaled. He seemed frightened himself. I didn't know if this was good or bad.

"You have to let me out," I said. I kept my voice low and calm.

He swallowed. He dragged his top teeth against his bottom lip. The windshield wipers beat on, though it was no longer raining.

"You have to let me out. Just pull over. Let me out. You missed the exits. That's not a crime." I said this last word heavily. "But I want to get out now."

He shook his head, just slightly, starting to realize, perhaps, that he didn't have to answer me one way or another. Another semi roared past us, its driver staring straight ahead. We were passing the western subdivisions of Lawrence, the new developments of houses with big lawns and three-car garages. One house already had Christmas decorations up, an angel with a trumpet in the front yard, a dark wreath on the door.

"I want to get out," I said again, and then, hearing the threat of a break in my voice, I closed my mouth and turned away. Against my will, my parents appeared in my mind's eye, and also my sister. I saw them the way they had looked in the last family portrait we'd taken together before the divorce. My mother and father stood arm in arm behind Elise and me, my mother's hand on my shoulder, my father's hand on Elise's, Elise and I standing close enough to graze arms; we were all connected, a circle of shoulders and hands. In the picture, which had hung over the fireplace in our old house and now sat in the storage room of my father's condo, everyone had been smiling. I thought of Tim, the way his hands felt in my hair, the note he'd left on my cheek.

"You have to let me out." I stared up at the ceiling of the cab until my eyes were dry. I leaned forward and looked at his face. "Listen to me. I have a mother and father and a sister. I have friends, and they love me. They love me. My parents love me. Do you understand? I am someone's daughter. Let me out." My voice was quiet, calm, but very firm. "You let me out right now."

He held up his hand, his fingers flexed, as if trying to block me from his view. He looked in his rearview mirror and wiped his hand against his brow.

I turned away again, looking down. I couldn't jump out. I would hurt myself, and I would be out in the cold, no one to help me, and, at the very least, unable to run. The sun had broken through the clouds, and the ice on the trees and fields sparkled like a million shards of broken glass. *The intense blaze of a sun-flooded jewel.* My mother loved Mark Twain, and at the end of every ice storm I could remember, she'd quoted this line, staring happily out the car or kitchen window. I kept the words in my head, holding onto them, my hands tight fists inside my mittens. *The intense blaze of a sun-flooded jewel.*

The truck rolled on. We passed a billboard advertising a hotel in Topeka with an indoor pool, just fifteen miles away. A hawk circled high overhead. I had been on this stretch of interstate before, on a high school field trip to the state capitol. But that had been on a sunny day in April, cows grazing in sunny pastures, a colt galloping alongside a fence.

I turned my head slightly toward him, my gaze moving around the cab. An ice scraper rested on the dashboard, much closer to him than to me. A large flashlight lay in a mesh bag that hung from the back of his seat. A ticket stub stuck out of a built-in ashtray just by the steering wheel. My gaze rested there, and my breathing slowed.

We were on a turnpike.

I stayed quiet, facing straight ahead. To get off the turnpike, he'd have to stop to pay a toll. There would be a toll worker. Some people had special tags that let them glide through on credit accounts, but I didn't see any such tag on his windshield. He was from out of state, just passing through. I lifted my chin, breathed in, and looked at the road ahead.

He reached over to turn down the heat. When I looked over at him, his temples and forearms were shiny with sweat. "I'm going to let you out," he said. "Just not here, not on the road. I'll let you out in Topeka. Or at the next exit. Whatever."

"Okay," I said. "I believe you."

"I wasn't going to hurt you." He looked at me and laughed, as if the very idea were ridiculous. "I just got distracted, you know, with you talking. You talk a lot. I'm not used to having somebody talking."

"Sure," I said. I managed what I hoped was a convincing smile. "Sure. I can see that."

We were still far outside of Topeka when, just up ahead, I saw the flagpole signs for a cluster of gas stations and restaurants. The exit was halfway up a hill. It was a turnpike stop, a closed loop, no escape from the tolls.

I raised my hand and pointed, as if that had done me any good before. "Here," I said. "I'll just get out . . ."

"I know," he said, irritated. He shifted gears, and unbelievably, wonderfully, the truck really did start to slow. I picked up my book bag without lowering my head, my eyes on the exit sign, the driver in my peripheral vision. I could see cars in the parking lot for a Hardee's, and a couple in matching NASCAR coats walking carefully back over the ice to their car.

"Listen . . ." He turned to me, leaving one hand on the wheel, the other raised to me, palm forward.

I didn't listen. We were still far from the restaurant. We were no longer moving, but the engine was running. I opened the door and jumped. My feet gave way on the ice, and I slid forward, hitting my face against the open door. I got up, fell again. I heard the door slam, gears moving. I looked up and breathed in exhaust. By the time I was on my feet again, the truck was rolling away.

The lobby of the Hardee's was nearly empty. A man sat in one of the booths by the window, playing solitaire and drinking a cup of coffee. A girl my age in a brown uniform swept behind the counter. She looked up at me and her face changed.

"You're bleeding," she said, with disapproval.

I took off my glove and reached up to my face. My fingers came down bloody.

"I fell," I said. "I fell outside on the ice."

"That sucks." She picked up the broom and resumed sweeping. "Yeah. I been here since midnight, but I know that ice out there is just terrible. Nobody from the morning crew even showed up. I was supposed to be gone a half hour ago."

Speakers hung from the ceiling on either side of the counter, playing a tinny, wordless version of "I Can See Clearly Now." The girl with the broom looked up at me. I looked at her. I wondered later, when I was calmer, warmer, and not so tired, why I did not tell the girl right then about the trucker, if only to explain why I was so rattled.

"Did you want to order something?" She asked this as if it were a ridiculous question. "Or did you want to wash up first?" She lifted a hand with a plastic glove and pointed to her left. "There's a restroom around the corner."

In the bathroom, I held a napkin up to the cut on my bottom lip. I stared at myself in the mirror, trying to decide if I really had bumped my head. My pupils looked slightly dilated. My cheeks were splotched with red, maybe from the cold. My hands were still shaking. I would call my mother. She would be calmer than my father. She'd always been the softer parent, more comforting, and more understanding of mistakes.

I emerged from the bathroom, a clean paper towel pressed against my lip. I could smell warm bread, something with cinnamon. The lobby's stereo was now playing "Hang On Sloopy," but I could barely hear it after passing through the double doors to the vestibule where the payphones were. I took a receiver off a hook and looked through my bag. My fingers moved underneath my physiology book, into zipped pockets. I pricked my finger on a safety pin; but in the end, I came up with almost a handful of change.

I could have tried to call Gretchen, or even Tim's roommate. They both had cars. They were both, more than likely, in class for the morning; still, I could have left messages, and either one of them would have come to get me eventually. But that might be hours from now. It was only my mother or my father who would come right away, who would drop everything at once.

I had to feed the payphone almost all of the coins to reach the different area code. I could see my bloody lip reflected in the shiny metal of the phone. I leaned against it and closed my eyes.

"Yeah."

I opened my eyes. I had been careful to dial the right number and the area code for Overland Park. But this was not the way my mother answered her phone.

"Who is it?" Her voice sounded a little hoarse. But it was her.

"It's me. It's Veronica."

There was a pause. I heard a car horn in the background, a gunning engine. "Veronica? Where are you? Why does it say restricted number?"

"I'm at a payphone. Listen—"

"Why are you at a payphone?"

"I don't have my phone. Mom. I need you to come pick me up. I'm at a Hardee's in Topeka. Or just before Topeka. It's on the turnpike."

There was a very long pause. I considered giving her more information, but I wasn't sure she was still there.

"Mom?"

"Why are you in a Hardee's in Topeka?"

It was her, but it wasn't her. She was already angry, ready to fight.

"It's a long story. I just need you to come get me."

"Why are you in Topeka?"

I heard another horn, Bowzer barking in the background. "Are you driving? Mom, listen to me. This is important. Pull over and listen to me."

"I'm not driving. What are you doing in Topeka? It's Friday morning, Veronica. You're supposed to be in class."

"I'll tell you later. I just need you to come pick me u—"

"Well I can't."

I held the receiver away from my face and looked at it.

"Call your father. He can come and go at work as he pleases. I can't."

I put the receiver back up to my ear. "Mom, you don't under—"

"No. No. You are the one who doesn't understand." She was yelling. It was worse than when my father yelled. I wasn't used to it. Her voice sounded strained and tight. "Anytime anyone ever needed anything, I was right there. I've done everything for everybody for twenty-six years. Well I can't do it anymore. Okay? I have to look out for myself today. I'm not your chauffeur any-more."

I heard a series of metallic pings, the coins falling deeper into the recesses of the phone. Even then, I stayed where I was, the receiver pressed hard against my ear. I did not understand that she'd hung up until I heard the dial tone.

6

IT COST FOUR MORE QUARTERS to leave a message on my father's voice mail. I used my remaining forty-three cents on a small cup of coffee. I managed to do that without crying, my lower lip trembling like a child's, my "thank you" barely audible. I sat in a booth by the window and turned my face to the glass. I wasn't really stranded, of course. I could have tried to call my father's office—even if he was in court, the secretary could have sent someone out to get me. I could have asked the man drinking coffee in the corner for a couple of quarters. I could have asked the woman at the register behind the counter. But the longer I sat there, the more I felt incapable of asking anyone for anything. I could still hear the dial tone, like a ringing in my ears.

By the time the orange-faced clock in the lobby read ten o'clock, people were walking from their cars into the Hardee's with quick, confident strides. The sun was bright in a cloudless sky, and much of the ice of the parking lot was already melting into tiny rivers that drained into an oily, rainbow-hued pool by the drive-thru. If I sat up straight and looked past my reflection, I could see traffic on the turnpike moving at a steady clip. Still, I did not move, or make any plans. I was missing my physiology lab, missing it that very moment. My dog shark would stay wrapped in its frost-proof plastic bag in the lab refrigerator, saving its secrets for another time, another student.

At half past ten, I took my physiology book out of my backpack. But I didn't open it. I just didn't want to. I could not remember the last time I had let myself just sit, and not get anything done.

When Elise and I were small, my mother kissed our scraped knees and shins. She did not air kiss—she put her lips right up to the wound because that was what made us feel better. My father, always a little squeamish, had pointed out that an air kiss would probably spread fewer germs, and my mother said she didn't care, our germs were her germs. If Elise and I had a germ, she wanted it, too. "No," he finally said. "I mean your germs, Natalie. You're giving your mouth germs to them." It was only then that she'd stopped.

At quarter till eleven, an older woman with bleached hair pulled back beneath her visor came out to sweep the floors around the booths. I could hear her whistling as she moved the broom close to my booth, and twice, when I looked up, I caught her watching me. A Greyhound bus rolled into the parking lot, and someone from behind the counter called for the sweeping woman to hurry back to the grill. But she lingered for a moment, still sweeping.

"Are you okay?" She winced as if she already knew the answer. She wore silver earrings shaped like dragonflies. She looked to be in her sixties maybe. She had a rose tattooed on her forearm.

"You're bleeding," she said. She clicked her tongue.

"I wrecked a car." I pressed my napkin harder against my lip. "Someone dropped me off here. I don't have any money to call anyone."

"Donna!" The person behind the counter was snapping repeatedly. "We've got a bus! Let's go!"

She glanced at the counter and then looked back at me. One of the side doors to the parking lot opened, and a long line of yawning and stretching bus passengers with muddy shoes made their way up to the counter.

"DONNA."

She held up her finger, still looking down at me. "I'll call Highway Patrol after this rush," she said. She leaned down to pat my arm, giving me an apologetic smile to show she wished there were more she could do.

Two hours later, an officer arrived. He had a South Kansas twang and a gray mustache that looked combed. We sat in the front of his patrol car while he filled out his report. He was surprisingly sympathetic, even after learning I had no proof of insurance and, really, no idea whether the car I had left by the side of the road was insured or not. He admonished me for not calling right away about the truck driver, though he agreed that it wasn't clear whether any law had been broken. He would have liked to have been able to talk with the guy, he said, and run a background check. But he didn't keep bugging me about it. He turned his heater on high and offered to turn it down if I got too warm.

"What you had, I think, is a certifiable case of a crappy morning," he said, putting the cap back on his pen. "Sorry you had to wait so long. We were pretty backed up with the storm. Twenty-three accidents this morning, and that's just on this stretch between Lawrence and Topeka."

I nodded. I couldn't think of what to say. I was hungry. My lip hurt. "That's terrible," I said finally, holding my hands against the heater. "You must be exhausted." I was trying to stay on his good side.

"I'm actually fine." He slid the report into a folder. "A storm like this gets my adrenaline going. I feel bad telling you this, but I kind of like it."

He did seem energized as he drove me back to Lawrence, his

posture straight, his hands at ten and two on the wheel except when he answered the radio. After the third call came in, he apologized again and told me he didn't have time to drive me all the way back to my dorm. He said he could take me to my car and that a tow truck was on its way. I could get a ride home with the driver.

This seemed like a reasonable plan. But as it turned out, the tow truck driver—who did not seem at all energized by his long and busy morning—insisted on taking me to my dorm before dropping off the car at a garage. He wanted me to get my checkbook before he took the car anywhere. That seemed reasonable as well. The end result, however, was that I arrived in front of the dorm in a tow truck pulling Jimmy Liff's famous—and now severely rumpled—MINI Cooper, "FASCIST PRICK" still faintly visible on the door. When we rolled up, thirty or forty people—many of whom only knew me through noise complaints—stood under the dorm's front portico, waiting for the bus.

I opened the door and slid out of the tow truck. The crowd was silent for several seconds, then someone said "Oooooooooooo," in a way that sounded pleased.

My cell phone was on my desk, next to my watch. There were four messages from my father. On the first, he sounded worried. On the second, he sounded worried and a little irritated. From then on, he was just yelling. My sister had left a message as well.

"Call Dad," she said. "He thinks you're dead in Topeka."

I sat on my bed, took off my hat, and dialed his number. When he heard my voice, he was quiet for almost five full seconds before he started in.

"Do you know where I am, Veronica? Do you know where I am right at this moment?"

"I don't." I sat on my bed. "Where are you?"

"I'm in the parking lot of the Hardee's on the turnpike in Topeka, where they apparently only let robots answer the goddamn phone."

"You drove out to find me?" I rested my head against the cool, cinder-block wall by my window. Outside, the sun was still shining, and I could hear the soft fall of melting ice.

"No, honey. No. I just drove thirty-five miles into the prairie because I wanted those little cinnamon rolls they make, and I couldn't find a Hardee's in Kansas City. Yes, I goddamn drove out here to find you! I was in court when you called. Why didn't you have your phone with you?"

"I forgot it."

He sighed.

"I'm sorry," I said. I was suddenly warm. The dorm's heating system, when it decided to work, forced dry, hot air through the vents, and the knob for my vent had fallen off. I stood up and shook off my coat.

"You're sorry." He groaned. "You left that message, scared me out of my mind. They told me you'd gotten a ride home with a cop. You're okay?"

"Yeah."

"Why were you in Topeka?"

"It's a long story. I'm fine now."

There was a beat of silence. "What are you mixed up in?"

"Nothing. I'm just tired. Can we talk about it later?" I stood up and opened my desk drawer. I was dizzy with hunger, but in no mood to go downstairs and across the parking lot for lunch. I had a jar of peanut butter stashed away for emergencies. I got it out, along with a spoon from the dining hall.

"Does this have to do with that Tom guy? Were you with him? You got in a fight, right? And he left you there. Give me his number. We'll have a little talk."

"Tim."

"Who? Who's Tim?"

"Tim is my boyfriend. Not Tom. I've never dated anyone named Tom."

"So he left you there?"

"*No.* He's in Chicago. He had nothing to do with this."

"Chicago? So nobody goes to class anymore? It's a Friday, right? But he's in Chicago, you're in Topeka. So it's not really college, right? It's sort of a voluntary attendance kind of thing. I pay tuition, while you travel the world and scare the shit out of me."

"Dad." I could feel my voice start to break. I hated it when he yelled. I worked to keep my voice low, steady. I tried to channel Elise. "A Hardee's outside Topeka is hardly traveling the world. I'm sorry I scared you. But I would really like it if I could explain all this later. I am having a very bad day."

"I walked out on a client, you know. Walked right out on him. Honey, I pay for your phone because I want you to have it for precisely this kind of situation. It doesn't do any good if you don't carry it."

"I'm sorry." This would be good practice, I thought, for talking to Jimmy Liff. I opened the jar of peanut butter, but the spoon slipped from my hands and fell into the crack between my desk and the foot of my bed. I looked back into the jar.

"You could have left a more detailed message. It was cryptic, what you said."

I got down on my hands and knees to retrieve the spoon. To my dismay, I saw it had fallen in a small pile of general dorm floor detritus— dust, an apple core, the chemistry study guide I had searched for in vain the previous month. I frowned, disgusted with myself. Brooms, mops, and vacuums were available for checkout at the front desk, but I had yet to bother.

"Hello? Veronica?"

Someone was knocking at my door.

"What is that?" my father asked. "What's that racket? Where are you now?"

I opened my door to find Marley Gould, one hand raised, ready to knock again, her other hand holding her French horn case. She was still wearing her long, puffy coat and matching hat, and she looked even younger than usual, her cheeks rosy, her eyes bright from the cold.

"I heard you were in a car accident!" She pointed at me. "You hurt your lip?"

"Yes, but I'm okay. I'm on the phone, though. Do you . . . do you need anything?"

"Veronica? Hello?" The phone had slipped to my shoulder, but my father's voice was still easy to hear. "Are you talking to someone else? Could you give me your full attention for just a moment? Would that be too much to ask, considering I just drove forty-five miles to come find you?"

"Sorry. I'm here." I smiled at Marley and mouthed an apology to her as well, easing the door closed between us. "Sorry," I said again. "That was one of my residents."

"Tell me what happened."

I ate a fingerful of peanut butter and swallowed. "Right now?"

"Yes."

I sat back down on my bed. I was going to have to tell him sooner or later. And I needed to ask him about insurance, and what he thought I should do.

"I was dropping friends off at the airport."

"What? Then why did you call from Topeka?" His voice sounded different, quieter. He'd switched to his headset. "That's the opposite direction from the airport."

I took in another fingerful of peanut butter, trying to think. My sister and I had learned early on that lying to my father required extremely quick thinking and steely nerves. Elise had pulled it off a few times—when she was a teenager, she would go round and round with him about whether traffic really could have been bad enough to make her miss her curfew, or whether there was any way to prove that she'd known someone in the backseat of her car had been drinking a beer. Even with her speed and bravado, he usually found the hole in her story. I myself had long ago decided that lying to him wasn't worth the trouble. I hadn't tried it since I was a child.

"How did I get to Topeka?"

He inhaled slowly, exhaled quickly. "Yes, Veronica. I'm asking how you got to Topeka."

I gave him an abbreviated version.

"You hitchhiked?" He was suddenly much louder. "You did the exact thing I told you to never do?"

"But it worked out," I said cheerily. "He just took me to, you know . . ."

"The Hardee's on the turnpike."

"Right!" I swallowed more peanut butter.

"In Topeka?"

"Mm-hmm."

There was no reply. I thought I'd lost the connection.

"Dad?"

"Why take you so far away? Why didn't he just take you to Lawrence?"

"He missed the exit."

There was a long, long pause.

"Dad. I am exhausted. I just want to take a shower. And since you're driving, and I'm home safe, maybe we can talk lat—"

"Aren't there two or three exits to Lawrence?"

I nodded. It would communicate nothing on the phone, but it was all I could manage.

"Oh my God. Oh my God, Oh my God. OH MY GOD." The phone seemed to shake in my hand.

"Dad. Please calm down. I'm fine."

I heard a dull thud, a gloved hand hitting a steering wheel, perhaps.

"DID THIS PERSON TOUCH YOU?"

"No."

"DID HE HURT YOU IN ANY WAY?"

"No, Dad, no. I'm fine."

"Because if he did . . . If he did, I will find him and KILL HIM. Or I will . . . I will find him and PAY SOMEONE to KILL HIM. You are . . . You have to promise me not to do something so stupid again."

"I won't." I held my head in my hands, wishing I could have lied. "Sorry."

"Okay. I'm driving to Lawrence tomorrow. I have some time. We can have lunch. I'll pick you up at eleven. And don't worry. You're on my insurance. I'm not an idiot."

"Okay," I said. I would have to pay dearly for this assistance—there would be more lectures, and probably jokes about my driving for years to come—still, I felt comforted, and cared for. He was a yeller, but at least he cared.

I had almost hung up when he said my name. I brought the phone back up to my ear. "Yes?"

"So . . ." He suddenly sounded awkward. "I'm just wondering," he said. "Where was your mother in all this?" He cleared his throat. "I assume you tried to call her."

I moved my finger up to my lips. I could feel the raised line of clotted blood.

"Veronica? Did you call your mother?"

I looked down at my boots, still damp with melted sleet. "I tried," I said. "She wasn't home."

My sister called just as I returned from the shower. "So you're not dead?" she asked. "Not even injured?"

"I'm fine," I said. I was wearing just a towel, and in my closet mirror, I could see the bruise the seat belt had left. I traced my finger down it, just hard enough to hurt.

"No one calls to let me know the crisis is over. Last I heard, you were lost on the windy plains with nothing to eat but fast food. Dad called me from his car. He was loud. Even for him."

I almost smiled. "Why would he call you? What were you going to do in California?"

"He wanted me to call Mom."

My heart sank a little. Maybe my father just didn't have my mother's phone number. But I imagined that if he had, he probably wouldn't have been able to make himself call it, even when he was allegedly so worried. He loved me, I knew. But the divorce, even in a crisis, reigned supreme.

"So did you?" I eased into my robe and wrapped the towel around my wet hair.

"Did I what?"

"Did you call Mom?"

"Hold on," she said. "ONE MOCHA GRANDE PLEASE. THREE SHOTS PLEASE." I heard static, movement. "Sorry. I'm at a drive-thru. I came in at six this morning. Six! I have no life. Anyway, yeah, I tried to call Mom. She didn't pick up."

"Hmm," I said.

"So what happened? How did you end up in Topeka?"

I tried to tell her the story as quickly as possible. But she liked to cross-examine, too.

"You skipped class to take these people to the airport?"

"No."

"How did you wreck the car?"

"There was an ice storm, Elise. Lots of people wrecked their cars this morning."

"Okay. Don't get defensive. I didn't know about the ice. It's beautiful here. It's always beautiful." She clicked her tongue. "I wish I weren't wearing a suit. I have to wear hose. It's ridiculous."

I sat on my bed and pulled on a pair of wool socks. I could picture Elise in her Volkswagen, her hair pulled back in a twist, moving down a freeway with her mocha. Elise could drive in heavy traffic while talking on the phone, while drinking a hot beverage, no problem. If she didn't have a stick shift, she could probably type out a legal brief right there at the wheel. She didn't wreck cars. She never screwed up. Still, when I told her what had happened that morning, I gave her the full story.

"Oh my God," she said, real sympathy in her voice. "Honey. Did you tell the police?"

"Yeah. Too late, I think. But yeah."

"You must have been scared."

I closed my eyes, grateful for the understanding. I doubted the people who worked with Elise knew about her soft side. But it was there.

"I'm okay," I said, not too convincingly. I wasn't ready for the pity to stop. "That's not the worst thing, either. I called Mom from the Hardee's. She hung up on me."

Elise was quiet for a moment. "What do you mean she hung up?"

"She told me she couldn't give me a ride, and she hung up."

"What? On purpose?" I heard a seagull cry in the background. "Are you sure it was on purpose?"

"Yeah. I'm sure. She said she wasn't my chauffeur anymore, and she hung up." It felt good, this tattling. I had covered for her to my father, but I needed comfort, and my loyalty had limitations. I was gratified to hear my sister inhale, momentarily stunned into silence. I stood up and rested my forehead against my window. The glass was cold, though the sun was still shining. Melting ice dripped from the windowsills of the higher floors. Seven stories down, people got off a bus and trudged back up to the dorm's front door. They wore heavy coats and backpacks and, I imagined, the self-satisfied expressions of people who had made it to class and completed their lab work on time.

"She's lost her mind," Elise finally said. She sounded sad, or maybe just tired. "I knew she was bad. I understand she's having some . . . midlife, middle-aged crisis. But that's completely unacceptable. You're her daughter. You needed her help."

I nodded. I felt a little better with this shared indignation. But not much.

"So what are you going to do?" she asked.

"What do you mean?"

"Are you going to call her?"

"No."

"Veronica." The sympathy had left her voice. "Something is wrong with her. This isn't how she normally acts."

"Maybe she's got a new boyfriend," I said. "Maybe this one is only twenty."

"Stop."

I frowned. I'd liked it better when it was me Elise was worried about. "You call her," I said.

"I'm going to." Her voice changed again, her words quick and succinct. Now she sounded more like our father. "Believe me. I'm going to give her hell."

After I hung up, I lay down on my bed for what I told myself would be just a moment, a quick rest for my eyes. And then I would call Tim. It would be difficult to tell him over the phone what had happened. I might not tell him until he got home. I only wanted to talk with him. It would be nice just to hear his voice.

But as soon as I closed my eyes, I slept. And I dreamed about my mother. I think I dreamed of her for some time, though only a series of flashes stayed in my memory: her face in profile, resigned, sitting in the passenger seat of her van. I knew it was her van. I was sitting in the back, behind the driver's seat, and I could clearly see her face. But when I looked out the window, I saw how very high up we were, and all at once, I simply evaporated. She was in the passenger seat of a semi, and there was no backseat, nowhere for me to sit.

Jimmy Liff was surprisingly calm when I told him about the car. "Yeah, well, shit happens," he said. "It was the ice, right? Our flight was fucking delayed forever."

I shifted the phone to my other ear. He must not have heard me correctly. I had been scared to call.

"I had to have it towed," I said, though I had already told him this. I wanted him to understand that more than the fender had been damaged. "My dad's insurance will cover the repair, though. He's pretty sure it will."

Silence. I waited. My room was gray, almost dark, but outside, a sliver of the western sky was orange and pink, bright with the setting sun. It was almost six, and I was still wearing my robe. I had slept through lunch and dinner.

"Do you want the number for the garage?" I asked. "They said they would get to it sometime next week, but—"

"Yeah. We can deal with all that later." He sounded bored, or at least distracted. "We'll take a cab back from the airport on Sunday. Don't worry about it. We're just glad you're okay."

I was too surprised to speak. Jimmy Liff could give my mother a lesson in post-accident etiquette. I never would have guessed.

"But you've got to get over there to mist the plants." Now he sounded anxious. "Okay? I really don't want them to die."

Gretchen volunteered to drive me over, and she let me know from the start she wasn't going to just drop me off. She didn't think I should be alone; the truck driver story had creeped her out. "I don't care what you say," she said. "You're not going to study to-night." She was wearing a T-shirt with a picture of a kitten with enormous blue eyes that curiously resembled her. "I have a box of mac and cheese in my room. I'll bring it. I'll make you dinner." She pursed her lips. "You look really wound up, Veronica. Even for you, I mean."

I didn't argue. I needed the ride. And she was right: I was rattled. I kept thinking of the exact moment I'd lost control of the car, when I was spinning and careening forward on the ice, the wheel useless in my hand. I'd felt the same helplessness in the semi after we passed the first exit; but it was worse, much worse, because the fear of it lasted so much longer. Even now, my hands felt like they were shaking, though when I looked down at them, they were still.

On the way to Jimmy's, Gretchen stopped at a liquor store. I did not protest. In fact, I gave her ten dollars. When we got to Jimmy's, she made margaritas while I misted the plants. She found pretty drinking glasses and even little umbrellas, and she told me to just sit at the counter and sip while she worked on the macaroni and cheese. Again, I did not argue. I liked the taste of the drink.

"Do you think we can use some of their milk?" she asked. "Or is that *very expensive* too?"

She was referring to the note Jimmy had taped to the wine rack off the kitchen: *ALL VERY EXPENSIVE,* it read. *DO NOT DRINK OR EVEN TOUCH.*

"We can buy more," I said. The counter was stainless steel, and I could see my reflection in it, blurry and warped. The alcohol burned into the cut on my lip, but inside, I felt a pleasantly numb sensation radiating out from my mouth. I knew I should probably hold off a bit until after we ate. I usually wasn't much of a drinker.

"Please." Gretchen took a carton of milk out of the fridge. "I think he could spare a bottle of wine. Look at this place. He's got some serious disposable income." Her gaze moved over the shiny appliances on the counter and up to the skylight, now dark, above our heads. "Does that Simone girl live here with him?"

"I think so," I said. I had not told even Gretchen that Simone's real name was Haylie, or that I'd known her from home. *If the poor girl wants to be someone else, let her be someone else.* I took another long sip of my drink and looked around the big kitchen. This was where Haylie/Simone ate breakfast. It was strange that I should know this much about her new life as well as her old one. I wondered if even her mother or little brother or incarcerated father knew where or how she was living, or that she'd changed her name.

"What's this?" Gretchen touched a few buttons on the wall, and

Latin music that was loud but not horrible swirled out from some invisible center of the room. "That's so cool." She picked up her drink and moved in a slow circle. "I don't even know where it's coming from."

She turned the volume even higher. I swung my legs to the drumbeat. I wasn't sure if I should be worried about the neighbors. Outside, the lawns were neatly trimmed, and all the cars were hidden away in garages. It didn't seem like the kind of street where you could blast music late at night. I took out my phone to check the time and saw that my mother had called.

Gretchen turned down the music. "What's the matter? Who was that?"

"No one," I said. I had not told her that my mother had hung up on me that morning. I had not mentioned my mother at all. I was too embarrassed. Everything else that happened that morning was mostly bad luck and timing. But my mother's response, or lack thereof, seemed to point to something damaged in her, and maybe in me as well.

"It was Tim," I said. "Just Tim calling."

"Oh." She used a fork to take a piece of macaroni out of the boiling pot, but she continued to look at me. "Are you . . . are you in a fight or something?"

I shook my head, looking away. I wasn't a good liar when I was sober. And now I felt a little hazy all over. I held my glass with both hands. "He wants me to move in with him. Next year. He'll pay the rent, he said."

She blew steam off the piece of macaroni. "This is a problem?"

My phone beeped. I looked at the screen. My mother was calling again. I hit ignore. *Too late! Too late for you!* I took another drink.

Gretchen looked concerned. "Was that him again?"

"Yeah." I nodded, agreeing with myself. "Yeah. He's really, you know, he's really gung-ho about it. He keeps calling."

She wrinkled her nose. "To pressure you?"

"No. No." I put my hand over my mouth. I felt bad, making him look domineering, even crazy. He actually hadn't even called me since he left for Chicago. I needed to quit talking. "He just called to say hi."

She twisted around to turn off the boiler. She looked back at me, confused. "I don't understand. You seem upset that he called. You're upset that he wants you to move in with him?"

I nodded.

"You just said you were happy with him the other night. You went on and on about how happy you were."

"I did not go on and on."

"Fine. But your face was like . . ." She smiled. Her eyes suddenly looked vapid. "And you said you were so happy." She gave me a quick glance. "And you hate the dorm."

I sighed. She was the same as him. I was the only one who saw the problem. "Yeah, but what if we break up?" I raised my glass as if making a toast. "I won't have anyplace to go. I won't have my job anymore."

She nodded, pouring the pasta and water through a strainer. Steam rose to her face. "Okay. You're right."

"What does that mean?"

"It means you're right. Don't move in with him."

This was not what I wanted her to say. I put my elbows on the counter, my face in my hands. "But I want to," I said.

She started laughing again. I looked up, annoyed.

"Honestly?" She picked up her drink and took a sip. "I think you can sit here and torment yourself if you want, but I'm going to start looking for a new RA buddy. I bet anything you're living with him next year. You're not going to be at summer training. Why are you always so worried? It's okay. It's okay to do what you want."

I shook my head. Her voice was kind, and she was smiling, but I didn't like what she was saying. *That's okay for somone like you. It's nice that you could find someone who wants to take care of you. You're not doing so well in school.* I waved my hand in front of my face. I was a little tipsy. I might be a little paranoid.

"It would be one thing if you just wanted out of the dorm. But it's more than that, right?" She was stirring in the cheese. "You don't want to just live in his apartment. You want to live with him in his apartment."

I cleared my throat. I focused on my tingling lips, willing them to form words correctly. "Just because I want to doesn't mean I will," I said. "I'm trying not to be an idiot."

She shrugged.

I leaned back on the bar stool, my arms crossed. I heard what she was not saying. Apparently, I was as predictable as water, sure to seek the easiest route. My phone chimed in my pocket. My mother had left a message—a long one. All this time I'd been talking to Gretchen, my mother had been talking to my phone.

"Let's have people over," I said.

She thought I was kidding at first. She only pretended to reach for her phone. She didn't know me as well as she thought she did. I felt good about that.

I cannot fairly blame the decisions I made for the rest of that evening on alcohol. It is true I was not used to drinking, and that I had little experience with tequila. But I knew this. Before I even brought that first sip to my lips, there must have been something in me that had been shaken loose by the events of that morning, something that yearned for a sudden detour from the steady path I had long ago set for myself. My plan, I think, at least my subconscious plan, was to drink until I was wobbly enough to simply veer into a different direction.

It worked.

I was in an excellent mood when people started arriving. I only vaguely recognized some of them from the dorm, but I welcomed everyone, especially the people I didn't know at all, their stranger faces fresh slates on which I could impress my new, impulsive self. I ushered them into the living room with sweeping gestures. I thanked them for bringing more alcohol. I forgot all about being shy, and I also forgot about Jimmy, and Haylie, and the fact that we were in their house. I focused on being a good hostess. I nodded appreciatively when someone changed the music on the stereo and turned the volume way, way up. I took coats up the stairs to the master bedroom, laying each one out carefully on the enormous bed. I do remember the stairs becoming more difficult to climb as the evening wore on. I was wearing a black feather boa that someone had pulled out of Haylie's closet, and it kept catching beneath my feet.

I do not remember actually opening the door for Third Floor Clyde. Gretchen told me that I did. She specifically remembered the moment he arrived because, apparently, I let out a joyful whoop of recognition, moving past his friends to hug him before he even stepped inside. I do not know if the fact that I don't remember this moment makes it any more or less embarrassing. She said I took the coats of all the newcomers, but that I insisted, quite loudly in front of everyone, that Clyde help me carry them up the stairs.

"I wasn't worried," she told me later. "You weren't slurring your words or anything. You were sort of just . . ." Here she leaned to one side and fluttered her eyelids so that she looked sort of stupid. "You were just . . . listing a little."

Still, I can hardly claim that Third Floor Clyde took advantage of the situation. I don't think he had the chance. I have a distinct memory of his startled expression as I took the boa from around my neck and wrapped it around his. I remember thinking that Becky Shoemaker was right: I really *could* make things happen by just thinking about them. I had known Clyde would show up as soon as I decided to have a party, and now here he was. It was fate, or the antidote to it. We were up in Jimmy and Haylie's bedroom, by ourselves, standing beside the bed that was now piled high with coats. Or he was standing, I should say. I was actually dancing. Sort of. That's what I thought I was doing—moving gracefully and easily from foot to foot. Looking back, I think I was still just listing, and maybe vaguely aware that I had to pee.

His eyes moved from side to side as the boa settled around his shoulders. He said something, but I couldn't hear what. The music on the stereo downstairs had gotten very loud. He wasn't nearly as tall as Tim, and I remember that just this difference seemed appealing, physical proof that some small but permanent change in perspective was taking place in my mind. We were looking at each other closely, eyes level and bright with anticipation. He brought his finger up to the cut in my lip, softly tracing the outline.

And that was all it took. I pressed my injured mouth against his. There was no exchange of witty dialogue. Maybe I just don't remember it, but I think I would have. To be honest, I wasn't that drunk. My coat was buried under all the others, and I clearly remember the muffled beeping of my cell phone from the pocket. It could have been anyone's, I suppose, but I heard it as mine, and I remember feeling good about ignoring it.

7

"GOOD MORNING." The words were said sweetly, and very softly. Gretchen stood over me, still wearing the shirt with the kitten on it. Sunlight reflected off the enormous mirror beside Jimmy and Haylie's bed. I was lying on top of the covers, my coat thrown over me like a blanket.

"How you feeling?" She reached up to move her hair out of her eyes. A bloodstained paper towel was wrapped around one of her fingers, a hair elastic holding it in place. "I have aspirin in my purse."

"What happened to your hand?" My voice was croaky, hard to hear. My tongue felt large and dry.

"Oh." She looked at her hand. "Some idiot threw a bottle. I don't even know who he was. I picked up some of the glass."

I squinted at her, but said nothing. I was taking in information. There had been people in the house even Gretchen didn't know. Bottles had been thrown. I sat up quickly. "The wine rack," I said. What Jimmy considered very expensive would be irreplaceable for me.

She waved her bandaged hand. "Relax. I rolled it into the pantry before things got too crazy. It's fine. Nobody even saw it."

"Oh." My head felt heavy. I lay back down. "Thanks." I sat up again. "Oh no! What time is it?"

She looked at her watch. "It's half past nine."

"My dad is picking me up at eleven." My cheeks felt raw, scraped by stubble. I looked down. I was still dressed, zipper zipped, buttons almost all buttoned. The boa was still around my neck. "He's picking me up at the dorm."

"I'll give you a ride." Her voice was much calmer than mine. She gave me a worried look. "To be honest with you, Veronica, that's uh . . . that's not what I thought you were saying 'Oh no' about." She reached into the front pocket of her jeans and pulled out a small piece of paper. "Clyde asked me to give you his number."

I didn't take the number from her. She let it fall to the bed. I brought my knees up and pressed my face into my coat. I wanted to go down into the wool, so dark and soft, to somehow crawl inside the material. "What happened?"

"That's what I was going to ask you."

She was laughing. I didn't laugh, and she stopped.

"Nothing happened," she said. "He came downstairs and told me you fell asleep. I think you hurt his feelings. Think of it." She leaned over and lightly punched my shoulder. "Third Floor Clyde. Mr. Beautiful. You hurt his feelings. You'll be famous for this."

I looked up. "People saw?"

She nodded slowly, eyebrows raised.

I looked away. I already knew all this. I hadn't been that drunk. But I had no other explanation. What had seemed a rational and sensible action the night before no longer seemed rational or sensible at all. I stared up at one of Jimmy's framed paintings, a watercolor of a severed hand.

"I'll make coffee," Gretchen said, already starting down the stairs. "Take a shower if you want. But prepare yourself. We've got some cleaning to do."

I tried to stand, but the air around me smelled like stale beer, and my stomach lurched until I sat down. I reached for my phone and checked my messages. The first was from my mother.

"I am trying to apologize." Her voice was hoarse, and she paused to sniff. *"I talked with Elise. I am very angry at myself for hanging up on you yesterday. If you want to punish me, that's fine. But get it over with, Veronica. Okay? Answer your phone."*

People have always said my mother and I sound exactly alike on the phone. I didn't think we sounded the same. I certainly didn't want to sound as whiny and shaky as she did now. But when I lived at home, we confused people. Even my father had been fooled sometimes, calling from the office to say he would be working late.

I erased the message, pressing the button harder than I had to.

Tim had left a message just after midnight. He was out at a bar with the younger faction of his extended family. Chicago was freezing, he said. He'd heard we'd gotten some bad weather, too, and he wanted me to call to let him know the drive to the airport had gone okay.

I was sitting cross-legged on the bed, my shoulders rolled forward, my phone a few inches from my ear. I looked up and caught a glimpse of myself in Jimmy Liff's framed mirror. I looked stupid. Literally. My mouth was open, and my eyes were dazed. I was a stupid person, perhaps, not just with chemistry but with life in general. At the very least, I was a person who did stupid things, despite all my anxious intentions and fear.

The last message was my mother again. She'd called again early in the morning. She no longer sounded like she was crying.

"Veronica," she said. *"People make mistakes."* There was such a long pause I thought the message was over. It wasn't. *"I am still your mother,"* she added, exactly three times, like a mantra she was chanting to herself.

Within half an hour, I was showered and redressed, still a little bleary, but pretty much presentable, my hair pulled back in a perky ponytail that I hoped would make me feel perky as well. But after a quick tour of the downstairs, I didn't feel perky at all. Gretchen was right: the town house was in bad shape. Cans and bottles and plastic cups rested on every horizontal surface. A large plant had been overturned on the stairway. And there was trouble in the kitchen: Gretchen had tried to clean the stainless steel counters in the kitchen with a spray she'd found under the bathroom sink, and a thick, streaky residue stretched between the oven and the espresso maker. Most worrisome was the blood from Gretchen's finger that had somehow gotten on one of the white curtains in the living room.

"Oh no," I said.

Gretchen was at the base of the stairs, trying to repot what she could of the plant. "Your phone rang while you were in the shower."

I took my phone out of my back pocket. My mother had called again. I closed it and put it back.

Gretchen was still looking up at me. Her hands were full of soil, the overturned plant by her knees.

"What?"

She raised her eyebrows.

"It wasn't Tim."

"Okay," she said. But she kept her gaze on me, and I looked away first. I closed my eyes so I wouldn't see the mess around me, the overturned chair, the cigarette butts swimming in cups. Gretchen seemed calm, and that was reassuring. The party and my incredibly brief fling with Clyde probably seemed pretty tame in her mind. She went to parties where people did cocaine in bathrooms and had sex with strangers in the guest rooms, no big deal. But I didn't. I wasn't used to waking up feeling sick and achy and embarrassed. To me, this was a very big deal; and it would be a big deal to Tim. I would need to eat something soon. I felt sick.

I knelt on the floor beside her and cupped soil into my hands. "I'll have to tell him myself," I said. "Before."

She nodded, still moving soil. "That would be considerate."

"He's going to break up with me."

I waited for her to tell me this was not necessarily true. She did not. All around me, the soil was ground into the beige carpet.

"Well," she said finally. "Maybe that's what you wanted."

I understood what she meant. I had performed my idiocy for an audience. What had I thought would be the result? She was right: some part of me that was scared and anxious had wanted to ruin things with Tim. But not all of me. Not now.

I dropped the soil into the pot and patted it around the base of the plant. It had suffered from its fall—one of its long leaves was bent behind it like a broken arm. I didn't see how we would ever get all the soil out of the carpet. I looked up at the cathedral ceilings. The air smelled like cigarettes.

"I think I just really screwed up," I said.

I worried she would laugh. She didn't always read my face and voice so well. She sometimes thought I was serious when I was joking. She thought I was joking when I was not. But I must have looked so miserable that she knew not to laugh at me then. She only patted my arm, and then we got back to work.

When we were done, we carried the plant up the stairs, easing it back onto its wrought iron stand. We stood back and looked at it anxiously. It was okay. We'd repacked enough soil at its base so that it stood upright, and only a few of the long leaves looked crooked. I didn't know what kind of plant it was. In my physiology class the previous semester, we had studied all kinds—fungi, moss, deciduous, and evergreens—dissecting stems and stamens, peering at cellulose under microscopes. The tests had been hard, but I'd liked what I was learning. Afterward, I'd looked at any kind of greenery with more awe and respect, having some understanding of all that was going on inside, all that xylem and phloem, all that constant regeneration so perfectly contained. Even on that achy, sad morning, I was especially impressed with Jimmy's plant having survived its tumble down the stairs. It was still alive, shiny leaves extended, and therefore, under all that quiet greenness, it was working hard, and still growing.

My father and I got a booth by the window. "YA'LL COME ON IN!" was written in neon across the glass, the words encased in a cartoon bubble unreasonably placed over a drawing of a cow who was not only smiling, but wearing lipstick. We both ordered steaks. I was thinking that protein would help. My head no longer hurt, but I still felt foggy inside, my limbs tired and slow to respond. Between sips of soda, I smacked my lips together, moving crushed ice from cheek to cheek. Third Floor Clyde, I had to admit, had been a very good kisser.

"What are you doing with your mouth?" My father squinted at me from across the table. "You okay? You've been quiet this morning. Even for you." He seemed more amused than worried. He was looking at me the way he often looked at me—a little starry-eyed, his lips curved in a half smile. His long-sleeved T-shirt looked stiff, almost starched, with a neckline that was too high. He always looked nice when he was going to work, but when the weekend came, and he had to go casual, he had trouble dressing himself.

"You sure you didn't hit your noggin on the steering wheel?" He reached over and lightly mussed my hair. "I wonder if we should go get you checked out. We can stop by one of those walk-in clinics and just have them take a look at you. Sometimes you can have a concussion and not even know it."

"I'm just tired." I looked over my shoulder, searching for the waitress. I was hungry. I was more than ready to eat.

"You look like you have a rash or something on your chin. What's that? And you cut your lip."

I moved my finger to the cut on my lip. "That was later," I said. "Not from the car. That was when I fell. On the ice."

His nostrils flared. He set down his water glass. "Right. When you were getting out of the truck. The truck driven by that degenerate . . ." He paused, pointing at me. ". . . who, so help me God, if I ever find . . ." With his other hand, he squeezed his napkin, which, being paper, didn't put up anywhere near the kind of fight the actual truck driver might. Still, I was touched by the sentiment. He seemed anxious, his eyes moving in a repeated circuit—over the salad bar, across my face, and then left, to the neon letters in the window, and then up to the sky beyond. It was a bright and sunny morning, cloudless; but outside, the branches of trees were newly bare. The wind was blowing hard and cold.

"So . . . tell me again." He put his napkin in his lap and moved his hand over his mouth. "Tell me again what happened after you got out of the truck."

I cocked my head. I was unclear on why he needed this information again. I didn't see why it would matter, what it had to do with the identity of the truck driver, or the likelihood that my father's insurance would cover the bill for Jimmy's car. But I knew, from vast experience, that my father didn't like to be thwarted from a particular line of questioning. "I . . ." I shook my head at him numbly. "I fell on the ice. I got up, and he was already driving away."

He made a quickening motion with his hand, as if I were purposefully delaying what was important. He was about to speak when the waitress appeared, setting a plate before him.

"Sir? The Maverick? Well done?"

He opened his mouth to answer, but she had already turned toward me. "Seven-ounce?"

I nodded quickly, hoping to give her time to flee.

"Erin, I think we're out of steak sauce here." My father loosened the half-empty bottle from its little cage in the middle of the table. "Other than that, we're all set here, Erin. It all looks very good."

I shielded my eyes so he wouldn't see me wince. It would do no good to tell him to stop. When I was seventeen, my mother had tried to convince my father that people who worked in restaurants didn't necessarily appreciate it when he read their name tags and used their names casually, as if he'd known them forever. She'd been met with strong resistance.

"You sure about that, Natalie?" he'd asked, putting his hands behind his head, an elbow jutting out on each side, the left one accidentally nudging Elise's head. We were all in a booth, having brunch at a pancake house, and everyone was a little tense; earlier that morning, we had gone to my grandmother Von Holten's nursing home to wish her a happy ninety-first birthday. My grandmother hadn't recognized anyone except my mother, which made sense, as my mother was the one who had looked in on her the most for the previous three years.

"You're saying working people don't like to be called by their Christian names?" He'd looked at my mother through narrowed eyes, his elbows moving farther out. Elise, home from college for fall break and already feeling claustrophobic in every sense, growled under her breath and pushed his elbow away from her head. My father apologized and looked back at my mother. "You basing that claim on any actual evidence? Or are you just, you know, more *empathetically* down with the working folk than I am?"

My mother kept her eyes on her menu. "I'm basing my claim on how uncomfortable they look when you're so familiar with them."

"That waiter?" My father pointed behind him. Our waiter, a very bored-looking man in his thirties wearing a button that read "Ask me about our crepes!", had just disappeared in that direction. "He was smiling, wasn't he? He didn't look uncomfortable."

"He has to smile. That's his job. If he doesn't smile, he might not get a tip."

"When have I ever not tipped?" He held his raised palm halfway across the table. "I'm an excellent tipper! What are you talking about?"

She was still looking at her menu, at a glossy picture of an enormous, syrup-drenched Belgian waffle. "I know that, Dan," she said. "We all know. We all know that you are an excellent tipper. I'm saying that waiters and waitresses smile because most people will tip them according to how friendly they are. They don't smile because they like you, or because they think it's funny when you use their damn names."

Elise and I exchanged glances. My mother wasn't normally one to say "damn." She was still gazing at the waffle, the tips of her thumbs rosy, her grip on the menu tight. That morning at the nursing home, the nurse had walked us out to the lobby and told us that despite the evident senility, my grandmother's vital signs were all quite strong. "She's a tough old lady," the nurse had said. "I have a feeling this is far from the last birthday." I had looked up just at that moment and caught sight of my mother's silent reaction—a deep wrinkle in her brow, a parting of her lips—her fear and fatigue apparent for just a moment before she looked down, searching through her purse.

"Okay." My father leaned forward on the table, his face maybe six inches from the tip of my mother's menu. "So calling someone by his name is now giving them shit? I'm going to need a new etiquette manual, then. Maybe you could write it for me, Natalie. Because there's no way I understand the logic of that."

"You don't need a manual, Dan." Her voice was monotone, pointedly unruffled. "Just think about it. Or put yourself in his shoes. Ask yourself how you would feel if you had to be nice to someone because that was your job, and then that person kept saying your name over and over as if he knew you, when really, he didn't." Now, finally, she looked up at him. Her cheeks were pink, her jaw clenched. "Ask yourself how you would like that."

He stared at her for a long moment and then drew back, holding his menu up like a barricade. "Well," he said quietly. "Maybe you ought to consider that not everyone feels the way you do."

Elise pumped her fist. "The King of the Last Word speaks!"

My father put his menu down. "I just don't think he looked un-comfortable!" He turned to Elise, and then to me. "Girls? Did you think the waiter looked uncomfortable?"

"I know I'm uncomfortable." Elise smiled at her menu, then looked up at me. "Veronica looks really uncomfortable. Maybe we need to get our own booth."

My father gave her a sideways glance. "Maybe you need to pay your own bill."

"Maybe you should keep dreaming."

My mother and I both sighed, the exact same way, at the exact same time. We looked up at each other and smiled. This banter between my father and Elise was normal, playful, nothing to cause any worry. In fact, it had a calming effect, at least for me, after the far more unusual bickering between my parents. I was used to Elise pushing back at him, giving him a hard time. But my mother, when she did disagree with him, usually did it softly, and with a smile.

"Thank you so much." My father took the new bottle of steak sauce and, after the waitress walked away, gave me a look. "Easy there, Jaws. Nobody's going to take it away from you."

I held my napkin up to my mouth. "I'm hungry."

"Okay. Well." He made the hurry-up motion with his hand again. "Sing for your supper, at least. You were saying what happened. After the truck."

"I went into the Hardee's."

"Right." He cut into his steak. "And then what?"

"I went to the bathroom."

"And then what?" His eyes seemed tender, sympathetic. The air around me seemed to go still and quiet, though I could still hear the restaurant's music playing, the soft twang of a steel guitar.

I took another bite. I chewed, swallowed. He waited.

"And then I . . . called you."

He nodded. "Wait, I'm a little cold." He put on a tan sports coat.

He had a pen in the pocket, and he paused to make sure it was fastened in. "Okay. You get yourself away from the truck. You fall. You're bleeding. You go into the restaurant to use the phone. Who'd you call first?"

For a moment, I thought this was what he was getting at. I actually thought he was hurt because I had tried to call my mother first. And I was relieved, even touched. It was just that old divorce story—each wounded parent wanting to be the chosen one. I considered lying, but I got scared.

"Dad. I knew you would be in court, or at least working. And Mom was closer."

He nodded. "And what did she say to you?"

I swallowed. It was a trick question. We both knew it.

"Elise told you."

We sat without talking for several seconds. The people in the booth behind us were laughing about something. A child's shrill voice cried out.

"I'm sorry, honey. I can't believe she let you down like that. I'm so sorry. I can't explain it. I can't understand how a person can change so much."

I looked away, considering the situation, and how what he was saying pointed to things not being as bad between them as I thought. Maybe they were not completely severed. He could still apologize on her behalf. I managed a smile. I appreciated his understanding, his apparent concern for us both.

He leaned forward, lowering his voice. "Can you tell me exactly what she said to you? Before she hung up?"

"She just . . . she sounded a little crazy." I shrugged. I picked up my knife and fork again. The steak tasted amazing, salty and firm. "She feels bad about it now. She's left messages, apologizing. She said she was having a bad day."

"But she knew you'd been in a car accident, correct? She knew you were out on the highway somewhere?"

I frowned. Correct. He was using courtroom language. "I don't remember," I said. I took another bite. He smiled patiently. He leaned forward a little more, reaching past my fork to touch my hand.

"Try." He appeared annoyed, or disappointed. "Just tell me what she said to you. Tell me exactly what she said."

I was about to ask him what he was getting at, why he was so fixated on this small point, when, while trying to gather the courage, I found myself gazing at the pen in his pocket, which, now that I looked at it, didn't look like a pen at all. It was rectangular. And it appeared to have several openings on the tip.

He saw me looking and sat up quickly.

I stopped chewing. I put my knife and fork down.

"What's in your pocket?"

He gave me a blank look. I think it was the first time in my entire life that I had ever stumped him.

"Is that your voice recorder?" I shook my head. It was impossible. I did not believe it. It was the voice recorder my mother had given him for Christmas. It was sleek, expensive, designed to look like a pen. She had hoped he could use it for work.

"Were you recording just now? What I was saying?"

"Fine. I'll turn it off." He touched a button on the recorder and picked up his knife and fork. He reached for the steak sauce, his mouth tight.

"Why would you . . . ?" I was at a loss. My hands were limp in my lap.

"She's crossed a line, okay?" He pointed at me with his fork. It wasn't a threatening gesture, more of a lazy one—he was still eating, and he didn't want to put his fork down. And yet he needed to point. "What your mother did, leaving you out there, was completely unacceptable. And it needs to be documented."

Warm saliva pooled in my mouth. I looked down at my steak. My stomach no longer existed. "Documented for what?"

"Don't worry about it. It has nothing to do with you. It's not your problem." He looked up and made the quickening gesture. "Why aren't you eating?"

I did not move. "You're going to use this in the divorce? You're going to use this against her?"

He rolled his eyes, still chewing. He brought his napkin up to his lips. When he spoke again, his voice was very quiet, but his words were clipped and hard. "You bet I am. You better believe it. She's completely delusional about my assets. She thinks I'm hiding piles of money from her."

"Yes," I said dully. "You've both told me."

"Okay. Be sarcastic. Be sullen. But at least consider what I'm saying. Let's review the facts. Your mother, as you know, had an affair. She made the choice to break the vows, the legal contract." He popped a piece of steak in his mouth and went back to cutting. "So she is solely responsible for the demise of the marriage, but because of the law, she still gets to walk away with half of everything I've earned, everything I've worked my ass off for, for almost thirty years. And even that isn't enough. She thinks she's still getting a bad deal!" He was still cutting the steak, his knife scratching against his plate, his voice getting steadily louder. The laughter at the next booth stopped. "She had it pretty good, you know? She never had to work. She always had a nice home, her garden. Nice clothes. She got her hair done. I guess I thought she was a little appreciative. Well you know what? I guessed wrong."

That wasn't fair. My body knew this before I did. I felt something like a current moving through me, pulling my hands up from under the table. "She took care of us," I said. "She took care of your mother. You make it sound like she was sitting around. She . . ." I tried to think what it was that had filled my mother's days while we were at school. She didn't play tennis. She didn't just get her nails done. She'd called the insurance companies and argued over bills. She'd picked me up at school when I was sick. She'd picked up other kids when they were sick, if their mothers were working.

My father stopped chewing. He stopped cutting his steak. He was still holding his knife and fork, but he was just staring at me.

The waitress reappeared. "How is everything?"

My father smiled, though he kept his eyes on me. "It's all wonderful, Erin. Thank you."

I looked down at my plate and listened to the receding footsteps of the waitress. I could hear my own shaky breathing. My napkin was in shreds in my lap.

My father took a long drink of water. "I paid for her mother's hospital bills. Let's not forget that. She helped my mother. I helped hers. We were a team. I thought."

I slid my plate away and sat hunched over, my elbows on the table.

"You must be exhausted." He went back to work on his steak. "I don't think I've ever seen you be so . . . contrary before. I have to say . . . I'm a little impressed."

"Great. That was my goal." I could feel tears welling, but I fought them back. I was angry, not sad, and I wanted him to understand the difference.

I stood up. I didn't look at him. I snatched up my purse and my coat.

"Hey!" I heard his startled voice behind me. I kept going, blurry-eyed, past the smiling hostess at the register, past the large statue of a Holstein in the lobby, and out through the double doors to the parking lot. I was aware of the rain, the wind in my face. My coat was still balled up under my arms. I got to the edge of the parking lot and stood there for a moment. I was maybe three miles from Jimmy's, two from the dorm. I put on my coat and started toward Jimmy's, my head bowed against the wind.

I knew he would come after me. I couldn't imagine that he wouldn't. But I really wasn't sure if I would get in. He was no better than she was. There were many ways to leave someone stranded. There were many ways of hanging up.

I'd only gone a couple of blocks when his car pulled up alongside me. The passenger window lowered, and he ducked to catch my eye.

"Okay. I'm sorry, honey. Okay? Please get in."

Cars honked behind him. He ignored them. I kept walking, my hands pushed deep in my pockets. He kept rolling slowly along.

"What? You gonna walk home in the rain? It's far, honey."

I stopped and looked at him. Whatever he saw in my face made him lower his gaze. Cars were still honking. Someone yelled.

"I'm sorry." He cleared his throat. "Okay? Okay? I am. I shouldn't have done that in there."

Another car honked. He held up one gloved finger to me, asking me to hold on for a moment. He rolled down his window, turned back, and let loose with one of the longest, and loudest, streams of obscenities I have ever heard in my life. The honking car screeched around to pass him. He made a series of gestures, screaming after it, and then turned back to me.

I leaned down a little so he could see my face. I wanted him to know how absolutely serious I was, how much I meant what I was saying.

"You're not allowed to use that against her," I said. "You're not allowed to talk about it, about her and me, with your lawyer at all."

"Okay. Okay." He leaned over and opened the door. "Just get in. Please? It's getting all wet in here."

I stood where I was, considering my options. I was cold. And wet. I wished, wished, wished that I had my own car. But I didn't. I opened the door and slid into the bucket seat. The heater in his car was working well. He angled all the vents toward me.

"You said it doesn't have anything to do with me." I spoke without looking at him, my purse cradled in my lap. "But you're the one it doesn't have anything to do with. It's between us. It's between her and me. You need to just stay out of it."

"Gotcha. Okay." He extended his hand. "This glove is leather. A dead horse. Beat it."

I shook his hand limply, still looking away.

"This thing has heated seats, you know. They're great. You'll feel it in a minute, even through your coat."

His voice was shaking a little. I said nothing.

"Please put on your seat belt."

We stared at each other. I looked like her. Everyone said so. You couldn't look at me and not see her eyes, her mouth, her strong chin. It must have been strange for him, to be so mad and done with her, and still have a daughter with so much of her face.

I put on my seat belt. He reached behind him and got a Styrofoam box out of the backseat. I could smell the steak inside. "I got the potato, too," he said, handing the box to me. I started to shake my head, and he set it carefully in my lap.

"You'll get your appetite back." He sounded tired. He put the car in gear, glancing up in the rearview mirror. "It'll all be okay, sweetie. I promise. Okay? Just wait and see."

8

GRETCHEN GAVE ME A RIDE back to Jimmy's. She felt bad that
she wouldn't be able to stay and help me clean—she had a study
group, and then she would be on duty at the dorm the rest of the
night. She offered to come over early Sunday morning, but I told her
not to. The party had been my idea. I would clean the rest of the
mess up myself.

But when I got inside, alone again, all I wanted was to take a bath.
The garden tub off the master bedroom stretched out, wide and
long, beneath a window with a view that, from the lower vantage of
the tub, showed only sky, which was a deep gray, the winter afternoon already fading. But the bathroom itself seemed to have its own,
tropical climate. Potted begonias and ferns hung from the ceiling.
The rim of the tub was populated by stone statues of friendly looking forest animals, some of which cleverly hid the speakers for the
waterproof stereo over the faucet, which I quickly learned to operate
with my toes. I used a small amount of Haylie's expensive shampoo.
I kept the water hot, the jets on high, the music loud. I knew I
needed to clean. I knew I needed to study. I knew I needed to call

Tim back, to at least let him know I was okay. But I didn't want to lie to him, and I didn't want to tell the truth. Actions had consequences. I knew that. I only wanted to put them off for a while.

Just as I got out of the tub, steam still rising from my skin, my phone rang. Tim's number flashed on the screen, and I picked up. I don't why. Habit. Guilt. A desire to hear a kind voice.

"Hi."

"Hey. You're okay." There was a pause. "Did you not get my message?"

I sat on the bed, still wearing a towel. The room was dim, but in the mirror, I could see a crescent of my face illuminated by the small, gray light of my phone. Outside, past the winter-dead golf course, the setting sun was a bright pink slash, the sky above it a deep purple. "I'm sorry," I said. "I should have called you back . . . Things have been a little crazy here."

"Okay," he said, his voice neutral. He didn't say anything else.

"I was in a car accident." I instantly regretted saying it. I should tell him everything or nothing at all. I was acting like my parents, campaigning for pity, adjusting a storyline to fit my needs.

"In that guy's car? That little car? Are you okay?"

"I'm fine. It was just a fender bender. I mean, more than that. The car had to be towed. But really, I'm okay."

He breathed hard through his teeth. "I knew it," he said. "Isn't that weird? I knew it as soon as I heard about the weather."

"What does that mean?"

"What?" He was confused. I could picture his expression, his dark eyebrows lowered.

"You just assumed I would wreck the car in bad weather?" My hands were clenched. I accidentally pressed a number on my phone. "You knew as soon as the roads got a little slick? You can make it all the way up to Chicago, but you already knew that little me wouldn't even make it home from the airport. Is that right?"

"What?" He started to laugh, and then stopped. "Veronica. That's not what I meant. I was just worried. I heard the ice was really bad. I would have worried about anyone out driving in it. Or you, especially, because you're my girlfriend." He paused. "Are you—are you okay?"

"I'm not a bad driver."

"I know you're not." There was a pause. "But that's not what I was saying, Veronica. I was just saying I was worried."

His voice was kind. I was a bad person. I was lying. Already, just by not mentioning Clyde, I was lying.

"Did you get hurt at all?"

"No." I rubbed the back of my neck. "I'm a little sore maybe." I glanced at the screen of my phone. There were no new messages. My mother had given up.

He wanted more details. He wanted to know how I'd gotten home, and whether or not I'd already told Jimmy. The more concerned questions he asked, the worse I felt. I stalled and hesitated. Finally, and honestly, I claimed fatigue. "I'll tell you when you get home," I said. "I'll tell you the whole story." I turned away from the mirror and lay back down on the bed.

He'd be home Sunday night, he said, but late. And he had classes all day on Monday. We could see each other on Monday night. He knew I had a test coming up, but he wanted to take me out to dinner, somewhere nice. He could pick me up at seven.

"Just come up to my room," I said. Guilt aside, I had to be strategic. I had to tell him in my own room. I couldn't wait until we were in his car to tell him. I wasn't going to tell him at some restaurant. I couldn't let myself get stranded again—an unhappy passenger in someone else's car, too far from home to get out and walk.

I decided I would clean in the morning. I would get up early, bright-eyed and invigorated, and get the town house back in shape long before Jimmy and Haylie came home. By eight o'clock, I had already misted the plants and changed into my pajamas. I sat on the couch, my legs stretched out, with the leftover potato and my chemistry book. I was still a good student. I was not a completely different person.

And truly, for at least a half hour, I diligently studied diagrams of benzene molecules linking their little black arms with other benzene molecules. *Ninhydrin and MDMA are colorless whereas the test reaction product is red because neither ninhydrin nor MDMA have enough conjugated p-orbitals to provide a HOMO-LUMO gap.* I worked through two sample questions. I considered the third. Ten minutes passed. Twenty. It wasn't yet nine o'clock. It was still early enough to call Tim and tell him everything, and at least not be a liar.

Focus. I looked back at the benzene diagram. I reread the equation. I closed my eyes. I opened them. I looked up at the clock. A single shelf, lined with books, sprouted from the wall behind the couch, fanged gargoyles guarding either side. *The Collected Works of Shakespeare* was prominently displayed. Apparently, Jimmy hadn't sold his copy back at the end of the semester, which was interesting, given that he hadn't seemed to have read any of the plays as we were studying them. But he did have a nice little library, right there within reaching distance of the couch. Vonnegut. Plato. Emily Brontë. Ginsberg and Burroughs. Plath. The bindings for the hardbacks cracked upon opening, the pages inside pristine. There were four books by Toni Morrison, a slim volume of CliffsNotes tucked inside *The Bluest Eye.* Looking down at the other end of the shelf, I saw *Jane Eyre.* I had read it for freshman lit, which had been taught by a graduate student with flaming red hair and wire-rimmed glasses who told us on the first day that the freshman reading list had been put together by the English Department, and that the books were not what she would have chosen to have us read at all, and that she was at least going to frame them for us in alternately Marxist, feminist, and post-colonial perspectives. She had frightened me on that first day, but I had come to like her as a teacher, though she and I reached a temporary impasse when the class started reading *Jane*

Eyre. I adored the book. Jane was a great heroine, I thought, with all her spirit and courage, and I believed the love story that unfolded between her and Rochester. The graduate student, however, firmly believed that *Jane Eyre* wasn't a love story at all; she presented us with a published article that argued that at the end of the book, when Jane is the young wife to the old, blind Rochester, she is no more than his Seeing Eye dog, an underling hired to maintain the colonial, patriarchal status quo. I didn't believe it for a second, and I was so indignant that I risked my English grade—my one dependable A for that semester—to argue on Jane's behalf in my midterm paper. I wrote that Jane was not his Seeing Eye dog, but his equal companion. Society may have cast them as master and servant, but in their minds, they were equals, because he loved her, and she loved him—there was ample evidence for this in the text.

The graduate student was fairer than I'd expected. She returned our papers a month later, and on mine, across the top, was written:

You are brainwashed by your culture. And you are wrong. But you are a good writer. A–

That night on Jimmy's couch, I reread almost all of *Jane Eyre,* reconsidering the Seeing Eye dog argument. I didn't mean to read so long. I just kept turning pages. There was the solace of focusing on someone with real worries: Jane, with her confined life in another century, lived in a far more dismal world than mine; her choices were fewer and far starker. And there was also the familiar pleasure of a good story, the slow revelations of someone's nature and troubles and thoughts; a word-created world to fall into.

I woke the next morning stretched out on the couch, *Jane Eyre* fallen to the floor. Sunlight streamed in through the living room's sheer curtains. In the dorm, mornings were loud. There was always a door opening, a door closing, someone laughing in the hallway, a stereo blasting, or an alarm clock going off in an empty room. But the town house was peaceful. I was happy when I wandered into the kitchen, even with the suds-stained counters and mud-tracked floors, but then I saw the little digital clock by the oven. It was almost eleven. Jimmy and Haylie would be home by four.

I circled frantically, picking up cans and cups. My bare feet stuck to the kitchen floor. I tried to prioritize my tasks. There was the dirt on the carpet where the plant had fallen. The blood on the curtain. Haylie's clothes, the boas, the shoes. The faint but distinct odor of cigarettes in the living room. The plastic bag of aluminum cans which Gretchen really should have taken with her, which I did not know what to do with, as I had no car, and no way to leave before Jimmy and Haylie returned.

Once again, I was stranded.

I tried calling Gretchen. No answer. My mother had called again, and left a message. I listened as I dug cigarette butts out of an aloe vera plant by the sink.

"If this is the only way I can communicate with you, I at least want you to know two things. One, you are not the only person in the world with problems. As your mother, I think it's my job to let you know that. Two, I am, again, very sorry I let you down. But, Veronica, I guarantee that, in the future, if you are in a crisis, and you need me, I will be there for you. You can call me, and I will be there. The other morning was an isolated incident. I think if you look at my entire record as a mother, you'll have to agree with that."

I emptied the cigarette butts into the garbage. I debated with myself for only a moment. She answered on the first ring.

"It's me," I said. "It's Veronica."

"I know." Her voice was breathy, distracted. I heard Bowzer's wizened bark in the background. I waited. She didn't say anything more. She was waiting for me to speak.

I kept my eyes on the plant. "You know how you just said I could call you the next time, you know, the next time I have a problem?"

"Yes?"

"I'm actually having one today."

"What?" She paused to tell Bowzer to be quiet. She did this politely. She said "please." To Bowzer. She came back to the phone. "What? Where are you? What happened?"

"No," I said. "It's not a crisis like . . ." I reconsidered making an out-and-out reference to the other morning. "It's not really an emergency. It's more of a little problem. But I could use your help." I paused. I felt suddenly shy, repentant. *You are not the only person in the world with problems.* "If you're not working, I mean. I don't know if you have to work today."

She laughed then, which surprised me. It wasn't her normal laugh. It was lower, a little gravelly, like Bowzer's bark. "I'm not working," she said. Her laugh faded into a tired sigh. "I'm at your service. What is it, honey? Tell me what you need."

She eyed the bloodstain from different angles. She turned the curtain over and held it up to the light. She looked a little rabbitlike when she wasn't wearing makeup, her eyelashes thin and hard to see. "You know what might do it?" she asked. "Meat tenderizer. Go check and see if they have any."

"Meat tenderizer?" I was on my hands and knees, picking tiny shards of amber glass out of the carpet. My mother had noticed them, glinting in the sunlight, when she'd first come in. She'd given me her leather gloves, sleek and close-fitting, to wear so I wouldn't cut my fingers.

"It's the best thing for getting out blood. Remember Elise used to get those nosebleeds? No, you were too young." She turned and sneezed into the sleeve of her coat. "Poor Elise. She'd just be sitting there, at the dinner table, on the school bus, on someone else's white couch, and then out it would gush, all this blood out of that little nose. The doctor said it would pass, and not to worry, but try telling that to a six-year-old. She'd get scared, and get her hands in it, and then it would just be everywhere." She held up her finger and sneezed again.

"Bless you," I said.

She looked at me. She appeared annoyed that I was just standing there. "Meat tenderizer." She snapped her fingers. "The kitchen. Go check. I thought we were in a hurry."

Jimmy and Haylie did not have any meat tenderizer.

"I'll pick some up." She was already moving back to the front door. She'd never even taken off her coat. "Is there a grocery store close by?" She stood with one hand on the knob of the open front door, her other hand jangling her car keys. "I want to pick up some microfiber cloths for the kitchen." She shook her head, mild disapproval in her voice. "They're the only thing to use on stainless steel. Don't spray any more chemicals on it."

"I don't know," I said. I went to rub my eyes, forgetting I was still wearing her gloves. "About the grocery store, I mean. This isn't really my part of town."

Her eyes met mine, and I looked away. I had told her I didn't want to talk about the town house, why I was there, who owned it, and why I needed to clean it very quickly. I had told her I didn't want to have to explain anything. I just needed help. On a normal day, this request would not have been honored. *I am your mother,* she would have said. *I need to know what's going on with you!* But today, at least, we both understood that she was still on probation, and that if I didn't want to, I wouldn't have to say a word.

But before she left, she reached up to cup my cheek. Her hand—it was the one that had been on the doorknob—was cold to the touch. I leaned away, wiping my gloved hands against each other over the open bag of empty cups by the door. I could hear the tiny clinking of glass shards as they fell. When the clinking stopped, I took off the gloves and handed them to her. "Thanks," I said. I kept my eyes away from hers. "You should put them on. It's cold."

She returned a half hour later with a bag of cleaning supplies, two chicken salads in plastic containers, and Bowzer. He appeared to have lost weight since the last time I saw him. A year ago, I would have had trouble carrying him in two arms, and now my mother held him easily in one. He peered up at me from under a mass of tangled graying fur.

I blocked the entrance. "Mom. No. I'm sorry, but no. Why did you bring him?"

He heard my voice and wagged his spindly tail. She handed me the bag of salads and tried to wave me aside. "Don't be a jerk, Veronica. It's too cold to leave him in the car."

"Then you should have left him at home. I can't have him in here. What if he pees? Or what if they're allergic or something? I've got enough mess to clean." I covered my nose, my mouth. "Mom. He smells."

She looked at me. She looked at Bowzer. The bag of cleaning supplies hung from her wrist, swinging back and forth.

"Here's the deal," she said. "I'm not leaving him outside. It's too cold, and he's having a hard time."

Bowzer gazed up at me with patient, cloudy eyes. He did not appear especially distressed. My mother, on the other hand, was breathing heavily, her nostrils flared. She was chewing gum. She never did that.

"I'll put plastic bags underneath him. But if you want my help, he's coming in."

I took a small step to the side. She rolled her eyes and carried him into the town house. "Here you go, sweetie," she said, setting him down in the entryway. He sniffed the air around him and took a hesitant step forward, claws tapping on the hardwood floor.

"He's going to pee," I said.

"No, he isn't."

"He's going to shed. And they don't have a vacuum."

"What? How can they not have a vacuum?"

"They don't. I looked all over." I shrugged. "They have a maid."

Her gaze moved up to a painting on the wall, one of Jimmy's. The lines were vague, the colors blurred together, but I had decided that if you looked at it long enough, you could make out a decomposing head.

"Who are these people, honey?" She'd stopped chewing the gum. All at once, she appeared very familiar, her old self, her eyes full of worry for me. "Who are they, and how do you know them?"

I leaned down to scratch Bowzer on his sweet spot, the little indentation between his ears. He turned, sniffing the air between us, and wagged his tail again. "Hey, Bowz," I whispered. "Remember me?" His collar hung loose from his neck.

"Of course he does," my mother said. "He always loved you best. I just do all the work." She took off her coat. It was her nice coat, the long black one that she only wore when she was dressed up, over skirts or dresses with boots. But today, underneath it, she was wearing her flannel nightgown tucked into khaki pants, no belt, and her gray cable cardigan hanging open. I didn't read too much into it. She had come to help clean on her day off, a Sunday morning, and so it made sense she'd not bothered with her clothes. But then she went to hug me, suddenly, no warning at all, and there was a musty, almost salty smell about her. Her hair was unwashed, shiny at the roots, and pulled back in a tight ponytail. She caught me looking at her, and she seemed embarrassed.

"It doesn't matter," she said quickly. "I've got my vacuum in the van." She pulled her coat back on. On her way out, she glanced back over her shoulder with a smile. "Don't just stand there, honey. I'm going to help. But I'm not going to do it all for you."

By three o'clock, all of Haylie's clothes were hanging neatly in her closet. The sheets were washed and dried and stretched back over the bed. Every empty beer can and plastic cup had been located and contained in the plastic trash bag by the door. The floors were vacuumed and mopped. I'd dragged the wine rack, undamaged, back out into the kitchen, where the counters sparkled, suds-free. There was no evidence of the party at all, not even a trace of cigarette smoke in the air. The entire town house smelled like the lemons my mother had cut open and microwaved. And she'd been right about the meat tenderizer—the bloodstain had almost completely disappeared.

She was rolling the vacuum back out the front door when she stopped and cleared her throat.

"Hey—it's okay if I take a shower? My bag is right out in the van."

I looked at her. I thought she was joking. She looked back, blank-faced, her hand raised like a hitchhiker's, her thumb tilted toward the stairs.

"You want to take a shower here?"

She leaned on the vacuum, and it started to roll forward. She almost lost her balance. She caught herself without a smile. "Well. I've been cleaning for a few hours now. Helping you clean. And I feel icky. I'd like to take a shower before I drive back." She paused to purse her lips in disapproval. "If that's not too much trouble."

I didn't know what to say. It was an odd request and, under the circumstances, a slightly unreasonable one. "Mom. They'll be back here in less than an hour."

She didn't say anything. She lowered her eyes to Bowzer, who was asleep in the corner of the entryway. My mother had made a little bed for him: Elise's old eyelet white bedspread, which my mother had brought in from the van and folded into quarters, with an empty plastic trash bag underneath that.

"I'd really like to not be here when they get here." I looked at my watch, then back up at her. "Can't you just wait until you get home?"

"No." Her voice, her expression, everything, made it clear she was not really asking. She turned the vacuum back in the direction of the front door. "I'll get my bag. I'll be fifteen minutes. Don't worry. You'll have plenty of time."

She did not take a shower. She took a bath. And it took her thirty minutes, not fifteen. When she finally came back downstairs, I was reading by the door with my coat on, my purse and backpack under my knees. Bowzer, sensing my presence, had rolled over onto his back beside me. I rubbed his chest, using my nails, and he seemed very pleased about it. His fur felt gummy and old.

"Oh." My mother looked down at me and smiled. "*Jane Eyre.* That's one of my favorites. A real love story."

She looked like a completely different person. She looked clean. She was wearing nice clothes, a cream sweater and brown cords. It was the kind of thing she used to wear to volunteer at the shelter— presentable, but not showy. Her wet hair was slicked back, the ends just starting to curl.

"You're ready?" I stood up. "You don't need to dry your hair?"

She shook her head, pulling on her coat. "I have a hat."

On my way out, I held the door open for my mother with my foot. She had her bag slung over her shoulder, Bowzer and his blanket balanced in her arms. As she passed, I smelled mint and rosemary. She'd also used Haylie's shampoo.

We made our way down the front steps. The party, and the resulting cleanup, had resulted in two full bags of garbage. I walked behind my mother, carrying a bag on either side of me. We were at the end of the driveway when she turned around.

"Okay, honey. I parked far." She leaned toward me, one arm out. "Let me kiss you good-bye." Bowzer emerged from his blanket cocoon and tried to lick her cheek.

"I need a ride," I said.

She bit her lip. She blinked. She looked even more rabbitlike, mute and anxious. All her hair was under her hat. "You don't . . ." She glanced up and down the street.

"I need a ride, Mom. I don't have a car." I tilted my head and stared at her. This request could not possibly be a problem. But given the way she stared back at me, I had to consider that she was, at least, surprised by it. Maybe she'd forgotten that I didn't have a car. Maybe she'd already forgotten I'd been in an accident on Friday. Maybe the details of my life were just details to her, not nearly as important as whatever drama was moving through hers and making her act like someone I didn't even know.

"Veronica." She appeared to exchange exasperated glances with Bowzer. "I know you don't have a car. But how did you get yourself here?"

It was a profound question, metaphorically speaking. Non-metaphorically speaking, it was just annoying. I set the garbage bags down and crossed my arms. Bowzer whimpered, wondering, perhaps, what the holdup was. My mother looked down at him and said nothing. I lowered my head, breathing in the cold air around me. I had been wrong. She had been wrong. The incident at the Hardee's, the hanging up, had not been an isolated incident. She really was different now. She was unreliable, distracted, preoccupied with something big that was not me.

I heard a door open on the other side of the driveway. My mother and I, aware that we were being watched, turned to see a tan, blond woman in a purple jogging suit. We smiled. The woman did not smile back. "Nice party," she muttered. She let her gaze fall to the two bags of garbage before she turned around and slammed the door.

I closed my eyes. "Can I just have a ride to the dorm? Or do I need to call Highway Patrol again?"

When I opened my eyes, she was looking at me as if she wanted to hug me, but she was holding Bowzer, and the blanket, and the strap of her bag was sliding down her arm. She jerked her head forward and raised her hand, an invitation to follow.

We were still several feet from her van when I noticed the stained glass lampshade balanced against one of the back windows. It had been my grandmother's. She'd had it in her house in New Hampshire, and then in her room in Kansas City, at the nursing home. A television screen faced out of the van's other back window, an end table resting on top of it.

My mother shook her head. "Just don't say anything, okay? Just don't ask." She sounded tired, and annoyed, as if I were pestering her about something we'd been over a million times. When she got close to the passenger door, she gestured for me to take Bowzer from her. I set down the bags and took him, watching her face as she fished in her coat pockets for her keys. She kept her chin tucked low, her jaw set, her eyes away from mine. When she opened the passenger door, she had to put her arms up quickly to keep two cardboard boxes from falling to the ground. Without a word, she set the boxes on top of the vacuum, which was lying on some blankets on the first long seat.

She opened the front passenger door for me and then walked around to the driver's side. My seat was littered with empty Diet Pepsi cans and a half-empty box of Wheaties. On the floor mat sat Bowzer's food bowl, alongside an old Cool Whip container full of water. I moved things around with my free hand and climbed in, still holding Bowzer. Once my mother was in her seat, he whimpered and tried to jump over the gearshift to her lap, but I held him back. He rested his chin on my arm, resigned. "It's okay," I said, stroking his chest. He still had the fat pocket, but everywhere else, he was so thin. I could feel his bones under his fur.

I was six when my father first brought him home in a plastic crate, with his tiny bark and big puppy claws, a red bow around his neck. My mother had been annoyed. She didn't want a dog. She had told my father a cat, maybe a cat, but a dog would be too much. She was defeated, outnumbered, the moment Bowzer nosed his way out of the box with a red bow around his neck. Elise and I shrieked with delight and then took him outside to play. It was a sunny autumn afternoon, and the air smelled like burning leaves. My father carved a pumpkin on the back deck while Elise and I ran in circles, letting the still unnamed puppy chase us and yip at our heels.

At some point, my mother came out from the back door, a dish-towel in her hands. She smiled at my father and then at us. She put her elbows on the railing of the deck and watched us play for a long time, her nose tilted up to the crisp autumn air. Not much later, my father cut his hand with the carving knife, and there was screaming and a blood-soaked dishtowel and a frantic trip to the ER. But before all that, while she'd stood on the deck watching all of us, I remember thinking that she looked happy.

We drove for several minutes without speaking. The roads were dry, but my mother was as cautious as ever, taking corners slowly. Someone behind us honked, but she didn't seem to hear.

We stopped at a light. There was no sound but Bowzer's wheezing breath, the rattling of the engine. I glanced at her, trying to guess. She was moving, maybe. She was moving somewhere that she didn't want me to know. She was moving in with a boyfriend, some boyfriend, someone who was not my father. Maybe the Sleeping Roofer had returned. It all made sense. That morning, she'd had the disheveled, wound-up look of someone who had not slept in her own bed the night before. I didn't care if it was the Roofer or not. She had spent the night with someone who was not my father, and I didn't want to know any more about it.

The light changed, and we started moving again. She turned on the radio, country music. I reached past Bowzer and turned the radio off.

"Why is all this stuff in the van? Are you moving? Are you moving somewhere secret?"

"You're not in charge of the radio." She reached over and turned it back on. A commercial had started, and she moved the dial. It was the college station. Eminem. She did not seem concerned. "I'm driving. It's my van. I decide about the radio."

Bowzer was shivering a little. I rewrapped the blanket around him. The van's heater still didn't work.

"I'm just taking a few things to Goodwill," she said. "It's not a big deal." She pulled into the dorm parking lot. A few people were standing outside the dorm. I held my breath, looking for Clyde.

"I'm just cleaning out, you know?" Her voice was flat. "Trying to live more simply."

I turned around and surveyed the boxes and furniture crammed around the back seats. "You're taking Nana's lamp to Goodwill?"

She moved her tongue around her mouth. She was chewing gum again. She smacked it. She was not a person who should chew gum.

"Mom, that's a beautiful lamp. And it was hers. You can't give it to Goodwill."

She fingered the keys in the ignition. "I can do what I want," she said.

"I'll take it. Don't give it to Goodwill. I want it."

"No."

"What? Why?" Bowzer turned and gave me a pained look, his silver brows moving from side to side.

"Just drop it." Her voice was low, authoritative. It was the voice she used when I was little, commanding me to take a Lego out of my mouth. "Okay, Veronica? Drop it."

She faced forward, not looking at me. She was chewing the gum hard and fast, her mouth closed, her temples pulsing.

I handed Bowzer to her. He nestled himself right into her lap, his chin resting on her left arm.

"Bye honey," she said. "I love you." She didn't look at me. We had never stopped at a Dumpster to get rid of the garbage, but something about her face made me know I should not mention this. I got out of the van, opened the sliding door, and pulled both garbage bags out. I carried them up the front steps to the dorm. It was not yet dark out; still, she waited at the curb, engine idling, until I was inside.

Just a few minutes later, despite myself, I started to have an inkling. By the time I was in the elevator, I at least understood that she had never been on probation with me. She was my mother, and always my mother. She could have pressed me about the town house, about Jimmy, if she'd wanted to. And she knew it. She was letting me keep my secrets, not out of guilt or respect or anything that had anything to do with me. She had simply set a precedent for the day, not asking for trouble, because she had secrets of her own.

9

THIRD FLOOR CLYDE was waiting outside my door.

He turned, hearing my footsteps, and for a moment, I was happy to see him. He was just so absolutely pleasant to look at, his hair curling around his ears, his smile easy and serene. He looked like he should be on a movie screen, twenty feet tall, playing someone beautiful from somewhere beautiful. He did not look like anyone who would naturally appear outside my dorm room in Kansas.

And yet, it didn't matter.

I started explaining right there in the hall. No one was around anyway, and, given what I had to say, it seemed awkward to ask him inside. And it seemed pointless, even mean, to let him say anything at all first; because nothing he could say would make any difference. It wouldn't matter if he turned out to be nice or smart or funny in addition to being the dorm's Adonis. I wouldn't care. I told him this, working to keep my eyes on his, to not be a coward and let myself look at the yellow cinder-block walls or the gray carpet. I clasped my hands in front of me and then behind me. I'd left the garbage bags in the first-floor trash room; my books were behind me in my backpack, and I wished I had something to hold. I told him that I had made a mistake the other night, and that I was embarrassed, but that my embarrassment had nothing to do with him. I told him that I had a boyfriend, and even though I had probably messed that up, I wasn't sure I had messed it up completely, and I didn't want to do anything to make my chances worse.

Marley's door was open. I could see her shadow on the hallway carpet; she was right around the corner, taking everything in.

"Okay," he said, his low voice steady. He was already turning away. "No problem. I understand."

I watched him walk away, worried that he did not understand at all. It was almost an old joke to reject someone and say there was nothing wrong with him, that the problem was with you. But in this case, it was absolutely true. What I was feeling now had nothing to do with him. But what I had felt on Friday night had nothing to do with him, either—which didn't say much for me. I used him, as if he weren't really a person. Whether he was wounded or not didn't matter. I was right to feel ashamed of myself.

"Hey, Veronica." Marley was behind me. "How're you doing?"

My first impulse was to ignore her. I didn't want to be mean, but I didn't want to talk to anyone just then. I wanted to turn around and move past her to my room and shut the door behind me. I wanted to stop saying and doing stupid things, and the only way to do that, it seemed, was to take a break from interactions in general. When I did turn around, however, she was standing closer than I'd expected, and she looked eager and desperate for conversation, even more so than usual. I glanced up and down the hallway. Every door but hers was closed. The dorm could be a lonely place on Sundays. In cold weather, especially, even the people who didn't go home seemed to disappear.

I looked at my watch. "You want to go to dinner?" I wasn't hungry—

I'd eaten one of the chicken salads my mother had brought just a few hours ago.

She nodded. Of course she nodded. She'd probably been alone all day. I wasn't sure what the course load was like for French horn majors, but it didn't seem very demanding for Marley. She always had time on her hands.

"I have to put my bag down." I unlocked my door and waved her in behind me. My blinds were still down from the previous night, and though it was still just late afternoon outside, I had to turn on the light to see.

"You need to decorate." She wrinkled her nose at my blank walls.

"I've been busy," I said. When I set my backpack on my desk, I heard the thud of my chemistry book. I still had to read, and try to understand, three more chapters before Tuesday.

"You need posters." She sat on the spare bed, one pig slipper crossed over the other. She was wearing the sweatshirt that had been signed, in various colors of Magic Marker, by the other members of her high school graduating class. "Seniors Reach for the Stars! Go Bison!" was ironed on the back in bubbly, hollowed-out letters. "I'm lucky, because a lot of my mom's friends are quilters, and they made me a quilt before I came to school. Have you seen it? It's pretty. I sleep with it at night and then I hang it up on my wall during the day so I can see it."

I nodded, feeling through my backpack for my meal card. I knew she had heard every word of my conversation with Clyde. At first, when she didn't bring him up, I thought she was being tactful. But the more she talked, the more it seemed that she just wasn't all that interested. She was still talking about the quilt, about its lace trim, and the way her mother's quilting friends had used her baby clothes to spell out her name. I tried to focus on what she was saying; I tried not to hear the ticking of my watch. I was going to fail the chemistry test anyway. I might as well be kind. I looked down and saw that

Tim's note, with the little drawing of the rabbit, had fallen to the floor. I picked it up and set it back on my desk.

The phone rang just as we were walking out. It was the dorm-issued landline, which I never used. The receiver felt heavy in my hand.

"Veronica?" I recognized, almost right away, the voice of Gordon Goodman, residence hall director—though he usually sounded friendlier than he did just now.

"Did you forget our meeting? Your performance review?"

I looked at my calendar. There it was, two days before the chemistry test, both of them listed in red ink so I wouldn't forget. I rested my forehead against the wall. I was still screwing up. I couldn't stop. It was like a free fall.

He said he would be waiting downstairs.

Marley took the news in stride, but I still felt bad. Running down the hall, I called over my shoulder that I was sorry, and that if she wanted to wait, we could go to dinner when I came back.

Gordon Goodman's office was just off the lobby, with an interior window that allowed him to see the front desk and the front doors. But now he had the blinds pulled down, and there was nothing to see, nowhere for me to look, except back at his disappointed face. Gordon was the one who had hired me. He'd interviewed me himself.

"I'm worried at this point." He leaned back in his squeaking chair. "It's December. The semester will be over in a couple of weeks. And you haven't done one program for your floor yet." He scratched his gray beard, grimacing. "And there have been complaints that you're never around. Or never available, at least."

I nodded, chewing as quietly as I could on my fortune cookie. He offered fortune cookies to everyone who came into his office. Today, my fortune read, *Wise men learn more from fools, than fools from the wise.*

"I'm sorry," I said, swallowing. "I know I've got to do a better job. I've been really busy with school."

He tapped his fingers on his desk, frowning. The bowl that held the fortune cookies was handmade, the edges wavy, the base striped black and green. One of Gordon's daughters, now grown, was a potter somewhere in Texas. He had pottery all over his office, mostly glazed bowls and cups, but also a tissue box, and a couple of bookends.

He leaned his elbows on his desk. "You're pre-med, right?"

I nodded and smiled. I waited for him to smile back. Usually, when I told people, especially older people, especially older men, that I was premed, I was met with instant respect and approval. Gordon continued to frown.

"I'm certainly sympathetic." He glanced at his bookshelves, which covered two entire walls of his office, floor to ceiling. Although the pottery coalition had made serious headway, the shelves mostly belonged to books—fiction, nonfiction, dictionaries and encyclopedias, textbooks from every subject. "I was in law school. I remember the pressure."

"You went to law school?" I was eager to change the subject.

He nodded. His gaze moved around the room.

"Then why—" I stopped. I didn't want to be rude. I supposed it wasn't a bad job, being a hall director. I had never seen him wear anything besides a sweatshirt and jeans, or a T-shirt and shorts, depending on the weather and whether or not he was out on his morning jog. That, I supposed, was a benefit of the job: every day was casual Friday. He had his own apartment in the dorm, with his own private entrance. I'd heard it was pretty nice. For being in a dorm. A drawback, of course, was that all of his employees were students, and he had to schedule performance reviews on Sunday nights.

He shrugged. "I didn't like being a lawyer. I kept thinking I would learn to like it, but I didn't. One day I just came home and said I wasn't going to do it anymore."

"Huh," I said. I tried to think of what kind of response would keep the conversation going in this direction. "Wow," I said. "That's crazy!"

He nodded. "That's what my ex-wife said. Only she was a little angrier. She was the one who put me through law school." He waved his hand in front of his face, as if trying to erase the words. "Sorry," he added quickly. "Too much information. Not your concern."

"That's okay!"

He met my smile with a blank face. The performance review would now resume. He pulled his eyeglasses away from his face and pinched the bridge of his nose. "Anyway, as I was saying, I am aware of the pressures of a demanding course load. But you've still got to do your job." He winced, clearly uncomfortable. "And I've got to tell you, Veronica. Right now, it doesn't seem like you're doing it."

My cell phone rang in my pocket. I apologized and pulled it out to silence the ringer. My mother was calling. I silenced it and apologized again.

"It's okay," he said. He shook his head. "It's okay about the phone, I mean. But . . . the not doing the programming, not doing your job, that's not okay." He leaned forward, his elbows resting on his desk. "I'm sorry about this. I can see you're stressed out, about this job, about school. I can look at you and see it. If you want to talk with me, if there's some way I might be able to help . . ."

He paused, waiting. He was so nice. I was aware of the pressure of tears, but if I didn't speak, I could contain them. I shook my head.

"Fine," he said. "But there's a reason Housing is giving you a free room. Some of these kids need somebody looking out for them. You've got to take the job seriously." He let his eyes rest on mine, unblinking. "Or you shouldn't have the job at all."

I did not cry in his office. I curled my toes up inside my boots, looked him in the eye, and promised I would try harder. I kept my voice even, my expression resolute. I said what my father would have said. I said I would honor the terms of my contract. I said I understood his concerns, and that I appreciated his understanding, but that things were about to change.

"Good," he said. "That's good to hear." He did not seem particularly happy. "You're sure you're okay?" he asked.

On the way back up in the elevator, I was alone, but I did everything I could to hold back the tears that had pooled beneath my eyes. I did not want to be crying when the doors opened to my floor's lobby, to Marley and her quilt and her Cheetos, or to another one of the freshmen on my floor I did not even know. I used all my old tricks: I yawned. I jumped up and down. But when my cell phone rang again, and I saw my mother's number flash on the screen, I stopped trying to get ahold of myself. I flipped open my phone and pressed it hard against my cheek.

"Hey." It was just one word, but I let all the sadness and shame I was feeling fall into the mouthpiece, hoping she would hear them.

"Veronica." The voice did not belong to my mother. It was a male voice, very low, unhidden anger in the tone. A ribbon of sweat went cold along my hairline. The pressure of tears disappeared.

"Who is this?"

"Jimmy."

I glanced at the screen of my phone. It was my mother's number. Jimmy Liff had her phone. I heard the grinding gears of the elevator as it slowed near my floor.

"Uh . . . one of your *guests* left their phone at our house this weekend?"

The elevator doors opened to the lobby of my floor. Marley was reading a book on the couch, her legs covered by the quilt. She looked up at me and started to speak. I pointed to my phone and kept walking.

"Shoot," I said. "It's my mom's." She didn't have a landline. There would be no way for me to tell her where her phone was.

"Your *mother* was here?"

"Yeah. Is that okay?" I stood outside my door, fishing my key out of my pocket. On my message board, written in the green dry erase marker, was: "SOMEONE (BLONDE) IS LEAVING HAIR TRIMMINGS IN SINK AND IT IS DISGUSTING. DO SOMETHING ABOUT IT." I opened my door and turned on my light.

"Did your mom come to your big party? The party you had at my house?"

I was silent. I could not think of anything to say.

"You know, Veronica, I tried to be cool when you told me you'd wrecked my car. My concern, as you remember, was for your safety." His voice was shaking with anger. I shut my door behind me softly. I sat down on my bed. This was it. This was consequence. There was no getting out of it now.

"And then I come home, and my neighbors are pissed, because it turns out there was some huge party here on Friday. Lots of drunk people. People pissing in the street, on the ice in these nice front yards. Not cool, Veronica. Not cool at all."

"Jimmy," I said. "I'm sorry. I tried my best to clean u—"

"A lot of my music is missing."

I closed my eyes. I had put his CDs back in the entertainment center myself, each one back in its right case. But he could say anything was missing. I wouldn't be able to prove, or even know, that he was lying.

"I'd say about three hundred dollars' worth."

The number seemed excessive, and arbitrary. "Jimmy, I don't have three hundred dollars."

"Well you better figure out a way to get it. I've got a good mind to call the police. My neighbors are witnesses. I *trusted* you. I was paying you for a service, and you caused damage to my property."

Someone knocked on my door. I ignored it.

"I don't know what you want me to do," I finally said. "I don't have that kind of money. If you think of some way for me to make it up to—"

"Well for starters, you can get your lying, two-faced ass over here right now. Our car is in the shop, thanks to you, and we don't have any fucking food here. We need to go to the grocery store."

I held the phone against my ear. He sounded nothing like the person who had shown me his orchids and ferns the other day. This was something new to me—being spoken to like this. He wasn't yelling. My father, when he was angry or even just excited, usually got much louder. But there was something hard in Jimmy's voice that left me even more stunned and stupid.

"I don't have a car," I said.

"That's not my problem." His voice was still quiet, and very calm. "If you're smart, you'll be here in half an hour."

Jimmy picked up the aloe vera plant by the sink and threw it into the garbage, which was on the other side of the kitchen, a good seven feet away. The terra-cotta pot cracked on impact. Haylie and I both jumped.

She recovered first, her hand on her chest. "Are you sure?" She laughed nervously. "It didn't look de—"

"It had cigarette ash in the soil." He stood in the middle of the kitchen, his arms crossed, his stance wide. "You know, from the cigarettes we never wanted in the house in the first place? Add that to the bill."

I looked up slowly, scanning the counter for my mother's phone. The kitchen still smelled like lemons.

"How many people were here, anyway? Huh? I'm asking you a question."

His eyes were a little pink, puffy around the edges. He was wearing a Chicago Bulls knit skully, the striped edge pulled low over his brows.

"I don't know," I said. "Not that many."

"That's not what the neighbors said." He stepped back, as if trying to get a better look at me.

Haylie checked her watch. "Can we just go? The Merc closes in half an hour."

Jimmy shook his head. "No no, honey. We're not going to the co-op. I'm going to need more than granola this week. I want Mountain Dew. I want processed meat." He reached up and gently touched his nose bolt.

Haylie clicked her tongue. She was already wearing her shiny red coat, and black boots that made her almost as tall as Jimmy. She leaned over and picked what I worried was dog hair off one of the knees of her tights. "But only the Merc has organic soy waffles." Her voice was high-pitched, a little girlish. She kept her head lowered, just her eyes looking up. "You can't get them anywhere else."

He suddenly looked pleased. He slapped himself lightly on the forehead. There was no problem, he said. He smiled, his eyes hard on mine. We could go to both stores. We were in no particular hurry, right?

I shrugged. That was all. If he wanted to go to two stores, I could take him to two stores. I had Gretchen's car for the night. When I'd called, she was studying at the science library. She said her car keys were in her room, and that I needed to try to calm down. "So you forfeit your house-sitting fee," she'd whispered. "That's enough. Don't let him push you around."

Jimmy was putting on his jacket, but still looking at me, and still standing very close.

"I need to get my mom's phone," I said.

Even without the dumb contacts, his eyes, green and very still, looked a little catlike. "Sure, Veronica." He smiled, and his eyes didn't move. "After we run our errands."

We went to the co-op first. While Haylie shopped, I sat on a bench by the automatic doors and watched shoppers come and go with their cloth grocery bags and bulk foods. I tried not to watch Jimmy pace. Every time he walked across the mat in front of the doors, they slid open, and then shut, only to open again after he turned and walked back across the mat again. He was on his phone, talking in a very loud voice to someone named Degraff about the stupid bitch who had wrecked his car and then trashed his house over the weekend. I didn't look at him. He didn't look at me.

He was still on the phone when Haylie brought her groceries to the register. She said his name, walked over to him, and he handed her several bills from his wallet without even looking up. After she paid, she put the change in her pocket and sat on the bench to wait for him with me, or at least near me. She sat very still, her paper bag of groceries on her lap. I gave her a long look out of the corner of my eye. As much as she had changed, with her dyed hair and her black eyeliner, she still looked, more or less, like the girl I had played princess with in fourth grade. Her mother had made snacks for us. My mother had made snacks for us. But when Haylie finally noticed my hard stare, she didn't seem undone.

"You really fucked up," she said with a shrug. "I talked to people today. You let your friends wear my shoes. My clothes." She took off a glove and examined a fingernail. "I don't feel sorry for you at all."

At the next stop, the regular grocery store, Jimmy told me I might want to have a seat again. "I'm feeling a little slow tonight." He pulled a cart free with a hard shake. "I think we're going to be here for a while."

I found a seat by the movie rental counter, wishing I had at least thought to bring my chemistry book. But I had not thought to bring it, and so there was nothing to do but just sit there and listen to the store's stereo system play light rock and watch people buy their groceries. I tried not to think of everything that was worrisome, pressing down.

"Veronica? Is that you?"

I looked up to see Rudy, Tim's roommate, moving toward me with his odd, bouncy walk, his toes pointed slightly inward. He'd just gone through the checkout line, and he was carrying a can of soup in one hand and a new *PC World* in the other. I greeted him as warmly as I could. Tim had told me once that I was the only girl outside of sisters and cousins that Rudy was able to talk to without breaking into a visible sweat. And even that had taken some time. The first few times I went over to their apartment, Rudy had stayed in his room.

But tonight, given that I was hanging out on a chair in the grocery store, I felt like the weird one.

"What are you doing?" He put the can of soup under one arm so he could get his keys out of his pocket. "Do you need a ride or something?"

"No . . . I'm just . . ." I gestured vaguely into the aisles. "I'm just waiting for some friends." I spotted Jimmy in the greeting card section. He picked a card out, read it, and put it back before getting out another. He looked up at me, saw me watching, and waved. Haylie stood beside him, flipping through an *Allure*.

"So Tim gets back tonight," he said. "I'm sure you know that."

I nodded. I tried not to let my face change.

"You might move in, huh? After I move out? He said you might."

I made a small, circular motion with my head, neither a nod nor a shake. The store's stereo was playing "Get Outta My Dreams, Get into My Car."

"You should," he said. "It's a great apartment." He looked away. He seemed nervous. He had never had to talk with me without Tim standing right there. "Plus, you know, I think it would make him pretty happy." He looked newly embarrassed, but he pressed on. "I figure it's the least I can do, you know—move out and make room for you. He's been a good friend."

After Rudy left, I looked back up into the aisles. Jimmy was still looking at greeting cards. It was almost ten. Tim was well into his drive home, probably in southern Iowa already. Jimmy looked up and waved again. I waved back, smiling. He thought he was tormenting me, I'm sure. But I no longer felt a hurry to get anywhere. He was only wasting his own time.

I got back to the dorm just past midnight. When I first saw my mother sitting outside my room, I assumed she had come back for her phone. I walked toward her, shaking my head. I had asked for her phone again when I'd dropped Jimmy and Haylie at the town house. Jimmy said that he wasn't sure where it was, but that he would look for it, and that he would probably find it around the time his car was fixed. I tried to think of how I would explain all this to my mother, and I tried to calculate how long this conversation might take. Half an hour. Maybe more. She would have all kinds of questions and concerns. I needed to read at least a chapter of chemistry before I went to bed.

She didn't look up as I approached. She sat with her back against my door, her legs stretched out, one rubber-soled boot crossed over the other. She had her long gray coat spread out on top of her like a blanket. I stopped walking, and she looked up. She'd been crying.

"Hi," I said.

She started to stand. The bottom of her coat caught under her boot, and she almost lost her balance. I held out my hand, and she took it, righting herself with a smile.

"Hi," she said. "I met one of the girls on your floor." Her voice was hoarse, quiet. "Marley? She plays the French horn?"

The bass drum of reggae music hovered overhead. I took off my mittens and put them in my pockets. I waited, my eyes on hers.

She held up one finger. She pulled a tissue out of her pocket and blew her nose. "I'm here because . . ." She looked at the wall behind me. "Veronica. I'm here because I need a place to stay."

My mind moved quickly to the acceptable. Her van had broken down. She had lost her keys, but she could get a spare from the office in the morning. The unacceptable—that she had had a fight with the boyfriend I imagined she was moving in with—hovered in the back of my mind.

She nodded, patient with my slowness, my steady refusal to understand.

I looked down. She had been sitting on a stack of folded sheets and blankets. I recognized the chenille throw that she used to keep on our living room couch, and the flower-print fitted sheet for the twin bed I had slept on for years. All at once, the floor seemed far away, and not at all dependable.

"I need to stay with you for just a while," she said. She reached over with her ungloved hand to touch my shoulder. "I'm sorry, honey. I'm sorry. It's too cold to sleep in the van. You don't know this? You don't know this already? Honey. I don't have anywhere else to go."

10

SHE WAS TOO TIRED to get into the whole story. In a nutshell, she said, she'd been evicted from her apartment because of the dog. Yes, she was having some financial troubles, which she was certain she could work out shortly. But she hoped I would understand if right now, she just wanted to go to bed. Her socks had gotten wet. She needed to borrow some dry ones before she went back down to the van to get the rest of her things and Bowzer.

She didn't ask if she could bring Bowzer up to my room. The dorm had a strict rule against any kind of pet visitation, but I made no effort to stop her. I couldn't think or worry about anything besides how very wrong the situation seemed. Why did she suddenly have so little money that she couldn't even go to a motel? Some secret addiction? I couldn't imagine it. Gambling? She'd never seemed interested. I wondered how long she'd been out of her apartment and where, up till now, she'd been sleeping. *In the van?* I could not bring myself to ask her.

I didn't really have the chance. As soon as she put on my socks, she left to go get Bowzer. She was worried about him, even with his blankets, being down in the van for so long. "I'll be right back," she told me, pulling on her hat. Her cream scarf had gotten stained with something, maybe ketchup, since I'd last seen her. "I'll have him with me, so don't lock your door." She stepped into the hallway and glanced back and forth before peeking back at me. "I'll come up the back stairway. No one will see him. Don't worry. And he's all peed and pooped out for the night. I'm sure of it."

I stood still after she left, staring at my closed door and listening to the vibrating pipes above. I blinked. I shook my head. I tried to come up with a sensible course of action—I would only have a few minutes before she returned. I could call Elise. But there was nothing she could do in San Diego, not tonight, not right now. I could call my father and insist that he help her. I could remind him that though they were no longer married, I was still his daughter, and she was still my mother, and that if he cared for me at all, he must still care for her a little. But that would be a long, loud conversation. My father could, and no doubt would, counter that the divorce—which she had caused—had put a financial strain on him as well, and that he was not responsible for her poor decision-making or whatever it was that had sucked up all her money. He was living simply, he would say. He hadn't gotten himself into a jam. Any concern for me would be overwhelmed by his refusal to be concerned for her.

And anyway, she would see my calling him as a betrayal. "He wants to see me poor," she had sniffed to me once, early on. "He wants to punish me. He wants to see me without anything at all."

I looked at my watch. She'd already been gone two minutes. I searched my room for anything I might not want her to see, as if I were fourteen again, locking my diary out of fear that her obsessive curiosity might get the best of her while she was putting my laundry away. I considered that her priorities were different now, and that she might be just a little too preoccupied with her own troubles to worry about my every thought or decision. Still, I picked up the note Tim had left for me, folded it carefully, and tucked it inside my desk drawer.

When I heard the door to the stairway open, I hurried across the room and peeked out into the hallway. She was jogging toward me, her boots heavy on the carpet, her gait awkward. She had both straps of a duffel bag looped around her neck, and her hands cradled her belly. It was Bowzer, of course, hidden inside her buttoned-up coat; but as she panted toward me, she just looked pregnant. A girl stepped out of her room with a dried green face mask, headed toward the bathroom; she passed my mother with nothing more than a friendly hello.

Once we were in my room again, the door shut safely behind us, she eased Bowzer out from under her coat and set him gently on the spare bed. "There you go," she whispered. He looked like a little black and gray lamb; his legs were so thin compared to his body. He whimpered, watching her take off her coat. She reached into the duffel bag and pulled out two Cool Whip containers, one full of dry dog food, the other empty. "We can put his water in this one," she said, handing it to me. "It's probably better if you get it, right?" Her tone was overly careful, polite.

I pointed out that she would have to use the bathroom eventually. It wouldn't be a problem, I said. We were allowed to have overnight guests for up to two nights in a row.

"But you should probably keep a low profile," I added breezily, as if I were just offering a friendly tip, something to make her stay more enjoyable. I wasn't sure how many nights she thought she would need to stay.

"Okay," she said. "I'll just do it all now." She reached into the duffel bag and got out a ziplock bag that contained a toothbrush and toothpaste and several bottles and creams. "Can you stay with him while I'm gone? If we leave him alone, he might whine."

She was almost out the door before she stopped and turned back.

"One thing," she said. She looked nervous. "I don't want you to tell Elise about this. Or your father. I'd rather this stay between you and me."

I rubbed my eyes. I shook my head, not so much refusing her as showing her my frustration. I had already planned on calling Elise in the morning, as soon as it was late enough in California. She would know what to do. She and her husband had a one-bedroom apartment, with no room for another person, much less a person with a dog. They were both just out of law school and, Elise had told me, still very much in debt. But I knew she would think of some way to help. Elise, more than anyone I could think of, always knew what to do.

"I don't know why you can't tell her but you can tell me," I started.

Her eyes narrowed, as if she suspected I was being stupid on purpose. When she saw that my question was sincere, she sighed. "Yes, you do," she said. She scratched her forehead with the hand that held the plastic bag, obscuring her face for a moment. When she brought it back down, to my surprise, she was almost smiling.

Bowzer whined anyway, as soon as she left, even with me standing right there. I moved him to my bed, scolded him, and then petted him lightly on the head, which probably only confused him. I *had* been his favorite while I was growing up—he'd follow me around the house, and sit by the door when I went to school But in my absence, his obsessive love had clearly been transferred to my mother. He was silent while I made up the spare bed with the blankets and rose-print sheets she had brought with her. I held them up to my nose and breathed in. They smelled clean. They smelled like the detergent she'd always used.

When she returned, she looked at the bed and smiled. "Oh," she said. "Thank you. Thanks for doing that." Something was different. For as long as I could remember, she had gone to bed with some clear cream with a pleasant smell spread over her face that made her skin glisteny and smooth. Tonight, her face did not glisten. The overhead fluorescent light cast shadows under her eyes.

"Do you need anything?" I asked. "Are you . . . are you hungry?"

She shook her head, her eyes on the dark window, the orange streetlights bright over the parking lot. "I just met another nice girl," she said. "Just now in the bathroom. Inez? From Albuquerque? Do you know her?"

I frowned. "You're supposed to be keeping a low profile." I did not know Inez. I looked at my chemistry book, waiting for me on my desk. I would not be able to study tonight, not unless I wanted to leave, and then wake her when I came in.

"I just said hello, honey." She put the ziplock bag back in the duffel, her free hand moving down Bowzer's back. "I didn't want to be rude. You don't know her? She lives right down the hall. You know, I don't think I've ever met anyone from Albuquerque in my entire life."

I got out my little bucket and headed for the bathroom, hoping that she would take a cue from me and change into her pajamas while I was gone. I had not seen her undressed since eleventh grade, when she and I joined a gym together. The joint membership had been my idea: I'd wanted to take yoga, but I knew that she might not be thrilled with the idea of me signing up for one more class or hobby, so she could spend two more afternoons a week driving me there and back. So I'd pitched the yoga class as something we could do together. I didn't just want to take yoga, I said. I wanted to take it with her!

My motives were not purely selfish. I really did think it would be good for her. Both of the grandmothers were still alive then, and my mother was spending a lot of time driving to the two different nursing homes, checking in on them and running their errands. She'd put on weight that year, not a lot, but enough to make her frown at herself when she passed the hallway mirror. Still, she would pick me up from driver's ed and tell me that she was too tired to cook or even fix a salad, and more often than not we would go through a drive-thru, switching seats after we ordered so I could practice driving home. She usually got a chocolate sundae, and she would start in on it right there in the car, mumbling driving tips and stayed suprisingly calm as I carefully steered and shifted. I couldn't wait until I had my license and I could drive by myself, but in the meantime, driving with my mother wasn't so bad; I much preferred her company to my humorless driver's ed teacher or my very excitable father. She let me choose the radio station, as long as I kept the volume low enough so I could hear her instructions and warnings.

And then one evening, as we were about to pull up our steep driveway, I asked her if we could keep going, if I could circle the neighborhood just one more time. She shrugged, digging her plastic spoon into her cup. "Fine with me," she mumbled. "This is the best part of my day."

That night, I looked up "depression" on the Internet. Experts suggested exercise, rest, and time with loved ones. I decided that yoga, and more time with me, might help.

But as it turned out, she wasn't interested, at least not in yoga. She said she wanted something more intense—she'd recently had a dream about lifting something immense far over her head, and in the dream, she had been amazed both by how heavy the object was and also that she was able to lift it. And if the last two years had taught her anything, it was that she didn't want osteoporosis. She looked at the schedule and saw that the gym offered a weight-lifting class called "STRENGTH CAMP" at the same time as the yoga class I wanted to take. What a coincidence, she said. What a sign. She said I was thoughtful to think of her. We could get some together time in in the car.

When she first started, she was miserable. She was too self-conscious to wear anything but baggy black sweats and a big shirt, and she came out of class red-faced and clammy with sweat. At home, she moved stiffly, wincing when she vacuumed, when she bent over to put on Bowzer's leash. But then little bulges appeared in her arms. In the grocery store one day, without warning, she raised her hand, squeezed her fist, and made me feel her biceps. She started doing push-ups on the living room floor while my father watched the news. In late spring, she told my grandmothers and their attendants that she couldn't help with any appointments before ten in the morning, and she signed up for A.M. Taebo. She modeled the punches and swipes for me in the kitchen, moving like a shadowboxer, sometimes laughing at herself, sometimes not. Her legs grew lean and muscular. She bought tank tops in different colors.

By June, it was too hot out to get in the car when we were still sweaty from class, and so we brought towels and shampoo and fresh clothes for the drive home. In the locker room, she did not exactly parade around naked. She wrapped a towel around her before she stepped out of the shower stall. But I would occasionally look up at the wrong time and catch a glimpse of her body, and it always made me uncomfortable. I didn't know why. I had grown up seeing her naked, walking in on her while she was in the shower, on the toilet, and once—horribly, when I was nine—straddled on top of my father as he sat in his office chair. I was familiar with her full breasts and their dark, downward pointing nipples; the paleness of her belly marked by the crisscrossed scars from two Cesarean sections; the dark patch of pubic hair that had mystified and frightened me as a child; the tiny, snaky, blue veins on her outer thighs. This was all familiar. What was strange, and strangely disturbing to me, was the new leanness, the pronounced curve between her hips and her waist, the enviable tautness of her belly.

She stopped going to the gym sometime after the divorce. She was still thin, but it just looked like a tired skinniness, even a frailty—the muscles were gone from her arms. I didn't want to see her like this, either. Tonight, especially tonight, I did not want to see her even a little unclothed. I needed the illusion of order, of distance. We were not friends or even roommates. She was still my mother, just staying in my room for a short time.

When I walked back in, she was still wearing her coat, unbuttoned, the cream sweater and brown cords underneath. "Uh, can I . . ." She sat on the foot of the guest bed. Her legs were crossed, one hand resting on Bowzer. She'd taken off her boots, showing the pink socks she had borrowed from me. "I forgot my pajamas. They're down in the van, I mean. Do you have something I could wear?"

I gave her some leggings and a long-sleeved sweatshirt that I'd gotten during training, "TWEETE HALL STAFF" emblazoned across the front.

"Aww." She held it up to her chest, swinging her head from side to side, her curly hair brushing against her shoulders, her small, silver hoop earrings staying completely still. "I'm one of the gang now. This makes it all worth it. Really."

I studied her smile. It was hard to tell if she was just joking around, or if something had actually happened to her attention span. In any case, she seemed to take my silence as a reproach—she looked away as she slid her coat off.

"I'll tell you the whole story," she said, pulling up her sweater with a quick yank. The T-shirt underneath came up with it, revealing a beige bra and, when both arms were fully raised, the faint outline of ribs.

I sat at my desk and opened my chemistry book, to a diagram of some chemical reaction, something to look at besides her. "Why didn't you tell me you were having money problems?"

She said nothing. I did not look up to see her face, to find a clue in her expression. I heard a zipper unzip, her heavy sigh. I kept my eyes on my book, my eyebrows furrowed with feigned concentration. I could not say now, or even then, what kind of molecule I was looking at.

"If you need to stay up, I can sleep with the light on," she said.

I looked up. She was in my leggings and my staff shirt, getting under the covers of the guest bed. Bowzer, lying at the foot of the bed, stood, stretched, and made his careful way up to her arms. "It won't bother me," she said. "Your father used to watch television in bed, and I got used to it. Really, I'm tired enough, I'll go right out."

It wasn't true. They used to fight about the televison. My father liked to set it to a timer, so he could fall asleep with it on. My mother had a velvet eye mask, and headphones that played white noise; but she said she couldn't keep the flicker of the television, the hum of it, completely out. She needed to sleep in the dark, she said. That last year before the divorce, I had twice woken up to find her sleeping in Elise's old room.

"That's okay." I shut my book. "I usually go to bed about now." I stood up, looking around the room. She'd left her bags on the floor by her bed. They were zipped up, arranged neatly, and pushed out of the way.

"Do you need anything?" I stood by the light switch, my eyes on her bags. "You want some water or anything? I can go get it. It's no problem."

She shook her head. She already had her head on the pillow, her eyes closed, Bowzer spooned up against her. "Thanks, though," she said.

I turned out the light and stood still for a moment, trying to think if I should ask her to stop saying thank you. No, I decided. That would just make everything more awkward. That would make us both feel worse.

I had almost groped my way back to my bed when she started talking.

"I'm just out of money." Her voice came out of the darkness, monotone, objective, a newscaster reporting misfortune that had happened to someone else. "That's really all I can tell you. There's no secret. That's just all I know. I shouldn't have taken on the house instead of cash. That was my first mistake. I thought I couldn't bear to sell it, but then I had to anyway, and by then the market had slowed, and it took a long time to sell. I didn't talk to you or Elise about it because I didn't want to worry you. And then there was mold in the attic, water damage. Dan said that it happened after he left, that he wasn't respons—"

Here she stopped, apparently remembering that Dan was also my father. For several minutes, we lay in silence. I could hear an engine revving in the parking lot, a muffled television in someone else's room. *My mother is homeless,* I thought. *My mother is homeless and living with me in my dorm.* I was being dramatic. It wasn't true. She just needed a place to stay for a while, and only because of the dog.

She cleared her throat and started again. The sum of it wasn't anyone's fault, she said. It was more a series of unfortunate incidents, one after the other, boxing her in. Or out. In September, she'd cracked a molar on a popcorn kernel and had to get a root canal, and she was no longer on my father's health plan. She was still looking for a steady teaching job, she said, something with benefits; she was having a hard time with that, of course, since she hadn't used her degree in over twenty years. But she was subbing, and she was putting in fifteen hours a week at DeBeck's. She had thought she would be okay. She'd planned on just living simply until something better came along, or until the divorce settlement was adjusted.

"It sounds fair, just cutting everything in half." She paused to yawn. "But we had so much debt. And my . . . future earning potential needs to be taken into account."

Potential. Usually a good word. But here, it was turned around, as in lack of. I tried to think of something nice to say. "You sound like a lawyer," I said. "I'm impressed."

"Yeah," she said. "I'm quoting mine." She did not laugh. "Anyway, then I got evicted, because of Bowzer. I already found a place that will take dogs. I can afford the rent. But it won't be available until next week. I need to wait until next Friday anyway, when I get a check, so I can pay the security deposit. I lost the last one because of the dog."

She was silent for a while after that, but I lay awake, listening. Someone running down the hallway laughed, loud and shrill. And I could hear Marley's French horn, the same three notes played over and over. She wasn't supposed to play the horn in her room, not after ten o'clock. But it gave me some relief to picture her, oblivious to all the worry in this room, working through her music so diligently, those same three notes: one two three, one two three, one two three.

For some time, maybe minutes, maybe hours, I lay awake, eyes open, staring up into the darkness. Just two nights earlier, I'd ignored her calls. I was aware of everything shifting, new regret a sharp pain in my throat. The hurt felt real, and truly physical, and also, strangely, like something necessary and right. When I was young, lying in bed at night, the backs of my calves would hurt so much that I would sometimes cry out. Growing pains, my parents said. They were a myth, the doctor countered. But night after night, my legs hurt; until one night, they stopped hurting, and I was taller.

11

SHE GOT UP EARLY to take Bowzer out. She did not get dressed to do this—she only threw her coat back over the clothes she'd slept in and pulled her boots back over my pink socks. Her hair was messy, curls everywhere, but she didn't bother with a comb. She didn't even turn on the light, though it was raining out, and only the faint gray of an overcast sunrise glowed around the window shade.

When she noticed me watching her, she put her hand to her throat, startled. "Sorry," she whispered. "I didn't want him to have to wait."

"Why are you whispering?"

She was already buttoning Bowzer under her coat. He gave me one last confused look before his eyes and snout disappeared.

"Because you were sleeping." She was still whispering. "What time is your first class?"

"Nine," I said, lying. I only had a conference with my English professor at eleven, nothing before that. I rubbed my eyes and squinted at her, trying to think what other people would think when they saw her in the hallway, or down in the lobby. She didn't look pregnant now. She looked like she was hiding something lumpy.

"You've got to be careful, Mom. You can't just take him out on the front lawn. Seriously. I could lose my job."

"I know." She patted the pockets of her coat. "I'll take him back down the stairs to the van, and then drive to a park or something." She blew me a kiss. "And I'll make my bed when I come back. I'll make yours, too, okay?"

"It's raining," I said.

"I know."

When she turned to go, she walked into my metal trash can, knocking it on its side. She put her hands to ears, wincing.

"Sorry," she whispered.

Without waiting for my response, she stepped out into the hall-way, shutting the door behind her so softly I worried she hadn't closed it at all.

When I got back from the shower, there was a message on my phone from Tim. He got home okay, he said, and he wanted me to think about where I wanted to go for dinner, because anything was good with him; he just wanted to see me. His voice was always scratchy in the morning, deep and warm. "Love you," he said, before he hung up. There was a pause before he said it, not a hesitation, but more of a deliberate wait, as if he knew very well what he wanted to say, but just wanted to think about it first.

I sat on my bed, my hair dripping wet, my phone tucked under my chin. I didn't want to do anything. I might have sat there for a very long time if I hadn't been worried about my mother coming back. She'd been out with Bowzer for almost half an hour.

I texted him. "*In hurry. 7 2night is good. CU then.*"

I stared at the message before I sent it, making sure it was what I wanted. It was good: I wasn't lying, but he wouldn't spend the day worried. There was no need for a buildup. I would just tell him. And then I would lose my best friend and the only part of my life that, in the last year, had felt consistent and certain. I would feel better, maybe, after it was over, after it was all settled and done.

I was just putting on my coat to leave when she burst back into the room, the hood of her coat dripping wet and pulled up over her hair. The ketchup stain was front and center on the knot of her cream-colored scarf. She was pink in the face and breathing hard—worn out, I suppose, from climbing seven flights of stairs with a medium-sized dog under her coat. She also had a white paper bag, rolled over at the top, tucked under one of her arms. When she set Bowzer down, the bag fell on the floor. She looked at it and laughed in a way that seemed unhappy.

"Breakfast," she said finally, leaning against the wall. "Bagels. I was going to get coffee, but I didn't see how I would get it up here. Sorry. And you like strawberry jelly, right? On top of the cream cheese? I had them do it like that. They thought it was weird. But they did it."

"Oh," I said. Bowzer started sniffing around the bag, and I bent over to pick it up. "Thanks. But you know, I can pick up a bagel whenever I want at the dining hall, and it's right on my way to class. You should save your money."

She was still out of breath, not saying anything, but I could tell, just from her face, that I had said the wrong thing. My cell phone rang. I took it out of my bag and looked at the screen. My mother was calling, or not my mother, because she was standing in front of me looking miserable and humiliated. Jimmy. I closed my phone and put it back in my bag.

"Thank you, though." I opened the bag and pulled out the bagel with strawberry jelly bleeding out. "This will save me time." I already had my coat on, my bag over my shoulder.

"Your hair looks nice," she said. "But I like it curly, too."

"Thanks." I smiled. She was standing between me and the door.

"You'll be gone all morning?"

I nodded. I couldn't tell if she registered this news as good or bad. She appeared to be making calculations, maybe adding up hours in her head.

"What . . . uh . . ." I kept my voice light, unworried. "What are you going to do today?"

She slid past me, farther into the room. "I'm not sure yet. I've got to go find a *KC Star*. I'll go somewhere and read the want ads."

I said nothing. She took off her coat and draped it over her arm.

"Do you want to hang that up?"

"I don't see a hook," she said. "You've got one for your coat, but . . ."

I took her coat from her and opened my closet door. I had another hook inside the door for my robe. I took my robe down, tossed it on my bed, and hung her coat on the hook.

"Oh . . . you didn't have to do—"

She shifted her weight, but continued to stand in front of the door. I didn't want to ask her to move so I could leave. She already seemed so uncomfortable, like anywhere she stood would be wrong.

"Anything you want me to do before I leave?" She looked around the room. "I could sweep or something. I could clean the windows. It would make it brighter in here."

"They're fine," I said. "You don't have to do anything."

She looked at me. "I don't work until Thursday."

"Oh," I said. "Okay."

"My supervisor gave me some time off." She pushed her hair behind her ears. "I worked on Saturday, after I had to pack up everything in the van." She was speaking quickly, and rolling her eyes as if bored by her own story. "I was late, of course, and then when I got there, I guess I looked a little . . . unkempt." She reached into the bag for the other bagel. "That was her word, my supervisor's. She's a little bit older than you are. Or maybe younger." She paused to smile. "*Lindsay*. She suggested I take several days off." She tore off a piece of bagel, leaned over, and held it out for Bowzer. "I don't think I was allowed to say no."

Bowzer turned his snout away from the bagel. She frowned, looked at the piece he'd rejected, and popped it into her own mouth.

"Anyway . . ." She chewed politely, her hand covering her mouth. "Don't worry. I'll go somewhere for the day, a coffee shop or something. I'll get out of your hair. I won't come back until late." She frowned. "You know what, though? I think I've lost my phone. Maybe it's in one of the bags. Could you call it for me?"

I took a bite of my bagel, holding up one finger to tell her to wait while I thought of something to say. It would do no good to tell her Jimmy Liff had her phone. She would be better off just thinking it was lost until I could get it back to her. Also: if I started to tell her the whole story, I would never get out of the room.

"You can just call it from that," I said, nodding toward the landline on the wall. "I've got to catch a bus."

"Sorry," she said. "I don't want to make you late."

I wrapped my scarf around my neck and walked quickly to the door. When I opened it, there was Marley Gould. She was wearing her ruffled nightgown, but she also had on pink lipstick and blush. She moved her head, trying to see over me.

"Is your mom still here?"

"NO," I said, stepping in front of her. "MY MOM IS GONE. SHE ISN'T HERE ANYMORE."

Behind me, I heard my closet door open and the jingling of Bowzer's collar. I kept my eyes on Marley's, my smile wide, until I heard the closet door shut.

"Oh." She looked at my door. "Who were you talking to?"

"I was on the phone. Do you need something?" She already had her hair braided for the day, a pink ribbon tied around each end. She smelled faintly of orange juice. I wondered if she had already gone down to breakfast. Some people made the trek in nightgowns and pajamas, as if they were still living at home, just traipsing downstairs for pancakes with their parents and not to an institutional dining hall that served four thousand people a day.

"I just thought I heard your mom," Marley said. "I guess you sound like her." She stared at me intently. "I met her last night. She was really nice. She asked me all about music. Did she tell you?"

"She mentioned it," I said. I pulled up my coat sleeve and looked at my watch. A normal person would have seen this as a signal to move aside.

"She's pretty, too. I can't believe she's your mom." She shook her head and pulled one braid over her eyes. "Not 'cause she's pretty, I mean. I mean she looks young."

I stopped trying to get past her. I leaned back against my door frame, my arms crossed, still barring entry. But I smiled, more or less inviting her to keep talking. "Yes!" I said, my voice just a little louder than normal. "I agree. She is pretty. And she does look young!" I was still anxious to leave for the library, but I could picture my mother, well within earshot, crouched beneath my clothes with Bowzer. If there was ever a time she might need to overhear something good about herself, I guessed it was pretty much now.

Marley seemed pleased by my sudden enthusiasm. "She's funny, too!" She nodded at me, as if I had just convinced her of something. "She played the saxophone when she was in junior high. I'm sure you know that. But she was making fun of herself—I guess she used to get in trouble with her teacher for bulging her eyes when she played?" Marley pantomimed playing a saxophone with bulging eyes.

I said nothing. I did not know that my mother had ever played the saxophone.

"She was out here for a long time," Marley added. She tried to look over my shoulder again. "Waiting. Were you late or something?"

"No."

"Hmmm." She stepped back, studying my face. I took advantage of the space between us to step into the hallway. My mother had gotten whatever ego boost she was going to get from Marley, and it was time for me to go. I turned, shut my door, and searched my bag for my keys. *Configuration refers to the three-dimensional orientation of atoms around a chiral center. It can be designated R or S.*

"She lives close by?"

"What?" I looked over my shoulder. "Yeah. In Kansas City."

"Oh, you're lucky. I bet you get to see her all the time."

I had to laugh at that, a low, self-pitying chuckle. I wasn't sure if my mother had heard. If she had, even in her present situation, she might think it was funny, too. Only Marley wasn't in on the joke.

"I'm not laughing at you . . . ," I started.

When I looked up again, she was already walking away, her slippers silent on the floor. She disappeared into her room without another word.

The English Department was in the ugliest building on campus. Wescoe Hall was initially intended to be a parking garage, but the university changed its mind and decided to make it the humanities building, apparently pretty late in the game. It was just a sad thing to look at. The surrounding buildings were beautiful, all limestone and brick, many of them castle-shaped, with flags waving from terra-cotta roofs and high, arched entryways. The science library was particularly impressive, all soaring architecture and beveled glass, the gift of some generous alumnus. Wescoe, on the other hand, was short and squat, concrete gray; the first two floors were basements. The upper floors were okay—they put in a lot of windows, and the classrooms were large and bright. But as you descended into the lower floors, where the instructors had their offices, the halls started to feel like tunnels, illuminated only by flickering fluorescent lights. Smokers huddled at both belowground entrances, and sometimes, even inside, the air smelled a little like car exhaust, as if the building somehow knew of its original destiny and was still working to play the part.

But during my conference with my English professor that morning, I felt an urge to breathe deeply. I had just come from the science library, where I'd spent the last two hours under the high ceilings staring at molecules and trying to flip them around in my head. Actually, I'd spent maybe an hour looking at molecules before I fell asleep right there at a study table under all that beveled glass and beautiful sunlight, my head cushioned by my forearms. I woke with drool on my book, a page stuck to my cheek, feeling stupid in many ways.

But now, right next door, in Wescoe's dreary basement, my English professor was telling me that he was impressed with the draft I'd turned in for my final paper on *Far from the Madding Crowd*. I was the only student who had argued that the ending was sad, he said. Strong critical thinking, he said. Palpable enthusiasm for the subject matter. A real talent for this. I smiled back at him, feeling dazed and slightly warm, though his office was cold, and my hair was still damp and curling from the rain. It had been a while since anyone had told me I was doing okay at anything.

He said he'd been impressed with every paper I'd turned in that semester. He thanked me for the thoughtful comments I'd made during class discussions. It was so nice, he said, to see so much genuine enthusiasm for learning. He asked me if I was an English major and if I was planning to apply to graduate school.

"No," I told him. "I'm pre-med."

The words came out of habit. But this time, as I said them, I felt as if I were listening from the outside, nowhere inside my own head. My gaze moved around his office, at the shelves full of books on Hardy and Keats and Yeats, books I would very much want to read if only I had the time. Papers cluttered his desk, and a print of Virginia Woolf's face stared out from the wall behind him. On the other wall by his desk, he'd Scotch taped several crayon drawings of stick figures with smiling faces, "FOR DADY" scrawled across the bottom of one.

"Pre-med," he said, smiling as he slid my paper back across his desk. "Renaissance woman, huh? Good at everything. Well, you're smart to do medicine, then. You'll always have a job."

I did not correct him. I did not explain that I was not a Renaissance woman, good at everything, or that I was about to flunk out of my major. I only stood and thanked him when it was time to leave, my voice maybe a little too grateful, too loud for such a small office. Before I left, I took one last look around. The only thing missing was plants, and he probably would have had some if he'd had a window. What was important was that he had an office. He spent his days doing what I would love to do, and he did not appear destitute. There was no reason to assume he would someday need to move into his child's dorm room to save up for a security deposit. Perhaps doing what you loved, what you really wanted to do, wasn't a problem. Perhaps just being my mother was. I did think wistfully of our family doctor, and all the tangible help she gave to people here and on the other side of the world. If I did not get control of myself immediately, I would never be able to vaccinate children in Kenya, or maybe never learn to do anything that useful. But maybe I could find some other way to be good.

I felt strangely light as I climbed the stairs back up to ground level, even in my coat and boots, my bookbag swinging beside me. Outside, I stood under one of Wescoe's many overhanging slabs. A bus came by, but I didn't run out into the rain to catch it. *A talent for this. Genuine enthusiasm.* I stared into the falling rain, vaguely aware that I was smiling.

I should have taken that bus.

"Veronica Von Holten! What a pleasant surprise!"

Jimmy Liff walked toward me across the patio, something metal jingling in his pockets, both arms extended, as if he were coming in for a hug. When he got closer, his arms still raised, and it appeared that he was not going to stop, I took a step back, forgetting I was standing at the top of several cement steps. I had to catch myself on the banister.

"What's the matter?" He stood over me, stooping a little so his face was very close to mine. "You're not afraid of me, right?"

I glanced back over my shoulder, searching for another bus. I didn't want to be afraid of him. I told myself not to be. Anybody could yell and throw plants and study gangsta rappers on BET until he could perfectly mimic the raised arm walk, the sneer, the Chicago Bulls hat pulled low over his forehead. But his focus was unsettling. Just a few days ago, he thought my name was Valerie. Now even my last name rolled off his tongue.

"How did you get to class this morning?" His voice was friendly, but he poked my shoulder, fairly hard, with two fingers. "Did you walk all the way in the rain?"

"I took the bus," I said. I put a foot down on the first step to keep my balance. He was still under the overhang; I wasn't. Rain tapped on my head and shoulders.

"Ah. Lucky you." He kept his eyes on mine. The area around his nose bolt was definitely infected. It looked red, puffy, the skin rising over the bolt's edges. "The bus doesn't go out where we live. The nearest stop is about a mile away. Did you know that?"

I looked over my shoulder again. No bus. When I turned back, he didn't seem to have moved at all. Even his eyes were very still.

"Are you even a little bit concerned with how I got to class this morning?" He was not yelling. His voice was still very calm. "Or Simone? Did you think about her? Do you ever think of anyone besides yourself? No? No concern? Well, I'll tell you anyway." He watched me, saying nothing for several seconds. He didn't seem to need to blink. "I had to call a friend, someone who had nothing to do with wrecking my car. Because you wouldn't answer your phone. Did you just not hear it ring this morning? Sleeping in, maybe?"

He flexed his eyebrows, waiting. Rain slid over my forehead, dropping into my eyes. For some reason, I did not think I should move to wipe it away.

"Or maybe you just figured it's not your problem?"

I started to turn away. He stepped in front of me.

"So how do you think Simone and I should get home? Walk in the rain? Try to hail a cab in Kansas? Well guess what? If I have to call a cab, you're paying for it. We'll add it to your bill. You don't want to answer your phone? Fine. But it's going to cost you. And let me tell you something . . . you're going to pay."

I looked into his eyes, searching for any potential understanding. It made sense that he would be angry about the party. Anyone would be annoyed. And there was a chance he really was missing some CDs. But even if he really had lost three hundred dollars' worth of music, it was hard to understand why he was looking at me with so much rage, why he was so bent on making me pay. I thought of his house, his car. Three hundred dollars plus cab fare was a lot for me, but it couldn't be much for him.

"Jimmy," I said. "I don't have any money." I held out both hands, as if to show him. "I would give you rides if I could. But I don't even have a car."

He clapped his hands hard enough to make a cracking sound that echoed off the concrete wall behind him. But his voice was still calm and quiet. "Oh, okay. So I guess you're off the hook then. I guess it's not your fucking problem that I can't get to class and back because my car is going to be in the shop for another three days."

He was smiling now, but his voice was getting loud. People walking by turned to look at us, took in my face, and looked away. There was nothing to say and nowhere to go. If I walked away, he would follow.

"Maybe I should just stay home until the car is fixed and fail all my classes? Does that sound more fair to you?"

I swallowed. He did have a point. I had wrecked the car. His logic was not completely off. I shook my head. I was doing it. I was doing what I always did with Elise and my father—stopping to consider the other point of view instead of just defending without pause. I knew this, but half of my brain was still trying to think of how I could make amends. I could call my mother and ask to use her van. But she was gone for the day, reading the classifieds in the public library or some coffee shop, staying warm and out of my way. And I couldn't call her anyway. Jimmy still had her phone.

"I don't know what you want me to do," I said.

He sighed. He looked as if he really felt bad for me.

"You're really not that smart, are you, Veronica?" He shook his head, answering the question for me. "Book smart, maybe. You do okay with school. But you just can't apply it to the real world, right? I have to spell it all out for you?"

Here again, though I knew I shouldn't, I wondered if he had a point.

"My last class gets out at one," he said. He spoke slowly, enunciating each syllable, as if he were talking to a small child. "So does Simone's. That gives you a whole hour to figure something out. You can pick us up at the fountain." He lifted his chin, his gaze still steady. "Don't you dare be late."

Gretchen wasn't in her room. Neither were her keys. I considered calling Tim, and quickly decided I shouldn't. At half past noon, I ran across the parking lot to the dining hall, searching the tables for anyone I knew even remotely. But all the people I asked said they didn't have a car; or, if they did, they were on their way to class, already late, their keys locked in their rooms. I suspected some of them were lying, and really, I couldn't blame them. I could guess what I looked like: bug-eyed and breathing hard, rain-soaked hair in my eyes—not the sort of person you would just toss keys to without a worry. When the third-floor RA—who I knew had paid for her Jeep by waitressing two summers in a row—looked away and mumbled something about wishing she could help, I lost the will to ask anyone else.

On the way back up to my room, I leaned my head against the back wall of the elevator and closed my eyes. My heart was still pounding, but I could already feel myself calming, sweat cooling under my sweater, my skin clammy beneath. It was a relief, really, to just give up, to admit there was nothing more I could do. I reached into my pocket and turned off my phone. Jimmy would call soon, and he would call later. For now, I just wanted to go to sleep. My mother would be gone all day, and I would have my room to myself. I was only putting off misery; but all I could think was how good it would be to lie down in a dark room by myself for a while, and not worry about what was coming.

I opened my door to find my mother and Marley sitting on the floor next to my bed, a large bag of M&M's between them. Marley was braiding my mother's hair. Bowzer slept peacefully on my bed. Both beds were made, the pillows fluffed. The windows looked suspiciously clean.

"Oh! Veronica! Hey!" My mother looked up at me as best she could without moving her head. Marley was making pigtails, one on each side; the braid she had already finished curled up a little at the tip. "How's she doing back there? I don't see how she's going to pull it off. I've got layers, I'm pretty sure."

"Natalie, keep your head still." Marley shook her head and smiled. She was wearing the pig slippers and a dress that was denim on top, a flowered skirt at the bottom. Her horn case lay open on the guest bed, the horn brightly gleaming in a snug bed of crushed blue velvet.

My mother's eyes rested on mine. "Sorry, honey. I was on my way out, but then your friendly neighbor stopped by, offering chocolate and music." She scrunched up her nose and smiled back at Marley. "How could I resist? And hey, have you ever heard her play?" She nodded back at Marley, as if I might otherwise not guess who she meant. "It's really something! It's one of the most difficult instruments to play well. Did you know that? Someone else told me that once. You wouldn't know it, watching this girl. She has to think about her breathing and her hands and even the way she's holding it. Marley, you'll have to show Veronica when you're done."

"Okay," Marley said. She looked up at me. "What's the matter? You look really weird."

I didn't want them there. I didn't want either of them in my room. I lowered my eyes and put my hand over my mouth. "Mom," I said, looking down. "I need to borrow your van."

"Why?" She moved her head to look up at me. Marley clicked her tongue and gently pulled back on the braid.

"Can you just give me the keys?"

My mother looked up at me, saying nothing. I knew, from vast experience, going all the way back to my earliest years, that the conversation would not continue until I apologized. *You don't take that tone with me, young lady.*

But apparently, these days, I could. "Okay," she said. She leaned forward, reaching for her purse on the edge of her bed. Marley moved with her, still holding the braid. I stared at the bag of M&M's on the floor.

"They're mine," Marley said. "You want some?"

I shook my head. I just wanted the keys.

"Veronica saw me play once." Marley was up on her knees, twisting an elastic around the end of a braid. "She came to the football game when the band played." She tilted her head, still looking at the back of my mother's head. "Or at least she *said* she did."

What happened next, what I did next, is difficult to defend or even explain. I will say I was tired, going on little sleep, and too much worry and adrenaline. I was in no mood for any complaint from Marley, no matter how subtle, no matter if what she was saying was true. I saw my mother look at me, wondering if I was, in fact, a liar. I saw Marley in a horror show of a dress and the pig slippers, the very picture of an easy target, and something ugly and fast in me decided, *You! You are the one who must be punished!*

"You know, Marley. You might take some responsibility for yourself, for making friends, instead of just pestering me all the time.

Maybe if you tried not dressing and acting like you were twelve years old, the other freshmen wouldn't avoid you."

They both stared up at me. My mother pulled her head back a little. I was already embarrassed, aware now of how I must look to them, and how I must have sounded; but in my swirling head, despite my embarrassment, or maybe even because of it, I felt I had no option but to stand my ground.

"I'm tired of feeling sorry for you." I kept my eyes on just Marley, though I could feel my mother looking up at me as well. "I'm tired of you being so pathetic. This is my room, by the way. I didn't invite you in here. And sorry, no, I didn't go to the football game. I'm not your mommy. I don't want to be."

My mother stood up quickly. "That's enough," she said, her voice very low. "Just stop talking, Veronica. Just stop talking right now."

Marley stood quickly. She smoothed her flowered skirt and looked at me, her eyes small, her mouth open, as if she still couldn't believe what I had just said, as if she were waiting for me to smile and say I was only kidding.

I stepped aside, giving her room to leave.

"I'm sorry." My mother touched Marley's shoulder. "I really have no idea . . ." Both of her braids turned up at the ends, like Pippi Longstocking's. She looked at me and spoke through clenched teeth. "I don't know what has gotten into my daughter."

Marley shrugged, and leaned down to close her horn case. I could see pink splotches on her pale cheeks, the same kind I got when I was trying hard not to cry. I put my hands against my face, my hands cold against my cheeks, my cheeks hot against my hands.

"Honey," my mother said. She was talking to Marley. "You don't have to go." She gave me a hard look. "Or if you want to go, I'll come with you."

Marley shook her head. "I've got to go anyway. I have class." She gave me a look of misery or hatred or maybe both, and ran past me out into the hallway.

When I finally looked up again, my mother had her head tilted away from me. She took a small step back and watched me from the side, birdlike, as if she couldn't bear to look at me full-on. I stalked over to my desk, unzipped my backpack, and started pulling out books.

"What is the matter with you?"

I said nothing. It was a question with too many answers. *Where do I begin? Where, oh where do I begin?* I didn't know what to do with myself. I stacked three pencils in a row. I scooted my chemistry book toward me until it was in line with the edge of my desk. I looked at my watch. It was after one o'clock, and still raining hard. I didn't care. I didn't care about Jimmy.

"Answer me." My mother leaned forward. She was trying to see my eyes. "You have no right to speak to her—to speak to *anyone* like that. Do you understand? Veronica! Are you listening to me?"

She grazed my arm with just her fingertips. When I didn't move, she sat on the foot of my bed.

"Honey?" she said, her voice soft, a little shaky. "Are you . . . are you doing drugs?"

I actually laughed, only for a second, but the pressure caused tears to spill out from under my eyes. I glanced down at her. She wasn't laughing.

"No," I said.

"Then what is it? What in the world would make you act that way? How could you say that about not being her mother, when she just lost hers? What is *wrong* with you?"

I looked up. Lost. For a moment, I really thought that she meant that Marley had lost her mother by leaving home and coming to college. What I'd said still wasn't so bad. My mother was overreacting, looking at me like that.

I shook my head. "I don't . . . What do you . . . ?"

"Her mother just died last spring. Cancer." She turned her palms up, holding them out, as if holding something fragile and round between us. "How do you not know that?"

I looked at the floor, at the bag of M&M's. I looked back at my mother's face. I tried to think what I knew of Marley's mother, what she had told me. She played the piano. She gave lessons out of the house, and she accompanied the church choir. Those details had all made it into my long-term memory somehow. If I had been told she'd also just died of cancer, I would have surely remembered that, too.

"What?" I asked. "Why are you looking at me like that? How was I supposed to know if she didn't tell me?"

But already I understood that I had just outdone myself. Out of all the stupid things I had done since Friday morning—the car, the party, Third Floor Clyde—yelling at Marley was the most shameful, the error I would remember the longest.

My mother crossed her arms. "She told me in about ten minutes. What's the longest you've ever talked to her?"

Bowzer woke and started scratching his chin with his back paw. My entire bed moved with the vibration he made, the mattress rattling in the frame. I wanted to get up and lie down next to him, the way I might have done when he was a puppy and I was a girl. I wanted to press my face into his fur and scratch him behind his ears until he sighed with pleasure and forgot about his aching bones. Even my mother would not ever forgive me, perhaps. She might still love me, but she would not think of me the same. She loved Elise, too, but for different reasons. I had always been the nice one.

"Isn't it your job to look out for the freshmen on your floor? Veronica, that girl is just dying of loneliness. Don't tell me you can't see it."

I closed my eyes. "Mom. If you had any idea how much stress I'm under . . . You were just telling me that I need to focus on my schoolwork . . ."

She waved her hand. "Don't give me that. You took this job. You signed on for it, and it's important. If you're not going to do it right, you shouldn't do it at all." She started to say more, and then stopped. She looked at me, frowned, and started again. "You're doing all this studying so you can be a doctor? You know, doctors have to deal with people, Veronica. And I'm pretty sure the stress doesn't stop in school. Is this how you're going to treat patients? You sure you want to go into a caring field?"

I started crying. I worried she would think it was a ploy, but really, I just couldn't help it. She handed me a tissue. When I looked up to take it, she did not smile.

"I'll talk to Marley tonight," I said. "I'll apologize."

"Okay." Her voice was neutral, her expression blank. She seemed to be waiting for something.

"What?"

"This isn't how you act. This isn't like you. What's going on?"

The landline rang. We both flinched. It rang again, and again, and again.

My mother's gaze moved from the phone to my face. I shook my head. I had no answering machine for the dorm phone. But anyone normal would have given up by now. Nine rings. Ten rings. It was Jimmy. He would let it ring all day.

She looked at the phone. She looked back at me.

"Things have gotten a little crazy," I said.

She leaned forward a little, squinting. The phone was still ringing.

"I've done some pretty stupid things lately. I've gotten myself into a mess."

She nodded. Her eyes moved to the phone. The ringing seemed to be getting louder. I put my hand over my eyes. "It's the guy whose car I wrecked. That was his town house I stayed in. He's mad because I had a party, after I wrecked his car. He wants rides all the time, and he doesn't care that I don't have a car. He wants a ride back from campus right now."

"Oh." My mother cocked her head. "Well. Do you want me to answer?" She did not give me a chance to reply. Her hand moved quickly to the phone.

"Hello?"

Apparently, while waiting in the rain, Jimmy had lost his ability to stay calm. I could hear him through the earpiece, though I was sitting several feet away. Some words were clearer than others: "bitch," "better," "NOW." I watched my mother's eyebrows move up, up, up, her eyes growing wider beneath them. She looked at me. She again appeared to be waiting for something, some critical word from me.

"I don't know," I said. "I don't know what to do anymore."

She rubbed her lips together, looking back at the phone with narrowed eyes. She moved her fingers down one of the braids to the pink ribbon Marley had wrapped around the end. One of her eyebrows lowered, and the other stayed high, deep lines appearing across her forehead. She put her hand on my shoulder. "Yes," she said into the phone. "I think I do understand. As a matter of fact, I do."

I couldn't believe he thought she was me. Her voice was lower. She sounded older, at least to me.

"No problem," she said. "Just wait there. We're on our way."

12

"THIS PERSON HAS MY PHONE? Why does he have my phone?"

We were in the van. Wet dog smell hung heavy in the air, but it was raining too hard to roll down a window. Bowzer rode between my mother and the steering wheel, his front paws resting on her right arm. He was panting, but he held his balance fairly well, gazing out the blurry windshield and occasionally barking at nothing.

"Turn here," I said. "Left." Jimmy had told my mother/me to pick him and Simone up at the Union, where they would be angrily waiting and staying dry. I was to call when we got very, very close to the doors. He hadn't said whether I should call his number or my mother's. I assumed he had both phones with him.

"You must have left it there when you helped me clean," I said, wiping mist off the side window. She was driving carefully, slowly, the pavement slick beneath the tires. But really, any speed at all would have been too fast for me. I wanted to just stop or, even better, turn around. I did not think that what was about to happen would be a good thing. I did not think my mother understood the situation. I did not think she had adequately imagined Jimmy Liff. I knew I should be grateful that she wanted to help me. But I couldn't help but think that between my two parents, my father would be much more helpful in dealing with someone like Jimmy. My mother, well meaning as she was, was just an older, worn down, and temporarily homeless version of me.

"And he's not giving it back?" Her voice was calm, an adult extracting the facts of a story from a wounded child. *He meant to break your pink pony? You're sure it was on purpose? Did you see him do it?* She still had both of the braids in, the ends sticking up from under her hat. Her scarf was still stained with ketchup.

"He keeps saying he doesn't know where it is. He's mad, Mom. He's mad about the car. He's mad about the party. I don't know if you can just ask for your phone back. Honestly, I don't think he'll give it to you. Not until his car is fixed."

She glanced at me, then back at the road. "Why didn't you tell me about any of this? Why didn't you tell me this was going on?"

We sailed past open umbrellas, people running with coats and newspapers over their heads. I waited, saying nothing. I didn't want to hurt her feelings.

She glanced at me again.

"You seemed like you had enough to worry about," I said. "You know what I mean? You sort of have your own problems."

She was quiet. A gust of wind made the rain blow sideways. A plastic garbage can rolled off the curb and into the road. She swerved hard to the left, and then back. Bowzer sighed and moved to her other arm.

"I know," she said. "But I still want to help you with this."

I could see the roof of the Union rising up over the hill. Dread weighed heavy in my chest. "I don't know that you can, Mom. He's kind of a scary guy."

She rolled her eyes. "He's a college kid living by a golf course."

"He deals drugs."

She glanced at me. "How do you know?"

"I don't. Just rumors."

She tapped her fingers on the wheel and glanced at me again.

I clapped both hands over my eyes. "NO! I DO NOT DO DRUGS."

"Lower your voice, please." She looked at me with brief displeasure. "Fine. Well, good. That's something that would scare me." She shrugged. "This guy, he doesn't scare me." Under her breath, she added: "Not at this point."

She did not, in fact, look even a little afraid. She was concentrating on driving, on getting us up the rain-slicked hill without sliding into the car in front of us or the car behind us, Bowzer still perched on her arm. She was wrong not to be scared, I thought. I was afraid of him, and it seemed unlikely that I had only been afraid out of my imagination and worry, the whole dilemma a creation of my own head.

She glanced at me. "What? Does he carry a gun or something?"

"I don't think so."

"Okay. That's good. Is he going to hit me?"

There was laughter in her voice, a happy mocking.

"Mom. Don't laugh. You don't get it."

"Switchblade?" She bulged her eyes. Bowzer was licking her chin. "Nunchucks? No. Wait. A shank? Like in prison movies?"

"It's not funny. He's creepy."

"He likes to swear a lot. I got that. He likes to use the 'f' word on the phone." She held Bowzer steady as she turned the wheel. "Is that supposed to make me afraid of him? His potty mouth?" She shook her head, her lips pursed. "I have absolutely had it with people using that kind of language." We stopped behind a line of cars. "And who's this Simone person? Is that a girlfriend? His moll? What?"

"It's Haylie. Simone is Haylie Butterfield. Remember? I told you she changed her name to Simone? She's Jimmy's girlfriend. And she's evil now."

She pressed Bowzer's head down to better see my face. "Little Haylie Butterfield? The girl you used to play with?" She held the flat of her hand just beneath her shoulder, which I guessed was the approximate height of little Haylie Butterfield when my mother knew her best.

I nodded.

"She was in your Girl Scout troop!"

She appeared stricken. She was driving fine, even with Bowzer still resting on her arm, but her jaw was clenched, her eyes wide. My mother had been our scout troop's leader when Haylie and I were in fourth grade. The meetings were held in our basement, sunlight streaming down from the high windows, though she'd regularly opened up the kitchen to all fifteen of us so we could earn our cooking safety badges. My mother had, of course, performed all her scout leader duties with zest. She supervised cookie sales and first aid classes, and also a visit to a farm that trained Seeing Eye dogs. She taught herself to tie seven kinds of knots so she could teach us. Even so, I would not have thought that she would have taken all those campfire songs, with their rhyming lyrics about loyalty and kindness, so much to heart that years later, Haylie Butterfield's rejection of Scout values would be what finally made her snap.

We were in front of the Union. She eased the van into a delivery zone, right next to the curb. I took out my phone, but I didn't dial.

"Mom," I said, as gently as I could, a swelling moving up in my throat. "I don't want you to have to meet them. You could just wait in the Union with Bowzer while I take them home. I did this, Mom. I'm the one who screwed up. Really. You'll be helping me enough if you just let me borrrow the van."

She appeared to listen to my little speech. But when I finished, she only shook her head. "Everybody makes mistakes," she said. "He's harassing you. It's not okay."

"I just don't think you're in the best shape right now." Again I tried to make my voice gentle. I didn't want to hurt her feelings. "I don't know that you'll be able to help so much, with . . . everything you have going on."

She looked away, blinking quickly. I assumed she was about to cry. But she only took a deep breath, her gaze moving to the windshield, the wipers beating back and forth.

"I disagree," she said. "I think this is actually an excellent time for me to help you. Because you're exactly wrong. I really don't have anything else going on right now. Or nothing important. Nothing good." She glanced down at Bowzer, smoothing her hand across his back. "I know you messed up. And I know you're not blameless. But I don't like anybody talking to you like that."

I nodded slowly, my eyes on hers. She looked at me and shrugged. Her words were worrisome, but something hard in her eyes made me feel a little encouraged.

Jimmy seemed unsure about climbing into the back. My mother had already used the little button by the steering wheel to unlock and open the sliding side door. But he just stood there in the rain, a smaller version of himself in my side-view mirror, his messenger bag flat over his head. He seemed concerned with the amount of stuff in the back, the lamps, the bag of dog food, the cardboard boxes. Haylie peered over his shoulder from several feet back, waiting under the portico to see what he would do before she ventured out into the downpour. Neither one had an umbrella.

"There's room for both of you on that first seat, I think." My mother leaned back between our seats, her mouth in a bright, tight smile. "You might just have to move that afghan. You can put it on the floor. It's okay. I have it there for the dog."

He bent forward, maybe just to see what was underneath the afghan, but Haylie must have taken his movement as a green light. She dashed out into the rain with her arms over her head, her heeled boots skipping over puddles. I heard her push herself past him before she fell into the seat behind my mother. I tucked my hair behind my ear and looked at her over my shoulder. She was wearing the shiny red raincoat, but her hair was wet and plastered against her face. Mascara trailed under each of her eyes. She glared at me and opened her mouth to say something that I imagined would not be nice. But then my mother turned around, too. Haylie's mouth closed, and her eyes widened. A kangaroo might have been sitting in the driver's seat. She looked that uncertain, that surprised.

"Hi!" My mother held Bowzer close to her chest and turned back a little more in her seat. "My goodness! Haylie Butterfield! How long has it been? Oh, and look at your hair, so dark now. Veronica told me you'd changed it."

Haylie nodded, glancing to her right as Jimmy climbed into his seat.

"You remember me, right? Veronica's mom? We all made granola bars in my kitchen?" She tilted Bowzer so he was facing Haylie. "Bowzer was there. You remember Haylie, don't you, Bowz?" She spoke to him kindly, softly. "You were just a puppy then, but you remember her, right?"

I heard grunting behind me. "I can't shut the fucking door! How does it shut? Hello? It's fucking raining!"

"Let go of it, please." My mother sounded like a flight attendant—polite, but confident in her authority. "I've got the control up here." She touched the button by the steering wheel, and the sliding door buzzed to a quiet, pnuematic close.

"It stinks in here."

His knees pressed hard against the back of my seat. I sat still, staring straight ahead. My mother turned around and looked at him.

"What?" He shifted his weight, his knees jabbing higher on my back. "Why are we just sitting here? We're soaked, if you can't tell. Are we going to fucking move?"

My mother did not answer. She continued to look at him. Her expression was difficult to read.

"I'm Veronica's mother," she said finally. "That was actually me you just spoke with on the phone."

Silence. I listened to the rain, my fingers tight around the diagonal strap of my seat belt. But I felt something close to hope. My mother was very nice, and she usually brought out niceness in others. Also, there was just the fact that she was older. He might act differently around her.

Jimmy's knees moved again. "Enchanted, I'm sure. Why are we just sitting here? And Jesus, what the fuck stinks?"

I thought she would make him get out. Once, when Elise and I were young and nagging her from the backseat about something, she'd made us get out and walk. *I've had it!* she'd yelled. *I've had it with the whining! Both of you, get out! Get out now!* We hadn't been far from home, less than a mile, I think; but still, when she pulled over and told us to get out of the van, we hadn't really believed she would do it until we were standing together on the sidewalk, watching the back of the van as she drove away.

But she didn't make Jimmy and Haylie get out. She only turned around and put the van in gear. "Buckle up," she said cheerily. The childproof locks clicked in unison, and we glided away from the curb.

"So, Haylie, how's your mom doing?" My mother glanced briefly over her shoulder.

There was, of course, no answer from the back. I assumed my mother was not trying to be mean. She'd really just forgotten about Haylie's name change. I turned back a little, just enough to see Haylie's face. She wore bright red lipstick that set off her pale cheeks and matched her raincoat. But she was shivering, staring out the window, her arms crossed tight over her chest.

"Who the fuck is Haylie?" Jimmy asked.

She glanced at him, and then at me, and then out the window again. It should have been satisfying, maybe; but the look on her face was so miserable that I only felt embarrassed for seeing it.

"Haylie?" My mother tilted the rearview mirror toward her. "I'm sorry. Did you hear me? I asked how your mom was doing?"

I looked at my mother and shook my head. "It's Simone," I said. "She goes by Simone now."

"Oh. That's right. Sorry. Simone? What's your mom up to these days? I haven't talked to her since . . ." She glanced back over her shoulder, her eyes slightly lowered. "Since she moved. I've been wondering about her. And your little brother. What is he, fourteen now? Where's he going to school?"

"They're fine," Haylie said. Her teeth were chattering.

My mother waited.

Haylie cleared her throat. "He's in Oregon," she said. "He's staying with my aunt."

My mother asked no more questions. She must have understood, as I did, that Haylie's little brother living with relatives implied that Haylie's mother was probably not fine at all. It was just five or so years earlier that Haylie's brother, dressed like a robot, had come to our door for Halloween candy. Haylie's father, pre–embezzlement charge, had stood out on the sidewalk with a video camera. Neither of them could have known, as Haylie and her mother could not have known, how much everything would soon change for them all.

"Again." Jimmy sounded tired, put upon. "Who the fuck is Haylie?"

"Excuse me," my mother said, glancing back at him. "You're going to have to watch your language."

I held my breath. If he got angry enough, trapped in the backseat with the childproof locks and nowhere to go, it seemed likely that I would be the one he lashed out at. He could, theoretically, reach over the seat and thump me on the head, or yank up hard on my seat belt. I wondered if she had considered any of this.

"Thanks for the lesson, Mrs. Old Person. But if I were you, I'd be a little more worried about my selfish bitch of daughter not having respect for other people's things."

We stopped at a light. My mother turned back to look at him again.

"Here," she said quietly, using both hands to lift Bowzer over the gears and into my lap. Maybe she was just tired of driving with the weight on her arm. But I imagined Jimmy was staring hard back at her, and she wanted the dog out of his view.

The light changed. Bowzer fell into me when we rolled forward. I put both arms around him, my right arm under his chin. I would get dog hair on my coat, I knew. And he smelled so bad that I had to take shallow breaths through my mouth. But he was also deaf, oblivious to Jimmy, and I was comforted by his presence, and his long, contented sigh.

"She wrecked your car because of an ice storm." My mother glanced in her rearview mirror. "It happens."

"Uh-huh." I could tell by Jimmy's voice that he was leaning back, farther away. "And trashing my house with a party? That just happens? I see where she gets her morals. Shit's missing, okay? Like three hundred dollars' worth of music. Does that just happen, too?"

My mother glanced at me. I was still sunk down below the headrest, so I felt safe to shake my head a little back and forth.

"You'll probably just have to get over that." She turned onto the main road that would lead us out to the town house. She'd always had a good memory for directions. "You know? Chalk it up to poor judgment from all of you? Life isn't fair, Jimmy. Sometimes you just have to cut your losses and move on."

I held my breath and watched the rain, the puddles in potholes bubbling.

"Wow. That's so Zen of you, Mom." His words were clipped. "Great. Now we know where you stand. How about this—I'll invite some of my friends over to your house. We'll see how you get over it." He leaned forward. I felt the pull of one of his hands on my seat. "I can find out where you live."

She glanced up in the rearview mirror and smiled. "You're going to have your work cut out for you there."

Of course he didn't understand, even with all the furniture and junk in the back.

"Don't be so sure," he said. "I know a lot of people. I know people who know their way around gates and intercoms. I can find out where you live in a day."

She turned another corner and glanced at me, still grinning, her eyes wide, her eyebrows raised. "Okay. Well. When you find out, let me know!" There was a long silence. Unbelievably, stupidly, I laughed.

"Oh. You think this is funny?"

I stopped laughing. My mother squinted at the windshield, her head cocked, as if she were really considering the question. "Not this," she said. "Not this specifically. It's not funny. But other things are."

I sat very still, waiting, trying to remember what I had learned in the self-defense unit in high school gym. If he came after me, reaching around my seat, or if he went after her, I would bury my dorm key in between my fingers and hit him as hard as I could. I would go right for the bolt in his nose, or, more precisely, the tender pink skin all around it. I would put Bowzer on the floor mat, holding him safely between my feet, and use my elbow like a lance.

"This is fucking bullshit. You know what?" His knee dug into the seat again, just behind my spine. "I'm done with this. I tried to be nice, but now I'm done. My car will be ready by Friday. Until then, I'll just call a cab." He leaned forward, looking at me. "And you can pay for it. You. Not me."

"She doesn't have any money." My mother leaned forward and

wiped the mist off the windshield with the back of her glove. She had the defrost on high, but all the talking, and Bowzer's steady panting, had fogged up the windows. "See?" She gestured behind her, to the back of the van. "I don't have any money either. This is a blood from a turnip situation, Jimmy. I don't know if it's fair or not, but that's the way it is."

He yelled some more. He moved around a lot in the backseat. My mother watched him warily in her mirror, as if he were a sack of groceries she worried would overturn. But we were almost there. We were driving alongside the golf course now, rain falling hard on the soggy grass, all the gentle slopes deserted. Haylie rode with her face completely turned to her window. And Bowzer rode calmly on my lap, protected by old ears and senility, blissfully unaware.

We pulled into the driveway. Before the van had even stopped, Jimmy started pulling on the door.

"Let me out," he said. "Let me out of this fucking stinking car."

"Just one moment." My mother turned around. "Don't call my daughter anymore. She can't help you. She doesn't have a car."

He was still trying to force the lock, hitting the door with his hand. I turned halfway around. Haylie remained perfectly still, facing out her side window.

"I'm keeping your phone," he said. "I'm not giving it back."

He sounded pathetic. He sounded like a little boy. Maybe he had the whole time, but I only heard it then. I turned around the rest of the way. "You're going to steal my mother's phone?"

"Just turn the fuck back around," he said. "I don't want to look at your face." He winced as if truly pained. "I can't stand to look at your face. I can't stand people like you. Miss Goody Two Shoes, phony bitch. You go running to Mommy and Daddy anytime there's a problem." He pointed at himself. "I don't know anything about that. I've been on my own since I was fifteen. Completely self-supporting." He thumped his chest. "On my fucking own. Nobody helping me. Nobody."

His hand trembled a little at his chest, and the conviction in his eyes seemed real; but there was something about the way he delivered the speech that seemed like he had delivered it, maybe verbatim, many, many times before. He was stuck in it. I saw it right away. You could get stuck in a speech like that.

My mother took Bowzer from me. I continued to look at Jimmy until he looked away.

"Let me out of this fucking car." He pounded a fist on the window.

My mother clicked open the locks. The door slid open behind me. When Haylie started moving, too, both my mother and I turned around. I don't know what else we thought she might do. She lived in the town house. All her stuff was inside. She didn't look at either one of us before she followed Jimmy out into the rain.

"He still has your phone," I said. I started to open my door, but my mother held my arm and pulled me back.

"Let him have it." She looked over her shoulder before backing out of the driveway. "If it makes him feel better to have it, he can have it. I'll need a new number anyway."

"He could make calls on it," I said. I was feeling grateful and also guilty. I wanted to go back and at least try for the phone. "You could get charged."

"Yeah. I'm so worried about my credit."

I smiled, and then I felt guilty about that. It really wasn't that funny. But she seemed fine, not just about the phone, but about everything, as if she really believed what she'd told Jimmy: sometimes fair just wasn't going to happen; after a while, you had to cut your losses and move on.

She drove with her shoulders back, her chin raised, Bowzer balanced, once again, on her left arm.

"Thanks," I said. "Thanks for your help."

"No problem." She reached over to pat my leg, but she didn't look away from the road.

My conversations that night, with Marley and with Tim, blur together in my memory. It is somewhat surprising, since visually, at least, they were very different experiences. When I spoke with Marley, she stood in her doorway, looking up at me with small, piercing eyes. Tim and I talked in his car, parked just outside the dorm; even sitting, I had to look up at him, the top of his head almost grazing the roof. And he was smiling, happy to see me, at first.

In both cases, my apologies were not accepted. In both cases, I tried to explain myself, and failed. But neither one yelled or got angry. They weren't like Jimmy, bent on making me pay. They just wanted to retreat, to get and stay away from me. And really, that felt worse.

I had meant to talk to Tim in my room. But my mother was taking a nap, stretched out on the guest bed with Bowzer at her side, her hat rolled down over her eyes. "Just a catnap," she'd mumbled, before drifting off, the window still gold with afternoon light. Two hours later, she was still asleep, and I went down to the lobby to wait for Tim.

I told him everything at once: what I'd done, how much I wished I hadn't; how much I already missed him; and how I had just been scared about moving in. He didn't say anything. He put his hands on the wheel, hugging it toward him a little. We peered at each other under the orange glow of a parking lot light, our expressions remarkably similar, eyebrows lowered, lips pursed. I told him I still wanted to be with him. I told him I was still having a hard time with my parents' divorce. I maybe went on a little too long, until finally, he interrupted me and told me, in the nicest way possible, that what he wanted was for me to get out of the car.

And so I did. His reaction was what I'd expected, in my head at least. It was what I deserved.

But I thought things might go better with Marley. I didn't want to take advantage of her loneliness, but I assumed it would work in my favor. Even after she started to close her door on me, I asked her if she wanted to go to dinner. She said she'd eaten. I have to admit, I was surprised. Up until she actually closed the door in my face, it seemed impossible that even Marley might decide that she didn't need me around after all.

13

NATALIE WOKE IN DARKNESS, forgetting, for a moment, where she was. Her knit hat was still rolled down over her eyes, and even after she pulled it off, she couldn't see. Out of habit, she moved to her left; in her apartment, she'd always slept far to the left on her queen bed, even after a year of sleeping alone. But now, trying to rise, she bumped her forehead on the cool, cement wall of her daughter's dorm room. She lay back down. Bowzer, lying beside her, sighed from deep in his throat.

"You're okay, boy." She reached over to rub the fur behind his ears. Even the back of his head felt thin. But he rolled toward her, hind legs kicking. She smiled. He still got some pleasure out of being alive. When he didn't, she would take him in. She would.

She got up, this time on the right side, and groped her way across the room to turn on the overhead light. She didn't know where Veronica was. Her books and backpack sat on her desk. Her coat was on the hook. There was no note saying where she had gone or when she might be back. Of course, she didn't need to leave a note for her mother. Veronica was an adult; she could come and go as she pleased.

Natalie cracked open the door, and peeked out in both directions. She hoped Veronica was down the hall, talking with Marley. Earlier, she'd wanted to remind her to do it, but she'd stopped herself. She could still get away with reminding her daughter to take care of her teeth and to sit up straight, but regarding the big things, it seemed to her, the die was already cast.

She closed the door and turned, looking around the room. She was pretty sure Veronica would go talk to Marley. Despite what the incredibly unpleasant Jimmy had said, she did not think her younger daughter was selfish or thoughtless, at least not characteristically so. She'd been careless lately. She'd shown some poor judgment. But she had always been sensitive to other people's feelings. Elise was, too, under all that bluster, but between the two of them, Natalie thought of Veronica as having the softer heart. She was maybe four the day they were stopped at a railroad crossing, watching a coal train roll past, just the two of them in the old station wagon. For years, they'd spent their days together; Dan was at work, and Elise was in grade school. On the day she and Veronica were stopped for the train, Natalie had just read an article in a parenting magazine that advised her to seize educational moments, so she turned around to explain to Veronica what coal was, what it was used for, and where it came from. Veronica listened patiently in her booster seat, little legs dangling, brown eyes thoughtfully watching the train roll by, until Natalie got to the part about dinosaurs.

And then there were tears. Veronica raised her arms to her mother, like some pleading, painted saint in a Little Mermaid T-shirt. "Why did they all die? Even the moms? Even the kids? Did it hurt?"

Natalie almost laughed, but caught herself: the anguish on her daughter's face was real. As the train thundered by, she did her best to convince Veronica that extinction, when it came to dinosaurs, wasn't that sad. For one, she pointed out, dinosaurs weren't that nice. They sometimes ate each other! They had sharp teeth and claws! More importantly, if they hadn't all died, they would probably be eating people, if people were even around. She tried to keep her voice cheerful, upbeat.

"They had to make room for us, honey, for everything new. And now we have coal! And oil, honey! It makes the car go!"

Even after the train had passed, and their own car was once again moving forward on the energy of dead dinosaurs, Veronica was inconsolable.

Natalie sat on the guest bed, looking up at the baby blue walls. It was possible, of course, that four-year-olds in general were sensitive, not Veronica in particular. She might be a very different adult. Her dorm room was distressingly bare. Only a science poster hung on one of the walls. There was a calendar pinned to the bulletin board, next to a picture of the tall boyfriend standing on his head. The shelves held only books and notebooks and folders. Natalie shook her head. She would not snoop. She was a guest in this room. She was a guest before she was a mother.

Even when Veronica was still living at home, Natalie had only allowed herself the most benign sort of detective work: she would borrow her daughter's novels, partly because she wanted to read them, but also so she could see what lines Veronica had underlined. When Natalie sat down to read a book, she just read it. She didn't use a pen. But Veronica's copy of *Sense and Sensibility* had had something underlined on almost every page. Natalie paid close attention, searching for significance: *Elinor was to be the comforter of others in her own distress, no less than in theirs.* It was distressing. Did Veronica think of herself like this? Did she think she had to comfort everyone? Did she think she had to comfort . . . her mother? Natalie worried. Those years after her own mother had died, and Dan's mother was still dying, she had maybe leaned on her daughter too much. And what was Veronica's own distress? Did she have some secret distress her mother didn't even know about? Other underlined passages perplexed her: *and yet there is something so amiable in the prejudices of a young mind, that one is sorry to see them give way to the reception of more general opinions.*

What did that mean? It sounded cynical. What amiable prejudices of her daughter's had already given way?

When Natalie tried to ever-so-casually ask about these lines, Veronica had only shrugged and said she thought they were interesting. Still, alone in the dorm room, Natalie eyed the shelves and stood up from the bed. There were mostly science texts now, but there were a few novels.

When the door opened fast, she jumped.

Veronica stood in the doorway. Her face was pale, her eyes mournful.

"Sorry," she said. "I should have knocked." Her eyes were level with her mother's, and her hair was long enough, even curly again, damp with rain, to reach the shoulders of her green sweater; still, Natalie could clearly see the child in her, especially now with the shiny eyes. Her face hadn't changed that much.

"Don't be silly. It's your room. Honey? You've been outside? Without a coat?"

"I was in a car," she said. "I just ran out to a car to talk with . . . someone."

The boyfriend, Natalie assumed. Tom. Tim. She couldn't remember. There was no excuse. If she said the name wrong now, she was finished. The next time Veronica said his name, Natalie would write it down, keep it in her purse, commit it to memory forever. As soon as her own life calmed down a little, she would pay attention to the details of her daughter's.

"Honey? Are you okay?"

"I'm fine." Veronica turned away and let her dark hair fall forward. "But I need a little time by myself." She leaned against her dresser, her back still turned. "In here," she added gently.

"Oh yes. Yes. Of course." Natalie moved in a quick circle, searching for her coat. She had never before been the kind of mother who accepted the first "I'm fine" from one of her daughters. She had been the kind who softly prodded for more information. In her experience, if you poked enough, they would tell, because really, they wanted to tell. But now, although Veronica clearly wasn't fine, Natalie had no choice but to retreat at the first request. That was the problem, or the main problem, with being both a mother and a charity case. It was Veronica's room. If she wanted her to leave, Natalie had to go.

She stopped turning. Her coat was in her daughter's closet, where the robe was supposed to hang. She opened the door and pulled it out quickly. "I'll step out and run some errands," she said, which was stupid. What errands could she run? It was after seven, and she was a woman without a refrigerator. She pulled on her hat, avoiding her daughter's eyes. Had Jimmy called again? Or was it something with the boyfriend? Was the boyfriend mean to her? Maybe the talk with Marley hadn't gone well.

Bowzer, sensing her imminent departure, whimpered and tried to rise. One of his legs gave way, and he fell back on the bed. He groaned and tried to get back up. He couldn't be without her at all anymore. It was like having a small child again.

"No. Stay." She held her palm up to him in hopes he wouldn't pain himself further. She looked at Veronica. "He can stay here with you?"

Veronica walked across the room to the bed and sat next to him. Her green sweater was nice, and made out of some soft material that looked like it might love dog hair. But she put both arms around the dog and eased him to her lap.

"You don't want to talk at all?" Natalie asked. She couldn't help herself. But she was ready to go, one hand on the doorknob. She just wanted to be sure.

Bowzer strained forward. Veronica only shook her head with a fast and unconvincing smile. "I'm okay," she said.

Call if you need me, Natalie wanted to say, though she couldn't. She didn't have a phone.

She probably should have brought along something to read. She would have to kill time at a coffee shop or a restaurant. It was too cold and dark for walking, and she didn't want to waste gas just driving around. She could try to find the public library. Or she could do what someone productive and virtuous would do in her situation. She could go get the newspaper and search the classifieds for a better job.

She stopped at a machine and got a paper, lifting it out of the box with dread. It was always so dispiriting—seeing adverisements for teaching positions and knowing, as she did now, that although they asked for someone with her degree, she was not what the good schools were looking for. She was too old, too out-of-the-loop, not up on all the new lingo. In the last few years, both before and after the divorce, she'd applied for twenty-eight teaching positions, and she'd gotten two interviews, both at junior highs with metal detectors at the doors and emergency alarms in every room. They were the bottom-rung schools, the ones where the fresh-faced graduates of teaching programs did not apply in droves; and apparently, they were the only schools that would consider hiring a middle-aged woman who had not directed a classroom in over twenty-five years. This realization—that she was, in all her lack of experience, yet another hardship to be thrown at the poorer children of Greater Kansas City—was so upsetting that at the first interview, she came across as sour and depressed; and, no surprise, she didn't get the job.

But at the second interview, she'd really tried. Really, she told the very young and dreadlocked principal, the fundamentals of education hadn't changed that much in a quarter of a century. He'd stared at her skeptically over the tops of wire-framed glasses. Of course they had a little, she was quick to concede, with computers and the new federal laws. She'd kept up with all of that. She read the paper. But *drive* and *caring* and *creativity* were the foundations of good teaching, and she had those traits in spades! She'd used them every day as a stay-at-home mother! No, she didn't speak Spanish. But she'd always wanted to learn!

The principal had furrowed his young brow and smiled politely, so there seemed no option but to keep talking. She said she'd tried to find records and references from her years as a teacher, but she was having some trouble, as the school where she'd worked had been demolished because of asbestos, and the principal was dead. Not of asbestos, she'd added quickly. Just old. And now dead.

She found a franchise diner on one of the main drags, the dorms visible from the parking lot. Her waitress was young, maybe in high school, with a sweet, wispy voice and blue eyes that looked up at the ceiling as she recounted the evening's specials. Natalie felt bad for only ordering a bottomless cup of decaf; she'd waitressed in high school, and she remembered the bad luck of having a beverage-sipper parked at one of her tables for much of the night. But the waitress didn't seem annoyed. Her eyes moved over Natalie's newspaper, at the one job desciption Natalie had already circled with blue pen. She appeared suspiciously sympathetic.

Natalie looked down at the newspaper until the waitress walked away. She didn't want sympathy, not from someone so much younger, not even Veronica's age. It felt too much like revulsion.

She had her pen poised, ready to circle again.

The irony here, perhaps, was that all those years ago, when Natalie herself was a fresh-faced student at the University of New Hampshire, she had only majored in education because it seemed like a practical choice. Her mother, a very practical woman from Maine, had strongly advised it. Teaching jobs were always plentiful, and teachers kept sensible hours. Natalie would be able to keep working after she had children. Also, Natalie liked to read, and she'd always been good with the little ones. Perfect. That Natalie had never really dreamed of teaching was beside the point.

"I'm not asking you to dream about it. I'm just asking you to get licensed." Natalie's mother had a thick Down East accent, full of a wary pragmatism that could make her daughter's musings, when she repeated them, sound dumb. "We both know what part of college you like best. But you can't major in sorority, dear."

She forgave her mother's condescension. Her mother hadn't even gone to college. It was just never an option, not at that time, in that little coastal town, the only income lobsters and tourists. Her mother's brothers went, but she didn't. That was okay at first, because she married Natalie's father. But when Natalie was eight, her father died.

"You want dreams?" her mother asked. "Okay. Dream about being able to support yourself. Believe me. It's a dream you want to take seriously as soon as possible, whether you marry Danny-boy or not."

But the real argument for teaching, in Natalie's mind, was that she didn't have any better ideas. The truth was, she didn't really dream of anything when it came to a real job, something she might have to do every day for the rest of her life. Nothing sounded that great. She liked to read, but she didn't like writing. She liked math until it got too hard. Her favorite courses, no matter what the subject, were always introductory. She hated that about herself, how stupid and shallow it made her sound. But her favorite part of college really was sorority life: She loved the shared meals in front of the big stone fireplace, the charity fund-raisers. She loved the camaraderie, the group projects, and the way everyone came to her for advice.

And she loved Dan. Her mother could call him Danny-boy all she wanted, but he was as smart and funny and warm as Natalie's father, and he looked at her like she was Helen of Troy. She loved the way he looked at her.

"And it doesn't hurt that he's going to make a lot of money," her uncle Pat had added, laughing. Natalie had been so offended. She loved Dan because she loved Dan. She would have loved him if he'd been a barber. She hadn't been that calculating, not at all.

"I believe you," Uncle Pat said with a wink. "But it's a fortunate coincidence, you have to admit." He sat up, coughing, seeing her face. "Oh come on, honey. I'm just playing with you. Don't get mad. Don't be like that."

The fifth time the waitress came by to refill her coffee, Natalie apologized. "I'm sort of camped out here," she said, smiling hard. Minus two quick bathroom breaks, she'd been sitting in the booth for three hours.

"No problem." The waitress was still cheery, though she looked a little young to be up so late. "Bottomless cup means bottomless cup. You can sit here all night if you want."

Oh good, so there was an option! Natalie kept smiling until the waitress walked away. For the cost of just one bottomless cup, she could sleep in this booth! She would stay warm and dry, and have good service. In the morning, she could splurge on pancakes, and wash her face in the bathroom sink. She wondered what the friendly waitress would do if she really lay down and fell asleep right here, her coat balled up under her head. It might be worth it to find out, and less humiliating than crashing in on her daughter again.

She took another sip, staring out the window into the night. It seemed right to lament her decisions, to blame all her wrong choices. She'd worried they were wrong even as she was making them. Most of her sorority sisters had not gotten married right out of school. They went on to graduate school, or law school, or medical school. Or they went traveling. Or they joined the Peace Corps. She remembered the way some of them had looked at her when she told them she was engaged. Yes, she said, she would take his name. Yes, she was moving to Kansas City. They all smiled and said congratulations and admired her ring, but she saw the judgment, even dismissal, in some of their eyes. Or maybe she was just paranoid and feeling unsure of herself.

"I'll get a job there right away," she told them, though no one had been rude enough to ask. "You can get a teaching job anywhere."

For a recent graduate with good grades, that turned out to be true. Natalie didn't have any trouble finding a job, even after she moved to Kansas City, or, as the editor of her sorority newsletter had put it:

even after she *followed her new husband to Kansas City.* In 1981! One of her "sisters" wrote that! And made her sound like a puppy, just because she wasn't going to law school, just because she didn't hyphenate her name, just because she didn't submit a picture of herself wearing a blazer with huge shoulder pads and one of those blouses with those stupid bow ties. She hadn't *followed* Dan. Was she not supposed to marry the person she loved because he was moving? Kansas City was where the law firm was. Someone had to give. Someone had to be flexible. And because the person she happened to love would be making approximately five times as much money as she would be making, it seemed reasonable and right that the flexibility might be required of her.

Natalie's mother didn't see the problem. "Please," she said. "Your cousins were in day care from day one, and they all turned out to be decent people. And I know plenty of kids who stayed home with moms who turned out to be wingnuts you'd never want in your house. And no, honey, I am not talking about you."

Dan's mother, however, wasn't as convinced that putting the beautiful baby Elise in day care so early was a good idea. She flew in from New York for the birth, and she stayed for several weeks. When she first saw the breast pump lying in wait in the nursery, she eyed it with suspicion.

"You're going to so much trouble?" she said, or maybe asked. Leni Von Holten was a short, apple-shaped woman who inflected her voice at the end of every sentence, question or not, so Natalie was never certain if she needed to respond. "You're pumping the milk? It can't be comfortable? So you can go to a job that you don't need, that you don't even like so much? Dan makes enough money to support you both? You really want to spend your days taking care of other people's children while someone else takes care of yours? This beautiful girl? This perfect little breadloaf who will only be a baby once?"

Natalie had careful, practiced responses to all her mother-in-law's questions: she explained that she did enjoy teaching; she shouldn't have complained so much the previous year, which had been particularly difficult, with more emotionally disturbed children than usual and a few particularly abrasive parents. Next year would be better. Really, she was looking forward to getting back to work. She'd found the best child care available, and she was sure that Elise would be fine.

But even as she said these words, her voice full of conviction, she felt herself wavering inside. Dan *did* make enough money for her not to have to work. Her paltry teaching salary hardly mattered—and next year, much of it would go toward covering child care so she could work. Her life would be a snake, swallowing its own tail. She would make herself miserable out of principle.

Still, in the fall, she went back to work, just as planned. The first time she dropped a wailing Elise off at day care, she steeled herself and tried to think what her mother would say—*You're doing the right thing! You're being an excellent role model! She'll be fine!* and not what her mother-in-law would say—*What are you, crazy?*

By early November, she had started to think that her mother-in-law might be right. She felt crazy. She was exhausted. Elise rotated through illnesses: colds, pinkeye, bronchitis, pneumonia, the flu. The day care director said it was typical, with her being around so many other children. Natalie used up all her sick days and family days for the entire year before Thanksgiving. Even Dan took a day off, in the middle of trial, but he couldn't pull that more than once.

When she wanted to complain about how tired she was, she called Dan's mother, and not her own; even as she dialed, she knew what this meant, which direction she was already leaning.

"I *wish* I could have stayed home with my babies," Leni said, and this time, her voice did not rise up at the end, and there was no hint at all of a question. "I never had the option. I had to work. We couldn't have paid someone to help at the store. But if I could have stayed home with my boys, of course I would have." She had to set down the phone for a moment—Dan's father was already shaky on his legs and needed her help to get down the stairs. When she got back on the phone, her voice was curt.

"Natalie, honey. I have to go. And I love you. You're already a daughter to me. But I have to ask you, why are you doing this? You know? Why make a good life hard?"

Right after the divorce, when Natalie didn't yet understand just how poor she would turn out to be, she'd paid fifty dollars to go to something called a Career Empowerment Seminar. For her money, she'd gotten lunch, including a salad and dessert, a laminated list of empowering mantras, and hours of advice that pretty much boiled down to the speaker's favorite phrase: *Do what you love, and the money will come.*

The other women in the audience seemed encouraged. Natalie seemed to be the only one who knew the formula wasn't universally true.

All those years, when the girls were little, she had been doing what she loved. She had mothered with passion. She had comforted and dressed and bathed and taught her young daughters every day of the week, because she believed she could do it with more caring than anyone else in the world. And she had loved it all, or at least most of it—the hikes to the park, the winter days inside, the making of snowmen and sock puppets. When the girls had field days in grade school, she volunteered to help hand out water balloons or retrieve Frisbees, and her own girls always seemed so happy to see her there at school that she felt sorry for other kids whose parents couldn't make it—they either didn't want to be there or they couldn't be there. She felt lucky that neither was true for her. In that way, in many ways, her mother-in-law had been right.

And later, there were the days she spent with Leni, and also her own mother, during the years when they both needed help. Natalie wouldn't say she loved those days the way she had loved the days with her children, but again, she was grateful that she got to be there. No one else would have looked after those two old women as carefully. The workers at the homes did the heavy lifting, and she was grateful for that as well, but she got to sit at her mother's side for two weeks straight at the very end. You couldn't hire someone to do that. And she was with Leni at the end, too, which was good, because who could they have hired to keep vigil so many days in a row, and to care enough to go find the nurse and remind her that Mrs. Von Holten really did need more morphine, PLEASE, now?

If that wasn't passion, what was?

And yet, look where she was now.

It was hard to know what Leni, if she weren't dead, might say if she could see Natalie parked in this booth with the decaf and the classifieds. She might have some sympathy. During the last years of her life, she was closer to Natalie than she was to her own son. And she seemed to sense that something was wrong. Her dementia varied from day to day, and sometimes she would ask, over and over, if Natalie was happy, if Dan was a good husband, if the marriage was still strong.

"Yes," Natalie would answer, because why distress the old woman further? And why distress herself? Was she happy? Generally, yes. She was comfortable. Was Dan a good husband? In a manner of speaking. It depended on what standard you used. Was the marriage still strong? Yes. In fact, it felt like a train rolling along a slight decline. It required little energy. It just kept going. Something would have to happen to make it stop.

And then one day, in the middle of that aching year after her own mother died, she came home from the grocery store and asked Dan if he thought of her as a separate and complete human being. She wasn't sure what made her do this—what, exactly, set her off. Her mother's death had left her restless, ready to say things as soon as she thought them. And on the drive home from the grocery store that day, it occurred to Natalie that Dan didn't really listen to her when she talked. He liked to talk to her about his work—the funny thing a client had said, the arrogance of some judge. He was a good story-teller, and she was a polite and interested listener, so this was how most of their conversations worked. But when she tried to talk, and tell him about her day—about her conversations with repairmen and dry cleaners and nursing home attendants—she couldn't keep his attention. His gaze wandered. He would start reading something, anything—the back of a cereal box on the table, old text messages on his phone. If she called him on it, he would apologize. And then he would do it again.

When her mother was dying, she'd noticed all this, but she'd been too preoccupied to really think about it. And then her mother died, and she had some time to think about it, and it started to really bug her. On that particular morning, coming home from the store, she was thinking about it. When she got home, Dan was right there, coming out to help her with the bags. Veronica was at a friend's house and thus unable to overhear. And so she asked.

"What?" He had on an undershirt and sweatpants, and the bifocals he needed when he read. He squinted at her over them, as if he were having trouble seeing her, though she stood only a couple of feet away. She held a paper grocery bag in one arm. Her purse was still slung over the other.

"Do you think I'm interesting?" She switched the bag of groceries to her other arm. She focused on keeping her voice neutral, no judgment at all. She wasn't trying to pick a fight. She really just wanted to know. "Also, when you think of me, when you picture me in your head, do you see me as a separate entity? Or do you only see me in relation to you?"

He took off his glasses and rubbed the bridge of his nose. And he said absolutely nothing. It was, in twenty-six years of marriage, the only time she'd caught him speechless, too stumped even to nod or shake his head.

"I'll get the rest of the groceries," he said, as if that were the question she'd asked. "Don't let the dog follow me out." He walked past her, out into the garage. She stood where she was, still holding a bag of groceries, a stalk of celery just under her nose. When he came back in, holding four bags, two in each arm, he made a big production out of having to walk around her to the counter. Bowzer hurried behind him, head raised, sniffing the air.

"What?" he asked. He looked at her only briefly before he set the bags on the counter. He took a box of ice cream out of a bag, holding it up in front of his glasses, checking the ingredients perhaps.

"I asked you a question." Her voice was quiet, no threat at all in it. But she held the bag of groceries like a shield in front of her, ready and waiting. His reluctance seemed a bad sign.

He bent down to pet the dog. When he looked up at her again, he sighed. He stood and leaned on the counter, one hand on his hip, and just then, he looked so much like his mother. It was more than just the shape of his face, the wide forehead, the thin lips. It was his eyes, his expression. Just that morning, when Natalie had walked into Leni's room at the nursing home, she had given her that exact same look—disoriented and a little frightened, fighting to understand.

She wanted to simplify it for him. She was ready to spoon-feed it to him, in fact. "Dan," she asked, still calm, neutral. "Do you think I'm smart and interesting?"

He seemed nervous.

She looked away and laughed.

"Sure," he said.

She looked back at him. "Sure what?"

"Sure you are." He rolled one hand in circles away from his chest. "And of course you're a separate person."

"Do you still love me?"

He didn't have trouble with this one. He nodded thoughtfully, his bottom lip sticking out. It was the expression of someone who had just been asked if a certain meal at a restaurant was any good.

He saw the way she was looking at him. He rolled his eyes. "We've been married a long time," he said, shrugging a little, as if this were something she, too, might shrug off as well. "Oh Nat," he said, his annoyance now tempered by pity. "What do you want from me?"

She explained it as best she could. She put the bag of groceries down on the counter so she could use her hands. She wanted her life to mean something. There had to be something it was about. Veronica would be leaving for college soon, and then it would be just the two of them, and if he didn't love her anymore, what did she have?

"I didn't say I didn't love you," he countered.

She shook her head, though she understood what he meant. Of course you could love someone without being in love. You could settle into comfort, into friendship, even routine. Of course that happened in marriage over time. She would have been able to accept all that, if that was really what was happening between them. But she was suspicious of the way he had phrased his last claim: *I didn't say I didn't love you.* He was avoiding saying that he did. Something else was going on here. This was not comfort or friendship or routine.

And yet he was trying to convince her. She couldn't think. She had to sit down. She walked into the dining room, leaned on the table, and sank into the closest chair—Elise's, when she was home.

"Honey," he said. He followed her halfway, leaning against the frame of the dining room's entry. "Come on. Can I get you something to drink? Do you want some tea?"

She shook her head. Bowzer's cold nose nuzzled against her limp hand. He circled twice beside her chair before he lay down, his head resting on her feet.

"We have a good family," he said. "You're a wonderful mother. And you're being so good to my mother. I can't tell you how much I appreciate all you do for her."

She shook her head. She wanted him to stop talking. "We should get a divorce," she said.

"What?" He had a double chin when he pulled his head back. And still, *still,* even now, even in this horrible moment, she still could love him if only he would try to say the right thing. He looked at her over the bifocals. "What are you talking about? Why do you want a divorce?"

"Because you may love me, but you don't find me interesting. And you don't think I'm smart enough to notice."

He started immediate damage control. He hurried over to the table. He sat down next to her and tried to hold her hand. She wouldn't let him.

"Oh come on," he said, as if she were being petulant, a child making a fuss. He sat up and tapped his forehead with his finger. "You know what? This is silly. I *am* in love with you, Nat. Of course I am."

She moved her hand across her face. It came back wet. She was crying. She hadn't even known.

He shook his head, resolute. "I don't want to get a divorce."

"Why not?"

He laughed—just briefly—a short, hard exhale through a smile of disbelief. It was as if she had asked the stupidest question in the world. When her face didn't move, when she didn't even blink, he realized he had to say something. And that's when she understood. Because he hesitated, and because he seemed so certain, and because she understood him well, she knew, she *knew,* that he was thinking about money.

"What about the girls?" He tried to take her hand again. "You want to do that to them?"

She jerked her hand away. He'd gone right for her weakness. Of course he had. He knew what he was doing. But after Veronica left for school, it would be just the two of them in the house. And what did it matter to him if they were more or less roommates? He had his work. He'd always had his work. She'd had the girls. Next year, he would still have his work, and she would have nothing.

"They'll come home for holidays," he said. "What? You want them to have to go to different houses? Thanksgiving with me? Christmas with you? You want that for them?"

She shook her head, looking away. She knew she was crying now.

"I am dedicated to the marriage," he said, and the way he said it surprised her so much that she turned back to look at him. He was sitting up straight, his face solemn. "I have never been unfaithful. I will never be unfaithful." He sounded very tired, as if recalling years of great sacrifice. "And I love our family. I love the girls. We have a comfortable home. If we just stay steady now," he made his hands into blades and pointed them down the length of the table, "we can get through this bad time and still have a decent retirement."

It took her a moment to understand that when he said "this bad time," he meant the way they were stretched financially from Elise's wedding and tuitions and the nursing homes and the falling stocks, and not "this bad time" in their marriage, which apparently, for him, didn't seem all that bad.

And then, a moment later, she did a curious thing—she pretended, even to herself, that she had not understood this at all. She pretended that she had heard a promise of improvement, of a future full of conversations in which he actually looked at her when she was talking and seemed interested in what she had to say. She pretended all of this because then it did not seem so strange for them both to get up and put the rest of the groceries away, and for him to go to work on his laptop, and for her to take Bowzer for a walk. Because really, what else was she going to do?

She had to be pragmatic.

The next time she went to the grocery store, she found herself gazing at the tabloids in the checkout line; she felt superior only for a moment. Celebrities got divorced and remarried all the time, she realized, not necessarily because they were shallow, or fickle, or quick to throw in the towel.

They got divorced because they could afford it.

Who knows how long she might have gone on like that if it hadn't been for Greg Liddiard? An entire year passed between the morning of that grim conversation with Dan and the day work commenced on the roof. And for a week after that, Greg Liddiard and another man had sawed and hammered and thrown down shingles without much attention from her. It was summer, so she wasn't subbing, and she hadn't gotten many hours at DeBeck's. So she was mostly at the house, paying bills, working in the garden. She went through the girls' old clothes to see what she could donate. She played a Neil Young CD one afternoon, and later, when she was going out to check the mail, the older, shorter of the two roofers, the one who would turn out to be Greg Liddiard, called down to thank her for the music, saying he could hear it up on the roof and that he liked her taste; but she'd only nodded and smiled. She wasn't looking for trouble.

The next day, both men said they needed to come in to check the buttresses in the attic, and to get there, they'd had to walk by the bookcase at the end of the hall. The other man walked right past it to the narrow stairs Natalie had just pulled down, but Greg Liddiard stopped to ask her about the books. He'd been a lit major in college, he said. He had a master's even. He'd done a thesis on Nabokov. Did she like Nabokov? She was wearing one of her tank tops from Strength Camp, and as she looked at him while he was looking at her, she was suddenly aware of her bare arms. He had a friendly face. And he listened when she talked.

Really, this was all it took. Greg Liddiard could have said anything about poetry. He could have been an idiot, though he was not. She was that starved for interaction, for real eye contact, even. She was standing by the window at the end of the hall, the afternoon sun shining so hard that her skin felt hot and she had to move away from it. Later, after he moved past her, when she turned and looked up at the sky, she saw that it was a cloudy day.

It was just one indiscretion, and never even fully realized. But as Dan liked to say, she had made her bed, and she could lie in it. Or sit in a booth at a diner, with all her worldly possessions packed in her minivan.

She supposed she should regret that first moment in the hallway with Greg, that first time she let herself look back at him, right into his pale, attentive eyes. But really, even now, she didn't. He was in Alaska now, married, a new father, and not the great love of her life. But if he hadn't come along, she might have still been living with Dan, going to sleep with her eyes and ears covered so she wouldn't hear the television after he finally came to bed. It was a more comfortable life than the one she had now, but she wouldn't pretend it was preferable.

This is what she would tell her daughters, both of them, if they would let her. But Elise got angry when she talked about Greg. Veronica clapped her hands over her ears. She understood—they thought she meant to talk about sex; and yes, of course, that was private, and nothing they wanted to associate with their mother. But so much that was private could be helpful, instructional, and what she wished she could tell them was that what happened with Greg had little to do with sex and more to do with bravery. Even before she met him, she had grown tired of living cautiously. She wished she could tell them that as scared as she was now, she didn't regret what she'd done. Passion wasn't always rewarded. And yet that wasn't the point.

Of course, neither of her daughters—the lawyer or the future doctor—was asking for any advice or wisdom from her at the moment. Just the night before, when she had come to Veronica's door, when she'd had to tell her daughter she had nowhere else to go, Veronica had looked at her with a mix of sympathy and horror, and it had made Natalie want to run back out into the night, into the cold, to the van. She wanted her daughter to feel sorry for Marley; that was fine. She didn't want her to feel sorry for her. She wanted to be someone her children could admire.

She thought she still could be. She felt sure of it for a while that morning, after she helped Veronica, after they'd gotten Jimmy out of the van; and she wanted to hang onto that idea that she could give each of her daughters something now, even after she had failed, even while she was falling. She did have something to give them. Because she knew she could get back up.

It was almost midnight when she closed the newspaper and stood to put on her coat. She'd only circled two ads, but she'd read the rest of the paper, cover to cover, except for Sports. She took just the Classified section and left the waitress five dollars. On her way out, the waitress waved and thanked her. Natalie, lifting her head, thanked her back.

14

I KNEW, EVEN AS I TOOK the test, that I was failing it. *List below the hydroxybutanol structures that have R configurations.* I'm not sure why I made myself stay the entire hour and a half. *What spinning pattern in the H-nmr spectrum would you expect for H atoms colored green in the structures below?* I probably could have walked out in the first fifteen minutes and gotten the same grade.

But I worked as well as I could through each question, calm and unhurried. Deep down, I had already accepted what was true. Two out of three wouldn't make it to medical school, and I would be one of the two. But for that last hour and a half, I did my best, right up until the TA cleared her throat. Apparently, even though I wanted things to change, I still needed to be pushed from the ledge. I wasn't ready to jump.

But the results would be the same. I put on my coat, handed in the test, and walked out into the cold morning. The sky was a bright, cloudless blue and the bells of the campanile were chiming. Across the street, two men on ladders used ropes to lift a giant Christmas wreath over the front doors of Strong Hall. The men did not speak to each other, but their movements seemed coordinated; the wreath slowly rose, perfectly centered. I found a bench and sat down to watch. I could do things like this now. It was over. There was nothing to cram for, no deadline looming over me. I didn't have anywhere I needed to be.

And so the ache in my chest returned. During the exam, and only during the exam, I had been free of the heavy sadness that I'd gone to bed with the night before. Now, again, I had nothing to distract me. The bench was concrete, and the longer I sat there, the colder I felt. But I didn't get up. The wreath turned blurry in my eyes, and I pulled my hat down low on my head.

"So how'd it go?"

I looked up. Tim stood in front of me, no coat, just the same sweater he'd been wearing the night before, his hands in the front pockets of his jeans. I started to smile, but the expression on his face stopped me. His dark hair was combed, his chin cleanly shaved, but I could tell, just looking at his eyes, that he hadn't slept.

"I was at the library." He nodded behind him. "I saw you over here. I just thought I'd come over and see how it went. The test, I mean."

I shook my head. I hated that I was the reason he looked so tired and sad. If I reached out, or even tried to go near him, he would stop me—I could tell. But he kept looking at me, waiting. He really did want to know about the test.

"I failed it," I said.

He shook his head. "I'm sure it wasn't as—"

"No. I did. I really did. But I'm fine with it. I don't care." I looked at the sidewalk by his feet and focused on not crying. If I did, he would feel sorry for me, and that wasn't right. I tried to pretend I was yawning.

He shifted his weight and crossed his arms. He gestured for me to scoot over. He sat on the bench, as far away from me as possible, and started rooting around in his book bag. He took out a calculator, another calculator, a book titled *Thermofluid Systems,* a can of Coke, the

Sports section from some newspaper, and an orange. "I thought I might have some Kleenex," he said. "I had that cold a couple of weeks ago."

I smiled, wiping my cheeks with the back of my mitten. "Thanks for checking," I said. I looked away from him, out across the street. The wreath was up above the doors now. The workmen stood below, looking up, one of them pointing at the red bow.

"If you didn't want to move in with me, you could have said so." Tim looked at me out of the corner of his eye. "If that really was the problem."

I nodded, still looking at the wreath. This time last year, my parents were married. I was getting ready to go home for Winter Break. The Roofer was maybe already on the scene, but I didn't know it yet. On Christmas Day, my family opened presents in the morning, and we ate turkey at the dining room table, and then we walked to Mr. Wansing's for the neighborhood pie party, just like we did every year. When we were little, it was the Wansings, the husband and the wife. Mrs. Wansing died when I was in third grade, but I have a clear memory of her carefully getting down on her knees to look me in the eye and ask, very seriously, if I wanted pumpkin or pecan. After she died, my mother hadn't thought that Mr. Wansing would keep inviting everyone over. He did, though. He bought pies at the store, and they weren't as good as the ones that she had baked, but everything else was the same. He set out polished silverware and whipped toppings the exact way that she had done. He also put a framed picture of her on the big table where all the pies were, so it seemed like she was gazing out over them, smiling at their familiar guests.

And just last year, we had all gone: my mother and my father, Elise and Charlie, and me. I hadn't thought much about it. I hadn't known it would be the last year, how much everything was about to change.

Tim rested his elbows on his knees. Even with his knees bent, his long legs stuck out far from the bench. A man walked by, and he pulled them in. "I was just asking," he said. "I wanted to help you. You hate your job, right? I was trying to help."

"I know," I said.

He rolled his eyes. "Okay. That's not completely true. I wanted you to move in. For me."

"But you wanted to help me, too. I know you did."

He gave me a long, appraising look. His gaze moved from one of my eyes to the other, and his mouth did something close to a smile. "I forget you're younger." He looked unhappy again. "It makes a difference, I guess."

I nodded. Despite popular belief, it wasn't always so great to be both young and in love. And yet, even at that moment, I had to sit on my hands to keep them from going to him. It felt like a physical pull.

We sat on the bench for a while, not speaking. Someone walked up and gave each of us a flyer for a garage sale.

He rubbed his eyes and looked up at me. "So what do you want, Veronica? You want to date around? You want to see other guys and then get back together? I'm not going to do that. I can tell you that right now."

"No. That's not what I want."

"Then what? Do you know?" He pointed at himself. "Because I do." The tops of his ears were pink, maybe from the cold, maybe not. He squinted up at the sky. "Eventually . . . I want what my parents have. That's not a terrible thing. They're pretty happy. Okay? I know you're cynical right now. But sometimes it all works out. You would know that if you'd ever met them."

This was probably true. Two stories about Tim's parents stood out in my mind. The first was that before Tim's eldest brother was born, his mother had been in a car accident that burned her left arm and some of her neck so badly that she was in the hospital for months, and Tim's father had stayed with her every moment that he could, reading to her or just sitting there with her so she would know she wasn't alone. The second story was that just last year, the two of them had been asked to leave a movie theater because they were laughing too much at a movie that wasn't supposed to be funny.

"I wish I'd met them," I said, only because it was true. He turned and looked at me, mad.

"Why?" he asked. "What's the point? Just curiosity?"

I shook my head, as if that were a reasonable answer. He waited.

"I want . . ." I rubbed my eyes, trying to think. "I want to be with you, but . . ." But what? I didn't have the word for it. It was the feeling of being in the semi, all those exits rolling by. "It would be so easy to move in with you. It's what I want. But it might not be good for me." Even as I said this, I heard how cold the words sounded, and I hoped he would hear in my voice that I didn't mean them coldly at all. "I meant everything I said last night. It was just a dumb thing I did. I still want to be with you." I reached across the bench and tugged on the sleeve of his sweater. I let my hand rest there on his sleeve, and he didn't pull away for a while.

But eventually, he did. He was quiet as he packed his things back into his bag. When he finally started to speak, I thought I was going to get an answer one way or the other. But he only looked up at the blue sky and said that the weather was supposed to turn again and that it might snow. I closed my eyes.

"Look," he said, standing up. "I don't know what I think. I need some time."

I opened my eyes, surprised. He must have seen it, because he shook his head. "I don't know," he said firmly. "I don't know what I'm going to do yet."

I nodded somberly. I understood what he meant. But I was still hopeful. Really, the fact that he was just thinking it over was as good an assurance as any. When did anyone ever really know what they were going to do? People who had been married for decades broke promises to themselves and to each other, good intentions or not. That was the way it was with love. You had to have a contingency plan, or be ready to come up with one quickly. No matter what he decided this week, he could, at any time in the future, change his mind.

When I got back to the dorm, I opened the door to my room to find my mother sitting next to Bowzer on the floor, or rather, on news-papers spread flat all over my floor, with a large bucket of sand in front of her. A dark-haired girl in a pink hoodie sat on her right. Gretchen sat on my mother's left. Three other girls who looked vaguely familiar completed the circle around the bucket. Everyone was taking turns scooping out handfuls of sand and dropping them into small paper bags.

Bowzer noticed me first. He wiggled the stump of his tail and struggled to his feet. A little pee dribbled out of him, forming a puddle on the linoleum.

My mother looked up. "Oh, hey, honey. How was the test?" She followed my eyes to Bowzer. "Whoops," she said, standing up. "I'll get that. It's just a little. I've got wipes in my purse."

"Hey, Veronica." Gretchen waved. She looked comfortable, re-laxed, as if she had been sitting there for a while. She had also taken the chemistry test that morning. We had caught the same bus and walked into the exam room together. But, of course, she had finished early. "I just came down here to get you for lunch," she said, shaking out a new paper bag. "And I walked in on this good time."

I looked down at Bowzer. I looked back at my mother. She'd al-ready dabbed up the pee with one wipe and was now using another to go over the floor.

"Oh," she said. "Don't worry about it." She tossed both wipes into the garbage and used another to go over her hands. "I explained the situation. They all like dogs. It's fine."

Everyone looked up, nodding in agreement. I took a step back, and tried to think where I should put my bag. I'd never had so many people in my room.

"We're making luminarias," my mother said. She air-dried her hands above her head. "For Christmas. Or I call them luminarias. What did you call them again, Inez?"

"*Farolitos.*" The dark-haired girl looked up and smiled. "They'll look really good if it snows." She shrugged. "They'll look good anyway."

Inez. Unless there were two girls named Inez on my floor, she was Inez from Albuquerque, the first person from Albuquerque my mother had ever met. She wore silver hoop earrings, large enough for the bottoms to graze her shoulders, and her hair was shiny black and very straight.

"It's just candles, bags, and sand." My mother nodded at Inez, smiled, and then looked back at me. "You missed the run to Hobby Lobby." She lowered herself to the floor again. "Have a seat, honey. You should make a couple. You just put enough sand in the bag to weight it down, then nestle a candle in. It's relaxing." She looked up again. "How was the test?"

I shook my head. My gaze moved over the pile of votive candlles in the corner.

"Where are you going to put them?" I asked. My voice, in itself, was a wet blanket. And what was I worried about? Really, we already had a dog in the room. Why not a dog and a fire?

"Outside," Inez said.

"Where outside?"

"Right outside. In front of the dorm. It'll look pretty, for once."

I caught Gretchen's eye. She looked back at me, frowning. She stopped filling her bag with sand. "Shit," she said. "You're right."

My mother picked up another handful of sand. "Right about what?"

"I don't know if they'll let us do it," I said. "Not on the property. Candles are pretty much banned."

"It's not a fire hazard," Inez said. She gave me a hard look, her chin jutting up. "That's stupid. Everyone does this back home."

I didn't know what to say. I didn't pretend to know anything about luminarias, and I'd never even been to Albuquerque. I only knew the dorm's fire code was strict. "We can try to put them outside," I said. "We could see if anyone says anything."

"Forget it." Inez leaned back on her hands and looked at a spot of newspaper on the floor. "I hate it here. It's stupid to even try." She looked up and out the window. Her brown eyes glistened, but her face was perfectly composed. "I can't wait for break. The second I finish my last final, I'm gone. I'm in my car. I'm going home."

I looked at the floor, and then back at her face. Here was someone who hated the dorm as much as I did, or more than I did. And this someone was younger than I was, and, in so many ways, farther away from home. I'd thought I had it so hard, being a little older than everyone else.

"Let's just keep making them," my mother said. Her own hands never stopped moving. "I don't know what else we can do with all this sand." She reached for another paper bag. "We'll figure out what to do with them later."

I had heard this line from her many times. Over the years, on cold afternoons and in Girl Scout meetings, whoever was under my mother's care had been encouraged to make more cookies than anyone could eat, more ornaments than anyone could hang, and more candle holders than anyone could possibly want. And if our creations burned, broke, or just looked stupid—no big deal. It was all about the making for my mother. She was never that concerned with the end result.

But Inez was listless as she dropped handfuls of sand into a bag, and the look on her face made it clear that she was only continuing to be polite to my mother. We worked without speaking. I could hear the sound of sand falling, the paper bags crinkling. Gretchen shifted and sighed.

My mother nudged me. "Do you have any holiday music?"

I looked up from my paper bag. "Do I have any holiday music?"

She nodded.

I shook my head. She seemed surprised, but no I didn't have any holiday music. I was a junior in college. I lived, essentially, in a high-ceilinged box. But she seemed disappointed, as if, after all these years, I had finally admitted that despite all her years of careful teaching, I didn't write thank-you notes, or wash my hands after using the bathroom. My mother had a lot of holiday music. Her favorites were Handel's *Messiah* and an album that ended with Judy Garland's sad voice singing "Have Yourself a Merry Little Christmas." I'd heard all that and more played over and over every December of my childhood. Her music was maybe packed in a cardboard box now, probably out in the van.

A girl across the room raised a sandy hand. "I have Jingle Cats."

We all looked at her. She was pretty, with long, curly red hair. She smiled, revealing braces.

"You know, the cats that sing? They're real cats. *Meowy Christmas?*" She looked back at all of us, incredulous. "Oh my God. You don't know it? My whole family loves it. And we're Jewish." She shrugged, shaking a bag full of sand. "They do 'Hava Nagila,' too."

The cats helped quite a bit. I put the CD in my little player, and almost right from the start it was funny. It wasn't so funny that you would die laughing, but it was hard to listen to and keep a straight face. By the end of "Silent Night," even Inez had cracked a smile. We all kept working, filling the bags with sand, which felt smooth and soothing in my hands. I felt as if I were decompressing, some hidden muscle in me finally relaxed. We were all quiet for a while, and there was only the sound of the cats and the music and sometimes some of us laughing.

Of course, I thought of who would love this, who should've been in the room. I touched my mother's arm. "Did you ask Marley?" I whispered.

She nodded without looking at me.

"Is she in her room?"

She nodded again. She still didn't look at me. But when I stood up, shaking sand off my hands, she reached above my boot and squeezed my knee.

The gray carpet in front of Marley's room already looked a little more faded than it did in the rest of the hallway—it was the only section that regularly got sunlight. She almost always left her door open when she was home—a steady, hopeful invitation to anyone walking by. Or almost anyone. From the hallway, I could see just the tip of one of her pig slippers on the floor. I hid behind the wall when I knocked.

"Come in."

I moved quickly to the interior of the room. As soon as she saw me, she looked back down at her work.

"What do you want?" she asked.

She was sitting at her desk, or what I assumed was her desk—the room was clearly divided in two. The bed behind me was as neatly made up as a store display, with a floral dust ruffle that matched the sham pillows. Sorority letters, painted blue with tiny daisies, hung on the wall overhead. On the bureau sat several framed pictures of tan, smiling girls in formal dresses, their heads resting on each other's shoulder, their arms almost always interwined. I squinted at each picture, trying to pick out Marley's roommate. It wasn't all my fault that I couldn't do it. She really wasn't ever around.

The other bed was unmade. The quilt that Marley always dragged out to the lobby was twisted across the bed, and a pillow, with a pillowcase that did not match anything, had fallen to the floor. In the corner of the room, wadded up on the floor, was the flowered dress she'd been wearing when I yelled at her. The French horn lay at the foot of the bed, looking beautiful and complicated with all its swirling tubes.

"What do you want?"

My gaze moved over her bulletin board. She'd tacked up a postcard of a boy with a french fry in his nose, and another of a ferret getting a bath. She had a large black-and-white poster of a man in a bow tie blowing into a French horn, but even that was just taped to the wall. There was only one framed picture, and it was on her desk. A woman in black glasses sat at a piano, with a little smiling girl next to her on the bench. I bent over and squinted to get a better look.

"Is that you?" I asked. "Is that you and your mom?"

She picked up the picture and turned it so I could no longer see the front. "Don't come in here and ask me things. Don't come in and ask about my mom. You've never even been in my room before." She looked up again. "What do you want?" she asked. "For the last time. I'm busy. Obviously."

I stood on my toes to see what she was working on. Sheet music was scattered across her desk, her own handwriting scrawled above and below and beside all the rows of notes. I don't know why this struck me as strange. I had an idea of people who played instruments just sort of magically picking them up and playing them. I knew they must practice. But I didn't think of them as studying music, thinking about it, the way I might think about a book.

"Will you please come down to my room?" I started to sit on her roommate's bed, but then thought maybe I shouldn't. "We're making luminarias. You already know that. You should come down, Marley." I ducked, trying to catch her eye. "Please? I really wish you would."

"I'm never going in your room again."

"I'm sorry," I said.

She looked up. Her nostrils were flared, and her eyes were blank with sadness. I understood then how much I had hurt her, and also how much she was already hurt.

"I appreciate that. Now please go."

I held up one finger, trying to think. Just that morning, during the exam, I had struggled to come up with solutions to one problem after another. I had gotten most of them wrong. But not all of them. I tried to think.

"What if I leave?" I asked. "What if I go right now, and I promise not to come back for several hours? I mean, it's me that's the problem, not the room. Right?"

Headway. She lifted her eyebrows. "That would work," she said.

I told her I just needed a few minutes to get my things. Baby steps, I told myself. She wouldn't forgive me all at once. And that wasn't the point anyway. She needed the company more than I did, and I at least owed her that.

Back in my room, I grabbed my bag and my coat and my keys and announced, to no one in particular, that I had to leave for a while, and that Marley would be coming down. My mother and Gretchen watched me move around, but neither of them said anything. I didn't know where I would go, what I would do with the afternoon.

Before I actually left the dorm, I stopped by Gordon Goodman's office. He frowned when I used the words "candle" and "paper bag" in the same sentence. But when I told him about Inez, and how homesick she seemed, he scratched his chin and looked thoughtful.

"Tonight?" he asked. "You want to put them out tonight?"

"Tonight would be best," I said. If we had to fill out forms and wait a week, Inez would be right: where we lived would not feel like our home.

"I'll make some calls," he said. "Come on in and sit down."

He had a tall stack of papers and a calculator on his desk, but he moved both to the side. I said I could make the calls myself if he told me who to call and gave me the numbers. He seemed pleased that I offered, but he waved me off. Housing would want to talk to him, he said. And he was already on a first name basis with almost everyone at the fire department, because of all the stupid false alarms.

"I think it's great that you're doing this," he said, the phone tucked between his head and shoulder. His smile was so approving that I felt guilty. He thought the idea had been mine. I couldn't tell him that my mother was the one who had organized everything, or that after two days, she was doing my job far better than I had in four months. All I could do was sit there and look grateful as he made four phone calls and spent a total of twenty-five minutes on hold.

I was grateful, and also, despite my misrepresentation, encouraged. Some people would always go out of their way to help, once they saw that you were really trying.

When we got approval, I texted Gretchen: they could put the luminarias out that night. I suppose I could have called, and maybe heard a group reaction to the news. But by the time I walked out of Gordon's office and past the beeping video games in the lobby and out into the afternoon, I felt so awake and calm in my own head that I didn't want to talk at all. The sky was still clear, the air cold, but I felt fine once I started walking.

The bookstore gave me two options: I could get cash back for my chemistry book, 30 percent of what I paid for it, or I could get 40 percent in trade. I picked out a used copy of *Middlemarch,* some gum, an organic peanut butter dog treat shaped like a candy cane, and a red knit scarf on clearance.

"You sure you don't want to keep it?" the cashier asked. He touched the cover of the chemistry book. "You look a little sad to see it go."

I wouldn't have said I was sad. But I understood what I was doing. At that moment, I was no longer thinking about quitting or even deciding to quit; I was actually quitting. And it was hard to look at that brick of a book and not think of all the long days and nights I had spent with it, trying harder than I'd ever tried at anything in my life. And now all that work, all that trying and worrying, was for nothing. I had failed.

The Union was decked out for the holidays, too. There were blinking lights and large banners wishing all of us a happy Christmas,

Kwanzaa, and Hanukkah. I used the change from the bookstore to buy coffee and some pistachio nuts. I found an empty armchair that faced a window big enough for me to see much of the sky, the first clouds of the probable snow hovering on the western horizon. I looked at my watch. I'd told Marley I would be gone for several hours, and I hadn't been gone for forty-five minutes. I crossed my legs. I uncrossed them. I crossed them again. I looked out at the sky. Whenever my father had taken his rare breaks from work, for holidays and family vacations, he often moved this way, jittery and anxious, unsure what to do with himself.

But I just needed to get used to it. For the rest of the afternoon, I read. *Middlemarch* was as thick as my chemistry book, but I turned the thin pages easily. I'd watched the movie of it with my mother and Elise two summers ago, right before Elise's wedding. We'd all been horrified when Dorothea married the old, unfeeling man, and we felt bad for her once she realized what a mistake she'd made. At the next commercial, Elise clicked her tongue. "No divorce back then. She's screwed. This is sad." But my mother had already read the book, and she told Elise to just wait. Sure enough, almost as soon as the movie came back on, good luck—and that's all it was, really—the creepy old husband died.

When the credits rolled, Elise clapped. "So she gets to be happy at the end. Aww. Nice." She clasped her hands beside her head. I was still thinking of the last line. *But the effect of her being on those around her was incalculably diffusive: for the growing good of the world is partly dependent on unhistoric acts.* There was more, but I'd already forgotten it.

My mother got up from the couch to stretch. "I don't know if I'd say she's happy." She'd looked at the stairs, her brow furrowed. My father had already gone to bed. "You should read the book," she said.

And so I did, for almost that entire, cold afternoon, sitting there in the Union. Even from the start, there was so much the movie had skipped over. *Since they could remember, there had been a mixture of criticism and awe in the attitude of Celia's mind toward her elder sister. The younger had always worn a yoke; but is there any yoked creature without its private opinions?* I underlined sentences, dog-eared pages. *Here is a mine of truth, which, however vigorously it may be worked, is likely to outlast our coal.* When I looked up, the setting sun was bright in my eyes. The sky was clear, with just a few wispy clouds edged in orange and red. It hadn't snowed yet, and maybe it wouldn't.

But Inez was right. I could see that as soon as I turned the last corner of my walk home. Even on dead grass and soggy ground, the luminarias were beautiful, perhaps because there were so many, all of them flickering in swirling patterns and lining the sidewalks around the dorm. A few people were out walking around them, quiet; and above me, in hundreds of windows, faces pressed against dark glass, so many hands cupped around eyes, looking down.

The fire alarm went off before dawn. My mother groped her way to my bed and grabbed my arm in the darkness.

"It's okay." I yawned before I opened my eyes. I sat up slowly and turned on my lamp. "It's just an alarm. We have them all the time."

I had to repeat all this twice. The alarm was so loud that even Bowzer could hear it; he was at her feet, trembling, and he looked as if he were trying to burrow into her shins, to work a hole right through her leggings and skin.

I held him back as she pulled on her boots, and she held him as I put on mine. In less than a minute, we were ready to go, with Bowzer buttoned under my mother's coat. Before I opened the door, she looped her arm around mine.

"I love you," she said. She looked at the floor. She wasn't kidding around. "I want you to know that. Okay? I think you're pretty great."

"Mom." I leaned toward her. "I love you, too. But really. It's just an alarm."

Out in the hallway, which was not, in fact, full of smoke, my mother walked slowly, with her chin lowered to keep Bowzer's head pushed down. All around us, doors were opening. Girls in pajamas stepped into the hallway swearing, their hands clapped over their ears.

"I need to go on ahead," I yelled. The alarms were louder in the hallway. "You should go find Marley, and have her wait with you. She doesn't have a car."

Just as we passed Marley's door, it opened. My mother turned back to me briefly. Both of her hands were occupied, so she sent me on with a nod of her head.

So it was Marley who was with her on the way down the stairs, and it was Marley who would tell me later how Bowzer popped his head out of my mother's coat just as they were filing out the double doors. The security monitor, Marley said, was meaner than he'd needed to be. She didn't know his name—it was the one with the pierced nose and the pretty girlfriend. My mother seemed to know him. He tried to take the dog. She wouldn't let him. He told her she couldn't leave, and that she had to come with him. And he kept calling her Mom.

Marley was surpised by what my mother did next, though when I heard, I wasn't. She'd become fearless, but she wasn't a fool. When Jimmy put his big hand on her elbow, she did what any middle-aged stowaway who had recently gone through Strength Camp might at least attempt when holding an elderly dog and confronted by vindicitive dorm security. She pointed over his shoulder, slipped into the crowd, and ran.

Gordon Goodman rubbed his eyes, one elbow propped on his desk. His white T-shirt was on backward, the tag sticking up under his chin.

"You can't have dogs in the dorm," he said. He turned and looked out his window, squinting at the rising sun. Just a half hour earlier, the fire trucks, unneeded once again, had turned off their lights and rolled away. I wondered if, on mornings like this, he regretted abandoning law.

"I know," I said. "I'm sorry."

He looked back at me, annoyed. We both knew he wasn't chastising me. He was just talking to himself, trying to sort through the problem. I'd already told him about my mother getting kicked out of her apartment, having nowhere to go.

Unfortunately, accidentally, I'd also told Jimmy Liff. He was on the other side of the interior window, pretending to fill out paperwork behind the front desk. Or maybe he really was filling out paperwork—on me and my mother. He stood just on the other side of the window, his head lowered, the top of his skullcap almost touching the glass. When I noticed him there, he looked up and smiled. I knew he'd heard every word.

Gordon tugged on his beard. "You don't have any relatives in the area?"

I shook my head.

"Any friends? Anyone she can stay with?"

"I think she's embarrassed. And it's hard, because of the dog."

On the other side of the window, Jimmy pouted. It was over the top. It was like he was making fun of himself, for just how much of a jerk he could be. Gordon saw my face change and followed my gaze. He stood, opened the door, and told Jimmy that he could finish up whatever he was working on later. His voice was stern, and that was a little vindicating, but not much. I didn't care what Jimmy Liff thought about anything, and I doubted my mother did either. But I hated that he looked so pleased, keeping his eyes on mine as he sauntered past the window one last time.

As soon as he was gone, I started begging. I told Gordon my mother would only need to stay a few more days, and that Bowzer wasn't bothering anyone. No one had complained. And it was my mother who had organized the luminarias. She was the one who drove everyone to the store for the bags and candles. She was doing my job better than I was.

Gordon raised his eyebrows. For a moment, I thought I had him. Of course he would relent. My mother was too nice of a person to have to sleep in a van.

But he shook his head. "I'm sorry," he said. "She can't stay, not with the dog." He frowned. He felt the tag under his chin, looked down, and tucked it back in his shirt. "Does she have anywhere to go tonight?"

"I don't know." I stood up slowly. My own head felt heavy on my shoulders. He was looking at his bookcase, at one of his glazed bowls.

"I'd like her to come back and talk to me. You think you can get her to do that? She's not in any trouble, okay? I just want to help."

"I'll ask her," I said. He was being polite. I kept moving to the door.

"Veronica!"

I turned around. He was on his feet.

"Are you going to talk to her today? Does she have a phone? Is there some way you can reach her?"

I nodded, though the answer to the last two questions was no.

She did call later that morning, from a pay phone outside a grocery store. But she didn't want to go talk to Gordon. No, she said, she wasn't scared of Jimmy. She hadn't appreciated him cornering her like that, telling her where she had to go. But she didn't care if he was around or not. She said she just felt bad about causing so much trouble for me. She sounded tired, but not particularly upset. "I'll come get the rest of my things later," she said. "I'll be fine, honey. Really. I just don't want to bother you for a while."

But I pleaded. I insisted. I told her it wouldn't take long, and that I would wait with Bowzer in the van. When none of that worked, I told her the real reason I needed her to come in was that I was about to get fired for keeping a dog in my room, and that I needed her to confirm my story, so my boss might give me another chance. I made my voice sufficiently righteous and whiny. It was for her own good, I told myself. Once Gordon met my mother, he could not possibly expect her to sleep in a van. She would charm him. He would understand that she didn't deserve any of this, even if she wouldn't get rid of the dog. He would bend the rules, and let her stay.

I was wrong. Twenty minutes after my mother walked into the dorm, she came back out to the van with a handwritten list of social service agencies and homeless shelters. Bowzer strained against my arm, trembling in his excitement over her return. As soon as she closed her door, I let him go, and he lunged, falling between her lap and the steering wheel.

"That's how he thought he would help?" I snatched the paper out of her hands. My eyes moved over words: "shelter," "crisis," "homeless," "emergency." He'd neatly written out phone numbers and hours and rules. By one listing, he'd added, "Ask for Carla, re: gas voucher."

"I though it was pretty nice of him." She took off her hat and put it on the dashboard. "It's not his problem. But you wouldn't have known that, talking to him." She took the list back from me and studied it. She didn't look that bad, considering she hadn't gotten a shower that morning and she'd spent most of the day in the van. She was wearing the scarf I'd given her. In the sunlight coming through the windows, it looked itchy, made with cheap yarn. And the red was too bright for her face.

"He gave me some career advice, too." She looked up at me, smiling.

I waited, but she waved me off.

"What? What did he say?"

"Later. Maybe." She kept looking at the list. "None of these places take dogs."

"Mom. That doesn't matter. You're not going to a shelter."

She started to say something, but when she saw my face, she stopped smiling, and all at once, she looked as if the skin of her face had suddenly grown heavy. She put her hand over her eyes and turned away.

"Mom. Let me call Elise."

She shook her head. She still had her hand over her eyes, her elbow resting on the steering wheel. Bowzer sighed in her lap, content.

"Then let me call Dad. I won't even mention you. I'll say I need the money. I'll make something up. I'll—"

She put her hand on my knee. "Please stop talking," she said. "Please? I just need you to be quiet for a moment. I have a little dignity left, and I'd like to keep it. I'll think of something else if you just give me a minute. Okay? I'll come up with something else."

I gave her a minute. And then two. And then five. And then ten. She didn't speak, and neither did I. I looked out the window, up at the sky, which was soft and gray this morning, though there was still no sign of snow. Tim. I could call Tim, and ask him to take the dog. My mother could stay with me. But I couldn't call him. Just a few days after Third Floor Clyde did not seem like the best time to ask him to take care of my mother's slightly incontinent dog. You couldn't push someone away and then lean on them. And although my mother was quiet, no ideas yet, I knew that if she knew everything, she wouldn't want me to ask him.

Also, I thought that if I waited long enough, she would give in. She would let me call Elise or lie to my father. She would realize there wasn't another option.

But she didn't give in. I don't know how much time passed. It got cold in the van. She sat with one hand on Bowzer's back and the other tapping the steering wheel. Her eyes squinted across the parking lot, though there wasn't anything to see. We might have sat there all day, the two of us. As time passed, that seemed more and more likely. I wasn't going to leave her there in the parking lot. And yet, despite her refusal to admit it, there really was nowhere for her—for them, at least—to go.

And then, there was.

Our salvation came in the unexpected form—and the very unusual sight—of Haylie Butterfield getting off a bus on the other side of the parking lot. It took me a moment to recognize her—not because of the dark hair, which I'd gotten used to—but because for the last five months, I'd only seen her transported in Jimmy's car—she never rode the bus. She was also wearing running shoes. She had on the shiny red coat and a long black skirt, and from the ankles up, she looked as glossy and glamorous as ever; but from the ankles down—running shoes. They were pastel blue with white stripes.

"Is that . . . ?" My mother looked out the windshield with narrowed eyes.

I nodded, watching Haylie make her way to the front doors of the dorm. Several other people had gotten off the bus with her, but she was already ahead of all of them. She moved quickly, with confident strides. She was almost up at the front doors when suddenly, as if she could feel my mother and me looking at her, she stopped and turned around. She put the flat of her hand above her eyes. And she started walking toward us.

I shook my head. I sat up straight. "She'd better not come over here," I said. "This better not be about the car."

"Now, honey," my mother said. "You don't know what she wants." But she pressed the button that locked all the doors.

When Haylie was maybe twenty feet away, she veered toward the driver's side of the van. I unlocked my door and got out. It was not my fault that my mother was having a hard time, at least not directly. But I wasn't about to let Haylie bother her now.

"What do you want?" I asked.

She looked at me, lowered her eyes, and tried to step around me. I moved again.

"What? You want to whine to us about your car some more? It's so sad that you have to ride the bus? Fine." I pointed at myself. "Whine to me, Haylie. Leave her alone."

She gave me a look as if I were the one tormenting her and not the other way around. Her nose was pink from the cold.

"I took the bus so I could come here," she said, her gaze lowered again. "I just want to talk to her. Her, not you. Is that okay?"

I shook my head. The bus didn't even go out to where they lived. I looked down at her tennis shoes.

"Just talk to me," I said.

The van's engine started up. We both turned as my mother's window shimmied down. She rested her arm on the door, and Bowzer's face appeared.

"What's going on?" My mother frowned at the cold air coming into the van and rewrapped the scarf around her neck.

"I'm supposed to give you this." Haylie reached into her pocket and pulled out an envelope. She tried to give it to my mother. When my mother didn't take it, Haylie looked up at the sky, which was almost the exact color of her eyes. And it was hard not to look at her, even then, or maybe especially then, and not consider how unfairly beautiful she was. Haylie Butterfield would be beautiful no matter what she did to herself. Black hair. Purple hair. Too much makeup. A bolt though the nose. It wouldn't matter. She couldn't get away from it if she tried.

"Jimmy told me you were staying at the dorm," she said. "What happened this morning. He told me. I called my mom, and she wants you to call her right away. She said you can stay with her. The dog, too."

Haylie tried again to hand over the envelope, and this time, my mother took it.

"Her phone number is in there. And I wrote out directions to her place." She pushed a dark strand of hair behind her ears. "She lives in an apartment by the Med Center. It's really small, and there's no yard. But she said you could stay there and bring the dog, if it's really only for a week. She's in nursing school right now. She's never home. That's why my brother's in Oregon."

My mother gave the envelope a worried look. She may have been thinking of Haylie's little brother, but she may have also been realizing that even this new, best option would not be painless. *If it's only for a week.* In any other situation, in our old life, this would have been such a hesitant invitation that my mother never would have accepted. She and Haylie's mother had been friendly, maybe more than acquaintances. But I don't think they were ever good friends. Now, however, my mother couldn't worry about imposing. So if this was all that could be granted, even with conditions, fine.

"Thank you, Simone," my mother said. She put the envelope in her lap.

Haylie looked embarassed. I couldn't tell if it was the "thank you" or the "Simone" she didn't want. But I understood right then that I shouldn't have been surprised that she'd come all this way to find us. Whatever she'd tried to turn herself into over these last two years, some part of her must have remembered what it was like to have everything fall apart. Really, it would have been more surprising if she had laughed at Jimmy's story and not worried about my mother at all.

"I'm sorry," she said. She looked at me for just a moment. "I'm sorry about this morning, what he did."

My mother nodded. "You didn't do it, hon. You're not him."

It was a nice thing to say, maybe the nicest thing possible, given the circumstances. But Haylie looked newly burdened. It was as if my mother, in exchange for the gift of the envelope, had presented her with a problem. She tightened the sash of her red coat.

"I've got to go," she said.

"Do you need a ride somewhere?"

She only considered it for a moment. "Not a good idea," she said.

"I'm on my way home." She turned and started walking back to the bus stop. Halfway there, she stopped. My mother and I didn't speak to each other; we didn't pretend to do anything but watch. Haylie stood still for a minute, maybe two, her hands in the pockets of her coat. She walked to the front steps of the dorm.

She was still there, sitting on the top step, when I got out of the van. She stared straight ahead, her elbows on her knees, her pretty chin resting in her hands. On my way up the steps, I asked her again if she needed a ride. My mother waved from the idling van, but Haylie again shook her head.

She was fine, she said. She was thinking.

15

My mother said that Pamela O'Toole, formerly Pamela Butterfield, was a kind hostess, especially considering how busy she was, and how small her apartment was, and the fact that she didn't really like dogs. My mother tried to be a considerate guest. She cooked. She tidied up. She kept her things in neat stacks behind the couch where she slept. She only used the shower when Pamela was at nursing school, and she took her sheets off the couch every morning. When Pamela came home, ready to study at the kitchen table, my mother took their dirty clothes to the Laundromat, or she went with Bowzer for long walks, or she just drove him around in the van. So it wasn't exactly *Kate & Allie*. The apartment was too small for both of them. But they had some good conversations: they talked of ex-husbands and daughters and former neighbors; they compared their descents and sometimes laughed. For the most part, however, my mother felt cramped and awkward and irrationally annoyed for having to work so hard not to be a burden, and she was always terrified the dog would pee, or worse, on the floor. During the week she stayed with Pamela, she said the three words she said more than any others were "thank you" and "sorry."

It got tiring, she said, being grateful.

There was more gratitude to come. The paycheck my mother had been waiting for was not enough to cover both a security deposit and the first month's rent, and so she went to one of her friends at the mall, Maxine, for help. Maxine told her she was being ridiculous about the dog. She told my mother she was not thinking reasonably or making the best use of her resources. But she also gave my mother a loan. My mother said "thank you," ignored the advice, cashed the paycheck, and moved into an apartment with Bowzer.

She called me from her new phone, excited, but she did not invite me to spend winter break with her. I hoped this was because she wanted her own space for a while. I worried that she couldn't afford the groceries.

"You'll be more comfortable at your father's," she said. "You know you will. For one, I'm sure he has furniture."

It was true. My father's rented condo had come furnished, complete with paintings on the walls in neutral colors that matched the carpet and the curtains and the throw pillows on the leather couch. Because he spent so little time at home, everything was clean and new-looking. The glass table in the dining room was smudge-free. He'd lived there for almost a year, and he'd used the oven exactly twice. The guest room had its own television and a double bed, which I would be sharing with Elise when she arrived on Christmas Eve.

Elise had already called to break the news that she could only stay for Christmas Eve and Christmas Day. Work was insane, she said. Charlie, who did tax law for an even bigger firm, couldn't take any time off at all. My mother wondered about her new son-in-law spending the holidays by himself.

"He'll be fine," Elise told my mother and, later, me. When she called me, she was on a headset, buying groceries at midnight, Pacific time. "You all don't understand the kind of time we put in. You can't imagine it. The work just doesn't stop."

By "you all," she of course meant my mother and me. My father needed no instruction on the kind of hours a law firm might require of a new associate. He was still working all the time himself. The whole week before Christmas, he left for his office before I woke up, and he usually got home after I ate dinner. But he seemed happy that I was there. Every night, he stayed up late, long after he was yawning and blinking, to tell me stories about his day—a judge falling asleep, a juror surreptitiously picking his nose.

"You're not laughing," he said.

I tried to laugh.

He looked at me over his bifocals. "You okay? You seem kind of down."

I shrugged. If I only told him that Tim had broken up with me, he would automatically take my side and call Tim names. On the other hand, if I gave him the particulars—namely, that it was all my fault—he might ask me, just what had I expected, acting like that? He would have to take Tim's side, given the parallels between Third Floor Clyde and the Roofer. I didn't see them as parallels, but he might see them that way.

"You're bored, right?" He put a frozen burrito in the microwave, setting the timer and turning it on without taking his eyes off me. "I mean not right now, while I'm here. I mean during the day. I feel bad, you're here by yourself."

I shrugged again. It was true that my options were limited. My father's car was with him all day, and it was too cold to walk anywhere. But I'd actually gotten used to my holiday schedule, which involved reading the last four hundred pages of *Middlemarch* and regularly looking up and out the window to watch rain or snow fall into the tiny, man-made lake for which my father's entire neighborhood was named. I made myself grilled cheese sandwiches. I watched the news and infomercials. Even with all this, I had several hours a day to spend on my default activity—lying on the guest room floor and feeling bad about Tim.

My father offered to pick up a study guide for the MCAT. "You've got all this downtime," he said. "You might as well put it to use."

I told him I needed a break from studying. I left it at that. I didn't want to talk to him about my chemistry grade, either, though report cards would be mailed out in less than a week.

But I liked the idea of a distraction, of somehow putting my time to good use. I'd told my mother that if she wanted to come pick me up, we could go to a movie, or I could help her get set up in her apartment. But she was back to work at the mall, going in for long shifts to make up for the time she'd lost. And anyway, she said, she didn't want me to see the apartment just yet. She wanted to clean it up a little first.

On my third night in the condo, my father brought home an ice cream maker. We assembled it and read the directions, and went to the grocery store to get ingredients. We spent the rest of the evening making a runny, vanilla-flavored dessert that we slurped like soup while watching *Law & Order*.

"I'll have to go to the gym after this." He leaned back on the couch, looking down at his empty bowl. "Maybe tomorrow night."

I nodded, looking at the television, a commercial for an asthma drug. The actor playing the doctor looked like Tim. Every day, I thought of things I wanted to tell him; but I couldn't, because he didn't call. I looked down at my bowl of ice cream. I'd only finished half, but I put it on the floor.

My father leaned forward, stretching his arms. "I'll hit the tread-mill, the elliptical. And the weights, too. I'll just stop in on my way home from work. I'll shower there. So I might be home really late tomorrow."

I nodded again. My father had just recently joined a gym; he said he usually got himself there three or four times a week. He'd already lost much of his belly. He looked good in general. He seemed to be making more of an effort with his clothes, even when he wasn't at work. For as long as I could remember, he'd spent his evenings in an old white T-shirt and a pair of blue sweatpants that my mother hated. Now he padded around his condo in new T-shirts and khaki shorts that looked like something Tim would wear. He had nice, striped pajamas, and a sleek robe for after he got out of the shower.

"You sure you don't mind?" He bent over to pick up his dessert bowl and mine. "I don't want to slack off too much over the holidays. But you might even be asleep by the time I get back."

"I don't mind." I kept looking at the television. The asthma commercial had thrown me into a downward spiral. Tim would get a new girlfriend. I would see them together on campus.

"Honey?" My father stood up, holding the dessert bowls.

"Dad. Go to the gym tomorrow." I forced myself to smile. "Don't feel bad. I think it's great that you're taking care of yourself."

He looked away. He looked back at me, biting his lip.

"I'm so nervous," he said. "I hate this."

I looked up at him. He picked up the remote and turned off the television.

"I'm seeing someone." He set the dessert bowls on the glass table a little too hard. One of them tipped over, spilling vanilla. He cursed under his breath. "Okay? There it is. I'm seeing someone. I'm sure that's strange for you. Believe me, Veronica. It's strange for me to look at your sweet face and tell you this, but I have a woman friend. She is a part of my life. I've moved on. That's who I want to see tomorrow night."

I did not move. I did not react. I did not want to know any more, but if he kept talking, I would have to listen. I could not keep clapping my hands over my ears like a child. My father looked down at me over the tops of his bifocals, watching my eyes. I didn't think I had ever seen him look so unsure of himself.

"She's a very nice woman," he said. "Susan O'Dell? You met her years ago, at my firm's Labor Day party? She brought that huge watermelon? She could barely carry it, remember? Auburn hair? Slim? She came to Elise's wedding." He held up his hands. "Nothing was going on. She was just a business associate, a friend. But we've started spending time together . . ."

I tried to remember his firm's Labor Day party, or even just a flash of any woman carrying a watermelon. I came up with nothing. I focused on staying calm, and on not letting my lip curl even a little.

"You'll like her a lot. She's really smart. Great lawyer. She's not looking for a free ride, you know? She's worked hard her whole life."

My gaze hardened. I didn't know if he was making a comparison to my mother or not.

He took a step back. He smoothed his hair with his hand. "I want you to meet her," he said. "I want her to come over for dinner when Elise gets here. She can meet you both. Boom boom. It's done."

"Christmas Eve?"

He threw up his hands. "It's either Christmas Eve or Christmas Day, honey. Elise will be gone after that." He picked up both bowls and carried them to the counter. "I'm trying to work her into your busy schedules."

I stayed up late that night, though I didn't read or watch television. I sat in the dark in the living room, wrapped in a blanket because the leather couch felt cold. The central heat turned on with a hum. A poinsettia plant, a gift from my father's secretary, sat in the middle of the glass table. My mother would be alone on Christmas Eve. Elise and I would be having dinner with our father and Susan O'Dell.

My mother might not be all that upset about the evening, even if she knew. There was a chance she would spend Christmas Eve listening to Judy Garland and sobbing into her pillow, but it was more likely that she would use the time to fix up her new apartment. Or she would read, Bowzer lying beside her. Either way, Susan O'Dell's presence at my father's table wouldn't change anything about her night. They had shot off in different directions, my parents. One trajectory no longer affected the other. And I didn't have to feel sorry for her, or angry on her behalf, because even she no longer seemed angry.

I was just about to go to bed when Tim called. He was at his parents' house in Chicago, the only one still awake. The upstairs was full of siblings and in-laws and cousins, he said. He had two nephews in sleeping bags in his room. He was calling from a corner of the basement, between his parents' old luggage and empty ornament boxes, because it was the only place in the house he could be alone. His voice was noncommittal, his words clipped. He said he just wanted to wish me a merry Christmas. That was all. But I sat up straight and pressed the phone aginst my ear. It wasn't Christmas yet, and it was late at night.

"How's your family?" I asked.

"Good. Okay. My little brother is being kind of a dick. He's started smoking, and he acts like James Dean, out on the front porch. One of my sisters-in-law made fun of him, and he got mad, stormed out for the night. My mom cried. So there's been drama."

"Oh," I said, surprised. I tended to imagine Tim's family as if they lived in a Norman Rockwell picture, only wearing expensive, tasteful clothes instead of overalls and flowered dresses. But of course real trouble would occasionally arise, with that many people in the house.

"How's yours?" he asked.

"Okay." The central heating had clicked off. The condo was perfectly quiet. "Just, you know, spread out." I sighed until I laughed. There was too much to say if this was just a quick call. If he really only called to wish me a good Christmas, then anytime now, he would say he had to go.

"I miss you," I said.

There was a long pause, both of us silent. I didn't hang up, and neither did he.

Two days before Christmas, my mother invited me over. Her new apartment was less than a mile from her old one, a little closer to the mall. The entire complex—green with white shutters—was nestled into a slope, and my mother's apartment, which the landlord called ground-level, could only be entered by first descending five concrete steps. You opened the door to a big, brown-carpeted room with no windows except for sliding glass doors on the opposite wall. The eyelet bedspread hung from the curtain rod. A bowl of pinecones sat on the counter. She had driven in a nail by the sliding doors—a rudimentary hook for Bowzer's leash. "He doesn't have to deal with stairs if we go out this way." She gazed out the sliding glass doors to the little patch of frozen yard, and beyond that, the pines that muffled the roar of the interstate. "Really," she said. "It's perfect."

She still didn't have any furniture except my grandmother's lamp and a twin mattress that she'd found at a thrift store. Haylie's mother had helped her squeeze it into the van and then carry it down the steps and into the apartment and, finally, around the corner to the little square bedroom in back. The bedroom's light fixture was a translucent globe in the center of the ceiling that my mother claimed had been half-full of dead flies when she first moved in. "It was disgusting," she said, pointing up at the fixture, which, by the time I saw it, was shiny and clean. "After I got them out and washed the thing, it was actually brighter in here." She made a face and shivered. "It makes me wonder about who used to live here. I mean, who lets that many dead flies just accumulate?"

I said nothing. She had allegedly spent days cleaning, fixing the place up. I hated to think what it had looked like before. Maybe the flies were pets, I thought. Maybe they weren't dead at the time, but elderly flies the previous tenant couldn't bear to part with. Why else would anyone live here? Bowzer was asleep on the mattress, which my mother had made up neatly, the extra material of her duvet fanned out across the carpet. I bent down and rubbed the space between his ears. His eyelids fluttered, but that was all. He hadn't gotten up when I'd first come into the apartment.

"What do you think?" she asked.

I could tell by her voice that she wasn't asking about the apartment. I kept one hand on his head and shrugged. She'd already come this far with him, moving into this dark, dingy place that smelled of cat pee. I didn't know what kind of a lease she had signed, but it seemed to me that since she was already here, she might as well keep him around.

"He's just been lying there for the last two days." She sighed and smoothed back her hair. She was dressed for work at the mall, wearing nice black slacks and a black sweater. Her earrings were shaped like candy canes. "I called the vet yesterday. He said I could bring him in again, and we could talk about it. Maybe different medication." Her knees creaked as she lowered herself to the floor. "I don't know. He still eats. But I had to carry him outside this morning. Just last week, he wasn't this bad."

I ran my hand down his soft back. His breathing was shallow, quick. I didn't know what my mother would do when he died, how she would take it. She'd given up so much for him, because of some strange attachment to him or whatever he represented. And now he would leave her. It wasn't fair. The night Tim called, we had stayed on the phone for almost an hour, talking seriously, then joking. Since then, I had carried a good feeling with me like a jewel hidden in a pocket. I still had possibility. But what did my mother have? A dying dog in a depressing apartment. I didn't know what to say.

"I don't want him to be in pain." Her eyes were still focused on

Bowzer. "The vet said he'd be open the day after Christmas. I'll take him in then."

"I'll go with you," I said. "If you want me to. When you take him in, I mean." I waved my hand. "Whenever."

She drove me back to my father's before it got dark. She was a little distracted, steering the van slowly through the ice-speckled streets. She asked me if I'd gotten my grades yet. No, I said. She asked when I would be taking the MCAT.

"Never," I said.

She thought I was joking at first. When she realized that I wasn't, and that I really had failed organic chemistry, and that I had decided to change my major to English lit, she was quiet. She kept her gaze on the road. Her lips were rolled into her mouth, invisible. We merged onto the interstate, snow falling from the roof and rolling down the windshield as we picked up speed.

"You don't have anything to say?"

She almost laughed, though she looked unhappy. "I don't want to say the wrong thing." She glanced at me. "Have you thought about nursing? Pamela—Haylie's mom—you know, she's going back to get a degree in nursing. She doesn't have to take the MCAT. And she'll make good money. She said there are lots of jobs."

"I don't want to do medicine," I said. "I don't love it. I want to do something I love."

She looked both sad and faintly amused. She looked like she wanted to say something. We turned a sharp corner, and she held out one arm across my shoulders, as if preparing to stop me from flying forward, though I was wearing my seat belt, and we weren't about to crash.

"Sorry," she said, both hands back on the wheel. "Oh honey, you're certain about this?"

I nodded, though I wasn't certain of anything. I wanted her to reassure me, to tell me that I was doing the right thing, and that all that mattered was that I would be happy. But she didn't say any of these things. She looked down at the control panel. The check engine light had come on.

"What does that mean?"

She sighed, turning a corner. "Guess I'll find out when I take it in." After that, she was quiet again.

She pulled carefully into my father's driveway. If she wondered if he was home, she didn't ask. She told me she would pick me up at half past ten the next morning. Elise's flight got in at eleven. She knew an Indian place that stayed open on Christmas Eve. She would take us both out to lunch.

"I don't like Indian food," I said. A lie. I didn't want her to spend the money taking us out to a restaurant. She might have felt like she had to. "Why don't I make something?" I asked. "Lasagna? I'll borrow Dad's car and go to the store tonight." I said this as if it were a given that he would let me borrow his car. "I'll make something good. We can just eat it at your place, like a picnic."

She shook her head. "Other places are open," she said. "We don't have to have Indian."

I feigned hurt. "Are you saying I'm a bad cook? Are you saying you don't think I can do it?"

A car pulled into the adjacent driveway, a man and a woman in a sleek little car. They rolled into their garage without looking at us. The garage door closed, swallowing them whole.

My mother gave me a look. "Veronica. This is not about your lasagna. Let's just say that Elise and I are in very different places right now." She frowned. "Surely you understand."

I shook my head. It was the "right now" that confused me. Elise and my mother had never really been in the same place, even when they lived in the same house.

My mother sighed. "Your sister doesn't need to see the apartment. I'm not going to live there long." She smiled and unlocked the van's doors. "We'll have fun tomorrow. We'll go out."

———

Before she picked me up in the morning, she cleaned the van. She didn't just get all the boxes and blankets and small appliances out of the back. She took it to a car wash and dropped in quarters to use a vacuum. I imagine she was the only person there, snow flying in on the upholstery, all the doors opened to the cold. But the van looked good. There was no more dried kibble rolling around on the floor mats. The plastic straw wrappers, dog hair, and used hand wipes had been sucked away from every crevice and nook. A circle-shaped deodorizer that smelled like lilacs dangled from the rearview mirror.

She did not bring Bowzer. She'd thought about it, she said, but decided not to. We couldn't bring him into the restaurant, and the van would get cold. He was better off at home. He hadn't even noticed when she left.

Just before we got to the airport, she took the deodorizer down and put it under her seat. She caught me looking at her.

"It looked a little trashy," she said.

Elise got off the plane wearing jeans, a billowy shirt, and flip-flops. Her light brown hair was streaked with gold and pulled back in a ponytail. She carried no bag, just several folders full of paper. She started to yawn, but as soon as she saw us, she smiled. My mother and I got to her at the same time. When I went to hug her, she tucked the folders under her arm and tickled my ribs. She kept doing it until I laughed and screamed.

"Girls," my mother said. "Girls!" But she was laughing a little, too. She stopped when she looked at Elise's bare toes.

"Honey," she said. "It's snowing!"

"Don't worry. I brought boots." Even in flip-flops, Elise was taller than both of us. "And a coat. Do you remember my luggage? It's silver? Can you watch the carousel for it? I have to pee. I'm dying." She handed me the folders full of legal-sized paper. "Here," she said. "Hold these."

My mother and I watched her walk away, flip-flops slapping on the floor.

"She looks good," my mother said quietly. I knew what she meant. Elise was naturally tall and thin, but when she was under stress, she could lose so much weight that her head looked too big for her body, her face gaunt, all the color gone. These bouts never lasted long, but my mother had worried about them for fifteen years. Given the way my sister had described her life in California, I think both my mother and I had expected her to be too thin. But she looked fine. She looked healthy, even curvy, her backside swinging as she disappeared into the restroom.

"What'd you get her?"

"For Christmas?" I turned around on my tiptoes, searching for the bag carousel. "A candle holder." That was another lie. I had already gift wrapped my "Math Is Hard" Barbie for Elise. When I'd told her about it a year ago, she wanted one for herself, but she couldn't find another on eBay. I didn't want to talk about it with my mother, to have to analyze the doll again; why Elise might want it, why I no longer did. It just seemed like the perfect gift, not least of all because it was free and I didn't have any money.

"What did you get her?" I asked.

"Earrings." She frowned. "I don't know if they're right. I never know what she'll like."

By the time we left the airport, Elise was wearing a gray wool coat over a turtleneck and black pants that were somehow not wrinkled. She opened the side door of the van to put her bags in. "Why does it smell like bad perfume in here?" She waved a gloved hand in front of her face. "Oh my God. Lilacs? More like chemicals. Yuck!"

We rode with the windows down, snow coming in, Elise in the passenger seat. She told us about her irritating seatmate on the plane, a man who had not brought anything to occupy him during the flight. Apparently, he assumed it was Elise's responsibility to converse with him, and he kept attempting to talk to her about the pitfalls of his job as an auto-parts salesman, even though it was clear she was trying to read.

"He wasn't hitting on me," Elise said. "He mentioned his wife twice. He just seemed to think I should be there for him. I should have brought crayons for him, I guess, or maybe stickers. After a while, I handed him the in-flight magazine. I thought that was pretty pointed, but he just kept gabbing, asking questions. I said, 'Sorry I can't talk. I've got to have these briefs read by Tuesday.' So then he starts to ask me for legal advice! Some kind of property dispute with his cousin. He starts telling me about it. I'm serious. The whole time, I've got my glasses on, my head down. I'm clearly trying to read." She smacked both hands against her forehead, just the way our father would have done it. "Finally, I go, 'Excuse me, sir. I have work to do. I'm sorry you're bored. But it's not my problem. Don't talk to me anymore.' I hurt his feelings, I think. He sulked for the rest of the flight."

In the backseat, I listened and wondered what I would have done if I had been on the airplane, held captive by the chatty man. I would have been annoyed, but I might have felt sorry for him. So I would have talked to him, and gotten even more annoyed, mostly with myself. There was much to admire in Elise: her straightforwardness, her courage. I'd been admiring her for these traits and more my whole life. It was comforting to think that she would have been a bad RA, to think that she would have lost her temper with Marley long before I did. But I wasn't sure that was true. It had not been Elise's job to entertain the man on the plane. That was the point she had made. If it had been her job, she would have excelled at it. She would have done it better than anyone else ever could.

"That always happens to me," my mother said. "In waiting rooms, especially, I get next to a talker when I want to read a book. I'm never brave enough to be so firm."

She pulled into the parking lot of a pizza parlor, explaining that not much was open on Christmas Eve and that I had said no to Indian. When we got out of the van, she exited on one side; Elise and

I got out on the other. In those few seconds of separation, Elise hooked her arm in mine and lowered her mouth to my ear.

"How has she been?"

We were walking. I could see our mother's head through the windows on the other side of the van. She cleared the corner, heading toward us around the back. In just a few steps, we would meet up.

"She's fine," I said. "She's okay."

Ordering pizza with Elise always required negotiation. The rules went back almost twenty years. We could get pepperoni if I was willing to give up green peppers. She would forgo olives if my mother allowed pineapple. She only wanted breadsticks if we could get them with cheese. When we reached an agreement, she made the final order, stacking all of our menus and handing them to the waitress. My mother looked at the edge of the table, smiling with just half of her mouth.

I looked at Elise. "You didn't get a soda."

She shook her head and took a sip of water.

"You usually order right away. You're a caffeine freak."

"I'm turning over a new leaf." She poked my knee under the table. "So how's school? Are they letting you cut up dead bodies yet?"

My mother frowned. "Elise. We're about to eat."

I gave my mother an appreciative glance. She wasn't at all squeamish. She'd just given me an out.

Elise clicked her tongue. "If she wants to be a doctor, it shouldn't bother her." But now she was looking at my mother. "Your hair is different."

My mother touched the side of her head. "I've let it go. I know."

It was true. I hadn't noticed before, but now, even in the low light of the pizza parlor, I could see a definite horizontal line in her hair, almost at the level of her ears. Below the line, her hair was all dark, the same color as mine. Above the line, there were several curling strands of gray.

Elise nodded, with no further comment. "So how's the mall? Do you like it? Is it fun?"

My mother nodded. She took a sip of water as she smiled. "It's fine," she said. In the center of the table was a flickering candle in a small red holder and a list of weekly specials encased in plastic. The list was green on one side, red on the other, and a little uneven in the frame. My mother picked it up and fixed it.

"How's your new apartment? Where is it?"

My mother waved her hand as if clearing smoke. "It's an apartment. Not much to say. I want to hear how you're doing, honey." She reached over to pat Elise's hand. The diamond on Elise's ring glinted brightly in the low light of the candle.

At the table next to ours, a man and woman sang "Happy Birthday" to a little girl. We all looked over and smiled.

Elise leaned forward, elbows on the table. "You really want to know how I'm doing?"

I sat back, ready to listen. For almost a year now, Elise had been telling us how busy she was, too busy to come home for a visit, too busy to even stay on the phone. But now, finally, here she was in the flesh, and though she often reminded my mother and me that we couldn't possibly understand how much work she did, that really, we had no idea, I expected her to tell us all about it now. There would be funny impersonations of a demanding boss, maybe, or a needy client. She had my father's small, blue eyes, and they were glimmering the way his did when he prepared to command our attention.

"Hmm. How am I doing?" She stretched back, her pale arms raised, her gaze moving over our heads. "Pretty good, I guess." She smiled at me, and then at my mother. "I'm pregnant."

My mother knocked over her water glass. "Oh!" she said, jumping a little. "Oh! I didn't expect that at all!" She stood up to hug Elise, and her wrapped silverware fell to the floor.

Elise mouthed *Help me!* over my mother's shoulder, though she was clearly enjoying the excitement.

"Hug you?" I asked, standing up. "You said you want me to hug you?"

When the waitress arrived with the pizza, Elise waved us both away.

"Okay, you two. Down. Sorry, yes, it's wonderful, la la la, okay. I want to eat." She thanked the waitress and reached between us to take a slice. "Whatever's in there, boy or girl, it's always hungry."

I tried to stop staring. Her belly, if she had one yet, was hidden by the table. A boy or a girl. A niece or a nephew. Aunt Veronica, I would be. I used my napkin to sop up the spilled water. "Are you going to find out?"

She held up a finger, chewing. She covered her mouth with her hand. "Soon. In a month. I'm due in June."

"It's good you're hungry," my mother said, with something like doubt in her voice. Her face was still flush, excited. "With both of you girls, I was nauseous the whole time. Even in the second trimester." She looked down at the pizza and wrinkled her nose. "Just the smell of this would have sent me over the edge."

"That's how I was just until a month ago." Elise leaned back and rested her hand on her belly, and as soon as she did this, she looked pregnant. I couldn't see any bump or swelling, but it just looked like something a pregnant woman did. "I felt like I was on a boat for two months," she said. "Bobbing. Bobbing." She crossed her eyes. "Even in my sleep, I was bobbing. I had to keep bags in my car. More in my desk. One in my briefcase."

I ate and listened as they kept talking, about cravings, about fatigue. Elise had taken naps in her office, under her desk. My mother said she'd done the same when she was teaching, when her students had gone to lunch.

"Ginger helps," she said. "Not for being tired, but for the stomach. I used to suck on candied ginger, I remember."

My gaze rested on the candle in its little red holder, and their words moved over my head. This was a new situation. My mother and Elise were usually awkward together, hesitant, two strangers at a party hell-bent on talking but without much to say to one another. Now they had this thing between them. I already detected a shift, our old triangle changing slants.

"You have a good OB?" my mother asked. "You want to get references, Elise. It's important."

"Hmm." She took a long sip of water. "Well. We thought we would wait and find an OB out here." She blinked at both of us. "Since we're moving back to KC in the spring."

Bombshell number two. My mother looked too happy to breathe. It was like watching a game show where the prizes just get bigger and bigger, until the winning contestant goes into convulsions. My mother had just won a grandchild and both of her daughters living close to home. I was pretty happy, too. Maybe everything wouldn't feel so over, so sad, once Elise came back.

She reached for another piece of pizza. "Charlie got a great offer, and he knew how much I wanted to come back here. They want him right away. He'll start in February." She rolled her eyes. "I'm the one who gets to stay behind and pack up all our stuff."

"Oh, honey." My mother looked a little crestfallen. "That's a lot to do when you're pregnant." She shook her head, lips pursed. "And knowing you, you'll work right up until you leave."

We were quiet for a while. The birthday people had gotten up and left, and most of the tables were empty. "Crimson and Clover" played on a neon jukebox in the corner. We chewed and swallowed, all of us still smiling, but avoiding each other's eyes. A question, I knew, hung in the air. My mother had her hand over her mouth.

"So you'll get a job here, too?" I asked. I pretended to be fascinated with a string of cheese hanging off the side of my pizza. Half of what made Elise so intimidating was the way she could focus her gaze, making any question I asked feel stupid. "After the baby, I mean?"

"Nope." She picked something off her shoulder, her nails manicured, her polish clear. "I'm just going to stay home with Junior for a while. Or Juniorette."

"How long is a while?"

Elise chuckled, as if my mother had asked her about the weather in Australia, or how many seconds were in a year. "I don't know. First grade?"

My mother put her pizza down. "Honey, you can't be serious."

Elise stopped chewing. She gave my mother the look—the long, steady gaze that said to any opponent, *You are about to be devoured.*

"This is a problem for you?"

"Anyone want parmesan?" I held up the shaker. We all knew my dad's old joke: *It's a free topping. Learn to like it!*

"Elise. You love your work."

Elise raised her eyebrows and shook her head. "These days? Not so much. You know what it's like? Remember when I was little I used to love Rice Krispie treats? Remember I used to beg you to make them? And then one day Veronica was sick and you went upstairs to lie down with her, and I stayed down in the kitchen and made a huge batch of Rice Krispie goo and then ate right out of the bowl before you came back downstairs. You remember that?"

"I remember," I said, still holding the parmesan. Elise had thrown up the rest of the day, stealing my sickness thunder.

"Well it cured me. I haven't wanted a Rice Krispie treat since. It's been almost twenty years, and I can barely look at one at a bake sale. That's kind of how I feel about work right now. I've had a little too much of it lately, and to tell the truth, it'll be nice to have a little break."

"Five years isn't a little break." My mother spoke through a frozen smile. "You could go back a little sooner? Part-time?"

I chewed more slowly, the pizza heavy and dry in my mouth. I was unnerved by the way our mother's worried eyes moved back and forth between me and Elise. I didn't think it was a fair comparison.

I was only changing majors. What Elise was doing was more extreme.

Elise shook her head. "You know what part-time is at a law firm, Mom? About fifty hours a week. I'd like to actually know my child. And we can afford it. The cost of living is so much lower here." She cocked her head, her face impassive. "Is there a reason you need me to work? Is there something going on with you?"

My mother lowered her gaze. "I'm just surprised," she said.

"I don't know why." Elise took another bite of pizza. She used her napkin to daintily wipe her mouth. "I've always given a hundred percent to everything I've done. I don't see why this should be any different." She gazed out the window, out at big snowflakes, falling slowly, meandering to the ground. It was clear, from her placid expression, that she considered the matter closed.

My mother leaned forward, elbows on the table. "Because of money," she said.

"Jingle Bell Rock" started up on the jukebox.

"Money isn't a problem," Elise said. "I just told you that."

"Your money. You need your own money."

Elise straightened her posture. "Our marriage is fine. I'm not you. Charlie isn't Dad." She took another bite of pizza. My mother still wasn't eating. But Elise, like my father, had no problem eating and arguing at the same time. It was like breathing to them.

"You don't know the future." My mother's voice wasn't loud, but her tone was so firm, so certain, that someone at another table turned around. She fixed her gaze on Elise. "You should keep working. At least part-time."

Elise waved the words away. "You haven't practiced law. You don't know what you're talking about."

"And you haven't been divorced. You don't know how that works, Elise."

Elise stopped chewing. She put her pizza down. She wiped her mouth with her napkin and looked away.

"Honey, I'm just trying to—"

"You're confusing me with you," she said. She looked back at my mother. "I'm the one who invests our money. My name is on every document. I balance our checkbook. It's a partnership. It's equal. And it will still be equal when I stay home."

My mother covered her eyes with her hands. After a while, Elise glanced at me, worried. I looked away. A lot had happened since she'd last called me from California. There was much she did not yet know. I did not think our mother was crazy. I was not certain she was even wrong.

Elise reached across the table and squeezed her arm, her expression softer now. "You big hypocrite," she said, smiling a little. I just want to be as good of a mother as you were. And you were so good, Mom. You're telling me you regret it?"

I leaned forward, shaking my head, trying to make eye contact with Elise. She thought her questions were nice. She didn't know just how bad things had gotten. She hadn't seen all our mother's things in the back of the van.

My mother looked up and shook her head. She did not appear especially pained. "No," she said. "No, I don't. I don't regret what I did. But I don't want you to do it."

Elise sat back slowly, her smile turned into a smirk. In her mind, she'd just won the argument. "That doesn't make any sense," she said.

My mother shrugged. She looked at Elise and then at me. She pushed her half-eaten pizza away from her.

"It doesn't," she said. "I know."

Shortly after dinner that evening, Elise pretty much had the same argument with my father. It was just louder. Poor Susan O'Dell sat blinking into her eggnog as my father got increasingly agitated by the idea of Elise becoming a stay-at-home mom. He stood up and paced around the dining room, almost bumping right into the glass-topped table. Was she *crazy*? he wanted to know. Did she not understand that she was *brilliant and immensely talented*? Did she forget how hard she had worked? Did she realize what she was throwing away?

Elise sipped hot chocolate and answered every charge. She only raised her voice when he interrupted her. And when she needed to talk to me or Susan, to ask us to please pass the cinnamon or the whipping cream, her voice was calm and polite. The louder he got, the more her gaze wandered, to her watch, to her nails, to Susan O'Dell's pretty and alarmed-looking face.

"Should we give them some space?" Susan whispered, her eyes on mine.

I shook my head. "This is kind of how it goes," I said. I didn't actually say *Get used to it,* but I hoped she got the idea. She seemed nice enough. She was quiet, but alert-looking, with a suprising spread of freckles across the bridge of her graceful nose. She was maybe ten years younger than my mother. At dinner, she laughed appreciatively at almost everything my father said. He was charming. He told good stories. He pulled her chair out for her and asked her opinion on a recent ruling by the State Supreme Court. But after dinner, because of Elise, she got to see what he was like when he was mad.

"Was this Charlie's idea? Did he just want to take the job here, whether you could get one or not?"

"You're seriously asking me that?" Elise shook her head and yawned. She put her feet up in his empty chair. "How much eggnog have you had?"

They stared at each other.

"I can always go back," she said. "I get to keep my degree, you know. I also get to keep my brain."

My father did not smile. "You're stepping off the ladder, honey." He pointed down at her. "Don't kid yourself. They're not going to let you back on."

She met his eyes, her smile gone. She didn't like him pointing, maybe. She looked tired all at once. "I stepped off the ladder when I said I wanted to come home for Christmas," she said. "I stepped off the ladder when I asked for three days off instead of two."

I looked into the corner of the room, where my father had placed his poinsettia. Elise and I had placed all our gifts around it, almost hiding the plant from view. We'd assumed there wouldn't be a tree.

"Susan has a kid." My father nodded at Susan O'Dell, who looked suddenly ill. "Susan has a kid, and she always worked. She did it."

"I should go," Susan O'Dell said. She wasn't talking to anyone, just announcing it to the room.

"I changed my major," I said, with a similar volume and tone. "I'm not pre-med anymore. I'm doing English literature. I might go to grad school. For literature."

Everyone looked at me.

"I think I'll be happier," I added. "I'll try harder and do better. I'll always want to go to work, you know, if I'm doing something I love."

I lowered my eyes, studying my hot chocolate. My non sequitur had actually been thought out, though only for about ten seconds. I'd understood, all at once, that this was the time to strike. For one, Susan O'Dell's nervous presence was keeping my father somewhat in check. He was yelling, but not as much, and not quite as loudly, as he would have been if she weren't there. Furthermore, Elise's defection was so much more extreme. In a year, she would be a housewife. I would be in grad school. There was a big difference.

My father pressed both hands against the top of his head. He looked at Elise. He looked at me. "What the hell is happening here?" He looked at Susan O'Dell. "Talk to them!" he said. "They need a strong role model. Now!"

I didn't like it, even if it was just a joke.

"We already have one," I said, my voice firm, before even Elise could speak. I was as mad as I'd been at the steak house, right before

I'd gotten up and walked out. He was putting us all into boxes. I was with my mother and Elise, nothing like the bright and hardworking Susan O'Dell.

"Sorry," my father said, palms raised. "Sorry. I didn't mean . . ."

I didn't believe him. I knew what he'd meant. But I'd spoken, and he'd apologized.

Elise gave Susan a sympathetic smile. "Coming back next year?" She picked up her mug and stood, stretching on her tiptoes, and as she arched back, her shirt lifted, and I saw that her jeans were only zipped halfway, and a rubber band stretched between the button and the eye of them. "He has some good qualities, as I'm sure you know." She walked around the table to where he stood, leaning in against his crossed arms to kiss him on the cheek. "You just have to know when to ignore him."

By the time she shuffled into the kitchen, I wasn't mad anymore. I was just impressed with the advice. I looked up at my father and smiled, raising my mug in Elise's direction. If he wanted to put me in the same box as my sister, well, that was fine with me.

Christmas morning, while I was still asleep, my mother called and left a message. Bowzer had had a bad night. He'd been okay when she went to bed, but at two A.M., she woke to his quiet whimpers. He was having trouble breathing. He'd messed on the bed. He'd always been such a clean, fussy dog; but he either couldn't, or wouldn't, stand up.

"*The vet said he'd come in and meet me at his office. He said he'd be there by nine.*" She sounded tired, though she was speaking very quickly. "*So I won't be here if you come over this morning.*" She sniffed and exhaled. "*I'll call later, in the afternoon.*"

I closed my phone and woke Elise. She swatted me away at first, but as soon as she understood, she opened her eyes and sat up straight.

"I'll come, too," she said.

We dressed quickly. While she was in the bathroom, I heard footsteps downstairs and the jingle of keys. I pulled on my boots and ran down the stairs.

"We need to borrow your car," I said.

My father looked at me over the rim of a mug of coffee. He was wearing nylon running pants and a matching jacket. His car keys were cupped in his free hand. Either the gym was open on Christmas morning, or Susan O'Dell still believed that he had some good qualities, too.

He frowned. "I was just about to go—"

"Bowzer's dying," I said. "He's dying right now. We need to get over there. We need to borrow your car."

He squinted. He tilted his head. Later, I would consider that he was perhaps truly confused. Bowzer, in a different era, had meant something to him. You didn't let an animal sit tummy-up on your lap every evening for over a decade and not grow at least a little attached. But he hadn't seen Bowzer in over a year, and after he moved out of the house and into this neat condominium, he must have assumed that he would never see the dog again. So in a sense, for my father, Bowzer had already been dead for a year.

But if he was confused, he was also worried about me driving. He glanced out the window, at the morning sun shining on a fresh layer of snow in the driveway. He might have been thinking of my accident in Jimmy's car.

I took a step toward him. "I'm a good driver," I said. "There's nothing wrong with my driving. This is important, Dad. Please."

I kept my eyes on his. I could have offered to let Elise drive. He could have suggested it. But both of us thought better.

He handed over the keys.

"Thank you," I said. "I'll be in the garage, warming it up." I moved past him, into the kitchen. "Tell Elise when she comes down?" I glanced over my shoulder to make sure he'd heard. The expression on his face stopped me. He looked sad. He was looking at the floor, frowning, his heavy brows pushed low.

"Dad? Do you . . ." I shifted my weight. It was a bad idea. It wouldn't work. And yet, Bowzer was the family dog. "Do you want to come, too? It would probably be okay."

He looked up at me, tears in his eyes. He shook his head and jogged up the stairs.

Dr. Bree told my mother she shouldn't feel bad. He didn't think she'd waited too long. As he said this, he filled two slim syringes and set them both on a metal tray. He was unshaven, wearing jeans and a blue hooded sweatshirt. If he minded coming to his office on Christmas morning, he didn't let on.

"You brought him in just last month. And he was doing okay then." He had a latex glove on just his right hand, and he used his left to smooth down the fur on Bowzer's shivering back. My mother had brought him in wrapped in the afghan. She'd had me and Elise fold it over the exam table before she set him down. But the room was cold. The vet apologized; they'd turned down the heat for the holiday.

"It sounds as if things turned for the worse only recently." He looked up at my mother. "I think you've been good to him, Natalie. I would say you've done a pretty good job."

My mother nodded once. She was dry-eyed, quiet. She had one hand gently rubbing Bowzer's chest, the other unmoving between his ears. When Dr. Bree picked up the first syringe, she held her breath. Bowzer looked up then, his old eyes weakly peering up at the three of us.

"This one is just a sedative," he said. "Once it goes in, no more pain."

"Good dog," my mother whispered. "Good boy."

The only sound was his labored breathing. I leaned forward to rub his warm neck, my fingers grazing my mother's. Elise put an arm around her waist.

"Did you hear that?" she asked, ducking a little. "Did you hear that? Mom? I want to make sure. He said you did a good job."

We could leave the body there, the vet said. It would be cremated, the ashes scattered over his neighbor's farm, unless we wanted to make special arrangements. My mother shook her head. Scattered ashes would be fine. She asked if she needed to pay just now. She'd prefer it if he could send her a bill.

Even when it was just the three of us, walking back out to the van, she didn't cry. She kept her hands in the pockets of her coat, her purse slung over her shoulder. She'd left the afghan inside with Bowzer. She had nothing to carry out.

When we got to the van, she turned around. "Incineration. It's not a nice word."

I shook my head. "He didn't say incineration, Mom. He said cremation. It's different." I didn't know exactly how it was different, but cremation sounded much better.

She nodded, but she did not seem consoled. Her mouth was hidden by the red scarf, but her eyes looked worried. She'd done the right thing, of course. She had no money for special arrangements, and asking Elise to pay for it would have clued her in to our mother's circumstances. But now she was maybe thinking about fire, about images that might bother her later.

"Scattered ashes are nice," I said. The wind was blowing cold from the west. I put on my hat and stepped closer to the van. "Scattered over a farm, right? That's good." I shook my head, searching for words. I didn't want to say *fertilizer*. That was sort of the idea moving through my head, but I was looking for a softer word: I thought *change;* I thought *space*. "Like the dinosaurs," I said, my voice uncertain. "They turned into something else . . ."

Elise shook her head as if she felt sorry for me for trying to think. But my mother moved toward me quickly. She pulled her scarf down below her chin.

"I can't believe you remember." She leaned back, squinting. "You remember I taught you that when you were little? Do you remember that? We were in the car? Waiting for the train?"

Her face was full of happy expectation, so I nodded, though I had no idea what she was talking about. On that hard, cold day, I would have said anything to make her feel better. If she wanted to think she was the one who taught me about dinosaurs turning into coal and oil, fine. Maybe she was. I only knew it was true, and that it was for the best that they had all died when they did, so there would be room for everything good still to come.

Epilogue

For my nephew's first Christmas, I knit him a hat. I was still a beginning knitter, and it didn't come out the way I'd hoped: the rows were wavy on one side and straight on the other. But I'd measured right, and the hat fit snugly on his little head, which was still barely covered with shiny wisps of hair the exact color of my sister's. He was six months old. Elise and Charlie had named him Miles, after Charlie's father.

On Christmas morning, my hat sat on his head for maybe fifteen seconds before he yanked it off and started screaming.

"Don't take it personally," Elise said. Miles, still wailing in her lap, tried to grasp a blinking light hanging low on the tree. We were in our pajamas, sitting on the plush carpet of Elise and Charlie's enormous living room, which, Elise liked to point out, cost a mere fraction of what an enormous living room would have cost them if they had stayed in San Diego. She mostly pointed this out when my mother was around, though my mother had told her, several times, that she didn't have to justify anything.

"It's a great hat." Elise raised her voice so I could hear her over the crying. She held the hat up and smiled a little. The fuzzy ball on top was lopsided. "I like that you made it yourself. You gave him your time. That's sweet."

"You knit?" My father stood in the doorway to the kitchen, wearing the green turtleneck sweater that Susan O'Dell had given him for Christmas. He did not seem pleased or comfortable. My mother knew—we all knew—that my father hated turtlenecks. Susan O'Dell still did not. But Elise had invited Susan for brunch, and so my father was in the turtleneck, waiting. He looked at me over his coffee mug and frowned. "When did you start knitting?"

I stretched out my legs, leaning back on my elbows. "Since I realized I had no money for presents."

"Get used to it, Ms. Liberal Arts." He sipped his coffee and chuckled at his own joke. Elise looked at me and shook her head. *Ignore ignore ignore.* That was not impossible. I really didn't care what my father thought of me knitting. I'd gotten myself a little stand that propped up any size book on a table, so I could read hands-free. In the last three months, I'd knit a hat for every member of my family—all while reading *Moby Dick*, *The Turn of the Screw*, and *A Vindication of the Rights of Woman*. When I got tired of reading, I would look down, surprised by how much my hands had accomplished.

I didn't always read while I knit. In October, I put up signs in the elevators, and I soon heard from seven freshmen who either wanted to learn to knit or who knew a lot more about knitting than I did. We met every Tuesday at eight in the lobby of my floor. I got programming credit. And it was nice, for one hour a week, just to sit around and talk and, at the same time, get something done.

"It's a little . . . domestic, don't you think?" My father walked into the room and stood next to the tree, looking down.

"No flies on you," Elise said. "Knitting can only mean one thing."

She looked down at Miles and then at me. "Veronica got knocked up, too."

She was making fun of him. I was not pregnant. I did not plan to get pregnant anytime soon. In January, I would take the GRE and apply to four graduate schools.

My father nodded and sipped his coffee. "That's very funny, Elise. If you ever decide to go back to work, you could be a comedienne."

Looking at her face, you wouldn't think she had heard him. She leaned forward and tapped my knee. "Don't knit yourself any socks, sweetie. If you're going to be pregnant, you'll want to be barefoot, too."

He took another sip and gave her a weary look. "That's right," he said. "Laugh. Make fun of the guy who paid for college."

She brought Miles back down to her lap and bounced him a little, cooing soothing words. She was different than she'd been before the baby. She no longer had to have the last word with our father. They would fight the way they always had, and then, right in the middle of it, she would stop as if suddenly bored; and whenever she did this, there was often something in her expression, and the way she tilted her head, that made me think of our mother. Elise was picking up gestures and habits, maybe; she and my mother talked more often these days. Elise called her several times a week, asking what to do for a diaper rash, or a fever, or on a long, cold day with no distractions.

My father leaned forward, looking at Miles. "You need any-thing?" he asked. "Do you want me to get him a bottle?"

"He just had one. He's just fussy this morning. He was up three times last night." She looked at me. "Did you hear him?"

I shook my head. The guest room was on the first floor, and Miles's room was on the second.

"Huh," she said, shifting him to her other arm. "Neither you nor my husband. What heavy sleepers you both are."

Miles quieted, looking up at her face, one small hand pressed over his mouth as if trying to hide his awe. He had my mother's eyes, and he already smiled with just one side of his mouth, the exact way Charlie did. For a few minutes, we all stared at him, entranced, as if he were a fire in a fireplace.

"Susan should be here soon." My father walked around the tree and settled himself onto the couch, tugging at the turtleneck. He looked over his shoulder and pulled back the curtain from the window. He seemed nervous. He hadn't given Susan her present yet, but he'd shown it to us: a diamond engagement ring, beautifully cut. He had proposed to her before Thanksgiving; they planned to get married on a beach somewhere the first week they could both get off work.

My father had told me and Elise about their plans the day after Thanksgiving, when Susan wasn't around. He'd sat both of us down in his dining room, his face stern, his hands pressed flat against the glass table as if he were holding it down. He'd been defensive, ready for a fight. Neither of us gave him one. We both liked Susan. When he had chest pains the last week of October, it was Susan who made him go to an emergency room, where it was decided that he was not yet having the heart attack that he would soon have if he did not make some changes. It was Susan who made him take his medication, and it was Susan who actually got him to go to a yoga class with her twice a week after work. Also, she laughed at his jokes. She listened attentively to the stories—the new ones as well as the old ones we had already heard too many times. Elise and I saw Susan as fresh troops, a whole new person who was not at all tired of him, who was ready to absorb his energy.

"I know it's only been a year," he said. "Or not quite a year," he added, seeing that Elise was about to correct him. "But I'm not a kid. And I want to be happy. I deserve to be happy, don't I?"

We were only quiet for a moment. "As much as anyone," Elise said, with a lilt in her voice that made her sound happy as she went to hug him. I hugged him as well, my congratulations sincere. I did want him to be happy, whether he deserved it or not. I ignored the nagging sadness that Elise did not seem to feel, and focused on the pulse of his heartbeat against the side of my face.

As soon as he left the room, whistling down the hallway, Elise's smile faded. She looked at her reflection in the glass table and tucked her hair behind her ears.

"There's an expression," she said, and I was surprised to see tears in her eyes. "Women mourn. Men replace." She laughed a little, meeting my gaze only for a moment. "You know? He hasn't even gotten a new dog yet."

My father tugged again on the turtleneck, squinting at the Christmas tree. "I'm going to take this off," he said. "I'm just going to tell Susan that I don't like them. Okay? She's going to have to deal with it." He reached down and yanked off the sweater, revealing a T-shirt with a credit card logo written in neon across the front. It was the kind of thing you got for free for filling out an application. "Otherwise I'll be getting turtlenecks for the rest of my life. I'm sorry if it'll hurt her feelings. Okay? If we get married, she'll have to know the truth."

Elise pointed Miles's rattle at him and nodded. My father stared at her grimly.

"Good plan," I said. I reached under the tree for his gift and handed it up to him. "While we're being honest about gifts, here's yours. It's a hat," I said. "I knit it."

He put his coffee mug on the carpet. "Thanks," he said, with no sarcasm at all. He unwrapped the hat and immediately stretched it over his head. The ball was definitely lopsided. He looked silly, but if he knew it, he didn't let on.

"Feels warm," he said. "I like it."

Elise nodded, eyebrows raised. "I think I like you more in that hat."

"Thanks." He looked at me. "So. How's the engineer?"

Now it was my turn to be annoyed. My father knew Tim's name by now. Tim had spent Thanksgiving break with us, staying with me at Elise's house and gamely eating Thanksgiving dinner with my father and then my mother so no one would have hurt feelings. My father took us out for Indian food. My mother had ordered pizza. They had both liked Tim very much, which did not surprise me. What did surprise me was that each of them had later asked if the other one had liked him as well.

"He's good," I said. "He's with his family. He just called, actually. He sends greetings from Illinois."

My father nodded, impatient. That wasn't what he wanted to know. "Is he getting offers?"

"Not yet." I focused on picking pieces of tinsel out of the carpet. Tim would start getting offers soon. He was going to a job fair in February, where he would interview with recruiters from all over the country. He would need to make a decision, and whatever he decided wouldn't have much to do with me. It couldn't. I didn't even know where I was headed for grad school. I still wouldn't know in February. "It's only for two years," Tim had said, though we both knew it might be longer. "And they have these things called airplanes." Still, we both knew the odds, and the potential Clydes and Clydettes in our future, or futures.

Elise looked up when the front door opened, a cool breeze rustling the ornaments and tinsel on the tree. Charlie appeared in the doorway, wearing a light jacket and running pants, his blond hair covered by the hat I'd knit him, his cheekbones glistening with sweat.

"How lucky am I?" he asked, still breathing hard. "Out of the office for two whole days, and the weather is downright balmy." He pointed back at the door. "It's already at least fifty degrees out there." He stopped walking and pointed both hands at his head. "Or maybe I just felt warm in my new amazing hat."

I liked Charlie. I always forgot that he was a lawyer, too. He was energetic and loud, but not combative like Elise and my father. He'd told me that when he was young, it had really never occurred to him that he would be anything other than a professional skateboarder. After his father died, he put himself through college waiting tables at a restaurant that specialized in children's birthday parties. He still knew the words, and the accompanying hand gestures, to the restaurant's theme song, and when he was a little tipsy, you could get him to sing them in English and also in Spanish.

"Good for you!" my father said. "Out for a run on Christmas morning!" He liked Charlie, too.

Charlie put his hands on his slim hips and peered over Elise's shoulder. "How's the show runner?" he asked.

"Fussy. He's been fussy all morning." She reached back to touch Charlie's cheek, and pulled her hand back quickly. "Yuck," she said, laughing a little. "Don't get sweat on the baby."

"I'll take a shower." He kissed her ear and stood. "And then I was going to run out for a bit. We're having brunch at eleven, right? And then we're going to your mother's? What time do I need to be back here?"

She turned around, looking up. I couldn't see her face. But he raised both his hands.

"On Christmas morning? Where do you have to go?"

"Why do I have to say?"

My father and I both stared at the twinkling tree, feigning sudden deafness. Two nights ago, after coming home from the Christmas party at Charlie's firm, he and Elise had gotten into an actual fight, loud enough for me to hear in the guest room. She said she wasn't going to his stupid parties anymore if everyone was going to treat her as if she weren't a person, as if there were nothing interesting about her at all. He said something to her that I couldn't hear, and she walked out of their bedroom, slamming the door behind her. He opened the door and said, "Elise, don't slam the door." She said she didn't slam it, and for a while, they argued about that. The next day, when Charlie came home from work, I watched the baby while they went on a walk together. When they came back, they were in a good mood, smiling and holding hands, their cheeks pink from the cold.

Charlie crouched on the floor, between Elise and the Christmas tree. "Okay, I admit it," he whispered. "I have to go buy presents."

There was another pause.

"What? I've been busy."

"You waited a little long for that. It's Christmas Day. Nothing will be open."

There was a longer pause. My father looked out the window and announced, maybe to me, that it really did look warm out, especially for December.

"Okay. Go. Fine." Miles gurgled from her lap. "But don't get me anything. I don't want a present from a gas station."

I agreed with my father, facing him. It did look warm outside!

"Elise. I have been very busy. You know that. Why are you giving me a hard time?"

"You could do gift cards." My father pointed at Charlie. "You can find them everywhere, even on a holiday. I've done gift cards for years. Saves time, and everybody likes them."

Charlie nodded, polite and quick, and turned his gaze back to Elise.

"Fine," she whispered. "But just so you know, I've been busy, too. I got about four hours of sleep last night, in case you don't remember. And now I have to prepare brunch for five people. While feeding a sixth. And I still haven't taken a shower. So I'll be a little busy, too."

I leaned forward. She did look tired, the skin beneath her eyes puffed up. "I can help," I said. "You were going to make French toast, right? I can do that. And I'll set the table. I'll tidy up."

They both looked at me. Charlie smiled. "I'll watch Miles when I get back." He smoothed his hand down the back of her hair. "You can take a nap."

My father waved his hand. "Don't worry about cooking for me and Susan. We're still not eating carbs. I brought some almonds. We'll just eat those."

Elise looked at him and said nothing.

"So you'll be okay?" Charlie asked. He was already standing up, but he would wait for her answer before he turned away. From all I knew of him, I believed he would have waited even if my father and I hadn't been there.

She nodded, looking down at Miles, who was peaceful now, happy. Charlie leaned over to kiss the top of her head before he turned and bounded up the stairs.

The dorm was locked up for winter break, of course. When we first saw my mother on the other side of the glass front door, she mouthed for us to wait, holding up a chain with maybe fifteen keys on it. She slid the biggest key into the lock and, using both hands, turned it until we heard a click. I was the one carrying the bag of presents, but as soon as she pulled the door open, she leaned out and nuzzled Miles, who was wearing a Santa hat and riding face-forward in a carrier strapped to Charlie's chest.

"Welcome to the crypt," she said in her croaky voice, the one she'd used when we were little, when she read us stories about goblins and witches. She was wearing slippers and a bathrobe, and her hair was still wet from the shower.

When we got inside, Elise looked around with a wrinkled nose and clutched a bottle of wine close to her coat. "It is a little spooky in here." She peered past the unmanned front desk into the big lobby, which was only lit by two flickering exit signs. All of the heavy mauve curtains were pulled shut.

"Are you the only one here? In the whole building?"

"I hope I am." My mother tossed the key ring in the air and caught it in both hands. When she saw our anxious faces, she laughed. "It's fine. It's only weird when I have to come in at night. Once I'm in my apartment, it's okay. It feels the same as when the kids are here."

I smiled to myself, looking around. Even an assistant hall director was not supposed to call the residents in her dorm "kids." She'd been at summer training with me, and she, too, had been strongly encouraged by Student Housing to refer to the college students in her building only as men and women. She probably did call them men and women when she was working. She was every bit as conscientious about the job as Gordon Goodman had thought she would be when he'd advised her to apply for it. But now her guard was down, and the truth came out: in her mind, they were just kids.

"At least it's smaller than my building," I said. I still had on my hat and my coat. It was colder in the entry than it was outside. Apparently, they'd shut off the heat for break. "This one is only half as big, right?"

She nodded, fingering a rope of gold garland that lined the outer edge of the front desk. An easel sat next to the elevator, and the large sheet of paper clipped to it read "HAVE A HAPPY AND SAFE HOLIDAY!" in my mother's neat and even handwriting.

"Just four hundred in this one." She smiled, putting the keys in the pocket of her robe. "And I'd say only seven of them regularly cause me trouble." She turned her attention to Charlie, putting her arm through his. "Hello, handsome," she said.

"Hello, Natalie." He looked down at her and smiled. At Thanksgiving, he'd called her "Mother Von Holten," and she'd told him never to do it again.

She looked at Miles and clicked her tongue. "Let's get the baby into my apartment. It's a lot warmer in there."

It was. She had a space heater in her living room, and steam covered the bottom half of the big window. The air smelled spicy and good. A covered dish sat on a hot plate in the middle of the table, which was set for four with matching plates and napkins. Charlie walked over and lifted the lid of the dish to peek inside.

"Lasagna!" He used one of Miles's little hands to give a thumbs-up. I couldn't tell if my brother-in-law was really excited about the lasagna. Just three hours earlier, we'd had brunch with my father and Susan O'Dell. It was possible Charlie was hungry again. I wasn't. But my mother said she wanted to cook for us, so I'd come determined to eat.

"How'd you cook it?" He looked around. "You don't have an oven."

"There's a kitchen on the second floor." She nodded down at the wine Elise was still carrying. "I have a mini-fridge, however. So I'll take that." Elise gave her the bottle, and my mother looked at the label and smiled. "Ah," she said. "Very nice."

She'd gone to a lot of trouble; that was clear. In addition to traveling up and down a flight of stairs who knew how many times to cook the lasagna, she'd done some decorating. Her apartment always looked cozy, though it was really just two dorm rooms linked by a door in the wall between them. The only real difference between her apartment and any other room in the building, besides the extra space, was that she had her own small bathroom. But in November, she'd gotten herself a nice twill couch that looked like something an adult would have, and she'd put up pretty curtains. I knew the table on which the lasagna sat was just a folding card table she'd found on sale at a drugstore, but today she'd covered it with red fabric that was maybe not meant to be a tablecloth, but looked good anyway. White Christmas lights blinked around her potted ficus, and she'd hung mistletoe by the window. When Charlie accidentally walked under it, she jogged across the room and kissed his cheek, and then ducked to kiss Miles as well.

"Hey." I tapped on the edge of the big salad bowl, which was oddly curved, and painted a beautiful shade of green. "Is this what Gordon's daughter gave you?"

"Yes! Can you believe it?" She was squeezing Miles's dangling feet, making sure they were warm. "I only met her that one time she came to visit. I told her I liked what she did, what I'd seen in Gordon's office. And then she mailed that to me as soon as she got home. Wasn't that nice?"

Elise and I exchanged glances. When my mother wasn't looking, Charlie bobbed his eyebrows and grinned. I had told them both how often I'd seen my mother and Gordon Goodman eating together in the dining hall. Maybe they were just friends, comparing the horror stories and complaints that any two middle-aged people living among the young would have. I asked her about him once, and she'd brushed me off. She said she wasn't thinking of any of that right now. But I had my suspicions, or maybe just hope. Perhaps Gordon's daughter did, too.

"I'm going to hop into my room and get dressed," she said. "It'll take me a minute. Veronica, honey, would you turn on some music? My CD player is behind you on the sill."

She went into the other room, shutting the door behind her. I pushed the button on her little plastic stereo. It was Christmas music, "Rudolph the Red Nosed Reindeer." Miles, still suspended from his father's chest, started swinging his arms and legs. Charlie and I started to shimmy, too, trying to egg him on. But Elise seemed somber, staring at the table or, specifically, at the hot plate under the lasagna. She lifted the red fabric and, seeing the card table, pursed her lips.

"Don't say anything about the ring," she whispered. She looked at the space heater and swallowed. "And definitely don't say anything about a wedding on a beach."

Charlie and I both nodded. There was no reason to bring up my father's engagement, at least not today. At the same time, I wasn't sure my mother would be as upset as Elise seemed to think she would be. News of a beach wedding might annoy her, given her current income, but I just didn't think that she would think about it for very long. Because of our strange circumstance, living and work- ing so closely to one another, I got to see our mother in the day-to-day routine of her new life, and I knew more about it than Elise did. My mother and I were not chummy. We had decided that during the school year, we would keep our distance from each other, and live our respective lives. But I often saw her in the dining hall, though we didn't eat together. Sometimes she would set her tray diagonally across from whomever she found sitting alone, striking up conversa- tion, just in case the alone person wanted to talk. Sometimes she sat with Gordon, and sometimes with another woman who was the as- sistant hall director from another dorm, who looked even older than my mother.

I don't mean to say that my mother looked particularly old. She only did in comparison to almost everyone around her, all of us needy and unknowingly needy kids. She was aware of her age, she said, the clock ticking all the time. She worried about retirement. She would get some money from my father, but not enough to live on indefinitely. She was unsure if she would be able to pull it off, starting again so late in the game. In another year, she would have a master's in counseling and residence life, and then she could be an actual director, and make a little more money, and still get free room and board. Still, she said, she would have to live simply. Saving for her seventies, she called it. She had to make up for lost time.

In some ways, however—to me, at least—almost from the day she started her new job, she looked younger than she had in some time. Or maybe she just seemed happier, now that so much of what she was good at was being put to efficient use. Early one morning in September, a freshman in her dorm had crawled out onto the ledge of the sixth floor, wrapped only in a blanket, shivering, and refused to come back inside. The police had been called, and an ambulance.

But it was my mother, leaning out the window, who talked with him for almost an hour, and convinced him to come back in. I don't know what she said to him, or what he said to her. She wasn't allowed to give me the details, or his name, even after his parents arrived to take him home or wherever it was that he went to try to get better.

So maybe it wasn't that my mother seemed happier. It might be more accurate to say she seemed to have found her calling, or at least her second wind.

We exchanged gifts after dinner. Elise got our mother an ice blue cashmere scarf. She had told me in private that she hoped her gift would replace the "icky thing," meaning the cheap red scarf that she didn't know I had bought for our mother the previous winter. The new scarf did look better. My mother wrapped it around her neck and smiled at its softness, rubbing a knotted edge against her cheek.

"It's beautiful. Thank you." A moment later, she looked at me and winked. "I'll keep the old one, too, I think. You know. For around the house."

Charlie gave everybody gift cards, and apologies, and promises that he would get started on present-buying a little earlier next year. I, of course, gave my mother a hat, which she also put on right away, negating any sophistication that Elise's scarf had brought her. My mother gave Miles a teether shaped like a tractor. She gave Elise and Charlie coupons for several nights of babysitting, along with a little calendar for the coming year that showed when she did and didn't have to be in the dorm. I got the same little calendar, a plate of Christmas cookies, and a hand-sized white box with writing across the top: "THESE ARE COPIES. I AM NOT ACTUALLY GIVING IT TO YOU."

I opened the box and found a car key attached to a chain with a silver four-leaf clover.

"I wish I could give you the van," she said, wincing as if embarrassed. "But I still need it from time to time. You can have it whenever I'm on duty. Just check my calendar. You don't even have to ask."

I clapped. I stood up and skipped around the table to hug her. I wanted her to understand that she shouldn't be embarrassed, that it was a wonderful gift. She'd started letting me borrow the van from time to time, and even that had been great. But it would be even better to not have to ask, to just walk over to the parking lot of her dorm, with my own key, and go where I needed to go. My father had talked about getting me a car when I went away to grad school, but I wasn't sure he would go through with it. He occasionally still grumbled about Jimmy's car, about his insurance premiums going up.

"Thank you," I said, my face pressed into her new, soft scarf. "I'll be careful with it." I did not say it, but I thought: *because I know it is the only thing, besides the couch, that you own.*

"Okay, good," she said, matter-of-fact. "I was worried you would think I was cheap." I stepped away, and she glanced at her watch. "Oh! It's almost three!" She cleared her throat and grinned. "I have a surprise," she said.

"Cherries flambé?" Elise, who was nursing Miles, her coat draped over her chest, pretended to look under the table. "Geez, Mom. I was impressed with the lasagna. Mine never tastes that good, and I don't need a key to get to our oven."

"It is as good," Charlie said, his voice neutral.

Elise waved him off and looked at my mother. "Back to dessert. What is it?"

My mother shook her head. "I didn't make dessert. But the surprise has to do with dessert." She looked at each of us, one at a time, as if she hoped that someone would guess. When it became clear that no one could, she relented with a sigh. "Mr. Wansing called me this morning."

Only Charlie looked blank. He'd come to the neighborhood pie party just once, two Christmases ago, the first he'd spent with our family, and the last before my parents' divorce.

"He's still alive?" Elise asked.

My mother frowned. "Honey. You just saw him a couple of years ago."

"I know. What is he, eighty?"

"Maybe." She looked annoyed. "But that doesn't mean he's about to die, Elise. He's still having parties, for goodness' sakes." Now she smiled again. "And he called to invite us, which was very nice. I think we should go."

Elise and I looked at each other, unsure of what to say. It was a neighborhood party, after all. We didn't belong anymore. Also, every year, our father had come with us. He liked pie, and he got a kick out of Mr. Wansing's stories about playing minor-league baseball in the fifties. It would seem strange, and maybe a little sad, to go without him.

"How did he find you?" Elise asked my mother. "How did he get your new number?"

"He Googled me." She shrugged. "I have a landline in the dorm. And I never did change my name."

Of course. I pictured old Mr. Wansing sitting in front of a computer, typing in my mother's name. Had he bothered to type in my father's? He probably hadn't, and that made sense. After Mrs. Wansing died, my mother had been the one to call Mr. Wansing in icy weather, to see if he needed anything from the store or the pharmacy. And because she was the one who walked Bowzer, she was the one he regularly bumped into on his own slow morning walks. I believed Mr. Wansing liked my father. He thought my father was funny, "a real pistol," he said. But my father had not gotten a call this morning. If he had, he would have said something. I think he would have wanted to go. But Mr. Wansing had known he had to make a choice. And so he chose my mother.

So there it was. My father got remarriage and a disposable income. And my mother got the neighborhood pie party. When I considered all this, I changed my mind. It seemed okay for us to go without him.

We took two cars. Elise didn't want to move Miles's car seat, and we couldn't all fit into her Volkswagen. My mother and I took the van, and she let me drive, my new key in the ignition. There was no traffic; the streets in Lawrence had that eerie, empty feel of a city on holiday, all the banks and businesses closed, and so the whole way to Kansas City, I followed Elise's car closely, as if I didn't know the way.

"Do you think she's okay?" my mother asked. She nodded at the back of Elise's car.

I looked at her, surprised. "I think so," I said. "Why?"

"I don't know. She seems tired. I mean, of course she does. It's hard, what she's doing. It's hard in a way she probably wasn't used to." She appeared deep in thought, her gloved hands crossed in her lap.

"You gave her the babysitting," I reminded her. "That should help."

She looked at me and smiled kindly, as if there was much I didn't understand. She shook her head. "I'll talk to her," she said.

After that, she was chatty on the drive, humming along with carols on the radio and clearly in a good mood, but as we got closer to our destination, she grew quiet. We both gazed out the windows, passing landmarks of our old life: my grade school, the grocery store where my mother pushed shopping carts for thousands of laps, the Italian restaurant where my parents had gone for anniversaries and special occasions, the park where we took Bowzer to run off energy when he was young. Just two years ago, I might have closed my eyes out of boredom with the suburban scenery. I had watched it roll by too many times from the back of a school bus or my mother's van. But now that we were on the path to all that was lost to us, the very familiarity of the houses and quiet streets gave them an almost magical sheen. The past wasn't elusive. We could go back anytime we liked, just by following the old route home.

But at the last minute, I didn't. As we pulled off a main road into our old neighborhood, Elise turned onto the street that Mr. Wansing lived on; but I didn't turn, because it also would have taken us by our old cul-de-sac. The roof of our house—the roof that had begun the unraveling—would have been visible from the street. Maybe Elise could drive by it, but I didn't want to, and I didn't think it would be good for my mother to drive by it. By taking the next turn and then winding around, we would approach Mr. Wansing's from the opposite direction, and not see our old house at all. When my mother noticed that we were not turning with Elise, she looked at me, but said nothing.

The longer route took us past the Butterfields' house, or what had been the Butterfields' house. The fountain had a wreath on the front. The stone lion was gone now, replaced by a regular mailbox with a lock.

"I just talked to Pamela last week," my mother said. "She was a little down. Haylie couldn't come home for Christmas. It's their busiest time. But she really likes it out there, I guess."

I nodded. Haylie had dropped out of school and was working at a ski resort in Colorado. Her mother told mine she was making good money, saving it up. I didn't know if dropping out of school had made her break up with Jimmy, or if it was the other way around. Whatever the case, Jimmy had a new girlfriend, dark-haired, almost as pretty as Haylie. He didn't work at my dorm anymore, but I would sometimes see them in his car or walking around campus. He kept his arm laid across her thin shoulders, steering her around. Because he was big, and because he still shaved his head, he was easy to spot from far away, and so I always had time to cross the street or duck into a building before he saw me. For a long time, that's what I did. And then one sunny day in November, for no particular reason, I didn't. He was alone, and walking toward me, and I kept walking straight, my head raised, not looking away. We passed each other without incident, his eyes vacant, staring straight ahead.

We parked behind Elise, in front of Mr. Wansing's. There weren't any other cars. There were a lot of people inside—we could see them through the windows. They were all current neighbors. No one else had come far enough to drive.

"I'm nervous all of a sudden." My mother looked up at Mr. Wansing's house. Green Christmas lights blinked from the edge of the roof, though the sun hadn't yet gone down. "I haven't talked to any of these people since . . ." She shook her head. "I don't know what they know, what they think."

"Do you care?" I asked. I really was surprised. It was hard to believe that after everything she'd been through, a little neighborhood party would scare her. Elise and Charlie were already walking toward us. Elise wore the carrier this time, Miles snuggled inside.

My mother shrugged, her fingers moving over her new scarf. It was too warm out for a scarf or a hat, but she was wearing both. "I don't know." She looked up in the direction of our old house. "I used to love coming to this thing."

"Why?" I asked. I wasn't being sarcastic. I really wanted to know.

She laughed. She looked back up at the house. "I guess because we did it every year. If that makes sense."

It did. "Then let's go now," I said.

Once we got inside, she was fine. People were happy to see her—or us, but mostly her. She was hugged repeatedly. She was told how good she looked. Elise and Charlie and I sat in the corner on folding chairs, watching her and eating pecan pie, smiling at children we didn't recognize. Carols played on a tape player, but not so loud that we couldn't hear the talking around us. Some people told my mother they were sorry to hear about the divorce, and I heard her say, "Oh, thank you, but it's fine, actually," her voice more adamant each time. Creepy Mr. Shunke tried to hug her for too long, and our former next-door neighbor, Nancy Everton, cut in to save her.

"Oh Natalie, you just missed the Piltons," she said, handing my mother a piece of pumpkin pie so Mr. Shunke couldn't hug her again. "The people who bought your house? They're lovely." She lowered her voice. "They don't mow their lawn like they should, and they let your roses go to hell." She raised it again. "Really, they're very nice. Two little boys and one on the way. No wonder they had to go early. She was probably tired."

"Good for her," Elise said, distracted. Miles had woken up, squirming and crying in his carrier. After a quick consultation with Charlie, Elise leaned over and tapped my knee. "We're going to go," she said. "If you're smart, you'll come with us. She's in her element. Who knows how long she'll be?"

But I decided to stay. I wasn't miserable, just sitting there and watching people, and I didn't want my mother to feel pressured to leave. She was clearly enjoying herself, sipping wine and laughing with Nancy Everton. I ended up having fun, too. I talked to two girls I'd babysat when I was in junior high, who were both now taller than I was; and I talked to Mr. Wansing himself about his new computer and the warm weather outside. When my mother was clearly out of earshot, he lowered his voice and asked how my father was doing.

"Please tell him hello," he said, his pale blue gaze gentle under bushy silver brows. His voice was clear, his gaze unclouded. He might outlive his wife by another ten years, at least.

"I was sorry to hear about your family's . . . troubles," he said. He seemed hesitant, concerned that he might be offending me. But he clearly wasn't looking for information, or passing judgment in any way. He really sounded like he was sorry to have heard. "I always liked all of you so much." He frowned and looked into his wineglass. "I guess it happens now, these days. But it must be sad for you and your sister."

"It's fine," I said, feeling as adamant as my mother had sounded when she said the same thing. But there was real sympathy in his eyes. I didn't want him to think that he had gone too far, saying something too personal. It wasn't too personal. I had known him—we had all known him—since I was girl, and when his wife had died, I remember not knowing what to say to him, and not wanting to even look up at his bewildered face. I knew he meant well now, and that he cared about us. But it really was fine—the divorce, everything. "Really," I said, touching his arm. "Thank you. It was bad for a while. But I think it's starting to be fine."

On the way out, my mother apologized for staying so long. "I didn't even see Elise and Charlie go," she said, walking with me back to the van. She sounded a little dreamy, and she seemed surprised to see that it was getting dark. She'd only had one glass of wine, and she hadn't even finished it. She was just happy.

She wanted to drive, she said. When she started the van, the radio came back on, playing a wordless version of "Good King Wenceslas." "Hey!" she said, pointing at the dashboard, and I knew what she meant. It had been the first song on the program when we'd gone to hear Marley play just a few weeks earlier at Vespers. Actually, we didn't hear Marley play—or at least I didn't. There were four other French horns in the orchestra, and I heard only a general horn sound coming from their section, which was really just background for the choir. When I realized this was how it would be for the entire concert, I was a little startled, considering how much Marley practiced, all the time and effort she put in. I knew she was good—she was only a sophomore this year, but she'd told my mother she was second chair. For some reason, I assumed she would have at least one solo. But she didn't. She did all that work and practice just to add to something beautiful, a sound so big that she herself couldn't be heard. When it was over, she seemed happy, smiling out at the clapping audience. I don't know if she saw that I was there or not.

My mother hummed along with the radio, pulling the van away from Mr. Wansing's. She tapped the rhythm on the steering wheel for a while and then reached up to turn on the heater. When we neared the entrance to our old cul-de-sac, she slowed.

"Okay if I just pull in real fast? Will it upset you to see it?"

I shook my head. She was hunched over the steering wheel, already peering past me. "Will it upset you?" I asked.

"I don't know." She turned on her blinker, though there was no one behind us. "Guess we'll find out."

We saw the changes right away, even in the fading light. There was no way to know, in the middle of winter, if my mother's rose-bushes had really been killed. But they'd painted the door red, and the shutters, too. New trees, their spindly trunks held fast with ropes, followed the slope of the driveway to the street. An Irish setter sat placidly on the porch. The window of the room that had been my father's office was covered with superhero stickers. A light was on in my old room.

"Weird," my mother said.

"Yes," I agreed. "It is."

"But not that weird," she said, now maybe talking to herself. Her chin was raised, her head tilted. She was still wearing the scarf and hat. "I mean, people move. People move all the time."

I waited for her to say something else, something sad. But she was just quiet for a while, her hands resting at the top of the wheel.

When she did talk, she said, "I hope Miles is awake when I drop you off. I'll just come inside for a minute."

With that, she took her foot off the brake and followed the curve of the cul-de-sac back to the street. There wasn't anything more to say. It was just the house where we used to live, and we didn't live there anymore.

Acknowledgments

I would like to thank the women and men at Children's Learning Center in Lawrence, Kansas, for taking such great care of my daughter during the weekdays while I wrote this book.

I am very much indebted to Lucia Orth, Mary Wharff, Mary O'Connell, and Judy Bauer for their thoughtful responses to drafts. I feel fortunate to have met fellow writers whom I can learn from and also call friends. And thank you to Ben Eggleston for being such a positive presence in my life as well as Vivian's. It must be good for my head, and therefore my work, to spend time with someone I admire so much.

I am also grateful for the honesty and intelligence of my excellent agent, Jennifer Rudolph Walsh. Ellen Archer's kindness and support have been constant. My editor at Hyperion, Leslie Wells, is a discerning reader and a thoughtful advisor, and her enthusiasm has been so encouraging.